PRAISE FO
USA TODAY BES
DAVID MACK

"[*A Time to Heal*] is a tightly written, riveting book. A fast read that offers believable intrigue, stunning war descriptions, striking character struggles and nemesis confrontations. If [it] were the score for an opera, it would obviously be the crescendo to the curtain drop."

—Kathy LaFollett, The Lincoln
Heights Literary Society

"[*A Time to Heal*] is powerful stuff, which makes no attempt to pretend that it isn't referring directly to current-day events. The skill of author David Mack's plotting shines through. . . . This is *Trek* with no easy answers . . . and an unsettling ending. . . . It's dark, it's effective."

—Anthony Brown, *Starburst Magazine*

"David Mack clearly has his finger on the pulse of *Star Trek* as we once knew it and as we know it now, elevating him into the top echelon of expert storytellers in both *Star Trek* and in the world of literature. . . . [*A Time to Heal*] could have easily been ripped from today's headlines or the current techno-thriller novels of Tom Clancy."

"Mack makes you care about the lives lost, the lives touched by their losses, and the dramatic aftereffects that occur throughout [*Harbinger*]'s myriad events."

—Bill Williams, TrekWeb.com

STAR TREK
DEEP SPACE NINE®

WARPATH

DAVID MACK

**Based upon STAR TREK®
created by Gene Roddenberry
and STAR TREK: DEEP SPACE NINE
created by Rick Berman and Michael Piller**

POCKET BOOKS

New York   London   Toronto   Sydney   Harkoum

An *Original* Publication of Pocket Books

POCKET BOOKS, a division of Simon & Schuster, Inc.
1230 Avenue of the Americas, New York, NY 10020

This book is a work of fiction. Names, characters, places, and incidents are products of the author's imagination or are used fictitiously. Any resemblance to actual events or locales or persons, living or dead, is entirely coincidental.

ISBN-13: 978-1-4165-0775-8
ISBN-10:   1-4165-0775-2

This Pocket Books paperback edition April 2006

10 9 8 7 6 5 4 3 2 1

POCKET and colophon are registered trademarks of
Simon & Schuster, Inc.

Cover art by Cliff Nielsen

Manufactured in the United States of America

For information regarding special discounts for bulk purchases,
please contact Simon & Schuster Special Sales at 1-800-456-6798
or business@simonandschuster.com.

For all we've lost and all we hope to find.

What though the field be lost?
All is not lost; th'unconquerable will,
And study of revenge, immortal hate,
And courage never to submit or yield.
—John Milton, *Paradise Lost*

Beware the fury of a patient man.
—John Dryden, *Absalom and Achitophel*

A being breathing thoughtful breath,
A traveler between life and death;
The reason firm, the temperate will,
Endurance, foresight, strength, and skill;
A perfect woman, nobly planned,
To warn, to comfort, and command.
—William Wordsworth,
"She was a Phantom of delight"

HISTORIAN'S NOTE

This tale is set in January, 2377 (Old Calendar), immediately following events depicted in *Olympus Descending*, the Dominion tale in *Worlds of Star Trek: Deep Space Nine, Volume Three*.

1

Harkoum

HUNTER AND PREY RACED WILDLY THROUGH A JUNGLE OF rusted pipes.

Jonu gloried in the taste of her own sweat as she sprinted after the Cardassian Woman. The Klingon bounty hunter's boots kicked up divots of loose gravel as she ran. Ahead of her, the glimpses of her prey—passing beyond the next cluster of twisting gray pipes and steel supports, or ducking beneath the swollen metal belly of a perforated storage tank—grew more frequent. A bitter tang of chemicals tainted the humid air.

Nearly four kilometers behind Jonu lay the wreckage of both her own small ship and the Cardassian Woman's stolen shuttle. Their broken, smoking fuselages were scattered in smoldering swaths across the barren landscape that surrounded the abandoned ore refinery. Shooting down the small craft had been almost impossible. Jonu had been caught off-guard when the Cardassian Woman had ended the pursuit by reversing course and ramming Jonu's ship head-on. It was a testament to both women's piloting skills (and the engineering prowess of whoever had designed their ships) that both of them had escaped the crash landings at all, let alone walking away all but unharmed.

Jonu had been left with no other option than to hunt down her target on foot; it was proving to be an exhilarating necessity. Fleeting glimpses of the Cardassian Woman's silhouette impelled Jonu forward through the industrial maze. Her heart raced with the joy of the hunt as she imagined the bloodthirst of her *d'k tahg*. Her hand tightened around the short blade's grip.

The stark, beautiful desolation of Harkoum's mustard-hued, strip-mined lowlands was but a blur beyond the refinery's decaying steel skeleton. Overhead, ragged forks of blue-green lightning lit up a battalion of swollen, bruised-purple storm clouds, auguring the onslaught of another scorching acidic downpour. A dusk breeze swept through the refinery. The air was rich with ozone, fat with the promise of an imminent deluge. Twin suns glowed with fiery majesty as they sank below the horizon, crowned by the roiling storm front.

Closer now, Jonu told herself. She smelled the Cardassian Woman's sweat growing thicker in the air ahead. A sheen of perspiration glistened on her own face. Harkoum's stifling humidity denied her any relief from the blistering heat, even at a full run. The effort of this sustained dash burned in her thighs and calves. Knifing pains between her ribs flared with each rapid, huffing breath. The ponderous weight of her running footfalls amplified her suffering.

She savored it all with an elated grin. *Closer now . . .*

Thinking ahead, she considered tactics for her endgame with the Cardassian Woman. If her prey stumbled, an overpowering tackle would yield the greatest advantage of position, and Jonu would drive her *d'k tahg* deep between the target's shoulder blades, or into the throat above the sternum. If the Cardassian Woman tried to dodge, or double back, or circle to gain time and recover stamina, Jonu would press her attack and deny her foe any chance to regroup for another attempt at flight. And if the Cardassian Woman abandoned her escape and turned to face Jonu in battle . . . that would be the most glorious outcome of all.

Jonu reached the next corner. Making the turn past a lopsided, vertical jumble of broken equipment, she saw the Cardassian Woman directly ahead, no more than a dozen *qams* away. Her prey looked back, over her shoulder, at Jonu. The Klingon woman widened her grin, emphasizing her sharpened canine teeth. She decided that the Cardassian Woman's neck bones would make a lovely necklace when she was finished with her.

A flash of light. The sharp report of a detonation. A firestorm of shattered steel sliced into Jonu's flesh. Stinging gravel blinded her. She dropped her *d'k tahg* and lifted her arms to protect her face. The concussion of the blast slammed her sideways against a concrete wall. It pinned her there for a fraction of a second, which was stretched out of proportion by the adrenaline coursing through her.

The blast wave dissipated. Gravity took hold of her and deposited her facedown in the dirt. Though she still could not see, the sound of collapsing metal debris was unmistakable. She scrambled forward on all fours while trying to blink her eyes clear. Her effort to reach safe ground came to a halt as several tons of smoking iron crushed her legs into bloody pulp.

Jonu's howl was one not of pain but of rage. Her voice was deep and rich, like those of many Klingon women, and her anguished cry echoed and reëchoed off the refinery's myriad hard surfaces, until her indignant scream evaporated into the smothering darkness of approaching night.

The dust cleared. Strength fled swiftly from Jonu's body. Her lifeblood spread into a magenta-hued stain that was swallowed by the parched, unslakable dust of Harkoum. Thunderclaps shook the ground, and a low wash of pattering impacts heralded the coming of the rain.

The Cardassian Woman stood above Jonu, holding the Klingon woman's *d'k tahg*. She regarded Jonu with a dispassionate stare, one that Jonu appreciated as the gaze of a fellow professional. Dirty, bloody spittle pooled beneath Jonu's tongue. She spat it out. "I'm bleeding to death," she said.

"I know," the Cardassian Woman said.

Fixing her eyes on the honor blade that used to be hers, Jonu said, "You could give me a warrior's death." *And come close enough for me to get my hands around your bony, gray throat.*

"I could," the Cardassian Woman said. Then she slipped the *d'k tahg* under her belt, which was slung at a rakish angle over her loose, desert-tan jacket.

Furious, Jonu shouted, "Have you no sense of honor?"

"I do," the other woman said. "But I know better than to trust a Klingon who fights her battles for money. You're not a warrior . . . you're a mercenary. You have no honor." She turned to walk away as the first raindrops fell and pockmarked the freshly scattered dust around Jonu with dark, tiny craters.

"I can throw you my disruptor," Jonu called out. "You could finish this from a distance."

The Cardassian Woman turned back toward Jonu. "If you can reach your disruptor, you can finish it yourself."

"No," Jonu said. "It's not the Klingon way."

"I see. And I suppose you wouldn't arm the silent over-load on that Breen-made weapon of yours. After all, you wouldn't just be trying to trick me into catching a live grenade . . . would you?" The corner of her mouth turned upward, the slightest hint of an arrogant smirk illuminating her features.

Jonu found the mannerism strangely . . . *familiar.* Straining to focus on the woman's face in the gathering gloom, she asked suspiciously, "Do I know you?"

The Cardassian Woman lifted the hood of her jacket to cover her short bob of raven hair. "No," she said. "You only think you do." Then she turned her back on Jonu and walked away, her silhouette vanishing into the embrace of the night.

Rain followed in her wake, trailed by the pure black of a starless sky. Entombed in darkness, Jonu lay paralyzed beneath the toppled metal and machinery. Dizziness and fatigue took hold as her blood continued to drain away, and soon she surrendered her face to the blistering acid rain. She felt her final moments unfolding and steeled her spirit for its journey to *Gre'thor.*

Drawing her last breath, she realized where she had seen the Cardassian Woman's eyes before.

She exhaled a whispered prayer to her ancestors: "Drown her in a river of blood."

2

Deep Space 9

THAT FACE.

Captain Kira's eyes lolled in Taran'atar's direction, glazed, unfocused, dimmed of vitality, downcast just shy of meeting the Jem'Hadar's own unwavering stare. He did not know whether her failure to look into his eyes was the result of her fading strength or a silent expression of her reproach. She lay on her side, half-folded against the bulkhead, surrounded by a quickly spreading pool of her own bright-crimson blood. The ferric odor of it was sweet to Taran'atar, but he took no joy in it. His blade remained embedded in her chest, perfectly on target for her heart.

Next to her in the corridor, in front of the turbolift near his now abandoned quarters, Lieutenant Ro was sprawled on the deck. The acute angle of Ro's upper torso was a testament to the grievous nature of her injuries. Taking down the security chief first had been the wise choice. Kira was more experienced in personal combat, but trying to eliminate her first might have given the other Bajoran time to counterattack, thereby splitting Taran'atar's attention. He had chosen to remove Ro from the equation instantly, then focus solely on Kira.

He pressed the turbolift call button.

Looking down at Kira, a seething anger swelled inside him. Though it had been the Founder Odo who had dispatched Taran'atar to this miserable place, with orders to observe Alpha Quadrant species and cultures, all of Taran'atar's fury now was fixated on the Bajoran commanding officer of Deep Space 9. As much as she had done to earn his respect—especially because she had not needed to since Odo had expressly ordered Taran'atar to obey Kira as he would obey Odo himself—she now had come to represent everything that he hated about his exile from the Dominion, from other Jem'Hadar, from the life he had been genetically designed to lead unto death.

Kira's breathing grew ragged and faltered into weak gasps.

The turbolift doors opened, and Taran'atar stepped inside. "Runabout Pad A," he said.

In her dying eyes, Kira's shock and sorrow were evident.

Tired of the oppressive weight of her gaze, Taran'atar purged his mind of unnecessary thoughts and shrouded himself. The turbolift doors closed. As the car ascended toward its destination, he withdrew to its rear left corner and coiled himself to strike in case someone inadvertently joined him in the lift en route to the launch bay—or attempted to intercept him during his exit from the station.

The car's swift ascent slowed, and there was a faintly audible hum and clack of magnetic brakes and safety interlocks changing orientation as the turbolift switched to a horizontal track of movement. Seconds later the turbolift accelerated again, hurtling around the outer edge of the habitat ring.

In recent weeks Taran'atar had felt increasingly isolated and directionless, and the sense that he had deviated from the Jem'Hadar ideal had torn at him. A visit to the female Founder, held prisoner by the Federation at its secret Ananke Alpha detention facility, had only exacerbated Taran'atar's growing misgivings. For reasons about which he could only speculate, she had in essence denied her divinity and that of all the Founders. He had tried to ascribe her remarks to the strain of captivity, but that had been only the first of many equally weak rationalizations. Could a true deity go mad?

Bereft of purpose, he now was robbed of his gods.

For the past three days, he had sequestered himself in his quarters. His agitation and confusion had fed upon and reinforced one another until at last he'd exploded in a fury. Unleashing his rage on hallucinations of the station's denizens, all of whom he had grown to loathe, he had within minutes destroyed the spare, ugly furnishings of his quarters, broken one tine off his blade by hurling it against the wall, and compromised the integrity of an interior bulkhead by hurling himself against it.

That had sounded an alarm, which had provoked Kira and Ro into hailing him. He had ignored them, prompting them to investigate.

Now he was leaving the station.

The confusion, the indecision, the lack of direction that had plagued him for weeks was gone. Clarity had returned with action. Forward motion was its own reward. Doubt had been replaced by certainty, by an absolute trust that he would know what measures to take when he arrived at his next juncture. He was beyond the vague directives of Odo, braving the uncharted waters of free will.

A deepening hum accompanied the deceleration of the turbolift. It stopped, and the doors opened with a low hiss. Taran'atar's senses detected no one in the corridor outside the turbolift. The turbolift gate opened. "Fusion core," he instructed the computer. "Grid twenty-two." Still shrouded, he slipped out of the turbolift before the gate slid shut. As the turbolift car sped away, he skulked toward the door to the maintenance hangar adjacent to Runabout Pad A.

There were muffled sounds of activity from the opposite side of the door. Taran'atar glanced through the curved pane of transparent aluminum in the rust-hued, circular portal. On the other side, a Bajoran man in a Starfleet engineer's uniform conferred with Ensign Prynn Tenmei, the senior flight controller of the *U.S.S. Defiant.* Parked on the elevator pad in the bay behind them was the *Euphrates.* The hangar's top doors retracted slowly into the hull, opening the compartment to space. Only an invisible forcefield stood between the two Starfleet personnel and a violent decompression experience. The engineer pointed out some details on a padd, gestured at the *Euphrates,* then handed the padd to Tenmei. She accepted it with a small nod, then the two separated and moved in different directions. The man passed through a door on the left side of the hangar, while Tenmei walked briskly toward the runabout and tapped her combadge. A moment later, the small ship's navigational thrusters began warming up with a resonant hum and whine that Taran'atar heard clearly through the door. Tenmei paused momentarily to inspect the runabout's port warp nacelle, then she perused her padd once more. She turned off the small data device and bounded up the step through the open port hatch of the *Euphrates.*

Taran'atar pressed the manual door-open button. The circular hatch rolled away. He stepped through quickly and tapped the door-close button on the other side as soon as he was clear of the threshold. Still shrouded, he took a whiff of the air. Fuel vapors and the odor of freshly fused duranium bonds masked most of the body scents, but only Tenmei's and the engineer's were fresh enough to be noticeable.

Confident that he was alone in the hangar, Taran'atar walked quickly toward the runabout and slipped gracefully sideways through its closing port hatch. He had expected to depart Deep Space 9 alone, but this scenario, he knew, was not without its advantages.

Prynn settled into the pilot's seat in the cockpit of the *Euphrates*. With her left hand she powered up the drive systems, and with her right she transmitted her flight plan to Lieutenant Dax in ops. Though the runabout was far less complicated than the *Defiant*, she treated it with the same professional attention as she methodically worked through the protocol of a preflight check.

Routines and procedures had been a saving grace to her since her return from Andor. Her thoughts had remained anchored there—on Tower Hill, watching the lightning on the ocean and the wind whipping through Shar's flowing white hair—even as she herself had made the long journey back to Deep Space 9. Loneliness was not a novelty to Prynn. She had grown accustomed to the feeling, thanks in part to the absentee parenting style of Elias Vaughn, a career Starfleet officer who was never at a loss for urgent assignments.

Shar's absence, however, gnawed at her. She had let him go willingly; she had urged him to go, to leave her and embrace the start of a new path in his life . . . but now, back here, without him, she struggled not to succumb to regret. A future rich with possibilities that Shar thought he had lost had been offered to him, and Prynn hadn't been able to ask him to turn his back on his bondmates, on his family, on his people. *Give up his birthright for me,* she scolded her selfish side. *I couldn't do that. I wouldn't.*

Inhaling sharply, she turned her mind back to the task in front of her, a simple flight check of recent upgrades to the *Euphrates.* The ship, according to Lieutenant Nog, the station's chief of operations, had not been "a hundred percent" ever since Dr. Bashir and Lieutenant Dax had crash-landed it nearly eight months earlier on the planet Sindorin. The young Ferengi engineer's notes had also cited damage inflicted during Captain Kira's mission, weeks later, to save the human colony on Europa Nova. Although the regular duty pilots had reported that the ship had been handling just fine since its return to service in June, Nog had ordered a full upgrade of the ship's warp and impulse systems. So far the work was only half-done, but Nog wanted a short test flight, to set a benchmark for the next round of improvements.

Most of the pilots had concocted excuses to avoid this four-hour solo flight. Prynn had volunteered for it. Despite her new belief that some kinds of damage might never really be reparable, she shared Nog's commitment to hands-on upkeep and respected his attention to minuscule details . . . but the truth was that she just wanted to have four hours of perfect solitude, at the controls of a ship in flight. That the ship had just been retooled to be faster than ever was simply a bonus.

An indicator on her dashboard blinked green twice, signaling that her flight plan had been approved. With a quick, well-rehearsed series of taps, she closed the port side hatch and opened a comm channel to the station's operations center. "Ops, this is *Euphrates,* requesting liftoff clearance at Runabout Pad A."

"*Acknowledged,* Euphrates," responded Lieutenant Dax, who was standing watch in ops this evening. "*Deactivating forcefield and raising the platform to launch position. Stand by.*"

Through the hull Prynn heard the hum of motors and the whine of the platform's hydraulics lifting the runabout toward the stars. Then the *Euphrates* cleared the hull, and ahead of the small ship towered the station's inward-curving upper pylons and its central command module. She felt a gentle vibration in the deck under her feet as the platform locked closed beneath the ship.

"Euphrates," Dax said over the comm, "*you're clear for liftoff.*"

"Acknowledged," Prynn said, firing up the navigational thrusters. "See you in a few hours. *Euphrates* out." She guided the ship gently away from the habitat ring, pivoted toward an empty vista of stars, and engaged the impulse drive at one-quarter power. The station was left behind in a blur. In less than a minute, she had reached safe distance for free flight. She increased speed to full impulse and began to plot the test maneuvers Nog had specified.

There was a whisper-rush of sound in the cockpit behind her. She spun her chair—and found herself facing Taran'atar and the business end of a Starfleet phaser.

"Do not reach for the comm," he said. "Set a new course."

Dr. Julian Bashir materialized from the transporter beam and sprinted toward Captain Kira. Lieutenant Ro lay on the floor a few meters away. Bashir's satchel, jammed with surgical tools and loaded hyposprays, was slung loosely over his shoulder. Nurse Etana Kol and medical technician Michael Ingbar raced down the corridor from the other direction, both similarly laden with portable medical gear. Security guards Alberto Taveras and Franz Cortez—who had called in the medical alert—stood over Kira and Ro, looking stunned and horrified.

The captain's uniform jacket glistened with the wet sheen of her blood, which burbled grotesquely around the hilt of the knife that still protruded from her chest. Ro's back was arched in a disturbingly unnatural-looking pose.

"Move!" Bashir ordered. There was no time for courtesy. Bashir, Etana, and Ingbar pushed past Taveras and Cortez. At Kira's side, Etana raced to stanch the massive bleeding from Kira's chest wound. Ingbar moved to assess Ro's condition. Bashir knelt beside Kira and flipped open his medical tricorder, then reached into his satchel for a hypo of neurocine. If Kira was lucky, the drug would shield her brain from hypoxia for the critical seconds Bashir needed to assess her vital signs and beam her to surgery. He pressed the hypospray to her jugular and injected it, hoping for the best even as experience told him to prepare for the worst. The image of Kira's ruptured cardiac muscle took shape on the tricorder display. Her heart had been brutally shredded. He tapped his combadge. "Bashir to ops: Emergency medical transport! Five to infirmary, stat!"

The shimmering pull of a transporter beam enfolded the two fallen women and the three medical officers. They materialized in the central diagnostic lab as the infirmary's main doors slid open. Dr. Simon Tarses hurried in, followed by the new Bajoran surgeon, Dr. Aylam Edeen, a late-thirtyish blond woman.

"Tarses, over here," Bashir ordered. "Dr. Aylam, take Lieutenant Ro. Ingbar, you're with Aylam." The medical team snapped into action. Dr. Aylam initiated a full-body scan of Ro while Tarses and Bashir hefted Kira into the surgical suite and onto its lone biobed. The display readouts above the bed immediately lit up and flooded with metrics of Kira's condition.

"Near-total bifurcation of the cardiac muscle," Bashir said, masking his dismay at the sight of his sleeves slick with his friend's blood.

"Massive bleeding in the pericardium," Tarses said, his voice calm and clinical. "Puncture runs from the aorta to the inferior vena cava, through both atriums."

"We can't fix this," Bashir said. "Let's stop the bleeding and stabilize her for full bypass." He looked at Nurse Etana. "Pull up the captain's last physical and use it to match an artificial heart." Etana nodded and exited to the diagnostic center to start the search. Without taking his eyes off Kira's plunging vitals, Bashir called out, "Dr. Aylam, report."

"Fracture of the tenth and eleventh thoracic vertebrae," the blond woman reported from outside the surgical suite, her own attention on Ro equally intense. "Partial severing of the spinal cord between the tenth and eleventh thoracic. Rupture of the spleen, consistent with blunt-force trauma. Internal hemorrhaging."

"Stabilize her, then assist us," Bashir said.

"Yes, Doctor."

"Simon," Bashir said. "Get the surgical hood, we need to start now." Tarses nodded and bolted away to retrieve the arch-shaped component.

Bashir recognized Taran'atar's knife as he pulled it free of Kira's splintered sternum. Ruby-red blood drizzled off the blade's tines—one intact and one broken. Bashir dropped the broken weapon on a tray reserved for medical waste, then used an old-fashioned pair of surgical scissors to cut away Kira's uniform jacket and shirt, exposing her bare and bloody chest. With his foot he pressed a control on the base of Kira's biobed and activated the sterilizing forcefield over the entrance to the surgical suite.

Dr. Tarses returned, passing through the sterilizing forcefield, which crackled softly at his passage. He attached the surgical hood to Kira's biobed, covering her from neck to midthigh. The portable sterile environment hummed softly as it powered up. Its displays flickered on in stutters of color.

Outside the surgical suite, Dr. Aylam engaged a site-to-site transport and moved Ro off the floor to another location. Bashir presumed that Ro was being transferred to the adjacent intensive-care ward.

During his brief moment of inattention, Kira's vital signs flatlined.

"Push thirty cc of triox," Bashir said as he reached into his satchel and pulled out a cortical stimulator. He fit it snugly over Kira's temples. "Setting autonomic bypass." Its first pulse failed to produce even a flutter of response. He increased the power and shortened its cycle. A faint twitch confirmed that it was having an effect, but Kira's EEG remained static. Tarses infused her bloodstream with the oxygenating drug, then Bashir sighed as her vital signs restabilized.

"Hook up the ventilator," Bashir said. "I'll get the rapid infuser going." He shouted toward the doorway, "Nurse! We need type and cross, twenty units of whole blood, stat!"

Another pulse of the cortical stimulator produced a small hiccup on Kira's EEG, followed several seconds later by a steady wave of low-level brain function. To Bashir's relief, there was no indication of brain damage. He reset the cortical stimulator to standby mode, in case of another flatline.

Bashir activated the surgical hood's automated laser scalpel and made a vertical incision down the center of Kira's chest. Changing to a more powerful setting, he cut decisively through her already damaged sternum, opening a path into the chest cavity. Although the surgical hood's primary tools for internal surgery combined microtransporters and forcefield generators, minor physical invasions were still necessary for a major operation such as this. A precisely targeted laser beam cut away Kira's damaged pericardium, flooding her chest cavity with hemorrhaged blood. Even shielded beneath the surgical arch, the carnal odor of it was unmistakable.

A quick glance confirmed that Tarses had almost finished guiding the ventilation hardware through Kira's sinus, down into her airway. Bashir worked as quickly as his enhanced abilities made possible, threading lines from the arch's rapid infuser into the cardial sac. With the machine's assistance, he secured the connection to the ascending aorta in less than a minute. He was attaching the second of three lines to Kira's superior vena cava, when Nurse Etana reported, "Doctor, we only have four units of Captain Kira's blood type on hand."

Too focused on his objective to ask why or lay blame, Bashir responded, "Get a list of all Bajorans on the station with Kira's blood type. Send them all a priority request for blood donors." To Dr. Tarses he added, "Push four units of plasma into the infuser to keep her pressure up." Even though there wasn't enough transfusable blood to make the procedure viable, Bashir resumed work, completing his sutures on the superior vena cava, and finding an intact section of the inferior vena cava for the third and final infuser line.

"Let's keep going," he said to Tarses. "Start repairing the damage in the lower aorta. I'll rebuild the inferior vena cava."

With four units of blood and four units of plasma, he could keep Kira alive for another twenty minutes.

After that, his bag of medical miracles would be empty.

Dr. Aylam Edeen rushed through the door into the infirmary, behind Dr. Tarses. Her hands were shaking. She saw Captain Kira and Lieutenant Ro lying on the floor—Kira with a knife in her chest and blood pooling beneath her shoulders, Ro twisted at mid-torso like a child's cruelly abused toy.

Aylam's entire body began to tremble.

Today was her fourth aboard Deep Space 9, and the first on which she had been summoned for an emergency call. She was no stranger to gruesome medical crises, having seen more than her share during her internship and residency at the Musilla University teaching hospital, during the last years of the Cardassian occupation of Bajor. The victims of countless skirmishes—between the Cardassian troops garrisoned near the university and the Resistance fighters striking from nearby Tamulna—had given her a quick and blood-soaked education in emergency medicine. She had expected quieter times after she had enlisted in the Bajoran Militia's medical corps, but she had quickly learned that military medical service, even during peacetime, was rarely a calm profession.

Bashir was at Kira's side, flanked by Nurse Etana and medical technician Ingbar. "Tarses, over here," Bashir said, his voice calm, professional, and confident. "Dr. Aylam, take Lieutenant Ro. Ingbar, you're with Aylam."

Bashir and Tarses together lifted Kira and carried her into the adjacent surgical suite. While they assessed the captain's vitals with practiced ease, Aylam pulled her medical tricorder from her belt and made an emergency scan of Lieutenant Ro, calibrating the device on the fly for Bajoran physiology. It swiftly rendered a gruesome, detailed report that confirmed what Aylam had suspected on first sight.

Bashir chose that moment to demand, "Dr. Aylam, report."

"Fracture of the tenth and eleventh thoracic vertebrae," Aylam said, scrutinizing the scan results to make certain she didn't mispresent even the smallest aspect of the case to her chief medical officer. "Partial severing of the spinal cord between the tenth and eleventh thoracic. Rupture of the spleen, consistent with blunt-force trauma. Internal hemorrhaging."

"Stabilize her, then assist us," Bashir said.

"Yes, Doctor," Aylam said, even though it was a taller order than Bashir had made it sound. Stanching Ro's internal bleeding was her first priority, but fitting the surgical arch over Ro while she was twisted at this unnatural angle would be difficult, if not impossible. *I can try doing this by hand,* Aylam thought, weighing her options. *But one mistake and I may paralyze Ro for life . . . assuming that's not already the case.*

First things first, she reminded herself. She tapped her combadge. "Aylam to ops: Emergency site-to-site medical transport for Lieutenant Ro: Beam her to any available bed in the intensive-care ward." Aylam stepped away from Ro, who dematerialized a moment later. Gesturing to Ingbar to follow her, Aylam moved away, from the surgical suite to the intensive-care ward on the other side of the infirmary's diagnostic lab.

She remained several steps ahead of Ingbar as she moved toward Ro's biobed at the far end of the room, snagging an internal-tissue regenerator on her way. "Ingbar," she said, "help me get her internal bleeding under control." Following her tricorder's readout to Ro's spleen, Aylam activated the surgical device and began manipulating the damaged organ without being able to see it with her own eyes.

As a young girl, she had watched Bajoran physicians perform shocking field surgeries for Resistance fighters, often cutting into their bodies with crude metal scalpels, reaching into bodies to repair damage with cauterizing chemicals and threads sutured with curved needles. The noninvasive surgical wonders of state-of-the-art Bajoran and Cardassian medicine had been denied her then, but she had in recent years come to find the remote nature of their use—and now, those of Starfleet—oddly disorienting. Part of her still regarded the dangerous, subtle violence of the old healing ways with reverential awe.

Minutes later, Ro's spleen had been repaired sight unseen. She had other, less critical internal injuries that still required attention, however, and sooner or later, Aylam would have to address the issue of how to realign Ro's fractured and herniated thoracic vertebrae without causing additional damage to her already partly torn and bruised spinal cord.

Aylam returned to the other side of the bed, crouched in front of Ro's half-doubled-over torso, and began stemming the tide of numerous small internal hemorrhages caused by broken ribs puncturing Ro's lungs and upper intestine. The procedure went smoothly, with Ingbar quietly (and almost presciently) handing Aylam various surgical implements.

It was all but finished when Ro Laren's eyes snapped open, wide with terror. She let loose a shriek that jolted Aylam with fear. The young doctor stumbled backward, hollering in surprise at Ro's sudden outburst. The tissue regenerator slipped from Aylam's hand and clattered on the cold metal floor.

Ro's panicked, confused eyes darted around the room. "What . . . ? Where . . . ? The captain?"

Ingbar placed a reassuring hand on Ro's shoulder and spoke in a low, soothing tone of voice. "Relax, Lieutenant. The captain's in surgery. You're in the infirmary with her. We're patching you up. Just lie still."

Dr. Aylam got back on her feet and rejoined Ingbar at Ro's bedside. The wounded security chief closed her eyes and took a breath. When she exhaled, she opened her eyes and glared at Aylam. "Why can't I move?"

It was too early, in Aylam's opinion, to diagnose whether Ro's paralysis was temporary or permanent. Raising the subject of spinal damage, even in passing, was likely to provoke Ro into asking a number of increasingly pointed questions, and the situation would only grow more awkward as Aylam answered each one with yet another paraphrasing of "I don't know yet."

"We're still assessing your injuries, Lieutenant," Aylam said, cutting off Ingbar before he could reply to Ro's query. "We're going to give you something to help you relax and—"

"I don't want to *relax*," Ro said, the angry growl of her voice intimidating despite her current infirmity. "I want an answer: Why can't I move?"

Dr. Aylam was still considering her reply when, over the

comm, Bashir shouted, *"Dr. Aylam, report to surgery, stat!"*

"On my way," she called out, then turned back to Ro. "When I finish my examination, I'll make a diagnosis," Aylam said. "Not before. So I suggest you let us make you comfortable."

Ro signaled her surrender with a disgusted roll of her eyes. Aylam nodded to Ingbar. "Ten cc of adozine." He pressed the hypospray gingerly against Ro's throat and injected the mild sedative. The drug was delivered with a soft hiss. It eased Ro into a placid, half-conscious state.

Making her way back to the surgical suite, Aylam felt a slight tinge of guilt for postponing what was almost certain to be a very difficult conversation with Ro. Telling a patient that they were going to be all right was the easiest news to deliver; telling them that their death was imminent was always traumatic, but at least it represented a sort of closure.

Telling a woman in the prime of her life that she would likely spend the rest of it as a quadriplegic . . . that was a task for which Aylam's many years of medical tuition had left her woefully unprepared.

Major Cenn Desca, the Bajoran Militia liaison to Deep Space 9, led Starfleet security guards Broeking and Cardok into Taran'atar's quarters. The two guards advanced cautiously, each with a phaser in one hand and a scanning tricorder in the other, separating to either side of Cenn as they entered the main room.

Surveying the scene, Cenn was taken aback by the amount of damage. All the furniture had been smashed into splinters, apparently by crushing blows or being hurled violently against the walls. One bulkhead was buckled inward at its seam, the dent just deep enough to compromise some wiring and trip some structural integrity sensors in the wall. It looked like someone had fought a long and exceptionally brutal battle to the death inside this room.

Catching Broeking's eye, Cenn said, "Ron, report."

"No sign that anyone was in here except the Jem'Hadar," Broeking said. "I'm reading his DNA on everything—furniture pieces, the bulkhead damage, the companel . . . If he was ambushed, I've got zilch on whoever attacked him."

Cardok looked up from his tricorder. "Sir," the Benzite said, "I'm detecting small traces of fresh Jem'Hadar blood on the carpet and on some pieces of the furniture." He turned toward the door. "And the blood trail seems to lead outside these quarters."

Cenn tapped his combadge. "Computer, locate Taran'atar."

"Taran'atar is not on the station," the feminine computer voice said. Under any other circumstances, Cenn might have been concerned for Taran'atar. Knowing, however, that Taveras and Cortez had found Captain Kira and Lieutenant Ro both gravely wounded only a few sections away near the turbolift made him view this evidence in a less forgiving light.

He tapped his combadge again. "Cenn to ops."

Lieutenant Dax answered. *"Go ahead."*

"Taran'atar's quarters are wrecked, and the computer says he's not aboard the station—which might mean he's shrouded."

"Hang on; backup's on the way." A moment later, the station's alert klaxon sounded, then Dax's voice echoed crisply over the stationwide comm: *"Attention, all decks:*

Intruder alert. All security personnel, report in for new orders. Commander Vaughn, please report to ops."

Commander Elias Vaughn was already in a turbolift, on his way to ops, when he heard Lieutenant Dax's summons. Tapping his combadge, he responded, "On my way, Lieutenant."

He had just wrapped up after a long day, reviewing the latest reports from the three Federation starships that had, five weeks ago, embarked on extended missions of exploration in the Gamma Quadrant. On his way into the "Ferengi embassy to Bajor"—aka Quark's bar—for a dinner break, he'd seen Drs. Tarses and Aylam sprint wildly across the Promenade toward the infirmary, shoving aside passersby as they ran. Instinct, honed by more than eighty years of service in Starfleet, had compelled the centenarian command officer to follow them.

He'd stopped in midstep at the threshold of the infirmary as Captain Kira and Lieutenant Ro had materialized, one bloodied and the other broken, on the floor. In an instant, Vaughn had recognized the haft of Taran'atar's dagger in Kira's chest, and he'd known then that something disastrous had happened.

With Kira down, he was the ranking officer on Deep Space 9. He'd wasted no time, moving immediately to a turbolift and ordering it to ops, where he'd planned on relieving Lieutenant Dax, who was standing watch this evening. By the time Dax called for him, he had already begun formulating primary plans of action and a series of backup contingency protocols that he would hold in reserve until they were needed.

Bulkheads sank swiftly past the open front of the turbolift cab. A familiar deck edge appeared and dropped out of sight, revealing ops, which was buzzing intently with anxious orders and a sharply palpable sense of urgency. Vaughn stepped off the turbolift before it came to a stop and walked quickly down the stairs to join Ezri Dax, who looked like the calm center in this storm. "Report," Vaughn said.

"Captain Kira and Lieutenant Ro have been—"

"Attacked, yes, I saw. Our response?"

"Major Cenn is heading up the investigation, starting in Taran'atar's quarters, which is where Kira and Ro were going when they were attacked. I've ordered Nog to help Cenn direct the forensic engineering teams."

Vaughn nodded. "What about Taran'atar?"

"The computer says he's not on the station, but if he's shrouded . . ." Dax trailed off as Vaughn impatiently gestured his understanding of the limitations of Deep Space 9's scanning hardware. She handed him a padd, on which a thorough search protocol was detailed. "We've declared intruder alert and started a deck-by-deck sweep."

Vaughn frowned. "If taking out Ro and Kira was his first move against the station, he'll go for the system capacitance control in the lower core—from there he could override the fail-safes and initiate a core overload."

Nodding, Dax said, "That was my opinion, too. I sealed off the auxiliary and primary control and put twenty security guards in an ambush deployment, near the primary heat exchangers."

"To mask their body heat and scent profiles," Vaughn said, impressed by the recent improvement of Dax's tactical skills. "Well done. Have you deployed a search team?"

"Yes, sir. I put Bowers in charge."

"Good choice." Vaughn turned to the situation table in the center of ops. Eyeing the schematic displayed there, he imagined all the places that a Jem'Hadar could conceal himself, and all the routes that Taran'atar might take as part of a campaign to cripple the station and kill its crew and inhabitants. Layers upon layers of conduits intersected kilometers of crawlways, and decommissioned ore chutes and conveyer channels circuited the lower decks. If Taran'atar had the discipline to remain shrouded, he could use untraveled passages such as those to evade capture almost indefinitely.

The hunt had been engaged—though at the moment, Vaughn wasn't entirely certain if he could say who was hunting whom.

3

Kira

IMPOSSIBLY HEAVY, FALLING THROUGH THE VOID, BLANK AND formless, terror and wonder without voice . . .

Turning her torso to the right as she drew her phaser, Kira felt the cold bite of the knife piercing her flesh, like a serpent's fang made of ice. Taran'atar vanished, retreating into his shroud. Ro lay on the deck, unmoving but still luminous, still tethered to life.

The world was gone. Time had ended.

Moving between the quiet poles of light and darkness, a windless expanse, loneliness with borders uncircumscribed, the terrible burdens of temporal existence shed like a dry skin . . .

Memories slipped past, grains of sand falling away from her consciousness. The faces of those she had loved and lost flashed by, almost too quickly for her to recognize— Shakaar, Bareil, her father. And so many senseless deaths—Ziyal, Marritza, Jadzia. A lifetime of unavenged wrongs—the slaughters of Gallitep, the servitude of her mother, the knife in her chest . . .

Old memories fled, jumbled and all at once, then tumbled away, fading as they sank into the ether of oblivion.

Frigid rain slashed across the resistance group's base camp, washed sheets of mud down the hillside. Kira Nerys huddled under an oiled sheet of canvas and pressed her back against the broad trunk of a *kava* tree. Lightning stuttered across the mist-swaddled plains far below, each gnarled fork dispelling the night for a split second and burning its sickly green afterimage into her retinas. The enemy was close, and that meant no fires tonight, no lanterns; just darkness and the chill of winter.

Sinking. Nameless. Empty.

Major Kira cradled the dying body of Aamin Marritza, the guilt in his eyes unassuaged by the fatal, murderous knife wound in his back. . . . Kira wept as she stood beside Bareil. He lay dying on a biobed in the infirmary, his brain disintegrating by degrees, his continued existence a gruesome mockery of the life he had lived. . . . No warning but the sound of the shot, a flash of light followed by screams of horror, chaos spreading through the crowd like fire through dry brush, the swirling confusion of panic—and Kira watched Shakaar's body fall dead, at last joining his *pagh,* which she would later learn had been extinguished months earlier by the parasite that had usurped his body.

Caught in an endless tide, swept away, like a foggy mist in a gale, coursing between stars that shone cold and remote . . .

Giving birth to Kirayoshi for Keiko and Miles, love's first blush, the warmth of a first kiss, the taste of something sweet, the spicy flavor of a *hasperat,* the dusty rose of a sunset on a hazy summer day, the bittersweet glory of music that could move her to tears, Benjamin Sisko's smile when he returned to the commander's office on the station . . . all her memories of joy, great and small, were torn from her, plucked from her pleading grasp, stolen—

Whiteness. Bright and endless, yet suffocatingly close. The muffling, liquid warmth of the womb—

I'm Kira Nerys. Alone in an eternity of ethereal light, she reached reflexively for her chest. Her body was whole; no injuries, no rends in the fabric of her uniform belied her mortal fate. There was no ground under her feet, yet she stood upright. There was no apparent source of light, but it was everywhere, as if shadows had been banished from existence. Kira had never before been here "in the flesh," as Sisko had, but she knew without a doubt that this was the Celestial Temple.

A woman's voice, monotonal and deep with maturity, broke the deep pulse of otherworldly stillness, and Kira knew that she was not alone here, had never been alone here, that to be here was to be with Them, with the Prophets, outside of time.

"Our hand," said the image of Opaka.

A vision of Ro added, "Our hand is closed." Kira got the distinct impression that they were talking not to her but around her.

"I don't understand," Kira said. "What does that mean? Your hand is closed? Are you saying I'm unwelcome?"

More faces appeared from the shining white curtain of timelessness. Shakaar. Marritza. Bareil. Ziyal. Tekeny. Her father. Jadzia.

They came, one by one, from all directions.

Surrounded, she turned back and forth as they spoke.

"Our hand is uncertain," said the Shakaar Prophet.

"Its purpose unclear," the Jadzia Prophet said.

The Bareil Prophet was suddenly close to her, centimeters from her face. He studied her with a gaze as deep as the reach between galaxies. "Our hand is not ready."

"Not ready for what?" Kira was confused. "To take my hand? To let me into the Temple?"

"Our hand must be opened," the Ziyal Prophet said.

The Jadzia Prophet circled Kira. "It must reach out to our children."

Kira turned her head to follow Jadzia only to find a Prophet-as-Vaughn crossing in the other direction. "Our children need the guidance of our hand," he said.

"I understand," Kira said, even though she really didn't.

A new voice, rich and warm, turned her on her heel. "I'm glad you've come," said a vision of Ben Sisko. "It was time."

"Ben?" Kira swelled with hope. "Is it really you?"

"It's *part* of me," he said. "I'm not sure really what part. I exist now in linear time, on Bajor . . . but part of me also exists here. I've always been here, but it wasn't always this way, until it was."

She shook her head. "I don't really follow."

He smiled, and it gave her comfort.

"It's not important," he said. "At least . . . not yet."

Over Sisko's shoulder, see saw her final moments in the corridor on Deep Space 9, but from a remove, like a third-party observer, and all of it in that shapeless whiteness, like three actors performing without a set. Ro collapsed to the deck. Kira's own hand reached for her phaser. The knife left Taran'atar's hand and buried itself in her chest. Her blood spattered the deck as her shoulder slammed against the bulkhead.

"Ben," she said, suddenly afraid, "what's going to happen?"

"That's up to you," Sisko said.

"But am I . . . ?" The question stuck in her mind while she watched a vision of herself losing consciousness, a pool of blood spreading beneath her. "Is this death?"

"It's a place between life and death," he said.

"Is that why I'm here?"

"No," Sisko said.

"Then why *am* I here?"

The Opaka Prophet reached up and gently cupped her hand around Kira's right ear. "To set our hand upon the path."

4

The Alternate Universe—
Kalandra Sector

THE IMPATIENCE IN THE ROOM WAS PALPABLE. EVEN WITH her back turned, Intendant Kira felt the glowering stares of her fleet commanders, who sat on opposite sides of the conference table behind her.

Captain Klag, of the *Regent*-class battle cruiser *Gorkon* (named for the much-glorified Regent Gorkon, who led the Alliance to its decisive victory over the Terrans in the previous century), as usual was attired in bulky, ornate Klingon regalia, and he made a spectacle of his guzzling large quantities of bloodwine. Both his clothes and behavior drew attention away from the fact that he had only one arm, which allegedly he had lost in courageous single combat.

Providing a stark contrast to Klag's decorous raiment and boisterous manners were the simple, unadorned gray body armor and quiet demeanor of Gul Akellen Macet, commander of the Cardassian heavy warship *Trager.*

Both men, however, clearly had one thing in common this evening: They were annoyed at having been summoned to Intendant Kira's flagship, the Klingon-built dreadnought *Negh'Var*.

"We have the strength to crush them," Klag said. "We should be making a direct assault on the rebels at Terok Nor."

Gul Macet's nodding visage was reflected on the broad transparasteel window in front of Intendant Kira. "I concur," Macet said. "We could retake the station and break the back of the rebellion."

She shook her head, dismayed by their lack of foresight. "At what cost?" Turning away from the starscape to face them, she made little effort to mask her condescension. "The rebels have fortified it well, and they're poised to retaliate against Bajor itself. If we lay siege to Terok Nor, we lose Bajor; if they destroy Bajor, we annihilate them and their rebellion."

"You mean to push into the Badlands, then," Klag said. "A system-by-system cleansing of the rebel strongholds. That *will* be a glorious campaign." The one-armed Klingon sounded proud of himself. *He must think he knows my mind,* the Intendant decided, her stare concealing a sneer of contempt.

"Madness," Macet said to Klag as the Intendant settled into her seat at the head of the dull-black table. "Most of those settlements are little more than lures—bait meant to draw our ships into danger while the rebels fall back and regroup at Sindorin, where our sensors are all but useless."

Intendant Kira flashed a cruel grin. "Quite right, Macet. That's why I deployed the Ninth Klingon Fleet in a sneak attack on Sindorin two hours ago." That revelation drew an admiring half-smirk from Macet and an appreciative snarl from Klag.

Reaching for the pitcher of bloodwine in the middle of the table, Klag said, "Regent Martok let you use his beloved Ninth Fleet, did he?" He refilled his stein in one long, swift pour that splashed broadly on the tabletop. "What did that cost you?"

"More than you will ever know, Klag," the Intendant said, her tone stern and humorless. Though she had tried to keep secret as many details of her overall strategy as possible, she had been forced to reveal more than she would have liked to Martok in order to secure his assistance. Unlike the sexual favors she had granted in order to gain this starship, she had been forced to make real concessions this time. "Once the Ninth Fleet regroups with us, we'll be ready to move on to our next objective."

Macet dared to ask, "What *is* our next objective?"

"All in due time, Macet," Intendant Kira said.

Klag scrutinized her face, as if expecting her secrets to be laid suddenly bare in the crease of her worry-worn brow. It was, at least, a welcome change from his overt and incessant leers at the supple curves of her torso, which were flattered and enhanced by her snug, black body suit. "If it's not Terok Nor," he said, weighing his words as he spoke, "and the Badlands have already been cleared, then what are you scheming, Intendant? Not planning on trying to overthrow Martok, I hope?" The way he said it made Kira think that Klag wouldn't really mind if she did.

Her gleam of amusement was tempered by the dark designs taking shape in her thoughts. If all went well, however, usurping Martok's authority would be the least of her ambitions. Soon she would seal her pact with her new ally; from that day forward, she would never want for new worlds to conquer.

"Control of the Alliance?" she at last said softly. "That's always been your weakness, Klag. . . . You think too small."

5

Deep Space 9

MAJOR CENN STOOD IN THE MIDDLE OF TARAN'ATAR'S quarters. The forensic investigation transpired around him in roving patches of quietly intense activity. A forensic team sifted through splinters of broken polymer furniture on the floor, brushed aside motes of shattered glass. Inside the room, in front of the door, they had found a single dagger tine on the bluish gray carpet. A small, irregular scrape on the bulkhead beside the door marked the blade's point of breaking.

Lieutenant Nog patched in a portable scanner to the room's companel, whose tripolymer surface had a fist-sized hole in its center. The cavity spat out sparks and was surrounded by a webwork of cracks and fissures. Forensic specialist Lieutenant Michael Strang kneeled in the middle of the compartment and collected from the carpet samples of the amber-hued fluid that security officer Cardok had identified as Jem'Hadar blood. So far, Strang hadn't found any other types of organic fluid in the room, confirming Cardok's initial scan. That suggested to Cenn that the

Jem'Hadar had either inflicted his own wounds or had been up against an exceptionally tough opponent.

A soft chatter of beeps emanated from Nog's handheld device. Cenn turned toward the young Ferengi. "Are you in?"

"Yes, sir," Nog said, his eyes fixed on the display screen in his palm. "But there's not much here to see." He clicked through several screens of data. "It doesn't look like Taran'atar used the replicator more than a few times in the months he's been here. And the comm system . . ." His voice tapered off as his attention grew more focused. "That can't be right." Cenn waited with diminishing patience. Just as he was about to ask Nog to elaborate, Nog explained, "There's a huge discrepancy between his comm logs and his power usage."

Furrowing his brow suspiciously, Cenn stepped closer to Nog. "Can you be more specific, Lieutenant?"

"Yes, sir. Officially, he sent and received less than a quarter kiloquad of data since his arrival on Deep Space 9. But the power logs for this node show a lot more energy usage than that—enough for thousands of kiloquads of data."

The major leaned forward and eyed the data. "How many comm terminals are linked to this node?"

"Just this one," Nog said. "Lieutenant Ro ordered his comm system isolated on its own channel."

Cenn nodded. "Are there any simple explanations for this?"

With a shrug, Nog said, "A data error in the logs; mis-wired node relays; damage to the companel's memory buffer—"

"All right," Cenn said. "Noted. Run a full diagnostic and have your people check out all the hardware. If this is a glitch, I want it ruled out. But if it's not—"

"I'll call in the data recovery team now," Nog interrupted.

"Keep me posted," Cenn said, then nodded and stepped away to receive updated reports from the other specialists—all of which amounted to a variation on a theme: *We have no idea what happened here.*

The phaser rifle was heavy in Sam Bowers's hands as he met his search team in the corridor, at the scene of the attack on Kira and Ro. He was cautious not to step in the dark, and still glistening, puddles of Kira's blood. "Jull," he said, "report."

Ensign Jull Zehar looked up from his tricorder. The spiky-haired Bajoran security officer, one of the recent militia-to-Starfleet transfers, did a double take as he looked at Bowers, who had been in the middle of shaving when Dax ordered him to report here. Bowers's right cheek was shaved clean, along with the right half of his chin, but his upper lip and the left side of his face were thickly stubbled. Jull tried to pretend not to notice, but it was clearly too late for that. Averting his eyes, he said, "We've got Jem'Hadar blood and microscopic DNA traces on the deck. There's a strong trail from Taran'atar's quarters to the turbolift."

Jull pointed to the turbolift car. Security guards Hollim Azahn and Jarmus Lenn—both veterans of the station's Bajoran security detail during Odo's tenure, now looking as comfortable in Starfleet uniforms as if they'd worn them their entire lives—stood in its open doorway. Jarmus's phaser rifle bobbed slowly in her anxious hands; the blond woman was clearly eager to start the pursuit. Hollim was the more composed of the two. "This is the turbolift that stopped here at the time of the attack," he said calmly. "More blood and DNA traces inside."

"Hang on," Bowers told the handsome, thirtyish senior petty officer. "We're doing this by the book." He turned to face Jull. "You confirmed that the blood in the corridor originated in Taran'atar's quarters?"

"Yes, sir," Jull said. "Positive."

"No sign he doubled back? Maybe to set an ambush?"

"Negative," Jull said. "Decay rates in all samples are consistent with continuous progress from the quarters to the turbolift."

Bowers herded them all toward the turbolift with a wave of his arm. "All right, let's move out." As the four personnel crowded into the lift car, he continued, "Who has the activity logs for this thing?"

"I do, sir," Jarmus said. "Its first stop after leaving this deck was Runabout Pad A. The second was the fusion core, grid twenty-two."

The mention of the fusion core gave Bowers a cold chill of remembrance. Only eight months earlier, another Jem'Hadar soldier, Kitana'klan, had nearly succeeded in destroying Deep Space 9 by sparking an overload from there. Calamity had been only narrowly averted thanks to the combined efforts of Lieutenant ch'Thane, Commander Vaughn, Colonel Kira, and Taran'atar. If Taran'atar was now the enemy . . .

Hollim asked, "Where do we start the search, sir?"

Bowers made a snap decision. "Computer: Runabout Pad A." The turbolift shot upward, a hum of magnetic coils ramping up quickly then fading into a steady low drone. "If he's heading for the core," he said to the others, "there's more than enough people waiting for him already. We need to cut off his routes of escape." The rest of the team nodded in agreement—except Jull.

"But sir, flight ops are locked down," Jull said. "And Statham and Frazelli are up there. If we head for the runabouts and we're wrong—"

"If I'm right," Bowers said, cutting Jull off, "then Statham and Frazelli are the only thing between Taran'atar and one of our ships—and they'll need all the backup they can get."

Vaughn paced anxiously inside Captain Kira's office while the team in ops continued to search for Taran'atar and investigate the attack. So far the situation seemed unambiguous, the evidence incontrovertible: The Jem'Hadar observer had, without any obvious provocation, assaulted Kira and Ro and left them for dead.

It doesn't make any sense, Vaughn's instincts protested. *Odo ordered him to obey Kira as he would obey Odo himself. Why would he break his oath to a Founder? How is that even possible?*

Alternative scenarios eluded Vaughn's imagination. Neither Ro nor Kira would have consciously antagonized Taran'atar, and the Jem'Hadar elder had, in the past several months, exhibited truly extraordinary discipline and restraint. Vaughn wondered whether the security recordings at the Ananke Alpha prison might have missed some subtle communication between Taran'atar and the female changeling. *If she ordered him to act against Kira, he might have had no choice,* Vaughn speculated. In all their talks, he had never asked Taran'atar what would happen if a Jem'Hadar received conflicting orders from two different Founders. Torn between the wills of two "gods," how could he possibly serve both in good faith?

It was as likely—or unlikely—an explanation as any other. As far as Vaughn was concerned, though, it didn't matter one damned bit. He picked up the baseball on the captain's desk. Kira had told him, more than once, about the ball's totemic significance to Captain Sisko, and she had confessed to having developed her own superstitious attachment to it, as well.

Turning the ball in his hands, he remembered the day he had asked Kira for the privilege of being her first officer. She'd related the details of her dream about the discovery of the Orb of Memory—details that had matched perfectly his own experience in recovering the ancient artifact from the freighter *Kamal* in the Badlands. Vaughn had always prided himself on being a rational man . . . until that day. That was when he'd finally felt the pull of destiny, giving his soul ballast against the updraft of oblivion. After decades of wandering, he'd found a home on Deep Space 9 and a simpatico ally in Kira Nerys.

Sorrow and anger trembled his hand. He put down the ball.

Isolated now in the office, he wanted to lead every search, process every clue, run every scan himself. Instead he had delegated those tasks to all the best-qualified personnel on the station, marshaled every resource and warm body at his command. He took a few slow, deep breaths, then sat down in the chair behind the desk.

After a brief pause, he powered up the display screen and requested a secure channel to Ananke Alpha. The administrator of the facility, Warden Lisanne Hexter, was notorious for not cooperating with inquiries about the goings-on in her facility, and that had become only more true since its conversion to hold the female changeling as its sole prisoner. The watchword on Ananke Alpha these days was "paranoid"—and rightly so, in Vaughn's opinion. He could only hope that the exigent circumstances, coupled with his unusually high-security clearance, would make the administrator more forthcoming with the information that Vaughn needed.

A soft double tone indicated that the channel was being established; within moments, the frequency would be open.

If there was anything to be learned from the prison's records of Taran'atar's meeting with the female changeling, Vaughn would know soon enough.

Most Ferengi felt a premonitory tingle in the lobes when an opportunity for great profit was close at hand. Quark, however, had long believed that he had been born with a different kind of blessing—an infallible sixth sense for danger. So far it had kept him alive, for which he was genuinely thankful, but he had yet to find a way to turn his survival instinct into real money.

Tonight the intuitive buzz of trouble had begun the moment Commander Vaughn had stepped into the bar, only to turn and sprint out again, across the Promenade toward the infirmary. Quark's first impulse had been to follow him, but then that "sixth sense" had told him to stay put. Moments later, Lieutenant Dax's voice over the station's PA system had sounded an alert, and the entire station had begun shifting into lockdown. All the patrons in his bar had scrambled out, leaving dozens of tables empty except for their dirty dishes and half-drained glasses. Even unflappable Morn had abandoned his wager on the dabo table while the wheel had been in midspin—on a triple-over bet, no less. Fortunately, the rules of the house were very clear: Any money left behind on the table went directly into Quark's pocket.

Several minutes later, the mess had mostly been cleaned up, and the staff had been sent back to their quarters—all except Treir, Quark's tall, seductively aloof Orion dabo girl, who had taken it upon herself to "recalibrate" the dabo wheel. She had performed a clandestine statistical analysis of its results for the past month and had made a very convincing argument to Quark that it was demonstrating a variance of 0.028 percent from normal—in the players' favor. "The dabo wheel in a Ferengi embassy is tilted *away* from profit," she had said a few minutes ago, after handing over Morn's derelict winnings. "There must be a Rule of Acquisition or something against that."

As usual, she was right. Her reward was to be entrusted with this most sacred of all Ferengi gaming duties. "Make it spin fair again," he'd told her. "But not *too* fair."

Watching her work, he felt all too aware of the passing minutes without business, without revenue. Sometimes the station's alerts were brief, and business would resume almost immediately afterward. Sometimes they were preludes to sieges that could last for days and leave his customer base shell-shocked and homebound for a week or more. Regardless, he had little choice but to sit tight and wait out the crisis.

He was flipping idly through screen after screen of profit-and-loss projections on a padd when a large commotion drew his gaze out, away from his bar. Even though the Promenade was supposed to be locked down and deserted except for security, a crowd was gathering quickly outside the entrance to the infirmary.

That's never *good*, Quark knew from experience.

He leaned across the bar counter and pressed his left lobe to the window to eavesdrop more effectively on the worried murmurs that wafted across the thoroughfare. Hoping for a bit of gossip or a timely warning to pack his latinum and make a run for it, he instead heard two names repeated in nervous voices.

Kira. Ro.

The padd fell from his suddenly numb hand.

He vaulted over the bar and landed on his feet, but the pulled muscles in his back reminded him that he wasn't a young man anymore and had never been a particularly athletic one to begin with.

Grimacing and gritting his sharpened teeth against the pain, he hurried out the bar's front entrance and moved quickly but stiffly toward the infirmary. Despite being a head shorter than most of the people in his path, he pushed through them with the practiced ease of someone who despised waiting in lines almost as much as he hated paying retail. Along the way he heard the whispered gossip: that Kira and Ro had been attacked; that they lay inside, dying; that they might already be dead.

The door to the infirmary was locked. He reached inside his jacket's inner pockets and shuffled through his clutch of isolinear rods, looking for one that would unlock the door. *Not sapphire. Not jade. Not topaz, unless I want to set off an alarm.* He plucked a translucent crimson rod from the bunch and tucked the others back in his pockets for safekeeping. The rod clicked smoothly into the override panel next to the door, which opened.

Noise from the Promenade crowd followed him in, but it dropped away to a dull undertone as the door shut behind him. In the operating room adjacent to the main infirmary compartment, Quark saw Bashir and Tarses swapping medical jargon with Dr. Aylam, the newly assigned Bajoran surgeon. A female nurse and a male technician assisted them. Most of what they were saying didn't mean much to Quark, but the way they were saying it told him everything that was really important: Captain Kira's surgery was going very badly. Something was wrong, and they were fighting to stave off the inevitable.

For the moment, the doctors were all so engrossed in Kira's surgery that none of them noticed his entrance. He took a cautious, creeping step forward—and felt something sticky under the sole of his shoe. Looking down he realized that he had stepped in a half-dried bloodstain.

He continued on, across the main room, toward the intensive-care ward entrance, in the back to the right of the main doors. Poking his head around the curved privacy wall, he looked for and found Ro. She looked like she might be asleep. Her breathing was slow and soft. Quark stepped lightly, not wanting to wake her if she was resting. He reached her bedside and looked down at her. She was pale, to the point that even her lips seemed blanched. For the first time since he'd known her, there was no edge in her countenance, no steely quality. *She looks . . . fragile.*

She lolled her head in his direction. Her eyes fluttered slightly. She moved groggily, and Quark figured she had probably been given some really potent painkillers. *Lucky her.*

"Quark," Ro said, a tremor in her voice betraying her heightened emotional state. "What're you doing here?"

"What does it look like?" He grasped her right hand and mustered a faltering half-smile. To his great relief, she returned it with one of her own.

The biobed display above her head was full of graphs and numbers and moving displays. Though he couldn't name even one of them, he had seen enough of them in action to know that the story they told about Ro's physical state was not encouraging. If any one of them was meant to represent her finances, he'd have to tell her that she was going broke faster than a Romulan trying to sell tribbles on Qo'noS. For now, changing the subject seemed like the wisest course of action. With genuine concern and curiosity, he asked, "What happened?"

"I don't know," she said. "The last thing I remember is . . ." She hesitated, apparently struggling with her memory. She continued, "I was in the turbolift with the captain. We . . . we were responding to an alert . . . in Taran'atar's quarters."

"I knew it," he muttered, anger flushing his lobes with heat. "That monster was bound to snap sooner or later."

She seemed confused. "It was Taran'atar?"

Indignant, he replied, "Who else would it be?"

"I didn't see who attacked us," she said.

"Of course not," Quark said. "He was probably doing that little invisibility trick of his." Giving her hand another squeeze, he added, "Probably too scared to face you head-on."

"Yeah," she said with pained but good-natured sarcasm. "I'm sure that was it." The increasingly tense discussion in the adjacent room drew her attention. "What's happening? Is the captain all right?"

"I don't think so," Quark said, realizing only belatedly that total honesty probably wasn't the best idea right now.

"I know you can hear what they're saying," Ro said. "What's going on?"

He knew there would be no stalling her, no distracting her. Closing his eyes, he listened carefully for a moment. In a hushed, grim tone of voice, he said, "Sounds like she's bleeding out." After a few more seconds, he added, "They've run out of blood for transfusion, and the gadgets aren't enough."

"Tap my combadge for me," she said.

"Why?"

"Just do it, Quark."

He reached out and gingerly tapped her combadge. It chirped once to confirm that it was active. Ro's voice was sharp with anger. "Lieutenant Ro to surgical suite!" Her volume made Quark wince and cover his auditory canals. "Dr. Bashir! Dr. Tarses! Nurse! Anyone! Get in here!"

Nurse Etana entered a few moments later and cast a flustered glare at Ro. "What is it, Lieutenant?"

"Is it true the captain needs a blood transfusion?"

"Yes, but—"

"We have the same blood type," Ro said. "Take mine."

"That's very generous, Lieutenant, but—"

"You're wasting time," Ro said. "Just draw what you—"

Etana stepped inside, clear of the entryway. "Calm down, Lieutenant. We have the situation under control." Quark became aware of the rising buzz of crowd chatter getting closer. He and Ro watched as the nurse led in the people who had been congregating outside. Quark only now realized they were all Bajoran personnel and residents, and he estimated that there were more than forty people in the main group.

The crowd milled about uncertainly in the confined space of the intensive-care ward. "Here is what you need to know," Etana said to them. "Captain Kira has been seriously injured and has lost a lot of blood. We don't have enough to transfuse her sufficiently for the surgery she needs to survive. Our records indicate that each of you has the same blood type as Captain Kira. We can't force any of you to donate blood, but we're asking for volunteers." Hesitant looks worked their way around the room, passed from one cluster of faces to the next.

Then, from the center of the group, a man's voice called out. "I will go first."

The crowd parted to let the speaker step forward. Emerging from the cluster of bodies was Vedek Capril, keeper of the station's Bajoran shrine. He stepped into the ward next to Etana, then turned and looked back at the crowd. "In the name of the Prophets, I implore each of you to join me in helping Kira Nerys in her time of need."

Ro's sarcasm was bitter and sharp. "Better late than never, right, Vedek? I see you brought an audience."

Quark winced; standing next to Ro when she was spoiling for a fight was like holding a metal rod in the middle of a lightning storm. Etana and Capril turned to face her. Around them, the other Bajorans craned and leaned to catch a glimpse of what was going on.

Capril met Ro's poisonous stare with a look of contrition. "Do you want to tell me what I already know?" He took a few steps toward her and Quark. "That I turned my back on Kira when Yevir had her Attainted? Or that I abandoned her after years of spiritual fellowship?" Taking another step, he continued, "Maybe you think I'm an opportunist? That I'm trying to curry favor or forgiveness, now that her Attainder has been lifted?" He stopped at the foot of Ro's bed. "Would you consider another explanation?"

Her mood changed from hostile to defensive. "Such as?"

"That I am ashamed of what I did—though I would do it again if such were my orders from the Vedek Assembly." He sighed. "You serve something larger than yourself, just as I do. Sometimes you obey, even when you don't agree."

An angry snort of breath conveyed her derision. "And sometimes you don't. You betrayed her."

"And now I'll give my blood for her," Capril said. "Make

of that what you will." He turned and stepped away, nodding to Etana that he was ready to make his blood donation.

"We can take four donations at a time," the nurse said to the crowd. "Please form a line, and we'll do this as quickly as possible." She led Capril to a biobed, then directed the next three volunteers to the other free beds in the ward, which quickly filled to capacity. Etana circuited the room, hooking up portable blood extractors to each of the volunteers' arms.

Quark lingered beside Ro, who continued to shoot withering glares at Capril. "You know," Quark said confidentially, "if you want to pick fights with people, you should wait till you're back on your feet."

Fear, rage, and grief darkened her expression. "I might never *be* back on my feet, Quark. I'm paralyzed."

Vaughn scrutinized the security recording of Taran'atar's brief visit with the female changeling at Ananke Alpha. It was being transmitted on a secure uplink from the top-secret prison facility. Warden Hexter had been unexpectedly forthcoming with the information, though she had cautioned him that they had spent the past week studying it in minute detail. There was absolutely nothing of interest, she had said, nor anything of relevance to the attack on Captain Kira. Vaughn had no reason to doubt her, but he intended to watch the recording and decide for himself.

He watched several angles of the enhanced video playback on one side of the screen; he skimmed the written transcript of the conversation on the other. As fascinating as the insight into Taran'atar's relationship to Odo and the other Founders was, it didn't offer much immediate understanding of why he had attacked Kira, why he had defied Odo's explicit orders—until the female changeling began to speak against Odo's loyalty.

"I would not presume to evaluate the loyalties of a Founder," Taran'atar said on the recording.

"Of course you wouldn't," the Founder said. *"You are not capable of doing so. But I am."* She continued for nearly a minute, recounting Odo's history among the "solids" of the Alpha Quadrant, then segued into a general criticism of Odo's efforts to affect a rapprochement between the Dominion and the allied powers of the Alpha Quadrant. Vaughn began to think that the female changeling's rebuke of Odo was a dead end until she said something that, with the benefit of tragic hindsight, chilled him to the marrow: *"And when he fails, he will abandon the Great Link, and he will return to Kira. Not just for weeks, but for as long as Kira lives."*

Vaughn paused the playback. Was that it? Had the female changeling's prognostication of Odo's dereliction of the Dominion in favor of Kira provoked Taran'atar to try to kill the captain, as a preemptive measure? Vaughn wanted to dismiss the notion as absurd, but it gnawed at him. Taran'atar's obedience to Kira had not been for the captain's sake but for Odo's. No matter that the Jem'Hadar elder had stood beside him and Kira against common enemies; at his core, Taran'atar remained loyal to only one master—the Dominion. More specifically, to its overlords, the Founders. It was not difficult to believe that if he had been led by a Founder to believe that Kira's continued existence posed a threat to the stability of the Dominion—or even to the Great Link itself—he would interpret that as a directive from one of his gods to intervene. To remove the threat.

A comm signal disrupted his ruminations. *"Commander,"*

said Dax, who was coordinating the search and investigation from ops. *"We've got a situation."*

"On my way," Vaughn said, terminating the connection to Ananke Alpha. He practically launched himself from the chair. The adrenaline rush brought on by the crisis was almost enough to mask the stiffness in his 102-year-old joints and muscles.

He strode through the parting office doors into ops and moved briskly down the stairs, to the situation table in the center of the room. Dax was already there, along with security officer Ensign Jang Si Naran, a slender young Thallonian with a goatee and a braided length of hair on the back of his otherwise bald, rust-red pate. "Report," Vaughn said to Dax.

"We think Taran'atar might already be off the station," she said. She tapped in a few commands on the tabletop display. The asymmetrically configured Cardassian interface lit up with several screens of data. "There's no evidence that he tried to reach the fusion core. Sending the turbolift down there looks like a diversionary tactic, something to split our focus."

Vaughn's ire was rising as he looked at Ensign Si Naran. "How did he get off the station?"

The young Thallonian activated his own screens of data on the situation table. "Lieutenant Bowers and his team tracked the target to Runabout Pad A," he said, projecting his steady baritone voice like a physical force. "The trail terminates there. We've ruled out double-backs or beam-outs."

"So where is he?"

Si Naran and Dax traded apprehensive glances. It was Dax who spoke first. *"Euphrates* left on a short maintenance flight about two minutes before the alert sounded."

She retrieved a copy of the station's flight logs. "According to the turbolift activity log, Taran'atar could've reached the *Euphrates* almost a minute before it lifted off."

As he perused the flight log, one detail captured Vaughn's attention: Prynn was the runabout's pilot and sole passenger. "Where's the *Euphrates* now?"

Dax checked the long-range sensors. "Bearing one-nine-eight, mark three-five," she said. "She's way off her flight plan and cruising at warp eight-point-one."

Vaughn was sure Dax had read the warp-speed data wrong. "Eight-point-one? A *runabout*?"

"Lieutenant Nog's been toying with some 'upgrades,' sir."

"Ensign Selzner," Vaughn bellowed to the communications officer. "Hail the *Euphrates*, priority one. Put it onscreen."

"Aye, sir," Selzner said as she entered the commands. Several tense seconds dragged past while she worked at her console, frustration slowly twisting her overbite into a frown. "No response, sir."

"Are you sure they're receiving us?"

"Yes, sir." Selzner checked her readings again. "I have a confirmed signal lock, but no response."

"Open a channel," Vaughn said. He waited until Selzner nodded to him that it was ready, then he continued. "Runabout *Euphrates*, this is Commander Vaughn on Deep Space 9. We know you're receiving us. Respond immediately. That's an order."

The silence weighed heavily on Vaughn, who hoped that Dax and Si Naran were wrong, that Taran'atar was still on the station, and that Prynn was out on another of her typical high-speed joyrides, music blaring so loud that it drowned out the comm. It was a reassuring lie, but he didn't believe it.

"Dax," he said. "Access the runabout's transponder and initiate a command override. I want that ship back *now*."

"Aye, sir," Dax said. She opened the command channel to the *Euphrates* while Si Naran retrieved its command prefix code.

With every passing moment, Vaughn imagined that he could actually feel the *Euphrates*—and Prynn—racing farther from his reach. Then a shrill alert tone from the situation table brought Dax and Si Naran's joint efforts to a halt.

Dax looked up from her work, her face taut from the effort of trying to hide her dismay. "The runabout's transponder is offline," she said. "We can't engage the override."

"Si Naran," Vaughn said, "get a long-range sensor lock on the *Euphrates* and track it as long as you can." Si Naran nodded once and went to work. Vaughn turned toward Dax. "Taran'atar's on the *Euphrates,* and I'm going after him in the *Defiant*. You're in command of the station until I get back."

"Good luck, sir."

Vaughn tapped his combadge as he moved toward the turbolift. "Vaughn to Bowers."

"Bowers here."

"Get to the *Defiant* and prep her to ship out, on the double. Round up a security team that has combat experience against Jem'Hadar."

"Aye, sir," Bowers said. *"On my way."*

"Vaughn out."

The turbolift arrived. He stepped inside and directed it simply, *"Defiant."*

Watching the decks rush past as the lift descended, acid churned in Vaughn's gut. His pulse was heavy and oppressive, thudding mercilessly in his ears, and his breath came quick and shallow. He concentrated on slowing his respiration and fought to steady his shaking frame, which suddenly felt as old as its years. *Cool head,* he told himself. *Don't lose control. Calm.*

Despite years of training, he couldn't unravel the knot of anger swelling inside him. He couldn't unclench his jaw. There was no trick he knew that would ease his swelling fury.

That bastard has my daughter.

Worst of all, he knew that was the optimistic scenario.

The pragmatist in him knew that Taran'atar, having seized the runabout, likely would have little or no use for a hostage—or, if he did, he probably wouldn't for long.

If that was the case, then Prynn was as good as dead.

6

Runabout *Euphrates*

STARS STREAKED PAST THE *EUPHRATES,* DISTORTED BY THE subspace effects of the ship's warp field. Taran'atar stood behind Ensign Tenmei, observing every movement of her slender hands over the ship's main console.

Without looking up, she said, "Where are we going?"

"Maintain your course and speed."

He hadn't expected to get this far. When he'd left Kira and Ro, he had thought that the likeliest outcome would be a close-quarters firefight that would end in his death or capture. If he had been forced to pilot the runabout or another craft off the station himself, he'd anticipated shooting his way out and being snared or destroyed by Deep Space 9's weapons array.

Instead, he was nearly a billion kilometers away from the station, with a hostage whose presence might prove valuable in curbing Commander Vaughn's tactical options. Objectively, he had scored a victory, but he still felt incomplete, his mission unfinished. Something was compelling him to stay in motion, had driven him to defy Odo and leave the station. But he didn't know what . . . or who. He closed his eyes. The harder he tried to remember what had led him to this, the more the truth eluded him. All that remained was *that* face. *Her* face.

He opened his eyes wide, his gaze sharp. Looking inward was a distraction. His training had always stressed that he be aware of his surroundings and his self, that he be in control, and that he stay attuned to where he was and to what he was doing.

For her part, Tenmei demonstrated those qualities admirably. After he had made clear that he was in command, she had quietly obeyed his orders. Though she was a hostage, she still comported herself with dignity and discipline. *Like her father,* Taran'atar thought. Aside from Captain Kira, Commander Vaughn had proved to be one of the few Alpha Quadrant denizens worthy of Taran'atar's respect. To a lesser degree, Dr. Bashir also had shown potential, but his obvious hesitation to embrace that which made him superior reeked of weakness to Taran'atar.

His previous experience with runabouts had led him to believe that they weren't capable of warp speeds greater than five on the Federation scale, but this one had been modified to be capable of speeds up to warp eight. Exceptionally fast as it was—and despite the small bit of extra speed they'd picked up with a wide slingshot maneuver around Bajor's primary star—he knew it would not be able to outrun the *Defiant* once that ship reached its maximum cruising velocity. By his best estimate, assuming a roughly one-hour head start for the *Euphrates,* the *Defiant* would still overtake them inside of ten minutes once it finally left the station and engaged pursuit.

Pushing the runabout for more speed was out of the question. Its hull already screamed under the stress of a velocity for which it hadn't been designed. The small craft shook violently as it sliced through eddies of subspace distortion, which lingered beyond the far rim of B'hava'el's outer cometary debris shell.

Confronting the *Defiant* would be an ineffectual tactic. Surrender was not an option.

He reached down and displayed a local star chart on the center nav screen. For a moment his focus on the dots and human-language symbols on the screen blurred. He struggled to overcome the fatigue that slowly crowded in on his thoughts. Fixing his attention required more effort than he was accustomed to.

It had been four days since he'd last slept and that had been during the journey back from Ananke Alpha. After three days he had begun to feel the need once more. *Resist,* he commanded himself, but the more he raged against the torpor, the more swiftly it dimmed his sense of clarity.

To slip from consciousness, to lose himself even briefly to oblivion was disgraceful enough, but his aging mind had since shamed him with a new defect: dreams. Aside from his alarm at "recalling" events that had never really happened, he was disturbed that the experiences were so shockingly vivid, as fully realized as any holodeck simulation and complete with tactile and olfactory stimuli.

Part of him was glad that this new imperfection hadn't manifested before his visit to the Founder. If it had, he would have been too ashamed of his debased state to face her. As it was, his conversation with her had taken an unexpected turn, leaving him unable to broach the topic of his infirmity; now his situation had worsened. He was certain that the advent of dreams signaled a serious degradation of his mental faculties.

His genetic imperative in this circumstance was clear: He was to seek correction from a Vorta or a Founder. However, there was no one to whom Taran'atar could go, given the fact that he had no way to contact Odo, who had barred him from returning to the Gamma Quadrant except on Kira's orders; that access to the Founder at Ananke Alpha was essentially impossible; and that all the Vorta had been recalled to Dominion space. No voice of counsel remained to lift his darkening shroud of madness.

Yet, looking at the star chart, he knew exactly where to go. First, however, there remained the matter of negating the *Defiant*'s numerous operational advantages. He locked in a set of coordinates and routed them to Ensign Tenmei's console.

"Adjust course as indicated," he said. "Maintain speed."

Tenmei entered the course change but did not verbally acknowledge the order as she would do for a superior Starfleet officer. Taran'atar respected her small gesture of passive defiance.

He checked the projected flight time to the new target point, then reconfigured the copilot's console to access the runabout's tactical system. He was pleased to find its ordnance package at full capacity. Looking at Ensign Tenmei, he said, "Retrieve an environment suit from the utility corridor."

She turned her chair and looked him in the eye for the first time since he had commandeered the ship. Her expression was neutral, betraying no sign of anxiety or animosity. After a moment of silent mutual regard, she stood up and walked toward the cockpit door. As it opened, he added, "Instruct the computer to keep the door open."

Prynn paused in the open doorway. With her back to him, she said, "Computer: Hold the cockpit hatch open."

"Acknowledged," the computer voice responded.

She stepped into the center compartment of the runabout, passed the emergency transporter, and opened the hatch to the utility corridor, which led to the aft compartment. She walked to the middle of the corridor and opened the equipment locker. Taran'atar looked back and observed her, making certain that she did not attempt to retrieve a weapon and conceal it behind or beneath the bulky, grayish-white pressure suit and helmet. She bundled it tightly and set the helmet on top of it, then closed the locker, picked up the bundle, and carried it back to the cockpit. Without preamble, she offered it to Taran'atar.

He took it from her. "Resume your duties."

With slow, quiet grace she sat down, swiveled her chair back toward her console, and resumed piloting the ship. He continued to watch her hands and her eyes. Her economy of movement was unusual for a human of her years, even one with Starfleet training. If she was pondering a tactical response, she wasn't telegraphing her intentions in the slightest.

Dividing his attention was a luxury he could ill afford under the circumstances, but as he began preparing for his inevitable encounter with the *Defiant*, he made certain to keep Ensign Tenmei inside the range of his peripheral vision. He had seen her kind before—and he knew not to turn his back on her.

Prynn didn't expect an answer, but she asked anyway. "Where are we going?"

"Maintain your course and speed," Taran'atar said, looming behind her right shoulder. He remained close enough to see everything that she did—even, she suspected, the movement of her eyes, in her reflection on the cockpit windshield. She was careful not to eye him too closely, but in fleeting glimpses she noticed telltale signs that he was distracted.

He closed his eyes. She used the brief respite from his scrutiny to steal a look at the readouts from the warp coils, which Nog had modified for this flight. The status indicators were all borderline; the system was at its limits.

By the time Taran'atar's eyes snapped open again, Prynn had returned her attention to the console in front of her. She made some small adjustments to keep the ship's course steady. Already she was considering her best options for sabotaging the runabout without destroying it. *Cutting the inertial dampener would scatter us across half a light-year.* She ruled out that plan except as a last resort. *Warp field collapse is the best bet,* she decided. It was risky; if she executed it too abruptly, she might breach the runabout's warp core. If she did it correctly, though, the resulting subspace disruption wave would draw attention from any starship within sensor range. *Better than taking odds on when he plans to kill me,* she mused darkly.

Part of the trick would be waiting until the right kind of starship was close enough to detect the runabout's engine failure; it wasn't enough to look for one that might be able to render mechanical assistance. Attracting a commercial freighter or other civilian ship wouldn't do any good; if anything, involving them in this mess would just put innocent lives at risk. Fortunately, the *Euphrates* was cruising toward the Cardassian border, which was still heavily patrolled by allied peacekeeping forces. *Just a matter of time,* Prynn encouraged herself. *Never thought I'd be praying to see a Romulan warbird, though.*

Taran'atar reached one hand over to the copilot's console and began interfacing with its companel. In the middle of inputting commands, he hesitated. Sneaking a sidelong look at him, Prynn saw that his eyes once more had taken on a faraway stare, like he was peering through the bulkhead into deep space.

With a gentle brush of her left small finger over the fuel intermix panel, she disengaged its safeties. It was the first of three minor tweaks she would need to make in order to collapse the runabout's warp field and cripple its warp drive.

His brief pause ended. He called up a star chart.

Breathe, Prynn reminded herself. *No fear . . . you out-skied an avalanche through the Tanglor ice chute on Jotunheim. You crossed the Burning Sea of Coridan in an open glider. You're not afraid of this guy.* She couldn't help taking another look at his stern reflection in the windshield. *The hell I'm not.*

There was little point lying to herself. In hand-to-hand combat, she knew she would have no chance against a Jem'Hadar as experienced as Taran'atar. As long as he was conscious and unrestrained, there was almost no scenario she could imagine that would enable her to escape. Even with his moments of distraction, he clearly wasn't incapacitated.

Still, she had started the process of disabling the runabout, and that was something. He wasn't saying much, other than issuing orders, so she'd been unable to determine why he had commandeered her ship, or why he had needed to leave the station. If it had been anyone else—a member of the crew or a local civilian—she might have been content to ride out the crisis and try to defuse the situation before it escalated any further. But considering who Taran'atar was and what he was capable of, she could only assume the worst: that he was taking some irrevocable action against the station, against Starfleet, or perhaps even against Bajor or the Federation as a whole.

Unless she received information to the contrary, she decided, she would assume that Taran'atar was acting as an enemy soldier, one who now had control of a Federation ship. It was her duty to deprive him, by any means available, of that control and—if extreme measures proved necessary—of the ship itself.

He would almost certainly kill her if she succeeded in crippling the runabout, but she had to assume he meant to kill her eventually, anyway. She decided not to factor that risk into her decision-making process.

A new set of coordinates appeared on her flight control monitor, transferred from the copilot's station. "Adjust course as indicated," Taran'atar said. "Maintain speed."

She entered the course change and made certain that the speed remained constant. For the moment Taran'atar seemed satisfied. He turned back to the copilot's station and began reconfiguring the main panel. The next adjustment she needed to make for her sabotage was to the warp field stabilizer, whose override interface was on the console above her head. She had just begun concocting an excuse to reach up and access that panel when Taran'atar turned and commanded her, "Retrieve an environment suit from the utility corridor."

Damn, she thought. *That's not a good sign.* Her hope for surviving this encounter diminished by another degree. Slowly she turned her chair to face him, committed to looking him in the eye regardless of the consequences. *If I'm going to die, I'll do it head-on.* Steadily, gracefully, she stood up and moved toward the hatch. *If I'm quick, I can make a break for the aft weapons locker. By the time he gets through the—*

"Instruct the computer to keep the door open," he said.

Naturally. She felt her ire rise at being given orders by an enemy. Steadying her temper and her voice, she said, "Computer: Hold the cockpit hatch open."

"Acknowledged."

Moving out of the cockpit, she passed the emergency transport pad and lamented that she had no time to set it to dematerialize Taran'atar and scatter his atoms into space. She opened the hatch at the back of the compartment and stepped into the utility corridor. On the port side of the corridor was the equipment locker. She opened it, removed a standard-issue EVA suit, and folded it neatly on the low shelf. Pulling a helmet from the rack on the back wall, she felt Taran'atar watching her. *Gotta give him credit. He's thorough.* She picked up the suit and helmet, closed the locker, and walked back to the cockpit. Wishing in vain that the gear had a live grenade tucked inside it, she pushed the bundle into Taran'atar's gray, leathery hands.

"Resume your duties," he said. He turned his attention back to the copilot's console. Prynn glimpsed it long enough to see that he was accessing the ship's weapon systems.

She turned her chair back to its forward-facing position. Out of the corner of her eye, she could tell that he was still watching her, even while he feigned interest in something else. Decoupling the warp field stabilizer would have to wait, perhaps for his next moment of lost or divided focus.

Checking the new coordinates she had plotted, she expected to find a planet, or perhaps an energy signature indicating a deep space rendezvous with another ship. She found neither.

Surveying Taran'atar's chosen destination, Prynn wondered for the first time if the Jem'Hadar elder had, in fact, simply gone insane.

7

Kira

In an endless sea of white, Kira asked, *"What path?"*

The Opaka Prophet let go of Kira's ear, which grew cold at the absence of her divine touch. *"The path."*

Kira blinked. She and the Shakaar Prophet stood together, just the two of them, on a lonely road that stretched into the eternal distance and vanished to a point in the horizonless, blank expanse. "We must offer our hand to our children," he said to her with the quiet patience of a teacher.

"In peace," said the Opaka Prophet.

"Or in war," said an ominous voice behind her back. She turned, her heart seizing with cold dread—

And she stood on the Promenade of Deep Space 9. It was dark and deserted, the space beyond its arching windows, starless, empty and black. Jake Sisko, his eyes aglow with the malice of the Pah-wraith, stood at the far end of the concourse. Kira's memory of this confrontation rushed back to her, the deep sense of wholeness and power and peace that came with being the vessel of the Prophets, who confronted the Pah-wraith and freed Jake.

"It is the vessel," the Jake-as-Pah-wraith Prophet said.

"You mean me?" Kira said. "Yes, I was."

A child took her right hand. It was Molly O'Brien. Tiny and adorable, smiling with sweetness and trust, she clutched Kira's hand. All of Kira's attention focused on the little girl.

The Opaka Prophet was on Kira's left. "What was . . . remains," she said.

Kira looked up at Opaka and realized that they were in the ruins of a great city, one that she had never seen before. Plumes of gray smoke twisted up out of the rubble. Alien beings picked through the debris, salvaging tiny items from lives turned to dust. Molly tightened her grip on Kira's hand. When Kira looked down at the girl, Molly looked back at her with a frighteningly ancient wisdom. "Our hand can stop this," she said in a child's voice chilled by an unnatural lack of affectation.

A few meters past the Molly Prophet, a pair of elegantly shod feet appeared, partially covered by the hemmed robes of a Bajoran vedek. Kira looked up at Yevir, the man who had Attainted her and cast her out of fellowship until Opaka had appealed to his mercy. He held a skull at arm's length. "Our hand is our action," he said, and the skull turned to powder in his palm, its particles scattered by a wind as cold as death.

The city and the people and the smoke all dissolved and melted away, and reality re-formed itself into a cross-shaped intersection of cobblestone roads in a parched, rose-red desertscape. Opaka remained steadfastly at Kira's side.

"Our hand needs guidance," the Opaka Prophet said.

"Direction," added the Vaughn Prophet.

"From me?" Kira was dumbstruck at the idea of the Prophets asking her counsel. "Are you asking me what *I* want?"

Several of the entities exchanged blank looks. A Keiko O'Brien Prophet said flatly, "It does not understand."

Kira tried to grasp what it was that the Prophets were asking of her, but it was all so vague.

"Our hand must bear our message," said the Shakaar Prophet, who was on the road behind her, kneeling at the boulevard's shoulder, watching a handful of sand fall through his spread fingers and drift away in the flow of a hot breeze.

Ziyal stood diagonally across from Kira, in the branch of the intersection to Kira's left. "Action and meaning must go together," the half-Cardassian, half-Bajoran young woman said.

Opposite Ziyal, Vaughn stood proudly, squinting against the harsh desert light. "Our hand must touch the linear."

Change rolled over Kira like an icy wave, turning the desert crossroads back into the shadowy thoroughfare of the Promenade. The Pah-wraith as Jake stood before her. "This our hand has done before," he said in a voice that rolled like thunder. "As the vessel."

Understanding eluded her. "You're talking about taking action in my reality? In linear time?"

"You are the vessel," said the Shakaar Prophet.

"I remember . . . but why? Why was I worthy? Why was I chosen?"

Sisko stepped forward to stand beside her. "Why was I?"

"But . . . you're the Emissary," Kira stammered.

"So?" He shrugged. "When the Prophets first met me, they didn't know what I was—they didn't understand linear time. But later they revealed that they'd set in motion a chain of events to ensure my existence. I was their creation in the past, but they were surprised to meet me in the present. They didn't know until they'd *met* me that they needed to *create* me. But does that mean that I was *worthy*? Or does it simply mean that I . . . *was*?"

The riddles, the paradoxes, the conundrums of linear and nonlinear time all left Kira with too many questions. "I don't see what that has to do with me," she said. "Or with this."

Every object and surface on the Promenade became radiant to the point of incandescence, then it all melted like wax and pooled into itself, revealing a nebula-streaked sky full of stars. The deck retreated under Kira's feet, and a tiny island of jagged rock formed behind her. Sisko vanished as a pillar of shimmering fluid rose from an opalescent, golden sea. The rising vortex made landfall beside her and detached from the vast ocean of the Great Link, and it became Odo.

She knew that it wasn't really him, but she was irrational and scared, and she let herself fall against him, seeking any solace, any shelter he would offer her. For a moment he embraced her, but then he gently pried her away and spoke to her in that rough-but-wise voice of his. "Our hand must reach our children."

"Our word and our action must be equal," the Vaughn Prophet said.

Whiteness enfolded Kira, until all that remained was her and the Opaka Prophet, who reached up and once again took hold of Kira's ear. "Our hand must fulfill the promise of our message."

Kira was desperate to understand. "What does that *mean*?"

"Walk the path," Opaka said, as the world changed again and transformed Kira with it. "Walk the path, and you will know."

8
Harkoum

DARKNESS DESCENDED, USHERED ONWARD BY A SCOURING wash of acid rain. Thunder rolled beyond the nearby foothills. The starport town of Iljar came alive; small oases of light slowly dotted its low sprawl of weathered brick façades and scrap-metal roofs. Most of Iljar's residents—all but a few of them temporary—preferred to hide from Harkoum's merciless daylight. Emancipated by the deepening shadow, they stirred for another evening of sordid entertainments and quasi-legal business dealings.

Grauq huddled in a deep alcove, whose weak overhead light fixture he'd smashed with his fist. Fragments of it crunched beneath his boots. He watched the entrance to the below-street-level docking platform across the muddy avenue. Berthed there, on the dingy circle of reinforced concrete, was the *Otamawan,* a small, six-seat cargo-runner. The beat-up little ship was capable of little more than a short hop within a star system or, perhaps, between two nearby systems.

It would be the Cardassian Woman's most likely target.

She wouldn't have many options, Grauq knew. Without currency, she was in no position to buy passage out of Iljar. She might try to barter work for transport, but Harkoum wasn't a world where trust was granted lightly to strangers. If she were stealthy, she could try to stow away—but then she'd run the risk of being carried farther from her destination rather than closer. After all the effort the Cardassian Woman had made to track the client to Harkoum, she wasn't likely now to leave any details to chance.

If she wanted out of Iljar, she would have to steal a ship.

There weren't many to choose from. Most of the freighter captains in town for the night had beamed down. The few other craft that were docked locally were either better secured, better defended, or would require more than one person to be flown safely—all except the *Otamawan*.

She will come for this ship, Grauq told himself again. *She has no other choice.*

Rain pattered heavily into a broad chain of dark gray puddles that filled the street in both directions; it pinged brightly on the rusted, corrugated metal roof above Grauq's head. A hooded figure walked quickly past, his footsteps splashing and echoing, and he made a quick right turn toward the cheap bordello. From a few blocks away, the shriek of a pulse pistol sliced through the soft white noise of the rain.

More than any other planet he'd visited, Grauq liked Harkoum. It was just as lawless and ungoverned as his homeworld of Chalna, and it had the added advantage of being mostly devoid of other Chalnoth. Aside from a handful of Klingons and Nausicaans, and a single Balduk mercenary employed by the same client who had engaged Grauq against the Cardassian Woman, most people on this planet were easily cowed. Money came easily; ships and women could be taken and discarded with equal ease. Talk here was cheap, and so were people's lives.

He was eager to face his prey. Anticipation for the fight and hunger for the kill nagged at him. Nervous energy made his lower jaw grind slowly back and forth, pressing his enormous canine incisors against the corners of his mouth. Last he had heard, the Cardassian Woman had rammed Jonu's flyer, knocking them both out of the sky. Unless the Cardassian Woman was a fool, she would flee toward Iljar rather than press deeper into the great southern desert, which the planet's first Cardassian settlers had called *Tarluk V'hel*—the Suns' Cauldron.

His right hand rested on the hilt of his knife. His left hand closed around the grip of his sidearm pistol. *Should I shoot her at range? Or take her by knife at close quarters?* Both methods had their merits, but in the end, he decided that the knife would be better. Victims' faces often went slack when taken down by a perfect shot through the heart; their passive expressions robbed the experience of its visceral thrill. But a knife killing, with a solid, final twist of the blade in the torso, always yielded a satisfying death mask.

Booming thunder rattled the loose pieces of the town and shook the wet ground under Grauq's feet. The rain, heavy before, now pummeled Iljar in torrential sheets. He could barely see the entrance to the docking bay across the street. The storm would offer good cover for the Cardassian Woman.

Grauq cupped his hand around a small canister on his belt and thumbed the dispenser tab. Two small, orange pills dropped into his palm. In a single, swatting motion, he tossed them into his mouth and swallowed. The dry, dusty pills stuck in his throat and burned slightly. He held out his enormous, gloved hand and caught a palmful of rainwater running off the roof. Ignoring the metallic bite of rust and the sour sting of acid, he slurped it down until the pills dislodged. Moments later the stimulants took effect, and his clarity sharpened.

The rain fell just as quickly, but he felt as though he could track every droplet at once, watching them trace weary paths across the ripples of metal and drizzle aimlessly through the cracks and channels of ancient stone walls. Moments still rushed past, but his thoughts rushed with them, suddenly equal to the myriad perspectives of space and time.

He hoped that none of the client's other bounty hunters found the Cardassian Woman first.

It wasn't that he needed the money, and he certainly didn't expect her to put up that entertaining a fight. He'd simply never *had* a Cardassian woman before. More than a few people had remarked that they were spitfires, given to fiery rages while being taken by force and utterly cold-blooded when it came time to exact their revenge.

Their collective reputation didn't concern him; he didn't plan on letting the Cardassian Woman live that long once he'd captured her. The client had made it clear that the target could be brought in dead or alive, but that dead was by far the preferable alternative.

Sharpening his knife in slow pulls against the whetstone on his bandolier, Grauq was more than happy to oblige.

9

Deep Space 9

NOG DIDN'T LIKE WHAT HE WAS SEEING AS HE DISSECTED THE activity logs in the companel's memory buffer. The data was fragmentary at best, all bits and pieces, virtual flotsam and jetsam in the isolinear pathways. None of it had coalesced into anything specific just yet, but only because it had been dissociated with prejudice: Someone had run a very sophisticated encryption and file-deletion routine to hide whatever all this used to be.

If there was one thing Nog loved almost as much as profit, though, it was a puzzle. The young Ferengi amended the data-recovery subroutine for the seventh time in less than an hour to compensate for the hashing these files had suffered. Somewhere in all of this there was a pattern. When he found it, he would be one step closer to "unbreaking the egg," as Chief O'Brien used to say, back in the days before Nog succeeded him as the station's chief of operations.

As satisfying as this task was, though, it didn't make it any easier for Nog to think of the *Defiant* shipping out without him. At Commander Vaughn's request, Nog was staying on Deep Space 9 to lead the forensic engineering team's investigation of Taran'atar's recent communications and information-related activity. Ensign Mikaela Leishman would head up the engineering staff on the *Defiant* in Nog's absence.

Nog understood the reasons for Vaughn's decision. He even agreed with them. But he still didn't like being left behind when the *Defiant* went into action. It just felt wrong.

That's the way it goes, he told himself. Thinking of Kira and Ro lying in the infirmary made his hands clench in anger. Breaking the encryption and reversing the data scrambling on Taran'atar's messages might be the only chance of learning why the Jem'Hadar had turned violent, and the only chance for bringing him to justice. *This is my mission, and I'm going to succeed.* He unclenched his hands. *I won't let the captain down. I won't let Ro down.* Taking a breath, he began a new round of decryption protocols. *I won't let* myself *down.*

His enormous, highly sensitive Ferengi ears detected Major Cenn's light-footed, perfectly paced footfalls as he approached.

"Anything to report, Lieutenant?"

"Yes, sir," Nog said. "I'm getting closer to reversing some of the data shredding and breaking the original encryption."

Peering intently down at Nog's work, Cenn said, "Is that sort of thing standard in Starfleet comm terminals?"

"No, sir." Nog held up his tricorder display for Cenn to see more easily. "It's not standard at all."

Cenn nodded. "Are we certain this isn't just routine comm traffic?"

"Not until we decrypt it," Nog said. "But I don't think this is routine. There's a serious mismatch between this memory buffer and the station's central comm logs." Highlighting the relevant data on the tricorder screen, Nog continued, "Even garbled, it's obvious there's a lot more data in this buffer than there should be. Since the buffer is used only for sending and receiving data on the main comm channel, Taran'atar either received a lot of information, or he sent out a lot of information. Or both. Based on the wear and tear in the router submatrix, I'd say he was probably transmitting more than receiving." Cenn looked away pensively. Nog lowered the tricorder and added, "Either way, he did an expert job of covering his tracks."

"How soon do you think we can uncover them?"

Nog shrugged. "A few hours. Less if I can get command approval to use more of the main computer for the analysis."

"I'll ask Lieutenant Dax to make the necessary arrangements," Cenn said. "Once you've restored the files—"

Nog interrupted, "I wouldn't say 'restored,' sir. They won't be perfect. More like reconstituted."

"All right," Cenn said. "When you've reconstituted the files, will you be able to tell me where Taran'atar sent them?"

On the tricorder display, a blinking indicator informed Nog that his new code string was successfully stitching some bits of a deleted data packet back together. He flashed a jagged grin at Major Cenn. "Ask me again in a few hours."

Ro Laren lay in the intensive-care ward, surrounded by blood donors and accompanied by Quark, who stood next to her bed and held her hand. "The doctors sound like they're almost done in there," he said, then gave her hand a gentle squeeze. She wanted to return the gesture, but she couldn't. There was no sensation in her hand—not from the pressure of Quark's grip or the warmth of his skin. Her hand remained motionless and distant, no matter how hard she concentrated on contracting its muscles.

Paralysis. Just the idea of it was enough to set her thoughts spiraling into panic and despair. She was waiting for someone—maybe Quark, maybe one of the doctors, or someone else—to trot out some idiotic platitude, such as *You're lucky to be alive.* Dismay gave way to rage. *Lucky to be a sack of meat? Lucky to be able to look down and see my body as a vestigial organ, a life-support system that doubles as an anchor? This isn't my idea of lucky.*

Dr. Tarses entered the ward and walked toward Ro. He paused along the way to confer with Nurse Etana, then continued until he reached Ro's bedside. Competing voices in Ro's head vied for expression. Her desperation wanted to ask Tarses what her chances were—could the doctors undo whatever had been done? Her pride refused to let herself be seen in such a weak and vulnerable light. Tarses didn't smile; he rested his hand softly on her shoulder. "Drs. Bashir and Aylam are still working on the captain," he said. "I'm going to have Nurse Etana prep you for surgery in a few minutes. Mr. Ingbar is hooking up a second operating platform in the surgical suite for you."

She nodded, a small gesture, and currently all she could muster. "How's the captain?" Asking about Kira was easier than asking about herself.

"It's too soon to tell," Tarses said. "There's still much to be done." The nurse joined him and handed him a padd. He gave it a quick look, applied his signature with the attached stylus, then handed it back to her. In a tone that Ro found alarmingly devoid of emotion, he asked, "Is there anyone you would like us to contact before you're anesthetized for surgery?"

Ro turned her head and looked at Quark, who squeezed her hand again and almost mustered a sad smile before his worry turned it into a crooked grimace. She looked back at Tarses. "No," she said, her words catching in her throat, choked back by her commingled gratitude and fear. "I'm all set here."

Tarses nodded, then he walked away. Ro guessed that he had returned to the operating theater. Nurse Etana moved among the other biobeds, thanking the blood donors and discharging them quickly but politely.

Blinking back tears, Ro said to Quark, "Keep a secret?"

The Ferengi grinned and cocked his head. "Have so far."

She laughed even as tears rolled from the corners of her eyes and tickled her ears. Her emotions felt like champagne erupting from an uncorked bottle, all jumbled together and defying her control. She reined in her mirth, only to face her grief, darker and deeper than before. Throughout her emotional round robin, she had Quark's undivided attention. Her confession crept out on a faltering whisper. "I'm scared."

He frowned. "That makes two of us."

Nurse Etana returned, this time carrying a surgical arch to fit over Ro's biobed. "Excuse me," she said to Quark as she lowered it into place over Ro's torso. The metallic shell locked into place with a soft click. Etana powered it up with a single touch of her hand on its main interface. Ro heard the bed's antigrav coils hum to life a moment before Etana detached it from its platform. The nurse guided the bed out of the ward and through the main room toward the surgical suite. Quark followed alongside, still grasping Ro's hand.

Dr. Tarses appeared in the surgical suite's doorway to meet Ro and Etana. He paused Ro's transfer at the threshold. "Ambassador Quark," Tarses said. "Regulations prohibit any unnecessary persons from entering this compartment during surgery." Quark stiffened at the curt dismissal.

"It'll be okay, Quark," Ro said. She wondered why she was the one comforting him. *It's not like* he's *going into surgery.* "Lockdown's over. You should get back to the bar."

Quark relaxed a little. "Good point," he said. "No telling what Treir's done to the place while I've been gone." He gave a last glance at Tarses and Etana, then looked back at Ro. "But I'll be right here when you wake up. That's a promise." With obvious reluctance, he let go of her hand.

Tarses and Etana guided the biobed into surgery. Quark, left behind, lingered on the edge of Ro's vision, then in her memory. The grim reality of her situation closed in around her.

Inside the surgical suite, she glimpsed Kira's face, hidden behind wires, gadgets, tubes, and a breathing mask. The room whirred and hummed softly with the sound of machinery keeping the captain alive. On either side of the captain, Bashir and Aylam worked in tense whispers. Ro's bed was secured to a platform parallel to Kira's. Nurse Etana stood behind Ro's head and prepared the delta-wave generator, which would guide Ro's brain into painless oblivion while her body was taken apart and put back together with the finest tools known to Federation science.

"You've suffered serious damage to two thoracic vertebrae," Dr. Tarses said as he appeared on her left, garbed in a fresh surgical smock. "Those fractures have caused tears in your spinal cord, which is why your legs are paralyzed. The loss of mobility in your arms and hands is likely due to a herniation-related bruising of the spinal cord near C-6 and C-7." Seeing the question in her confused expression, he added, "In your cervical vertebrae . . . your neck."

"Okay," she said.

"Repairing the damage in your neck shouldn't be difficult," Tarses said. "But the damage in your back is more serious, and we've had only limited success with repairing spinal cord tissue. We're going to do everything we can, but it's important for you to understand that we can't make any promises."

"Do what you can," Ro said. "Everything you can."

"We will," Tarses said, then he motioned for Etana to activate the delta-wave generator.

Ro's thoughts drifted and clouded almost instantly. Shadows swallowed the room from the edges inward. She sank into her own thoughts. As she surrendered to the comfort of darkness, she wondered whether she would awaken whole or as a pale facsimile of the woman she'd once been. Then light and memory faded, for what Ro could only hope would not be the last time.

Ezri Dax moved from one ops officer to the next, collecting status reports as she went. The station had resumed normal operations, except for a temporary quarantine around the investigation site near Taran'atar's quarters. She had just signed off on the engineering report from Ensign Kall Denna and paused at the situation table to compile her notes.

A synthetic tone sounded on Ensign Selzner's console. "Lieutenant," Selzner said. "Commander Vaughn is hailing us."

"On screen," Dax said.

Vaughn's face filled the hollow oval display suspended

high above the deck. Behind him the bridge of the *Defiant* bustled with activity. *"We're almost ready to ship out,"* he said. *"Do you still have a fix on the* Euphrates*?"*

"No, sir," Dax said. "Without the transponder we couldn't keep its signal locked. Ensign Si Naran is trying to boost our range now." She hesitated before adding, "We might have a better chance if we could triangulate our readings with sensor sweeps by ships in that area."

"No," Vaughn said. *"I don't want anyone else involved in this unless absolutely necessary. Even one stupid mistake could get Prynn killed. I'm not taking that chance."*

"I understand," Dax said. "But Starfleet might not."

"Don't tell them, then." He seemed to realize only after the words were spoken that they had come out . . . wrong. *"At least, not yet. Put off filing the official report until we can explain not only* what *happened but* why *it happened."*

"Yes, sir," Dax said, intuitively grasping the reasoning behind his order. Normally, an incident that incapacitated two senior officers would be reported to Starfleet Command as soon as possible. In this case, however, the fact that Taran'atar was the assailant would spark inflammatory questions for which the station's command team currently had no answers: *Was Taran'atar acting on orders from the female changeling? Is the Dominion trying to reignite its conflict with the Alpha Quadrant? Or is Taran'atar a rogue element?* Once roused, Starfleet Command would insist on taking action. Dax believed that Vaughn's instincts were probably correct: A clumsy, brute-force approach to this situation would only further endanger Prynn's life.

Assuming she's even still alive, Dax thought—but wisely kept to herself.

Vaughn looked away for a moment as he signed off on a junior officer's report. *"Any more word on Ro or the captain?"*

"Not yet," Dax said. "But Ro's in surgery now."

He sighed. *"All right, then. . . . We're all set over here. Defiant requesting clearance to depart."*

"Clearance granted," Dax said, nodding to the flight operations manager, who tapped in some commands on his panel and nodded back to her. "Docking clamps released, *Defiant*. You're clear to navigate. Good luck."

"Acknowledged," Vaughn said. "Defiant *out."*

The screen blinked off. Dax punched up an exterior view to replace it. She watched the *Defiant* fire its reverse thrusters and gently back away from the station. The ship pivoted 180 degrees and engaged its impulse drive. Moments later, it seemed to ripple and fade, then it vanished entirely as its cloak engaged. After a few seconds of gazing at the empty starfield, Dax turned off the viewscreen.

She walked up the stairs to the commander's office. It would probably be a few hours before Major Cenn's team was ready to make its next report. There was no way to guess when Kira and Ro might be out of surgery. And the situation with Taran'atar was now out of Dax's hands; the *Defiant,* with its vastly superior speed, power, and weaponry, would likely overtake the *Euphrates* in less than a quarter hour. What happened then was entirely up to two people: Taran'atar and Commander Vaughn.

Not exactly an encouraging scenario. The doors of the commander's office closed behind her. She walked to the desk, turned the chair, and sat down. She felt suddenly very heavy.

On the desk, the white orb of Benjamin Sisko's baseball

caught her eye. She reached out and picked it up. Turning it in her hand, she could almost feel the warmth of his hands still radiating from the leather. Her fingertips lingered on the coarse stitches as she turned it slowly, like a tiny planet.

"Computer," she said. "Open a channel to Bajor."

10

Defiant and Euphrates

LIEUTENANT GREG FORTE LOOKED UP FROM HIS TACTICAL display. "Commander, we have a sensor lock on the runabout."

"Good work," Vaughn said. "Patch it through to me here. Helm, adjust course to intercept."

Vaughn and Bowers stood on the portside of the *Defiant* bridge, at opposite ends of a large companel. The ship was traveling cloaked at maximum warp toward the hijacked runabout. On the left side of the companel was displayed a local star chart. Bowers shook his head. "I don't get it. What's his plan?"

"We can ask him that when we catch him," Vaughn said as he studied the charts. "Even at warp eight, he won't reach any planets before we're on top of him."

"If he had an accomplice, he might be heading toward a rendezvous," Bowers said. "Maybe with a faster ship."

"There's nothing on long-range sensors. If there's another ship out here, it's cloaked liked us." Vaughn called up a schematic of the *Euphrates* on the right-hand display.

"We need a way to disable his shields and knock him out of warp without risking fatalities, and we need it now."

"A low-power photon torpedo might be the safest bet," Bowers said. "But modulating the yield would be tricky."

Knowing that the rest of the bridge crew was listening in, Vaughn turned his head and raised his voice. "Ideas, anyone?"

Chairs turned as the crew met his gaze. Science officer Tariq Rahim spoke first. "We could try harmonizing our warp field with theirs and inducing a disruption wave. Collapse their warp field and knock 'em back to impulse."

"Not bad," Bowers said. "But if Taran'atar wants to go out in a blaze of glory, he could steer into us at warp and take us both out."

"Not if we keep our shields up," said Ensign Stefka Merimark, a tactical engineering specialist. "The runabout doesn't have the power to breach our shields, and we can take them out of warp before they get close enough to try."

Vaughn nodded. "Rahim, Merimark, you can make this work?"

"Aye, sir," Rahim said, and Merimark nodded her assent.

"Make it happen. Bowers, stand ready on phasers and the tractor beam. As soon as we have them at sublight, I want them to stay there."

"Yes, sir," Bowers said, then moved toward the aft tactical station. Vaughn returned to the captain's chair and checked the star chart on his tactical screen. Bowers had raised a good question, even if it hadn't been immediately relevant to the mission: *Where was Taran'atar going?* Everything that Vaughn had learned about him and about Jem'Hadar in general over the past eight months made it seem highly unlikely that he would flee without purpose or direction. The more Vaughn thought about it, the more convinced he became that Taran'atar's motive wasn't escape. If he was on the move, he was either regrouping with someone, or he was on the attack.

The only thing Vaughn was certain of was that, whichever scenario proved to be true, it was imperative that Taran'atar be stopped before reaching his objective.

Ahead of Prynn, on the other side of an angled sheet of transparent aluminum, was a vista of warp-streaked starlight. Reflected, apparitionlike, on the windshield was Taran'atar, who stood up behind her in the cockpit, holding the runabout's meter-long microtorpedo ordnance canisters, one under each arm. His back was to Prynn. As he closed the floor panel with his foot, Prynn reached upward. With a single, feather-gentle flip of her fingertips she decoupled the warp field stabilizer. *Two down,* she thought, congratulating herself. *One to go.* Behind her, Taran'atar stacked the canisters atop the EVA suit, next to the runabout's transporter pad. He still had made no mention of what purpose he intended for them, or for her.

She returned her attention to her console and saw that they were very close now to the coordinates he had selected. Just as the star charts had indicated, the sensors showed the rogue comet Nahanas tumbling through deep space, less than four minutes away at their current speed. Reaching across her panel to start a sensor sweep of the comet, she paused at the bark of his voice.

"Stop. Initiate no action unless I order it." He stepped up behind her and surveyed her controls. Apparently satisfied, he sidestepped back to the copilot's console. With quick stabs of his fingers against the control interface, he began to reconfigure the runabout's tactical systems. Observing the various system gauges on her console, Prynn realized that he was diverting all weapon power to the shields and inertial dampeners. A moment later, he deactivated several nonessential systems and reduced the life-support to minimum levels, terminating all support in the craft's aft cabin. The power from those systems he transferred to the structural integrity field.

She wondered what he was planning. Precautions such as these suggested that he was anticipating a sudden return to impulse power. Had he figured out her plan for sabotage?

Then it hit her: Knocking out the warp drive would be the *Defiant*'s safest way to capture the runabout without a firefight. Clearly, Taran'atar was expecting to be intercepted very soon. *But he just unloaded the microtorpedoes and took the phasers offline,* Prynn realized. *What's he going to do then? Ram them? And why are we on a collision course with a comet?*

"Set the helm to autopilot," he said.

Now what? She hesitated, her mind racing in search of options. With her trap not yet ready to be sprung, she did as she was instructed, locking in the current flight path.

He stepped backward until he was next to the door. He leveled his phaser at her. "Get up and move to the rear of the center compartment." She stepped over the threshold and walked to the back of the cramped space, near the door to the utility corridor. Taran'atar followed her in, then stepped to a control panel, where he entered a complicated series of commands.

The transporter's energizer coils powered up with a rich, mellifluous hum. A creeping dread filled Prynn's thoughts as Taran'atar, holding the EVA suit, looked at her and said simply, "Come here."

****

"Closing to intercept in sixty seconds," Bowers said.

"All hands to battle stations," Vaughn said. "Stand by to drop the cloak. Bridge to engineering: Are we ready to knock the *Euphrates* out of warp?"

"*Aye, sir,*" answered Ensign Leishman. "*Standing by.*"

"Bridge out. Mr. Forte, set phasers to five percent of normal power and target their warp nacelles. As soon as we're in tractor range, I want them—"

"Sir," Bowers cut in, his tone urgent. "The *Euphrates* is out of warp—and drifting."

At the helm, Ensign Amy Zucca hurried to compensate. "Reducing to impulse," she said, and the stretch of stars on the main viewer reverted to their normal, static appearance.

Vaughn squinted at the viewscreen. "Can we get a visual?"

"Magnifying," Zucca said.

The lower half of the screen was obscured by an out-of-focus, grayish blur. Near the top was the image of the *Euphrates,* tumbling and rolling like a random bit of space junk set adrift.

"Tactical, report."

"Minimal power aboard the runabout," Forte said, reviewing the sensor data. "Shields are down . . . no life signs on board."

Vaughn double-checked the *Defiant*'s position on his command display and noted that the runabout was just beyond the rogue comet Nahanas. "Mr. Bowers, does it look like the runabout had a run-in with that comet?"

"Checking." Bowers ran a quick sensor sweep, then turned back toward Vaughn. "Affirmative. We're reading small debris and pulverized rock and ice, scattered along a trajectory consistent with the runabout's position."

"Mr. Forte, keep sensors trained on the runabout. Helm, take us in closer to the comet." Vaughn tried to guess what had happened. *Did they bail out? Did she get the drop on him?*

The image on the main viewer changed, bringing the comet into sharp focus. It resembled a spiny sea creature, jagged and covered with towering spikes of crystalline rock. Spinning away into the vacuum above a cluster of sheared-off spikes was a cloud of ice crystals and fine dust.

"Sir," Rahim said, "I've got an intermittent signal—an SOS on a Starfleet frequency, from the surface of the comet." He looked up at Vaughn. "It's Ensign Tenmei's combadge, sir."

"Beam her up."

Rahim shook his head in frustration. "She's deep in a crevasse with a lot of magnesite. It's hard to punch through."

"Helm," Vaughn said, "lock on that signal, get us a clear line of sight for transport."

"Aye, sir," Zucca said. The spires of the comet loomed large as they passed beneath the *Defiant*. *Euphrates* drifted off the viewscreen.

Vaughn looked over his shoulder. "Forte?"

"Still on the runabout, sir. No change."

"We're directly above Tenmei's position," Zucca said.

"Drop the cloak," Vaughn said. "Arm phasers and stand by to transport."

The lights on the bridge brightened as Bowers said, "Cloak disengaged."

"Phasers ready," Forte said.

"Bridge to transporter bay," Vaughn said. "Lock on to Ensign Tenmei's signal on the comet surface and energize."

"Energizing now," Chief Chao replied over the comm.

"One life sign on the runabout!" Rahim said. "Jem'Hadar!"

Forte called out, "Runabout's raising shields!"

"Fire pha—"

Thunder rocked the bridge as something massive rammed into the *Defiant*. Vaughn was hurled from his seat as the bridge went dark. He plummeted to starboard and landed on top of Bowers, who was pinned to the starboard bulkhead. Around them, the other bridge officers fell and collided. They rolled with the motion of the ship, onto the ceiling, then back to the deck as the artificial gravity and inertial dampeners reset themselves.

Vaughn pushed his bruised, weary body back to a standing position and staggered to the center chair. The main viewer was a scramble of dark, wavy lines. The various station monitors on the bridge all were either dark or flickering with static. The bridge crew, though shaken and scuffed, appeared not to be seriously injured as they returned to their posts. Vaughn tapped his combadge. "All decks, damage reports." He turned his chair and looked at Bowers. "What hit us?"

"Still trying to figure that out myself." Bowers moved to one of the forward stations and tapped at it until it responded. "Patching in the backup sensors," he said. The main viewer crackled back to life. The *Defiant* was surrounded by a storm of rocky debris and dust. "No sign of the *Euphrates*, sir. . . . Hang on, I've got her—heading for Cardassian space at warp eight."

Around the bridge, the other duty officers checked in.

"Shields and cloak offline," Rahim said.

"Weapons offline," Forte added.

"Helm is sluggish," Zucca said.

"Engineering to bridge."

"Go ahead," Vaughn said.

"We took a beating down here, sir," Leishman said. *"Warp core's down, and we've got damage in the port nacelle."*

"Everyone all right?"

"Nothing a week on Risa wouldn't fix."

"How long to put us back in the hunt?"

"Won't know until I have a look at that nacelle," she said, *"but a few hours at least."*

"Economize where you can, and keep me posted," Vaughn said. "Bridge out." He heaved a sigh. Looking around, he saw Bowers huddled over the science station, conferring in hushed tones with Rahim. "Mr. Bowers, do we still have a transporter lock on Ensign Tenmei?"

Rahim and Bowers looked up at Vaughn, both of them with the same haunted expression. "We know what hit us, sir," Bowers said. "It was the comet. . . . It exploded."

Vaughn's jaw trembled. The blood drained from his face; he could feel it. Icy despair closed around his heart.

"The comet was rich in ultritium," Rahim said, filling the sudden, terrible silence that becalmed the bridge. "Sensors indicate a high-power explosive on the comet's surface was used as a detonator." Rahim's report began to trail off as Vaughn's attention turned inward. "We suspect the explosives were from the runabout's microtorpedo ordnance."

In a dry whisper of a voice, Vaughn filled in the detail he knew was coming next. "And they were linked to her combadge," he said, his eyes staring down at the deck, past it, into nothing at all. "So that our shields would be down for transport."

"Yes, sir," Bowers said. Lowering his head, he turned away.

Vaughn closed his eyes, then pounded his fist on the arm of his chair. "Should've boarded the runabout," he said in a low, angry voice. "Shrouded. He was shrouded. He was there all the time." A grotesque sensation worked its way up his throat, a feeling of rising bile that burned and choked its way upward.

He opened his eyes and rose from his chair. "Mr. Bowers, you have the conn."

"Aye, sir," Bowers said. Vaughn strode off the bridge, his steps measured and steady. The door swished shut behind him. Alone in the port corridor, he quickened his pace. Seconds later he was in the ready room. He ordered the computer to lock the door, then he sagged forward, his palms flat on his desktop.

Minutes or maybe hours passed; he didn't know anymore.

His breaths were short, shallow, and empty. He bit down on his sorrow, adamant in his refusal to give it utterance. A lifetime of control had taught him to bury pain, but now he was unable to subdue his rage or his grief. *Just like Ruriko,* the darkest of his inner voices said, the accusation cutting deep. *You killed Prynn just like you killed Ruriko.*

Jaw clenched to the point of agony, he struggled to silence his demons. Tension coiled the muscles from his temples to his shoulders. His face felt as hard as stone, petrified in a state of shock. *You killed her.*

Pride rose to his defense. *No, I didn't—he did. He tricked me . . . tricked me . . . used her as bait . . . wasn't my . . . not my . . .*

Excuses felt feeble, selfish, and hollow.

He slammed his left hand on the desktop and shut his eyes against the horror, against the ugly truth. Tears welled beneath his closed eyelids. He strained to hold them back. *You don't get to cry,* he raged at himself. *You don't have the right, you stupid bastard. You don't deserve tears. You don't deserve them.*

But she does.

Strength faded from his limbs. The floor beckoned to him as his knees buckled. He was being pulled downward, inexorably, mercilessly. The harder he struggled to dam up his tears, the more freely they ran from his eyes. The steel coil of his jaw unwound, and his mouth fell open to unleash a scream that now refused to take shape. On his knees, clinging to the edge of his desk like a sailor beside a lifeboat, he felt the true weight of his years bear down upon him. Suddenly his bones felt old and brittle, his skin as dry as a husk. He no longer felt like a man but like a handful of ancient dust, robbed of heat.

Grief was choking him.

God forgive me. . . . I killed my little girl.

He lost his hold on the desk's edge and pitched forward between the two guest chairs in front of his desk. Planting his hands on the rough gray carpet, he bowed his head, unable to hold it upright, laid low like Job. The past lashed out at him, assaulted him with memories of Ruriko dying in a blast of phaser energy, her hand outstretched toward Prynn. The woman he'd loved, whom he'd tried to free from the Borg collective, had reached out to assimilate the daughter whom he'd cherished as much as he had neglected. Forced to choose between them, he hadn't hesitated. Prynn had hated him for it; he'd hated himself. Forgiveness had been such a long road . . . one he suddenly felt he'd walked in vain.

Prynn's forgiveness—he still hadn't earned it, but they had at least finally started down the path to a new beginning. He had let go of his guilt; she had loosened anger's hold on her heart. There were so many things they had never spoken about, so many things he'd wanted to tell her, to ask her. Even the sound of her voice, or seeing that vivacious gleam in her eyes when she recounted one of her extreme-sport adventures, was worth more to him now than anything else under the stars. Vaughn couldn't imagine all that life and beauty being taken away in a flash of heat and violence, even though he'd always known it had been a risk, whether she had chosen to wear a Starfleet uniform or not.

She had been the future. The part of him that would have continued after he was gone. His fleeting grasp at immortality.

Now mother and daughter lingered side by side in his thoughts, their accusatory stares piercing his decades of stoic silence. *You killed us. You failed us.*

A bitter roar threatened to explode from him, to shake the bulkheads with his grief, but it was as though a tourniquet were tied around his throat. His suffering had no voice.

He pressed his fists together behind his head and covered his ears with his forearms. His soul was at war with itself, torn between wrath and discipline. Life as he knew it unraveled before him, his future promising nothing but oblivion now that his child was erased from it. Her absence left a vacuum in his psyche, one that he knew Opaka Sulan would be disappointed to know he planned to fill with hatred. With dreams of revenge.

I'll kill him.

His more rational demons chided him. *You can't kill him. You need to know why he did this.*

Shaking his head, he refused to be dissuaded so easily. *It doesn't matter why. He stabbed Kira. He broke Ro's back. He killed my little girl. He's going to die for this.*

The voice of reason would not relent. *You need to know why. If the female changeling ordered him, he might've had no choice. . . . You can't get any answers if he's dead. You need him alive.*

Grabbing the arm of one of the guest chairs, he pulled himself up to the edge of the desk. Seizing hold of that, he pushed his fragile, gray self back to his feet. Fighting the urge to clench his fists, he buried his anger, his hatred, his cold hunger for vengeance. Old training came back to him; the mission would come first, as it always had. Duty would trump all.

He thought of Prynn, alone on that jagged, desolate ball of volatile rock, being torn apart in a maelstrom of fire . . . and then he imagined disintegrating Taran'atar with a phaser beam, the crimson glow of the Jem'Hadar's vanished form yielding to a vivid green afterimage. A smirk of grim satisfaction tugged at the corner of Vaughn's mouth. . . .

You need him alive.

Vaughn picked up a guest chair and, with a guttural roar heaved it over his desk at the black polymer companel on the wall. The chair bounced off the panel, leaving only the barest abrasion on its surface. He stepped back, huffing for breath.

His composure slowly creeping back, Vaughn straightened his posture and smoothed the wrinkles from his uniform. He walked behind the desk, picked up the thrown chair, and carried it back to its original position. Using his sleeve cuff, he buffed most of the abrasion from the companel screen. Inspecting his handiwork, he looked for his reflection on the compañel's surface but, like the Fool gazing upon Lear, saw only his shadow. His weathered face and dimmed eyes betrayed nothing: no guilt, no remorse, no regret. He drew a deep breath, exhaled, and forced his face into a semblance of grim certainty.

Resolved, he turned and walked slowly back to the bridge.

Learn why Taran'atar went rogue, he ordered himself. *And* then *kill him.*

II

Runabout *Euphrates*

TARAN'ATAR WAITED UNTIL THE LAST POSSIBLE MOMENT TO act. The runabout's passive sensors detected the weapons lock from the *Defiant,* then a scattering of particle emissions from their transporter system. As they established a lock on the combadge of Ensign Tenmei, nestled deep inside a fissure on the comet, Taran'atar raised the *Euphrates'* shields. He shifted the impulse engines out of standby and accelerated immediately. The comet Nahanas was nearly a quarter million kilometers behind him when it exploded two seconds later.

As he'd planned, the *Defiant* was engulfed in the blast. With its shields down, it was pummeled by rocky shrapnel and buffeted by a massive release of energy from the comet's ultritium-rich crust. After thirty seconds, the *Defiant* had made no move to pursue the *Euphrates*; it appeared, for all practical purposes, to be dead in space.

Taran'atar set a new course and accelerated the ship to warp eight. He engaged the autopilot, then rose from his seat and moved to the cockpit's aft starboard station. As

was the standard aboard Starfleet runabouts, it was configured for engineering applications. He accessed the
transporter system, removed the security lockout he'd
encoded, and activated the rematerialization subroutine.
In a high-pitched shimmer, Ensign Tenmei reappeared on
the transporter pad.

She looked surprised. "What happened?"

"You may resume your post," he said. "Do not alter
course."

Warily she moved back toward the helm, taking small
steps. She stepped over the discarded environment suit,
whose emergency power cell Taran'atar had modified into a
detonator for the ordnance package; its built-in components
had made it remarkably easy to interface with Tenmei's
combadge, which had served as its trigger. He followed her
back into the cockpit and began methodically checking the
tactical readouts at the aft port station. Prynn settled slowly
into the pilot's seat and looked at the console chronometer.

"You held me in the pattern buffer," she said. "For over
six minutes."

"Yes." He recalibrated the sensors to seek out minor ripples in local tachyon currents, as a possible early warning
against nearby cloaked vessels. He found the Starfleet
vessel's instruments crude compared to those on a
Jem'Hadar warship, but with effort, he decided, they might
still be made useful.

After a few more minutes passed in silence, Tenmei
spoke again. "You could have beamed me into space."

"Yes," Taran'atar said, seeing no point in denying it. To
make certain she didn't mistake his restraint for weakness,
he added, "I still could."

That answer seemed to discomfort her. Glancing at the
navigation display, she said, "We've left the comet."

"Yes," Taran'atar said. "My objective there is accomplished." An irresistible force tugged at his eyelids. Already the exhilaration of action was ebbing, leaving his thoughts murky and mercurial. He yearned for the perfect satisfaction of the ketracel-white. The white fulfilled all needs, sated all appetites. There was no hunger, no thirst, no fatigue for a Jem'Hadar with the white in his veins. Like his brethren, Taran'atar had been born to the white, had lived by it most of his life, until it was discovered he had never truly had a physiological need for it. *That should have been my first warning,* he decided. *My first sign that I was flawed.* Now, as fatigue sapped his will, he wondered whether a new infusion of the white would sharpen him. Reinvigorate him.

"Why haven't you killed me?"

"You might yet prove useful," he said. Although he found her queries irksome, he at least appreciated that they kept his attention engaged and sleep at bay. "Until I have reached my destination, your presence gives me . . . options."

"I see," she said. "And then?"

He hadn't intended to involve a hostage at all, so he did not in fact have a plan for her final disposition. "I don't hesitate to kill, but neither do I kill without reason. When I've reached my destination, I will act as necessity dictates."

"Wonderful," she said. "How long a flight should I expect?"

"That is not—"

"Because," she continued, "unlike Jem'Hadar, humans need to sleep, and we have other biological functions that can't be suppressed indefinitely. So if you and I are going to be en route for more than a dozen hours, we should talk about how I might be permitted to address those needs."

Taran'atar nodded. "Not unreasonable," he said. "You

may eat once per day, at a time of my choosing. I will permit you brief visits to the personal hygiene facilities aboard this vessel, as needed. You may not close its portal."

"Thank you," she said. "And sleep?"

He thought for a moment, recognizing in her request an opportunity to stave off his own impending slumber. "Retrieve one of the emergency medical kits," he said. Tenmei got up and moved to the back of the cockpit. She opened a wall panel and removed a medkit. Taran'atar held out his hand, and she passed it to him. He set it on the nav console and opened it. Sorting through its assorted ampoules, he selected two of a mild stimulant that would suffice to keep Tenmei awake for the rest of the journey, and two of a far more potent compound that would do the same for him. He handed the two ampoules of mild medicine to her. "Use the first one when you become fatigued," he said. "Use the other twenty-two hours later." He inserted one of his doses into a hypospray and injected it into his jugular. Its effects were weak compared to those of the white, but it would suffice for now. His skin tingled slightly, and he caught the scent of Tenmei's hair.

She picked up her two doses and frowned. "I can't guarantee I'll be at my best if I'm chemically altered."

"All the more reason," he said, tucking his second dose into a pocket on his black coverall. He stood behind the copilot's seat and stared straight ahead, at the warp-distorted starfield. The ship was secure, his pursuer had been evaded, and sleep had been conquered for at least a short while longer. All that remained now was to monitor and control his prisoner.

So far she seemed compliant. She sat at her console and kept her movements to a minimum, almost as if she were mimicking him. He'd had very little direct contact with

Tenmei before an hour ago. It was possible, he supposed, that she was, by nature, deferential to power and authority, or perhaps disinclined toward violence or confrontation. Such an impression closely matched his least flattering preconceptions about humans. However, it did not track with the majority of his observations of human members of Starfleet, particularly those who, like Tenmei, belonged to the officer corps.

And he had to consider who her father was.

In Taran'atar's experience, human temperament, though malleable by circumstance, seemed in many instances to be inherited. Some traits had a knack for manifesting themselves more forcefully than others: tenacity, aggression, cunning.

He was going to have to monitor her very closely indeed.

12

Kira

GENERAL KIRA NERYS, SUPREME MILITARY COMMANDER OF the Bajora, rode at the forefront of her army, leading them south on the Dahkur road, home to the fortress of Parek Tonn.

Her robes, once a regal violet, had darkened with the dust of the road and the blood of war; her suit of loose armor plates and metallic mesh, which had been so resplendent when she had first sallied out to unify the continent under the golden banner of the Bajora, was now dark and dented. Only her sword remained as if new; sharp and bright, it had been honed and lovingly cared for through all these long months of dark endeavor.

Jayol, her *zhom*, loped along, his massive paws slapping the rock-paved road in a steady cadence. The enormous, lupine steed's gait was unflagging, as though the burden of General Kira and her saddle did not exist. As the hours of long riding blurred together in Kira's memory, she began to find the sway of Jayol's muscular torso as hypnotic as the sea. His blue-black fur had lost some of its luster after years of hard riding and exposure to the elements, but he had lost none of his speed, agility, power, or dignity.

Behind her was a procession of upright spears and lances, all adorned by tattered banners or bloodstained pennants that snapped in the bitter wind. Five regiments of heavy cavalry, trailed by four more regiments of archer-infantrymen, churned up a cloud of dust that heralded their coming to all those between them and the horizon who had eyes to see and the will to care.

Rising ahead of her, cut in a concave semicircle from the granite face of Mount Kola, was the city-fortress of Parek Tonn. Hewn from the cliffs and caves, the fortress had been ancient when Kira's grandsires had been young. Time and painstaking work had transformed it from a crude but strong natural redoubt into a marvel of engineering. Even from a distance it had been imposing—jagged gray blades of stone jutting upward to rend the sky. Now, as Kira and her army drew near to this greatest of all Bajoran strongholds, her heart swelled with pride and relief. Their long march would soon be at an end and her army could rest, home at last.

The faces behind her were masks of exhaustion, dull visages of pain and privation. War-weary and bedraggled, they talked around the night fires of farms to which they planned to return, of families they intended to raise, of dreams too long deferred. She had asked so much of them for so long, and they had answered her every summons, a braver and more loyal force than any general could dare think herself worthy of commanding. *When Parek Tonn is secure,* she promised herself, *I will release them.*

Even as Mount Kola filled her vision, her eyes remained fixed on the blighted landscape. This was not the Dahkur she had left behind. Where once a forest had stood, thick and lush, its canopy blazing green under the golden orb of day, a dead landscape of gnarled black tree trunks now sprawled under a leaden sky. Gone were the sawing music of the *lopa* bugs, the trilling songs of birds, the soft rustle of spring zephyrs winding through the vineyards on the hillsides. Only the anguished cry of the wind had a voice in this desolate place, in this land reduced to the chalky ash of an expired cinder.

Golden paws fell in step beside those of her steed, and she averted her eyes from the scene of destruction to greet General Jamin with a nod of recognition. He returned the gesture and smiled. She had always loved his smiles because the darkness of his skin made them look brighter by contrast, and because the warmth of his demeanor felt genuine. Of all her commanders, he was the one she trusted the most, the one whose counsel was always considered most carefully.

She nodded toward Parek Tonn. "You see it, too, Jamin?"

"Yes," he said, shaking open his scarlet cloak. "The fires are lit. The fortress is occupied, and in numbers."

It was suspicious. No advance force had been sent to prepare the fortress. Its gates should have been sealed, its walls secured by a single, loyal battalion of caretakers.

Imagining an unlikely scenario, she asked, "Could the Paqu have moved against us while we were in the east?"

"I doubt that," Jamin said.

They continued to ride, unspeaking, toward the fortress. The *zhoms'* claws clicked on the paving stones under their paws, and the metal clanks of armor and shields scraped along behind them. Night crested the horizon at their backs as the sun, redder than the flush of anger, set behind the mountain, and left the sky was streaked with radiant but fading hues.

It was in the deepest hour of the night, midway betwixt dusk and dawn, when Kira and Jamin reached the Fields of Berzel, where three roads converged at the foot of Mount Kola, within a quarter-hour's ride of Parek Tonn. "Tell the troops to make camp," Kira told Jamin. "We'll approach the gates at dawn."

"As you wish," Jamin said. He tugged lightly on the reins of his *zhom* and galloped back to issue the order to the other generals and then to his senior officers, who would spread the word down the line to the rank and file. Approaching the gates in darkness would be unwise; even if allied troops garrisoned the city, after nightfall it would be easy for a sentry to mistake friend for foe. Safer to hail the gatekeepers at dawn, under full colors.

The night was deathly still, sunrise was swift, breakfast was perfunctory—hard bread softened with tart wine, sharp cheese sliced into wedges, and dried fruit. With Jamin at her back and followed by an honor guard, General Kira led her people single-file across several narrow, offset paths that bridged four wide trenches in front of Parek Tonn. Excavated centuries earlier, the trenches ringed the approach to the fortress at regular intervals, starting several hundred *pates* from the gates. A defense against enemy siege engines, they were deep enough to be perilous to careless infantry or mounts that tumbled into them.

The rider behind Jamin carried the banner of the Bajora, which fluttered in the already stifling air, translucent in the long rays of morning. The group's shadows preceded them by many paces until they crossed the last bridge path and began climbing the slope toward the keep, their dim alter egos shrinking before them, foreshortened underfoot on the angled ground.

Magnificent and lofty, the curved fortress towered above Kira and her retinue, surrounded them on three sides as they rode slowly toward the mighty gates of reinforced wood, metal, and stone. Mounted on flagpoles atop the looming bulwarks, countless flags snapped crisply in the wind. Kira felt dwarfed, insignificant . . . like an ant beholding the heel of a god. Broad plateaus of stone, topped with towers of marble, dwelled behind the sawtooth barrier of the outer battlements.

Every watchtower was lit with a lonely signal fire. Shadowy forms moved behind the arrow slits or past the observation posts in the gatehouse. A distant chanting of unearthly voices and an eerie hum resounded from deep inside the fortress. Wisps of smoke rose upward from the city, sequestered far beyond the upper tier of battlements. Hushed in the cradle of stone was the whisper-roar of winter melt, cascading down from the mountain peaks to refill the city's artificial reservoir. Narrow flumes of spray plunged down from on high as the overflow was purged and released to run off and evaporate on the dusty slopes below.

"We're being watched," Jamin said, staring up at the gatehouse.

"I know," Kira said. She urged Jayol forward even as she signaled Jamin and the others to hold where they were.

When she had moved several steed lengths ahead of the others, she announced herself. "Hail!"

From above came the gatekeeper's echoing, deep-voiced reply. "Declare yourself."

"I am General Kira Nerys. This is my people's fortress. Open the gates, and welcome us home."

Her proclamation echoed, reëchoed, and faded away,

leaving only a confused silence that pressed in on her. As her patience waned, she debated whether to speak again; if she had not been understood, doing so might resolve the matter. But if she was being treated like a fool, letting herself be goaded into supplicating a gatekeeper would only compound her embarrassment.

At last the answer came.

"This is not your fortress. It is ours."

Stunned by the usurpers' brazenness, Kira stared up toward the gatehouse, eyes wide and bright with indignation, jaw agape. Mustering her anger into words, she shouted back, "Who dares to seize our home and deny it to my face? Show yourself!"

The gatekeeper emerged from the gatehouse, out onto the battlement, and peered down at her from the dizzying heights.

This was no man, nor was it a woman. As it straightened to its full height, Kira was transfixed with horror. Several pink limbs unfurled delicately from its tubelike body, and it gazed upon her with a single, slow-blinking eye of gray, which stretched all the way across its narrow face. As if displeased with her appearance or her entreaty, or both, the eye itself curved downward at its edges, into a frowning stare.

Although she resisted the urge to reach for her sword, General Kira could not hide her revulsion. "What *are* you?"

"We are the Eav'oq," the gatekeeper said. "We are the ones who have defended this fortress for millennia."

"You've—" Fury tripped up all the words trying to race from Kira's thoughts. "*You've* defended? But this is—"

"Our fortress," said the gatekeeper.

Visions of fiery sieges she had repelled from these walls

burned in Kira's memory: the Paqu, the Navot, the Janir . . . thousands of Bajora had perished to protect this venerated place.

Her weathered sneer added venom to her sarcasm. "And against whom, exactly, have you defended this fortress?"

Gesturing into the distance, the gatekeeper's long limbs undulated like ribbons in the wind. "From them."

She turned her head to follow his gesture.

A black wave rose in the south—a rough, dark line scratched on the far horizon, where the road vanished to a point.

Another army was approaching.

13

Deep Space 9

DAX STOOD IN THE MIDDLE OF OPS, LOOKING UP AT THE viewscreen and taking notes on a padd as she listened to Vaughn's report.

"At which point," Vaughn said, *"we engaged the transporter beam . . . triggering a detonator that linked Ensign Tenmei's combadge and what we suspect was the microtorpedo ordnance package from the* Euphrates." Every person in ops looked up suddenly, all attention in the room now fixed on Vaughn's face, which Ezri suddenly noticed looked haggard. He continued, *"The explosion set off the comet's ultritium deposits, destroying the comet and damaging our warp core and port nacelle."*

She hated to ask: "Casualties?"

"None aboard the Defiant," he said in a somber tone.

Old habits from her days as a counselor reasserted themselves. *This is insane—his daughter is dead. Why is he still in command? He should be relieved of duty, now, before . . .* She stopped herself. *Bowers is the XO on this mission. It's his call. Stay out of it.* "We have the *Rio*

Grande standing by," she said. "She can reach you in about five hours. Is there anything you need that we could—"

"No, we have everything here," Vaughn said. *"It's just a matter of making the repairs."* He sighed. *"Any update yet from Nog and Cenn?"*

"Not yet," Dax said. "Nog's still piecing old files back together. It'll probably be a few hours at least before we hear anything."

Vaughn nodded. *"And the captain and Ro?"*

"Still in surgery," she said. Her answer deepened Vaughn's long frown. She looked a bit more closely and saw the dark circles under his eyes, which looked mildly bloodshot. "We'll let you know if there's any change."

"Please do," he said. *"We'll check in at 2300 station time to let you know how we're doing with repairs.* Defiant *out."* He reached forward and cut the channel. The image winked out, leaving only the empty viewer frame.

Grim expressions had settled upon all the faces in ops by the time Dax climbed the stairs back to the commander's office. She went to the replicator and procured a cold glass of tonic water. Its bitter tang suited her mood. Moving to the window, her thoughts turned from Vaughn's suppressed grief to her own emerging sadness. She'd known Prynn for just less than a year, but the young woman had been unique, fiercely independent, and never at a loss for a tale of daredevil antics, which had made her seem to Dax like an unlikely friend for Shar.

Shar. Dax realized that someone would have to relay the news to the station's chief science officer, Thirishar ch'Thane. Shar and Prynn had become very close recently, and Prynn had traveled with him to his home on Andor for the funeral of his bondmate, Thriss. He was there now, united with his three current bondmates, submerged in arcane Andorian customs of marriage and mating. This would be the worst possible time to break such news to him—assuming that he could even be reached. Dax decided that it might be best to wait until there was some other, better news to go with it: word of Kira's and Ro's recovery, perhaps, or an assurance that Taran'atar had been brought to justice . . . one way or another.

She wondered what Vaughn would do when he caught up to the Jem'Hadar who had killed his daughter and plunged a blade into Kira's heart. Would he abide by the law, by regulations, and bring the renegade in alive if at all possible? Or would he provoke a confrontation, force Taran'atar into a corner, turn the hunt into a duel? Dax wanted to think that she knew Vaughn well enough not to worry that he would choose a vigilante's path, but when she thought of some of her past hosts' reactions to the deaths of their children, she realized that there was no predicting what he might do. A father avenging his child was capable of anything, especially when that father was as versed in the arts of war as Elias Vaughn.

Bashir watched the screen while his hands worked out of sight, inside the access panels of the surgical arch. Replacing a heart was supposed to be a routine procedure, but the severe trauma and blood loss that had preceded Kira's operation had made its outcome far from certain.

The transfusions had helped, certainly. Without them, her operation would have ended hours ago. Now Bashir found himself at the twelfth step in a delicate process. The artificial heart that Etana had prepared for Kira was ready and had been beamed into place beneath the surgical arch. Now Bashir and Dr. Aylam were working together to attach Kira's pulmonary artery and aorta to the synthetic organ.

The aorta was Bashir's task; Dr. Aylam was attaching the artery. He was making his second review of the newly formed microcellular bonds at the aortic junction when Aylam said, "I'm ready for the next step, Doctor."

"You can't be done already," he said, his tone just a bit too sharp to be fully professional. Aylam and Ingbar appeared taken aback, and he could tell from Aylam's reaction and the marked silence behind his back that Tarses and Etana were watching him as well. Calming his voice, he added, "Please inspect your new bonds and make certain there are no defects. The captain's been through enough trauma today. I don't want to risk any postsurgical complications if they can be prevented."

Dr. Aylam nodded. "Yes, Doctor," she said, then she began a methodical review of her own surgical handiwork.

Several minutes passed. Tarses and Etana worked quietly on Ro's injuries, painstakingly isolating and protecting her spinal cord at every turn while they regenerated her cracked and broken vertebrae. Bashir couldn't help but eavesdrop on them while they worked, eager as he was to know Ro's condition. Of course, there would be no way to assess that until she was out of surgery and into physical therapy. It might, in fact, be weeks before the full prognosis for her recovery would be known.

Finally, Bashir was satisfied that the artificial heart was as solidly incorporated into Kira as her original heart had been. "The moment of truth," he said. "Mr. Ingbar, stand by to deactivate the bypass. Dr. Aylam, unclamp the aorta." He watched with nervous expectation as Aylam deftly freed the clamp inside Kira's chest. The artificial heart responded exactly as it should, its myoelectric fibers contracting and relaxing in a smooth, even cadence, perfectly mimicking the most recent cardiological patterns in Kira's medical records. "Remove the clamp from the pulmonary artery." Aylam released the pulmonary clamp, allowing blood to flow freely into the artificial heart. Its beating was steady and smooth. "All right, then," Bashir said. "Let's remove the bypass connections."

The work was quiet and unhurried. Most of the labor was handled by the surgical arch itself; it retracted the bypass tubes and guided Bashir's and Aylam's hands as they regenerated the minor perforations that had been left at the connection points. At the end of the fourth hour since Kira had been beamed into the infirmary, Bashir said to Aylam, "Would you mind closing, Doctor?"

"Not at all, sir," Aylam said. She activated the osteofuser and repaired Kira's sternum, then laid down a layer of synthetic myomer and cartilage to repair the damage that had been caused by spreading open Kira's chest by force. Aylam worked quickly; she was putting the finishing touches on the regenerated upper layers of dermis by the time Bashir had reviewed Ro's chart and turned to join Tarses and Etana on the other side of the tiny surgical suite. Bashir nodded approvingly as he watched Tarses work.

"Looks like you've got most of it repaired," Bashir said, letting his upbeat tenor convey how impressed he was. "Genetronic replication?"

"Yes," Tarses said. "It seemed like the most promising course of treatment."

"Agreed," Bashir said. "It's funny—when I requested the prototype from Starfleet Medical, it was for research, not practice." A question occurred to him. "Do you have a plan for limiting its cellular replication matrix? The literature seems to suggest it can become unstable as it progresses."

"I combined it with Dr. Crusher's work on cybernetic regeneration."

Scrutinizing the specs displayed in front of Tarses, Bashir felt his eyebrows lifting. "Medical nanites?"

"They limit the genetronic matrix's activity at the molecular level, preventing accidental metastasization. I've programmed them for an operational life span of four days, disabled their ability to recharge, and limited their power supply to six days. At that point, they should pass into Lieutenant Ro's bloodstream and be purged by the liver."

"Fascinating work, Doctor," Bashir said. "I hope you plan on publishing your findings."

"Indeed, sir."

"I look forward to reading them." Bashir looked down at Ro, unconscious beneath the delta-wave generator, while Tarses and Etana guided a small army of submolecular machines to reconstruct her damaged spinal cord with replicated tissue. Wondering how successful Tarses's strategy for overcoming the chief flaw of genetronic replication would be, he hoped, for Ro's sake, that Tarses's finished article for the *Starfleet Medical Journal* would have a happy ending.

He rejoined Dr. Aylam beside Captain Kira. Aylam powered down the surgical arch. "Her EEG readings are borderline, but the scans don't detect any evidence of brain damage," she said.

"Brain damage isn't always obvious in physical scans," Bashir said. "The mind is a subtle balance of chemistry, electricity, and the intangible." He accepted a padd that Aylam offered to him. He reviewed Kira's bioscans from surgery and sighed. "There's nothing to do now but wait."

He signed the report with the stylus and handed the padd back to Aylam. "Let's move her to recovery and evaluate her condition when she wakes up."

Professionalism coupled with hope prevented him from adding, *If she wakes up.*

14

Border of Bajor Sector and Almatha Sector

Prynn prepared her sabotage by degrees.

To mute the active feedback for the panels at the pilot's station, she extended her little finger until it rested and pressed gently down on a sliding icon that controlled the helm volume. Dragging it slowly but smoothly, she nudged it in one motion to its lowest setting.

Behind her, Taran'atar busied himself making physical alterations to the isolinear matrix of the tactical station. She could see his reflection on the cockpit windshield. He gave no sign of noticing her adjustment to the controls' volume; routine chirps and tones continued to emanate from other consoles around the cockpit.

Reconfiguring her console with delicate touches, she gave herself direct access to several systems, which she linked together. Working on a few square centimeters of console in front of her was far more discreet than making excuses to access several other stations in the cockpit.

It was time to make her final preparation: She reduced the inertial dampeners' efficiency around the runabout's nacelles just enough to disable them as the warp field collapsed, but not enough to cause an explosion.

She linked all the deliberate malfunctions together so that she could trigger them in sequence with a single touch of a fingertip. Her trap laid, she nudged the level of audio feedback from her console back to its normal level.

Taran'atar closed the tactical panel, then stood and entered a few commands. He seemed satisfied with the results. He turned himself slightly toward her, then remained motionless.

Half an hour later, Prynn began to wonder whether something was wrong with him. "Are you going to sit down?" she said.

"On Jem'Hadar vessels, there are no seats. Comfort breeds weakness."

"You could have just said no."

It was hard to tell from his dim reflection, but she thought he might have actually smirked a little at her remark.

"I have noticed," he said, "that humans and other Alpha Quadrant species understand Jem'Hadar ways better when they are explained in context."

Watching him in the half-mirror of the windshield, she said, "I really don't give a damn about your *context*. Or about you. If you like talking about yourself, go ahead, but I'm not looking at our time together as a learning experience."

She wondered if her statement would provoke him.

He simply nodded once. "Fair enough."

Then he said nothing else for nearly an hour.

The region of space along their course seemed strangely devoid of traffic. According to the navigation screen in the middle of the cockpit, they had passed over the border of

Almatha Sector and were now legally in Cardassian territory. Not that Prynn expected to encounter any Cardassian ships out here; this area was an allied protectorate, likely to be patrolled by either Romulans or Klingons, leaving Gul Macet's forces free to concentrate on defending Cardassia Prime and other more densely populated systems of the Cardassian Union.

An alert trilled softly on the panel next to Taran'atar. He silenced it with a tap of his index finger and trained his unblinking stare on the screen as he analyzed the complex sensor diagram that appeared on his monitor. On the viewer above his head, he called up the star chart. His posture relaxed as he settled on a course of action. "Adjust course," he said. "Bearing three-eight mark one-five."

She was about to input the course change—executing flight commands came as naturally to her as breathing. Then she stopped herself. *If he's changing course, it must be to avoid something. Not an anomaly, regular sensors would read those.* Remembering where she was, the most likely answer became clear. *He reset the sensors to find cloaked ships. There's a Klingon or Romulan ship nearby, and he wants to evade them.*

Catching his glare, reflected in the viewport, she started to comply.

Just as she was about to enter the final coordinate and engage the course change, she let her thumb tap her carefully crafted preset.

Catastrophic deceleration pinned her against her console and hurled Taran'atar forward. He hit the copilot's chair, which made a loud cracking noise as its pedestal broke. Stars pinwheeled past the cockpit window as the uneven collapse of the ship's subspace field sent it spinning and rolling wildly through space at well past full impulse. A thunder-roar shock wave rattled it as a blinding flash of light pulsed from its warp nacelles.

Dull and heavy silence fell over the craft. The stars seemed to turn and roll in slow, chaotic spirals as the runabout drifted in a helpless tumble. Every warning light in the cockpit was lit, though most of the consoles were dark.

Mission accomplished, Prynn gloated.

Despite having been tossed hard enough to cripple most humanoids, Taran'atar recovered his wits quickly and took in the new situation. "Report. What has happened to the engines?"

"Their modifications were experimental," she said, which was true. The rest of her explanation wasn't going to be. "They weren't ready for a prolonged flight, especially not at full speed for this long. I was only supposed to do an impulse flight and some low-warp maneuvers, to set some benchmarks for Nog."

He tapped futilely at the copilot's panel, which refused to yield any useful information about the ship's status . . . then he turned his glare toward her. "You sabotaged the ship."

"I didn't have to," she lied. "I knew it was only a matter of time before something like this happened. All I had to do was not tell you."

The emergency channel beeped twice, signaling an incoming transmission. Prynn and Taran'atar both looked at it. He once more cast his fierce gaze at her. "How convenient for you, then, that it failed now."

She said nothing as the emergency channel continued to chirp, just as she'd hoped it would. Of course, she had considered triggering the sabotage as soon as it had been fully set, thereby crippling the *Euphrates* in deep space without any other ships nearby. That had seemed like a bad risk, however, because she'd seen no sign of any pursuit from Deep Space 9. While the *Defiant* might have been traveling cloaked, she would have expected them to have overtaken the runabout by now. After emerging from the transporter she had wondered whether Taran'atar had confronted the *Defiant* at the comet, but she had since dismissed that as a ridiculous idea. Even if Taran'atar had found a way to deliver the full force of the *Euphrates'* microtorpedo ordnance in a single blow, the *Defiant's* ablative armor would have suffered little more than discoloration.

If the Defiant *had caught up to us, this would be over by now,* she told herself. But that left her wondering why the *Defiant* wasn't intercepting them. It occurred to her that if Taran'atar's departure from the station hadn't raised any alarms, there might not have been any immediate reason for the team in ops to suspect anything had been wrong when she hadn't checked in on time from her test flight. In fact, they might only now be realizing that she and the *Euphrates* were, in fact, missing.

And still the comm signal was beeping.

Then a low hush of sound turned her head, and she caught a fleeting look at Taran'atar as he disappeared into his shroud. Then his voice was in her ear, hot and frighteningly intimate. *"Answer the comm,"* he whispered. *"Do not tell them you have been hijacked or that I am aboard. Do not attempt to send any coded messages. Do you understand?"*

Fear did not come easily to Prynn, but she still had a healthy respect for danger and knew when not to tempt its wrath. "Yes," she said. "I understand."

"Open the channel."

She reached up and activated the small viewscreen over her station. Its flurry of scratchy static resolved quickly into an image of a gaunt, wiry-looking Klingon man. He wore the uniform of the Klingon Defense Force. *"This is Captain Qurag of the Klingon patrol vessel* noH'pach. *Identify yourself."*

"Answer him," Taran'atar whispered to her.

"This is Ensign Prynn Tenmei aboard the Starfleet runabout *Euphrates."*

"We detected your engine failure," Qurag said. *"Do you require assistance?"*

Parroting Taran'atar's whispered cue, she said, "Yes, Captain."

"We are changing course to intercept you. Stand ready to receive a repair crew in two minutes."

"Thank you, Captain," Prynn said, on her own initiative but without rebuke from Taran'atar.

"Qurag out," the Klingon commander said. The screen went dark as he cut the channel.

"Now what?" Prynn said to her shrouded captor.

"Now you remain seated and still," Taran'atar said, a disembodied voice in the cockpit. *"Or else I will kill you."*

"Decloak," said Captain Qurag.

At the forward control console, pilot and first officer Sergoz executed the command. "Done, Captain," she said.

On the main viewer, the disabled Starfleet runabout tumble-rolled. "Intercept and ready tractor beam," Qurag said. With a thump of his gloved hand, he opened a comm channel to the aft engineering bay. "Koth, Orruk, get ready to beam over."

Chief mechanic Koth barked back, *"We've been ready."*

"Of course you have," Qurag said with mild annoyance. "Can't keep the pretty human woman waiting, now, can we?"

"You said it was an emergency," Koth said.

"I said *she* had an emergency, not us," Qurag growled. "Report to the transporter. Bridge out." He smacked his hand down, closing the channel. On a ship like the *noH'pach,* with its tight-knit, five-person crew, there were no secrets—and the past three shore leaves had made it painfully clear that Koth wasn't just partial to human women; he was obsessed with them. Qurag shook his head disapprovingly at the very idea. *Why would any Klingon choose such an unsturdy mate?*

"We're at intercept station, Captain," Sergoz said.

"Activate tractor beam." As the bright, golden beam snared the runabout and gradually halted its erratic motion, a gentle hum vibrated through the dark green-gray bulkheads of the small Klingon scout ship.

"Holding at station," Sergoz said.

"Disengage beam." As soon as the tractor beam vanished from the forward viewer, Qurag turned toward the operations station on his left. "Are they ready?"

"Yes," second officer Malk replied.

"Energize."

Qurag hoped that the Starfleet ship could be repaired, or that another Starfleet vessel could take responsibility for towing it back to Deep Space 9 and ferrying its pilot home. If the *noH'pach* was forced to take the runabout in tow, it would be unable to cloak, and its effectiveness as a deterrent to smugglers would be negated for the remainder of this cruise. Making matters even more unpalatable, there would be reports to file with Defense Force Command and Starfleet, and Koth would no doubt spend the entire journey to Deep Space 9 preening and boasting in a pathetic attempt to impress the human woman.

Sergoz silenced a sudden buzzing signal on her panel. "Koth is hailing us."

"On speaker." Sergoz punched in the command and turned to face Qurag, implying that the channel was open for him. "Qurag here," he said.

"The ship is without main power," Koth said. *"If its warp coils are damaged, as I suspect, we will need to tow it back to its base."*

"Very well," Qurag said. "Finish your inspection and report back."

"Acknowledged."

"Qurag out." Taking the cue, Sergoz cut the channel for him. *Fortune is not smiling on me today, it seems.* "Scan the sector for other Starfleet vessels," he said to Sergoz. "Let's see if we can make this someone else's problem."

Prynn watched two pillars of shimmering particles appear in the cockpit of the *Euphrates,* accompanied by a bright rush of white noise. They swiftly resolved into the forms of a pair of uniformed Klingon men. As the transporter effects faded, the two Klingons looked around and got their bearings. Both carried long, narrow boxes of engineering tools and portable scanning devices similar to tricorders.

The taller of the two stepped toward Prynn and displayed a broad, jagged smile. "I am Koth," he said, "chief mechanic of the *I.K.S. noH'pach.* This is my assistant, Orruk."

Orruk whirled toward Koth. "I am *not* your assistant," he said through bared teeth. "I'm the science officer."

Koth turned and loomed over the other man. "Captain Qurag sent you to assist me. At this time, in this place, you are my assistant." The pair muttered low Klingon curses at each other.

Prynn wanted to warn them about Taran'atar so that they could beam out with her and trap him aboard the derelict ship. She had no idea how to do that without getting them all killed. Instead, she interrupted, "Can this wait till after you fix my ship?"

Turning away from Orruk, Koth changed his demeanor instantly. "Of course," he said. They set down their tools and activated their scanners. Koth moved to the engineering panel.

Orruk tapped at the copilot's console, which remained dark and unresponsive. "Mains are offline," he said.

Koth nodded in agreement. "Reserves are intact but unable to deliver power to the impulse system." He lifted his wrist communicator and spoke into it. "Koth to *noH'pach*."

Several seconds later, Captain Qurag's voice squawked from the wrist device, sounding small and hollow. *"Qurag here."*

"The ship is without main power," Koth said. "If its warp coils are damaged, as I suspect, we will need to tow it back to its base."

"Very well," Qurag said. *"Finish your inspection and report back."*

"Acknowledged."

"Qurag out." The channel clicked closed.

Orruk stood just behind Koth; he seemed distracted. Looking through the open cockpit door, he sniffed the air.

"We're going to check your ship's nacelles," Koth said to Prynn. As he continued, Orruk sniffed the air again, then drew his disruptor. "But I think we'll need to—" He stopped in midsentence and turned to face Orruk. "What in the name of *Fek'lhr* are you doing?"

Aiming his disruptor slowly from one side of the runabout's central compartment to the other, Orruk said, "There's someone else here. I can smell him."

Koth drew his *d'k tahg* and skulked in a low crouch past Orruk into the central compartment.

Taran'atar unshrouded in the cockpit, between Prynn and Orruk. The Klingon science officer whirled and leveled his disruptor. Taran'atar knocked it away with his right hand and with his left palm struck Orruk under his chin. The Klingon's neck snapped with a sound like dry twigs.

Koth charged back into the cockpit with a battle roar. Orruk's body slumped as Taran'atar locked his hand around the dead man's throat—he was using him as a shield. Koth lunged forward, only to find himself impaled on Orruk's *d'k tahg,* which was in Taran'atar's hand. The Jem'Hadar let go of Orruk, then reached out and broke Koth's neck with one sharp twist.

Both bodies fell to the deck with a heavy sound.

Taran'atar stood over them, his face impassive. He sheathed the stolen *d'k tahg* under the belt of his coverall.

Prynn stared at the spreading pool of magenta-tinted blood on the deck of the cockpit and trembled with rage. "You didn't have to kill them," she said.

"They acted with lethal force. I defended myself."

She shot up from her chair and stepped toward him. "Defended yourself? You butchered—"

He backhanded her across the face. The force of the blow knocked her sideways. Her vision was already purpled as she hit the bulkhead. By the time she collapsed to the deck, it had faded to black, taking consciousness with it.

****

Malk, son of Roloc, cursed his father every morning and night for having condemned him to serve out his days on this tiny, unimportant, neglected ship. His father hadn't done it directly, of course; he had been an influential member of the provincial government on Qo'noS before becoming governor of Mempa . . . then the uprising against Gowron had come. Roloc had not opposed Gowron, but he'd also done nothing to stop Gowron's enemies from handing him a serious defeat in the Mempa sector. Gowron had never forgotten Roloc's lack of support, and after he'd risen to power, he'd made certain that Roloc's role in imperial affairs was diminished and that Malk's career would be quashed. Now, despite the fact that Gowron was dead and Martok had ascended to the chancellor's seat, Malk still languished aboard the *noH'pach,* a ship that rarely saw action against anything more threatening than crews of smugglers too drunk to realize they could no longer fight.

He dreamed of getting a transfer to a battle cruiser. Or to a ground-combat regiment. He had heard of glorious battles being waged on the imperial frontier, out toward the galactic rim. New worlds, new foes, new opportunities for honorable glory . . .

An intruder alert buzzed on his operations panel. He switched off its sound and turned toward Captain Qurag, who was staring at him and waiting for his report. "Unauthorized transport," Malk said. "Aft compartment. One human life sign."

"Go handle it," Qurag said.

"Yes, Captain." Malk got up, unsheathed his disruptor, and left the bridge. He stalked down the central corridor to the aft compartment hatch, charged his weapon, then opened the door. On the floor in the middle of the deck was the human woman he had seen on the viewscreen, the one from the crippled Starfleet ship. She was unconscious, and her hands and feet were bound with knotted coils of Starfleet-standard optical cable. He saw no one else in the cramped but otherwise open compartment. Sheathing his weapon, he moved to the woman and knelt beside her. She was still breathing, but a massive and fresh bruise discolored the right side of her face.

The tip of a *d'k tahg* erupted from Malk's throat in a spray of magenta viscera. He pitched forward onto the deck and watched his blood fall away through the floor grate, carrying with it his dreams of honor and glory.

Taran'atar marched toward the hatch to the *noH'pach*'s bridge. *I am dead. I go into battle to reclaim my life. I do this because I am Jem'Hadar.* The door opened at his approach.

Victory is life.

He aimed his phaser and snapped off two fast shots at full power. The Klingon commander and his pilot both vanished in flares of supercharged particles that faded into ashes.

Tucking the phaser back under his belt, he moved to the forward console and accessed the small patrol ship's weapons system. Engaging the engines, he piloted the ship through a wide turning maneuver and brought it full circle toward the runabout. When the *noH'pach* reached optimal distance, he targeted the *Euphrates* and fired the disruptors on the unshielded vessel.

It exploded in an inferno of red-orange vapors.

He powered down the *noH'pach*'s weapons and engaged the small craft's cloaking device. A low hum pulsed once through the ship as the cloak shrouded it from eyes and sensors. His journey could now continue, and in greater secrecy than before.

Making a mental note to deal with Ensign Tenmei later, he jumped the ship to maximum warp, back on course for Harkoum.

15

U.S.S. Defiant

BOWERS SWIVELED HIS CHAIR AS HE HEARD THE AFT PORT door hiss open. Vaughn stepped quickly onto the bridge. "Report, Mr. Bowers."

The acting XO rose from the center seat and stepped aside to relinquish it to Vaughn. "Main power and sensors restored, port nacelle repaired." He handed a padd to Vaughn. "Leishman assures me we can make warp eight-point-five."

Vaughn reviewed the details on the padd, then nodded. "Do we have a fix on *Euphrates?*"

"Not yet," Bowers said. "But its warp field dragged some charged particles from the comet in its wake, giving us an idea of their last heading. We're running a new sensor sweep now."

"What about the cloak?"

"Still offline, sir," Bowers said.

For a moment, Vaughn said nothing; the centenarian stared at the thin field of dispersing dust and rock fragments that once had been the comet. His stern, unyielding face betrayed nothing. He handed the padd back to Bowers. "Good work. Get us underway, maximum warp."

"Aye, sir," Bowers said. "Helm, set course one-three-seven-point-one mark nine, best speed." Ensign Zucca carried out the order, and the ship jumped to warp, leaving behind the shattered remains of Nahanas. Bowers turned back toward Vaughn. "I have all the available engineers working on getting the sensors back to 100 percent," he told Vaughn in a low voice. "The cloaking device seemed like a lower priority task, seeing as we've already lost the element of surprise."

"I'm not sure we ever had it," Vaughn said, his gaze still fixed on the viewscreen. He turned and looked askance at Bowers. "We probably have a while before we catch up to the runabout if you want to take ten minutes and go finish that shave."

Self-consciously, Bowers lifted a hand to his half-smooth, half-stubbled throat. "I'll be back in five minutes, sir," he said, then slipped out the aft starboard door toward his quarters. Before the door closed behind him, he became aware that someone had followed him off the bridge. Lieutenant Tariq Rahim caught up to him and gestured with an outstretched hand and a quick nod that they should continue walking.

As they circled through the corridor toward the forward starboard turbolift, Bowers said, "Mind telling me what this is about?"

Rahim's voice was a worried whisper. "Is Vaughn all right to stay in command?"

"Why? Because of Prynn?"

"C'mon, Sam," Rahim said as Bowers pressed for the lift. "The guy just blew up his daughter. And now he's going after the guy he blames for it."

It was no secret that Bowers had questioned Vaughn's emotional fitness for command after the discovery of Prynn's Borg-assimilated mother, Ruriko, during the *Defiant*'s extended mission in the Gamma Quadrant. Bowers had left it to Lieutenant Dax to confront Vaughn, but on a ship this size, everyone knew who really had raised the red flag.

Facing Rahim, Bowers masked his guilt with anger.

"Are you a Betazoid, Tariq?" Bowers glared at the science officer. "Maybe part Vulcan? Or a quarter Ullian?"

Rahim simmered at the insult. "It doesn't take a telepath to know he's got to be torn up inside. If he's on a revenge mission, you have a duty to—"

"I know my job," Bowers said sharply. "And so does Commander Vaughn." The turbolift door gasped open behind him as he continued. "Has he done anything irrational? Has he displayed any lack of emotional control on the bridge?" Emboldened by Rahim's shamed silence, Bowers continued, "We all liked Prynn. And we're all angry, and we're all grieving in our own way. Does that mean *we're* unfit for duty? Should I tell the skipper to turn the ship around?" He stepped into the turbolift. "Return to your post, Mr. Rahim. Dismissed."

16

The Alternate Universe— Kalandra Sector

GUL MACET STEPPED INTO THE LAVISHLY APPOINTED residential suite of Intendant Kira. Her private space aboard the *Negh'Var* was as grand as anything Macet had ever seen: sprawling open space, tiered into raised and lowered portions, and surrounded on three sides by resplendent starfield views that now were crowded with the gathered ships of her battle fleet. Draperies of iridescent, multicolored Tholian silk shimmered in the subdued light, fluttering slowly in the gently circulated warm air. Muted music, of lilting feminine voices and gentle strings, seemed to float down from above, imparting an otherworldly ambiance.

A fragrance of assorted Bajoran wildflowers reached Macet's senses as he was led through the sumptuous quarters by one of the Intendant's lithe Vulcan handmaidens. Gentle splashing sounds became more distinct as he climbed up a few short tiers to her bathing area. As he neared the top he saw her. She reclined comfortably with her eyes closed, chest-deep at one end of an oval pool of chalky-colored liquid whose surface was dotted with vibrant orange flower petals.

"The fleet is assembled, Intendant," he said.

She opened her eyes and smiled. "Very good."

"We also have received word from the Ninth Klingon Fleet," he said. "Sindorin has been reduced to radioactive glass. The remaining insurgent encampments in the Badlands are withdrawing toward Tzenkethi space."

That seemed to amuse her. "I doubt they'll receive a warm welcome there." She stood up in the pool and walked slowly up a few submerged steps until she was only knee-deep. The milky fluid fell in snaking rivulets down her naked body. Another of her handmaidens waded in promptly and helped the Intendant into her short, blood-red robe. Kira tied the garment shut as she turned back toward Macet and circled around the pool to stand above him, looking down with haughty affection. "Take the fleet to Regulon," she said. "Regroup there with the Ninth Klingon Fleet. When I rejoin you, we'll begin final preparations for a direct assault on Terok Nor."

"When you rejoin us?" It took a moment for Macet to believe that he had heard her correctly. "The *Negh'Var* will not be going to Regulon with the rest of the fleet?"

"No," Kira said. "If we're to assault Terok Nor, there's another matter I have to deal with first—one of utmost secrecy."

Always with her it's secrets, Macet brooded. The Intendant was a capable strategist and tactician, but her most serious weaknesses, in his opinion, were her egotism and her paranoia.

There was no point arguing with her, however. That path almost always led to disgrace and execution, and not always in that order. Macet nodded politely. "As you command," he said. "I will guide the fleet to Regulon and await your arrival." He began to turn away, then he paused and looked back up at her. "If I may be so bold as to ask . . . ?"

She ran roughshod over his gentle query with her sinister, condescending smile. "Be ready for my return, Macet. Because when we meet again . . . Terok Nor will be only the first stop on our road to glory."

17

Harkoum

DAWN BROKE OVER ILJAR IN PALE SILVER FLARES AND SEARED away the rain clouds. Harkoum's two suns ascended in unison, so close together that they could be mistaken for one. Dark gray shapes were transformed into rust-hued clusters of shoddy buildings; the morning light turned orange, and the brightening streets grew deserted as the town's heliophobic residents scurried for refuge in the dim indoors.

Sunrise turned to late morning; mud reverted to dirt in the street. Grauq stayed near the back of the doorway in which he'd passed the long, stormy night. A hot wind blew in from the north and rattled the loose metal sheets on the roof above him.

There had been no sign of the Cardassian Woman. The *Otamawan* was still securely docked below street level, attached to its temporary berthing by snaking umbilical lines that replenished its fuel and air reserves.

As dearly as he wanted to twist the knife in the Cardassian Woman's heart, the Chalnoth mercenary had wearied of this waiting game. His knife was back in its sheath, and the strap of his holster had been unfastened. He was just going to shoot her.

Assuming, of course, that she ever arrived; he was beginning to doubt his instincts. It didn't seem likely that she would have braved the Suns' Cauldron, but Grauq had seen other desperate people do far more foolish things. There was another town on the desert's edge, but it was more than twice as far as Iljar was from the site of the Cardassian Woman's collision with Jonu. If she had chosen to make her way there, she would still be nearly half a day's walk from its outskirts.

Not a chance, Grauq decided. *The flayers would eat her alive before she was ten steps past the Gula River.* He had seen the flayers ambush desert travelers before; the gigantic, wormlike predators would spring from beneath the sand, tentacles snaking wildly, their shrieks audible for kilometers around. Within seconds their prey would be paralyzed by sonic attacks, and inside of a minute, the flayers could strip all the flesh from the victim's body. Hunting in packs, they were fast, silent, and all but undetectable until the moment of attack. If the Cardassian Woman had tried to cross the river to reach the starport at Katulu, she was dead by now.

Another hour dragged by, hot, quiet, and still. Grauq checked the charge on his weapon, then resumed his singular focus on the *Otamawan.*

The small ship's aft hatch opened. Its chief mechanic, a wiry, middle-aged Efrosian man, limped down the plank. He clutched a scanner in one hand and walked beneath the vessel, inspecting its hull. The process was slow and excruciatingly boring to watch.

This was not a day that held much promise of being interesting. Grauq considered ingesting another dose of stimulants. Reaching for the dispenser, he hesitated. Experience warned him that he might be wasting the valuable synaptic enhancers. If the Cardassian Woman was dead, as he suspected, or if she had been captured by one of the client's other retainers, then he'd be neuro-spiking himself for no good reason. He resolved to wait. *They act fast,* he reasoned. *If she arrives, I can take them then.*

Fatigue was beginning to dull his concentration when a sound lifted his eyes and coaxed him out of the doorway, into the glare of daylight. It was the screeching whine of a launch thruster, one that he knew as intimately as his own voice. He reached inside his vest and found his field scope. More than two kilometers away, on the other side of Iljar, a shining metallic shape climbed into a blinding white stretch of sky. He pointed his field scope at it and peered through the device, hoping not to confirm his own worst suspicion. The scope's polarizing filters kicked in as he magnified the image. Taking shape in his gaze was his own tiny space-craft, the *Githzarai*, flying away from him, heading directly for orbit.

That bitch, he fumed, with equal parts disbelief and grudging professional respect. *She's stealing* my *ship.*

He put away the field scope, popped two stim-pills down his gullet, and drew his plasma pistol.

Down on the docking platform, the *Otamawan*'s weath-ered-looking Efrosian mechanic spotted Grauq coming down the ramp from the street. Before he could sound an alarm or challenge Grauq to identify himself, Grauq shot him between the eyes and continued straight toward the *Otamawan*'s open aft gangplank.

Inside the ship, the rest of the crew had been alerted by the sound of weapons' fire and were rushing in Grauq's direction, sidearms drawn. They were forced by the cramped quarters into moving single file.

In the lead was a strong-jawed Andorian. Grauq fired one maximum-power shot at the man's throat. The pulse passed through him and struck the Tiburonian man behind him square in the face. Both men collapsed backward and pinned the third person in line, a fat human female.

Last in line was a Caitian male, who snapped off a phaser shot that struck Grauq in the chest. The interaction of the beam and his ablative body armor arrested his forward movement. The odor of charred clothing and the cordite stink of overheated metal assaulted his acute Chalnoth senses. When the phaser beam ceased, the Caitian was stunned to see Grauq still standing.

Before the Caitian could fire again, Grauq shot back and hit him fatally in the chest.

Grauq walked on top of the dead Andorian and Tiburonian. Beneath them, the human woman struggled and freed her arm. Grauq stomped on her wrist, which broke with a small, wet snap. Her disruptor fell from her hand. He knelt down, drew his knife, and stabbed her once in the throat, pushing his blade until he heard it crack through the vertebra below her skull. Her eyes went dull, and he wiped off his blade on her Caitian comrade's pant leg before sheathing it.

Grauq stood and closed the aft hatch, then moved toward the cockpit. The interior of the *Otamawan* reeked of the sickly sweet odor of burned skin, and Grauq knew that the fetid stench of decaying flesh would soon become overpowering. Unfortunately, there wasn't any time to dump the bodies; he needed to get this ship airborne immediately and go in pursuit of his own stolen vessel before the Cardassian Woman used it to reach the client.

He crammed his bulky frame into the small pilot's seat and pressed a switch to detach the supply umbilicals. Firing up the engines, he checked the short-range scanner and locked in the signal of the *Githzarai,* which was already at orbital distance and beginning a circuit of the planet. From a tinny-sounding speaker above his head squawked the voice of Iljar flight control, requesting the *Otamawan*'s flight plan before liftoff. Grauq punched the speaker, and its fractured remains dangled next to him at the end of a frayed duotronic cable.

There wasn't much to fear when it came to defying the local authorities. Smuggling was rampant on Harkoum, and most of the businesses that still operated on this neglected sphere at the edge of Cardassian space weren't interested in drawing a lot of attention. Grauq didn't know of a single settlement on Harkoum that actually had a constabulary of any kind. Vigilantism was its own law on this planet.

The *Otamawan* lifted off sloppily; its antigravs were not well calibrated. In defiance of standard practice, Grauq kicked in the impulse engines while still in the atmosphere, and a few seconds later the glare of the sky dissipated into the darkling majesty of space. The *Githzarai* was still above the atmosphere and clearly visible on the *Otamawan*'s sensors.

And so was the massive Romulan warbird that hung in orbit, intercepting incoming and outgoing freighter traffic. Grauq swore under his breath. The allied "peacekeeping effort" had disrupted smuggling in the Almatha sector for months. It was easy to evade Starfleet vessels; the Klingons and the Romulans, however, had proved to be dangerous and unpredictable. Moving under cloak, they could appear anywhere at any time without warning. They could secretly surveil shipping lanes and star systems for weeks. Now they were at Harkoum. Grauq wondered if the client knew of their presence—and whether the client's presence on Harkoum was the reason the warbird had come.

Problems for another time, he decided. Tracking the *Githzarai,* he saw that it had settled into a steady low orbit. *The Cardassian Woman wasn't expecting the Romulans, either,* he realized. *Until they leave, she won't give away her destination.* A growl of satisfaction rumbled in Grauq's chest. The situation had turned to his advantage, after all. If the Cardassian Woman was trapped in orbit by the warbird's presence, then he had time to slowly close the gap between them and ready himself for an assault on her ship—and because the *Githzarai* was actually *his* ship, he knew a whole host of ways to disable it without destroying it. If his new plan went as hoped, he might yet get to enjoy seeing the Cardassian Woman struggling futilely beneath him, begging for the merciful release of his blade. . . .

The first pungent hint of decay wafted forward from the hold. Grauq reduced the *Otamawan*'s internal temperature settings to near-freezing and hoped that the Romulans, as a species, weren't inclined toward lingering.

18

Kira

"WE DON'T HAVE TIME TO NEGOTIATE," GENERAL NATHECH said. "We have until night at best. That southern army is getting closer."

"And they outnumber us," said white-haired General Ghavun.

Surrounded by her generals and flanked by Jamin, General Kira tried to calm their rising anger. "I know," she said.

Twisting in tight, anxious circles, Ghavun fumed, "Where did that southern force come from? And who is barring us from our own keep?" He stopped and took two angry steps toward the colossal mountain redoubt. "Why won't they let us in?"

"Because they don't have to," Jamin said, stroking his narrow goatee in a slow and thoughtful manner. "They control the gates, and that means they're in charge."

"Let them have it," said General Renla, the only woman in Kira's inner circle. Renla looked young, but she was wiser than her years, tempered by a life of loss and grief in wartime. "No fortress lasts forever. We can bivouac in Lonar for the season."

"No," Kira said. "Parek Tonn is occupied, but it's still ours. I won't abandon it—not to the Eav'oq and not to whatever army marches here from the sea."

A susurrus of confusion and indignation spread swiftly through the ranks of archers and cavalry gathered on the plains behind Kira and her retinue. Morale—already faltering at the end of a long and difficult winter march home through high country and merciless storms—was taking another humbling blow from this most unwelcome news. Rumbles of discontent grew louder by the minute; Kira knew that she needed to decide quickly on a course of action before what little discipline remained in her army collapsed under the burdens of despair and rage.

"Jamin," she said, "keep the rumors quiet while I seek another parley with the Eav'oq."

"You're going alone?"

She noted the concern on his face. "Yes, Jamin."

"As you wish." In a calm, low voice, he told the other generals what to say, then dismissed them to promote patience among the rank and file.

With a nudge from her knee and a tug on the reins, Kira guided Jayol back toward the lofty gates of Parek Tonn. Musky odors of sweat permeated the *zhom*'s thick fur as the morning sun climbed higher, bringing unrelenting heat that stifled the wind. Alone beneath the rough-hewn gatehouse that jutted from the mountainside, Kira called upward, "Hear me, Eav'oq!"

Again, the narrow, scowling eye appeared over the edge of the battlement and looked down upon her with suspicion. "We are here," the gatekeeper said. "And you are heard."

"If we cede you the fortress," she shouted, struggling to

overcome the intimidating vertical distance that stretched between them, "will you grant us sanctuary?"

"No," said the gatekeeper, without even a moment's pause to consider her plea. "It is not yours to cede. It is ours."

Rage coursed in her veins, but it failed to overcome the profound powerlessness that wrapped her in its dark folds. Imperious desires crowded her thoughts, demanding satisfaction, demanding redress, demanding blood—even though she knew that she was in a position to demand absolutely nothing. All she could do was ask the gatekeeper, "Why do you deny us?"

"You are no different than them," he said, gesticulating again toward the distant army on the horizon. "Takers of life, extinguishers of light. You come bearing weapons of war. How are we to greet you but as an aggressor?"

"We haven't come to make war on you," Kira said.

"But you come making demands," the gatekeeper said. "You order us to admit you into our fortress." Kira restrained herself from once again asserting that it was the Bajora's fortress to begin with and let him continue. "If we were to raise the gates, who would defend us from you?"

"I give you my pledge," Kira said. "We are not your enemies. I ask you again for sanctuary in Parek Tonn."

"No."

Wounded pride and her deepening concern about the dark army advancing from the south fouled Kira's mood as she rode back down the broad slope to rejoin her generals.

They huddled together in a circle. Nathech spoke first. "If they won't let us in, we should attack."

Ghavun nodded. "Agreed. We should take back what's ours."

Almost in unison, Renla and Jamin shook their heads,

dismissing the idea. "A waste of time and men," Renla said.

"We're not equipped for a siege," Jamin said. "No rams, no towers, no ladders or catapults . . . and not one tree left whole between us and the edge of the world. We might as well hurl our swords into the sea, for all the good they'll do us."

"But this is our *home*," Nathech protested. "It's *ours*."

"Jamin and Renla are right," Kira said. "The Eav'oq could cut us down at their pleasure, and we'd be lucky even to chip the cornerstones. We will not siege the keep."

Defeat lay over the circle, which grew quiet and pensive.

Jamin turned his gaze to the south. "The Eav'oq," he said. "They told us they'd defended the citadel before . . . against them." He pointed at the faraway army, whose razor-line of darkness had grown thicker. Everyone turned and watched the distant battalions slowly draw closer. "Do we want to be here when that army arrives? And if we do, what side of the fight will the Eav'oq want us to be on? . . . What side do *we* want to be on?"

"An alliance," Nathech said, appalled. "You're talking about an alliance with those usurpers."

"It makes sense," Jamin said. "If our goal is to be inside the fortress, then we should make it the Eav'oq's goal to *bring* us inside. With their enemy approaching, it should make for a tempting proposition."

"This is ridiculous," Renla said, rolling her eyes. "Why involve ourselves in their fight? We can move to the other side of Mount Kola and wait out the battle there."

Ghavun scowled. "And what happens if the Eav'oq lose control of the fortress to an even more hostile power? I should think we'd find our options far less palatable in that event."

Nathech made a bitter harrumphing sound. "Yes, far more *palatable* to turn ourselves into mercenaries in our own home."

"Enough," Kira said. "We'll ride under colors back to the gate and propose an alliance with the Eav'oq."

"To whom?" Nathech said sourly. "The gatekeeper?"

"You forget yourself, Nathech," Kira said, and with a glare from her steely eyes he was cowed back into loyal obeisance.

"Apologies, my lady."

Kira granted him her forgiveness with a nod, then she turned and stalked back to her mount. A squire held the stirrup as she planted her foot. Grasping the pommel of her saddle, she swung herself back up onto her *zhom*'s broad back and took the reins. All around her, the generals did the same. Jamin was already guiding his own lupine steed to her side, directing the standard-bearers to mount up and fall in as he passed by them. Masked by a rising dust nimbus, Kira and her circle rode slowly back up the slope, for a third audience before the gates of Parek Tonn. Minutes later they came to a halt on the ground where they'd stood before, ringed by a settling halo of disturbed earth. No need this time to hail the gatekeeper; he revealed himself high above on the battlements. Kira nodded to Jamin, indicating that he should speak for her.

"On behalf of General Kira Nerys of the Bajora, we come to offer a pact of truce, and our word of bond in alliance," Jamin said, his strong voice reverberating in the cupped well of the fortress walls. "Is there one among you whom you call your leader? One who can give us your word of bond?"

The gatekeeper turned away, as if to confer with someone. After several seconds he replied, "We have nominated our sister as our interlocutor in this matter," he said.

Then he withdrew from the edge of the battlement and retreated into the gatehouse. Kira watched the walls, searching for movement, and then she saw it—a flash of light on a parapet not far from the gatehouse. Someone emerged from inside the fortress—not an Eav'oq but an older, white-haired woman, one of Kira's own people, in white flowing raiment. "My name is Opaka Sulan," the woman said. "And I will speak for the Eav'oq."

19

Deep Space 9

BASHIR, TARSES, AND AYLAM GATHERED AROUND THE MAIN display screen at the rear of the infirmary's diagnostic lab. Enlarged on the monitor was a real-time medical scan of Lieutenant Ro's spinal cord tissue, magnified to reveal the ongoing repairs being carried out by Dr. Tarses's medical nanites.

"Truly impressive work, Doctor," Dr. Aylam said.

"Indeed," Bashir added. "First-rate." Pointing at a pair of nanites that seemed to be collaborating on the repair of a nerve fiber, he said, "Coordinated activity. Very sophisticated. What other applications do you see for this?"

"Quite a few," Tarses said. "Assuming this succeeds in restoring Lieutenant Ro's spinal cord to proper function, we can explore using this to rebuild all kinds of delicate nerve tissue—and maybe even conduct repairs on deep brain tissue without risking harm to surrounding structures."

Bashir marveled at the simplicity of Tarses's innovation, and, even though he knew that it was irrational, he felt a small pang of envy, as well. *Be serious,* he told himself. *You can't invent everything. Not every breakthrough in Federation medical science is going to start and end with you.* He almost had to laugh at himself. *You're enhanced, not omniscient.*

He knew that if anything was going to dispel his dark mood tonight, it would be watching Dr. Tarses go on and on about his revolutionary new procedure, completely oblivious of the fact that young Dr. Aylam hung on his every word. Bashir knew that look very well—Aylam was unmistakably smitten with Tarses, who was too enraptured with his own achievement to take any notice of the young woman's expressive body language. She was turned squarely in his direction, the end of her stylus perched provocatively near the corner of her mouth. Every few minutes she lifted a hand to sweep her blond hair from her face and stretch in a way that accentuated her figure. And through it all, Dr. Tarses made no indication of noticing any of it.

Bashir, on the other hand, couldn't help but be mesmerized by Dr. Aylam's flirtations. Until tonight he hadn't spent more than half an hour with her; various tasks had cut short his "welcome to Deep Space 9" tour on her first day aboard. For three days he hadn't been able to make time even to see her; now he couldn't take his eyes off her.

And again, he could only envy Dr. Tarses.

The young physician's dissertation about medical nanites was interrupted by the sound of the infirmary's front door opening to admit a nasal drone of annoyance. "Where is she?"

All three doctors turned to see Quark standing in the doorway, looking agitated. "I see all three of you standing here gabbing, so I know she's not in surgery," he continued, pressing on into the infirmary. The doors closed behind him. "So where is she?"

Bashir knew who Quark meant. "Back in the ward."

Quark took a few steps toward the ward entrance, then stopped when he saw that all three doctors were still staring straight at him. Visibly irked at the insistence on protocol, he said with vexed disdain, "May I?"

Gesturing toward the ward entrance, Bashir said, "I set out a chair for you."

That softened Quark's mood just a bit. "Thanks," he said, then walked quickly into the adjacent room.

Though he hadn't been privy to all the details of Quark and Ro's peculiar friendship, Bashir had noticed that the two seemed unusually close, considering Quark's usual relationship with law-enforcement personnel. Rather than risk disturbing its delicate equilibrium by inquiring about it, Bashir simply accepted the situation at face value and left it at that. So far, that had seemed to work out best for everyone.

As soon as Bashir returned his attention to the monitor, Tarses resumed his presentation. "Now," he said, "as you can see here, the postganglionic nerve—"

"That's a preganglionic fiber," Bashir interrupted.

Tarses did a double take toward the screen. "Are you sure?"

"Positive." Bashir made a sweeping, it-doesn't-matter gesture with his hand. "Please, continue."

The unexpected criticism seemed to derail Tarses's train of thought, and he stammered for a few seconds while he recomposed himself. Just as he was about to soldier on, the comm chirped.

"Nog to Dr. Bashir."

"Go ahead, Nog."

"Sir, I've found something in Taran'atar's comm logs that I think you should have a look at."

"What have you found?"

"I'm not exactly certain, sir," Nog said. *"Let's just say I'm looking to get a second opinion."*

Bashir wasn't certain why Nog didn't seek a consultation from one of his fellow engineers, but he trusted the young chief of operations to know who was best qualified to help him. "On my way. Bashir out." Backpedaling away from Aylam and Tarses, he said, "I'm sorry, if you'll excuse me." He turned and walked toward the door, then paused to add, "Do continue your presentation, Dr. Tarses. Dr. Aylam seems very interested in *everything* you have to say." Tarses looked quizzically back at Bashir, apparently unaware of the fact that, less than two meters away from him, Dr. Aylam was blushing.

Making an effort not to disturb anything, Bashir stepped carefully as he entered Taran'atar's quarters. Demolished furniture was everywhere, as if it had been scattered by an explosive force. There was no sign of the forensic teams that security had summoned hours ago; presumably, they'd found all that they were going to; whatever they had recovered had been sent to the station's science labs for analysis.

Nog stood and worked with a handheld data-retrieval device at the companel to Bashir's left as he entered. At Nog's feet was a tray from the replimat; on it was a half-eaten bowl of tube grubs and a glass whose bottom was obscured by the lonely dregs of now-decarbonated root beer. The young Ferengi looked up and smiled at Bashir. "Thanks for coming, Doctor," he said.

"No problem," Bashir said. He joined Nog, who had set up a hard-line connection by running optronic cables through the splintered fist-hole in the companel's surface to its inner components. From inside came soft electronic beeps and the gentle whirring of a ventilator. "What have you found so far?"

"More than I know what to do with," Nog said. "Massive data files, huge comm logs—all of it scrambled. I've been decrypting it one piece at a time and putting it back together. I don't have any complete files so far, but all the incoming signals I've recovered have one thing in common." He called up a moving waveform image on his tricorder's main screen. "This: a repeating wave, embedded in all the messages as a subcarrier."

It looked strangely familiar to Bashir. "What does it do?"

"That's what I wanted to ask you," Nog said. "I have my ideas, but I could be totally wrong." He rubbed his hands together and fidgeted nervously as he watched Bashir study the peculiar oscillating wave. "Any guesses?"

"It looks organic," Bashir said. Nog pressed a knuckle against his lips and nodded for Bashir to continue. "Fairly long frequency, more neuroelectric than cardioelectric. . . . I could be mistaken, but I think that's a brain wave."

"I thought so, too," Nog said, entering commands into his data device. "It reminded me of a waveform I calibrated in some of the *Defiant*'s sickbay upgrades last month." He superimposed another signal on top of the first. They were not an exact match but were quite similar. "This is a standard-issue delta wave," Nog said, "the kind we use for surgical anesthesia. It's pretty close." He turned toward Bashir. "Do you think the one I found might be a modified version? Maybe customized for a Jem'Hadar?"

"Maybe," Bashir said. A thought occurred to him; his instincts told him to follow it through, but his ethics brought him up short. "I could check this against some of

Taran'atar's recent medical scans," Bashir thought aloud. "But I can't report what I find without violating his medical privacy."

Nog rolled his eyes and heaved an exasperated sigh. "He stabbed the captain and broke Lieutenant Ro's back. I think he ought to—" The high-strung Ferengi pulled back on his anger. Considering the fact that Nog's left leg had been shot off by Jem'Hadar during the Dominion War—and the fact that he had never been shy about voicing his suspicion of, and dislike for, Taran'atar—Bashir thought that the engineer was demonstrating considerable restraint. "He's a Jem'Hadar—I don't think privacy is high on his list of priorities."

Bashir knew that Nog's opinion wouldn't sway a Starfleet Medical Board review if he was investigated for this breach of doctor-patient privilege, but he took the tricorder from Nog and established a link to the station's main computer. Within moments he had logged in to his medical database and opened Taran'atar's patient records. Skimming quickly past the results of the Jem'Hadar's physical, he called up the report he had filed several months ago, after Taran'atar had come to the infirmary with a new and peculiar affliction for his species: sleep.

It had taken a lot of effort to convince Taran'atar to let Bashir monitor one of his sleep cycles in the controlled environment of the intensive-care ward. The data that Bashir had recorded that night had represented a major breakthrough in Jem'Hadar biological research, even though it had defied simple analysis for lack of a baseline against which to measure it. Now, however, Bashir saw a pattern taking shape—and being duplicated—on screen. Removing the Starfleet delta wave from the screen, he overlaid Taran'atar's dream-sleep brain-wave pattern with the one that Nog had reconstructed from the comm logs.

"They're an exact match," Nog said. And they were.

Fear and suspicion began to twine in Bashir's gut. "This is Taran'atar's sleep-cycle brain-wave pattern," he said. "It's not just a rough approximation, like the delta-wave generators we use. This was tailored specifically to affect *his* subconscious mind. It was meant expressly for him."

Nog looked startled. "So my hunch was right? This is some kind of mind control?"

"Precisely," Bashir said. "Hidden in the background of a signal like this, it could induce a hypnagogic state within seconds, rendering the subject highly susceptible to suggestion. And since Jem'Hadar are programmed to be obedient—"

"Suggestions to him would be like commands," Nog said. "But Jem'Hadar are only supposed to obey the Founders and the Vorta."

"That's true," Bashir said. "But something like this might be able to circumvent the Jem'Hadar's hard-wired biological conditioning—"

"Like a backdoor in an operating system bypassing a hardware function."

"Right." Bashir closed out Taran'atar's medical file and logged out of the medical database. "Keep working on those files," he said. "We need to see what the delta wave was being used to do to Taran'atar. That might tell us who's using it. Once we know that . . . then we can start to ask why."

20

U.S.S. Defiant

ELIAS VAUGHN WATCHED THE WRECKAGE AHEAD OF THE *Defiant* slowly grow larger on the viewscreen. In his mind's eye he reassembled the jumbled, broken pieces and reached his own conclusion before Lieutenant Forte made his report from the tactical station.

"The wreckage is definitely from the *Euphrates*," Forte said, confirming what Vaughn already knew. "It was destroyed between five and six hours ago."

Vaughn kept his eyes on the spin-rolling kaleidoscope of scorched debris. "Any sign of Taran'atar?"

Ensign Rahim turned from his science console to answer. "We're reading biological residue from two humanoids," he said. "Both Klingon. No sign of Jem'Hadar DNA in the debris field."

Bowers checked his situation monitor. "That tracks with the damage to the runabout. The hull fractures are consistent with a single, high-power disruptor strike." He tapped at his console for a moment. "But if that's right, *Euphrates* got hit while her shields were down."

That seemed to intrigue Rahim. "A sneak attack?"

"Maybe," Vaughn said, not yet convinced.

"But why would a Klingon ship fire on a Starfleet runabout?" Bowers said. "Especially one with its shields down?"

Forte chimed in, "Maybe they got a look at who was flying it."

"Right," Rahim said. "If they scanned it and detected a Jem'Hadar aboard—"

"At warp?" Bowers asked. "Not likely."

Ensign Zucca turned her chair around to join the conversation. "Prynn might have sabotaged the runabout before she—" Zucca saw Vaughn's strained, brooding mien and skipped ahead to the end of her thought. "If the runabout was sabotaged, it might have fallen back to impulse before it was intercepted."

"All right," Bowers said. "I can buy that."

"So the runabout gets intercepted," Rahim continued. "Then the Klingons send a boarding party—"

"Wrong," Vaughn said, snaring everyone's attention. "The Klingons wouldn't have boarded the runabout if they knew a Jem'Hadar was on board; they'd have just blown it to bits." He got up and moved to Rahim's station. Pointing at the data on Rahim's screen, he continued, "More likely those two Klingons boarded the *Euphrates* because they thought they'd found it adrift. As soon as they were aboard, Taran'atar killed them. Then he beamed on to their ship, killed the crew, and destroyed the runabout himself. Which suggests a small ship and crew—probably a scout."

Incredulous looks circuited the bridge. As Vaughn expected, only Bowers had the courage to actually speak his mind. "Sir, is it possible the Klingons captured Taran'atar, then destroyed the runabout?"

"If they captured him," Vaughn said, "why would they destroy the runabout? And if a Klingon crew destroyed a Starfleet vessel, even one that had been hijacked, why haven't they notified Starfleet?" Neither Bowers nor the other bridge officers had any response. Vaughn sighed. "No, the most likely scenario is that Taran'atar not only has a huge lead, he now has a cloaked ship that's currently faster than us. There's no telling what direction he went from here."

Forte jumped in, "Won't the Klingons notice that one of their ships is missing? I mean, we shipped out on the QT because we wanted to capture the runabout without turning it into a major engagement. If Taran'atar captured a Klingon ship, what happens when they issue an alert?"

"I don't think they will," Vaughn said. "As a point of pride, the capture of one of their ships isn't something they'd want publicly known—especially not with most of Almatha sector under Romulan oversight." Vaughn needed something more solid than his hunch to go on before the search for Taran'atar could continue. Turning away, he said, "Mr. Bowers, continue analyzing the runabout debris. . . . I have some research to do."

Vaughn didn't see any reason to explain himself, even though he felt the apprehension from the crew as he vacated the bridge. Walking back to his ready room, he felt as though his thoughts were a dark blur of fury and grief, a flurry of tactics thrown together with revenge fantasies. He tried to let go of the anger, the passion that was impairing his calm judgment. Around him the *Defiant* was still and quiet, cruising slowly at a subimpulse maneuvering speed as it collected data on the debris of the runabout.

Sequestered once more in his ready room, he procured a mug of black, unsweetened coffee from the replicator and sat down at his desk. Activating the desktop computer interface, he wondered what time it was in the First City on Qo'noS, then decided that he didn't really care if he was waking up his old friend. *People as old as we are shouldn't sleep so much, anyway,* he decided. *Little enough time left to us as it is.*

His request for a secure diplomatic channel took most of a minute to process and connect. A flashing icon on the lower corner of his screen confirmed that his hail was being sounded on the other end of the subspace signal. He savored a taste of his piping hot coffee.

Then the image on his screen changed from the white-on-blue Federation laurel-and-stars emblem to the grizzled face of his old friend Lorgh from Klingon Imperial Intelligence. Lorgh looked tired, grouchy, and unamused. *"Oh, it's you,"* he grumbled. *"If I'd known, I'd have gone back to bed."*

Vaughn wasn't in a mood for verbal sparring, not tonight. "No jokes," he said. "Prynn's dead, and I think the bastard who killed her has one of your ships."

The old Klingon agent was now fully awakened. *"What do I need to know?"*

"I have reason to believe that a Jem'Hadar named Taran'atar has captured one of your patrol ships in the Almatha sector."

Lorgh worked at a panel adjacent to his monitor screen while he spoke. *"Taran'atar,"* he said. *"That was the observer? The one sent by Odo?"*

"Yes," Vaughn said, not at all surprised to know that Lorgh had kept up with current events on Deep Space 9.

"What was Prynn's part in this?"

"Taran'atar hijacked her runabout to get off Deep Space 9. By the time we had caught up to them . . ." Vaughn realized suddenly that he couldn't bring himself to say it. The words were too awful to hear aloud in his own voice. "We found the runabout destroyed a short while ago, along with the remains of two Klingon personnel, but no Jem'Hadar DNA. Damage to the ship was consistent with Klingon ordnance."

"I see," Lorgh said. Something on his other screen caught his attention. *"There is an imperial scout ship on a regular patrol near your coordinates, the* I.K.S. noH'pach . . . *And the ship is overdue to check in with sector command."*

"I don't suppose you can tell me where the *noH'pach* is now," Vaughn said, not really expecting Lorgh to divulge that information even if he had the capability.

"No," Lorgh said. *"But I can tell you that it's a* Haqtaj-*class vessel. The rest I'm sure you can do on your own."*

Vaughn nodded; being able to review the technical specs of the scout ship wasn't much, but it was more than he'd had before. "Thank you."

"If you find the noH'pach, *I think the empire would be grateful if you kept this incident out of any official reports."*

"Of course," Vaughn said.

"It would also be wise to avoid any Romulan involvement."

"I'll try, but I might need to expose a few of your secrets—ship schematics for the *Haqtaj* class, for one."

"Whatever is necessary," Lorgh said. Then he added, *"I hope your daughter had the honor of dying in battle. If so, I'm sure she's already being hailed in* Sto-Vo-Kor."

"No doubt," Vaughn said, his pain swelling inside him like a burning cancer. He had to end the conversation while his stoic façade remained intact. "I owe you one, old friend. Vaughn out." He terminated the transmission and reclined deeply in his chair. Staring up at the ceiling, he had to force himself to breathe. He struggled for calm, even as he doubted his mind would ever know peace again.

Prynn was gone, and he was alone.

Sam Bowers hadn't found anything in his fourth scan of the runabout's wreckage that the first three scans hadn't already uncovered. Frustration was making him irritable. He wanted to be in motion, in action, in pursuit of Taran'atar, wherever he might have gone, however he might have gotten there. But if Commander Vaughn was correct—and Bowers had admitted to himself that Vaughn's conclusions seemed quite reasonable—the *Defiant* was essentially blind to its prey.

The aft port hatch opened and Vaughn returned to his seat. Bowers closed out the work on his screen and moved to stand on Vaughn's right side. "No new information yet," he said quietly. "But the good news is that Leishman is making more repairs to the warp nacelles; we'll have full speed within the hour."

Vaughn nodded. "Well done." He lowered his voice. "I've made some progress, too," he said. "According to HQ's fleet deployment records, the Klingons had a small outrider called the *noH'pach* patrolling this part of Almatha sector. If Taran'atar captured a ship, that's probably the one."

Bowers doubted Vaughn's account of how he had come by the information about the outrider, but, given the circumstances, the acting XO wasn't inclined to press the commander's patience. "What do we know about the *noH'pach*, sir?"

"It's a *Haqtaj*-class vessel, crew of maybe five or six," Vaughn said. "She recently upgraded her cloaking device, and her computer has a significant amount of sensitive

Klingon military data, so it's important we find her before the Romulans do. I've forwarded the full specs for the *Haqtaj* class to your station. Look them over with Forte and find a weakness we can exploit."

"Aye, sir," Bowers said, then nodded to Forte, who followed him to the aft console. Calling up the specs Vaughn had provided, he routed the data to Forte's monitor, which was adjacent to his own. The blueprints in front of them were incredibly detailed, more so than any Starfleet scan could have yielded without substantial internal assistance.

Forte leaned sideways and whispered to Bowers. "How did he get this? These are classified Klingon schematics."

"This sort of stuff is always done on a need-to-know basis," Bowers whispered back. "We don't need to know."

It was evidently not the answer that Forte had hoped for, but he sighed and began studying the ship schematics. "Our first priority is finding it, right?"

"Right."

"I'll focus on its cloaking system, work up a simulation, and test it for trace particles and subspatial artifacts."

"Sounds good," Bowers said. "If it works, at what range could you get a sensor lock on them?"

"We'd have to be close to penetrate the cloak . . . maybe inside half a light-year."

"No, we need to do better than that," Bowers said. "It's been almost four hours. According to this, the *noH'pach* can make warp nine. I need at least a three-light-year range right now, and the longer it takes to see through their cloak the more range we'll need to compensate for his head start."

Shaking his head slowly, Forte said, "I don't think that's feasible, sir. Breaking through the cloak is one thing, but at the ranges you're talking about, we'd need a sensor array twice the diameter of the *Defiant*, with the power of two starbases to back it up. Even Deep Space 9 doesn't have that."

Bowers relented. Forte wasn't prone to defeatism; if he said the plan wasn't workable, then Bowers had to take him at his word. Leaving the tactical officer to continue working on punching through the Klingon ship's cloaking screen, Bowers returned to Vaughn's side for a hushed conference.

"We're working on seeing through the *noH'pach*'s cloak," Bowers said. "We can't run a scan powerful enough to make up for its head start, but I have an idea."

"I'm listening."

"Up until we lost Taran'atar's trail, his course had been extremely consistent—almost single-minded, in fact." He called up a star chart on Vaughn's right-side command panel, then superimposed a bright-yellow graph line depicting the route of the *Euphrates* after it left Deep Space 9. "The runabout was on the same general heading for nearly an hour after it left the station." He traced its path across the screen with his fingertip. "It deviated briefly to intercept that rogue comet and set a trap for us. But as soon as we were disabled, it continued on almost the exact same heading it had started on. And there were no major changes of heading from then until we found the wreckage." Turning toward Vaughn, he finished, "Sir, I believe that even if Taran'atar is traveling cloaked, he's still on the same heading as before."

Vaughn frowned. "Why would he cloak, then?"

"To confuse us," Bowers said. "To make us waste time debating his next move, when he's actually still on the same move he's been making since the beginning. If he was trying to conceal his destination, he would have chosen a more erratic flight path—but he didn't. He chose a straight line with one tactical deviation." Bowers felt his mind racing as he dissected Taran'atar's tactics. "I don't think evading capture is his primary objective; for him it's just a means to an end. His behavior suggests that he's most interested in getting somewhere quickly. I think he's on a deadline, making a straight shot for some kind of rendezvous." The conclusion seemed obvious to Bowers. He straightened his posture and said, "Sir, I recommend that we continue on Taran'atar's original heading, at best possible speed, and attempt to overtake him."

Vaughn sat and considered Bowers's suggestion. He nodded slowly. "You might be right," he said. "And I had thought of that possibility. But even if you're correct, we'd be chasing an enemy we still can't see, and Leishman would have to postpone the rest of the warp-drive repairs, leaving us too slow to overtake him." He sighed. "Be patient, Sam. Let Leishman get the engines back to full power, and work with Forte to pierce the *noH'pach*'s cloak. If we don't have any better leads by then, we'll continue on Taran'atar's original heading, as you've suggested. But until then, we're going to sit tight." With a grimace he added, "And I'm going to hate it just as much as you do."

21

I.K.S. noH'pach

"CURIOUS," KITANA'KLAN SAID. "DO YOU THINK THIS MAKES you free?"

Taran'atar didn't know whether to blame the stimulant drugs he had taken hours ago on the *Euphrates* or his own worsening mental decrepitude for conjuring the hallucination that had appeared beside him. He knew that his fellow Jem'Hadar on the *noH'pach*'s bridge was a product of his imagination; he had slain Kitana'klan himself, had broken his neck in his hands with a sharp crack of bone and thick ripping of muscle, roughly nine months ago. Kitana'klan appeared wholly corporeal; his voice sounded resonant and echoed slightly off the bulkheads around them. The scent of the white was heavy upon him.

"You are not real," Taran'atar said, as if that would instantly negate all possibility of further conversation.

Speaking now as the female Founder, his delusion said, "Who are you to judge what is real, and what is not?"

"I am a Jem'Hadar," Taran'atar said.

The delusion shook its head and now wore the smug

authority of the nameless Jem'Hadar First who had tortured him on Sindorin. "You don't even know what the word means."

"It means *soldier*."

"How can you be so old yet so naïve?" the Jem'Hadar First said. "Soldiers have value. You and I are expendable, utterly disposable."

"You were expendable," Taran'atar said. "You had no name."

"My maker didn't know how to name Jem'Hadar," he said. "But I didn't need a name; I knew what I was. Just as I know what you are, even though you won't admit it. . . . We are slaves."

Dignifying a waking dream by talking to it seemed like a preposterous waste of time to Taran'atar, but the urge to respond was overpowering, a compulsion that spurred him like a heartless rider dissatisfied by its mount. "I am not a slave."

Odo glowered down at him now, his rasp of a voice dry in its sarcasm and unflinching in its contempt. "Oh, really?"

"I serve willingly," Taran'atar said, his pride faltering into defensiveness.

Captain Kira now harrumphed bitterly. Blood oozed weakly from around the knife in her chest. "Some service."

That face. He was out of his chair before he'd had time to process the ferocity of his hatred. His hands were around Kira's throat—then he realized that he was choking Eris, the first Vorta to whose authority he had submitted, nearly twenty-three years ago. Her sapphire eyes radiated terror and indignation. He released her, stricken with shame that he had dared to lay hands upon his better. That he had hated her every day of his life was immaterial: The Founders commanded the Vorta, and the Vorta commanded the Jem'Hadar. It was the order of things.

"I submit myself for discipline," he said.

"Why did you stop?" Eris said. "You could have killed me."

"It is forbidden. My pledge is to obey. Obedience brings victory, and victory is life."

"You pledged to obey Captain Kira," Eris taunted. "Where was your obedience then, First?"

She was correct; he had riven himself from the will of the Founders by striking Kira down. In Eris's words he discovered an irresistible temptation: If he was capable of smiting one who was the beloved of a Founder, what more dire consequences could he possibly incur by beating a mere Vorta to a slow and misery-laden death? He roared and lunged at Eris.

She was gone, like a thought barely grasped. A thick, scaly gray hand whipped him about-face. He stared into the eyes of Mokata'klan, the Jem'Hadar First who had named him. "You forget your place!" He backhanded Taran'atar, who stumbled. The long-dead commander slammed his steely elbows down on Taran'atar's shoulders, driving him to his knees. Taran'atar bowed his head before the First who had led him in his inaugural battle.

"You are not a Jem'Hadar," Mokata'klan said, his breath hot with the odor of white. "You defied the will of a Founder."

For this Taran'atar had no response: His imaginary accuser had spoken the truth. He turned away from Mokata'klan, to see the female Founder eyeing him with scorn and pity. "Did you think that you were serving me by disobeying Odo?"

"No," Taran'atar said.

"A Jem'Hadar is obedience," she said. "Without it you aren't a Jem'Hadar at all."

"I know," he said.

Disgust tainted her every word. "What are you, then, now that you have failed as a Jem'Hadar?"

"I am dead. I must reclaim my life."

She scolded, "Do you expect another Founder to absolve you of blame for your betrayal?"

He kneeled and bowed his head abjectly, like a penitent youngling. "No."

"But you have left your assignment to present yourself to a Founder for correction, yes?"

"No," he said. "I have not. . . . I cannot. I will not."

The nameless First from Sindorin sneered at him. "You just don't want to. And why should you?"

"It is the order of things."

The Sindorin First said, "Yet you're not going to them."

"I am flawed," Taran'atar said. "Defective. Unworthy."

"Unworthy? Of what? *Them*?"

"I am a disgrace to the Founders, to the Dominion. I have known this since I was found to have no need for the white. In that moment I diminished. I became a lesser being."

"Making you suitable for lesser gods," said the delusion masked as Weyoun, the Vorta who had identified his abberant nature. "Surely you don't cling to the outrageous idea that they are the omnipotent, omniscient lords of creation?"

The truth pressed down on Taran'atar like a defeat. "The female Founder herself denied it. She proclaimed reverence for another, one whom she called the Progenitor. But what god would bow before another? I thought her confinement had harmed her, but how could a god succumb to such a trivial punishment? Perhaps she spoke truthfully; perhaps she is not a god . . . and neither is Odo."

"Then why continue to bind yourself to their will?"

"It is . . ." Taran'atar trailed off, realizing that all his hardwired platitudes were empty of meaning. He could parrot them by rote, but part of his mind had awakened to their falsity. "Because I have no choice," he said instead.

"The very definition of a slave," said the Sindorin First.

"I am not a slave."

"Of course not," said the Odo delusion. "If you were, you could not have defied me. But you did."

"Yes," Taran'atar admitted.

"So it *is* possible for a Jem'Hadar to defy the will of a Founder," Odo said.

"It should not be."

"But it is," Odo insisted.

"Yes."

The Sindorin First pulled Taran'atar to his feet and bellowed, "Then you have emancipated yourself!"

Taran'atar pushed away the nameless one.

"No," he said, his first seeds of awareness taking shape and growing into something greater but still out of reach. "I defied the Founders' will . . . but neither do I obey my own."

Captain Kira glared at him. Her smirk was malicious and knowing. "Then whom do you obey?"

He lunged at her with a war cry and outstretched hands.

She pulled his knife from her chest and drove it into his gut. Pain registered, sharp and cold in his lower intestine. His hands fumbled to grasp the weapon and pull it free . . . but when he looked down, he found only the unharmed, unblemished fabric of his coverall twisted in his fingers.

The delusion had vanished. He was alone again on the bridge, the autopilot engaged, the cloak still hiding the ship as it sped through the empty darkness toward Harkoum.

A sick feeling burbled inside him. He felt edgy and uncomfortably warm, and his body threatened to pull him, at any cost, down into the vulnerable lacuna of slumber, to the surreal disorientation of dreams. Staving off his loss of consciousness with drugs had originally seemed like a reasonable option. Now, hours later, as the stimulant's side effects asserted themselves, he wondered if his choice had been ill made. His hearts were pounding rapidly and were out of synch. The arrhythmia was no doubt at least partly to blame for his light-headedness and increasing shortness of breath. He forced his lungs to draw breath more slowly. Through willpower alone, he calmed his frantic pulse.

Equilibrium was slow to return. He was still clearing his mind of tangential thoughts when an alert sounded on a console at the back of the bridge. With the return of a task outside of himself, his focus snapped back. He stepped to the console and reviewed its indicators. There was a power disruption in the aft compartment of the *noH'pach*. Although the malfunction appeared to be minor, it had the potential to become hazardous if it was part of, or linked to, a critical system.

Drawing his phaser and heading aft, Taran'atar decided it would be prudent to correct the malfunction immediately—especially since it was almost certainly the product of sabotage by his unsupervised prisoner. *I should not have left her unwatched,* he chastised himself. *That was careless.* He unlocked the aft hatch as he approached. It opened. He stepped through.

Searing heat and piercing needle-jabs of pain turned his mind blank, and then he collapsed face-first to the deck.

Prynn awoke to the stench of decaying *gagh* and regurgitated bloodwine, which had commingled in a shallow access crawlspace below this compartment's hexagon-patterned floor grate. The side of her face hurt, but not from lying pressed against the metallic deck. Memories crept back into the front of her thoughts, until she recalled the stunning backhand from Taran'atar that had sent her flying against the bulkhead.

Peeking first, then looking around, she saw she was alone.

She tested her bonds. Her hands and feet were fairly well secured behind her. Craning her head and twisting her body, she was able to see that she had been tied with Starfleet-standard optronic cables, almost certainly from the runabout. Looking around at the unmistakable aesthetics of a Klingon warship, she wondered what had happened to the *Euphrates* and to Taran'atar. *Did the Klingons rescue me?* She shook her head at her own misplaced optimism. *Right, they rescued me, then they trussed me up like a sacrificial* targ *for the trip back to Deep Space 9. Guess again.* It wasn't hard for her to believe that Taran'atar had seized the small Klingon ship. What she found difficult to comprehend was why he was still holding her prisoner.

You can ask him all about it after *you escape,* she decided as she started to pull and push against the cables on her wrists and ankles. She was able to force only the slightest degree of slack in the synthetic fibers before they cut into her skin. She relented when she felt them start to become slick with her blood. *Relax,* she told herself, thinking back to her Starfleet survival training. *Stop trying to force it.* Think *your way out.*

The aft compartment seemed to be a multipurpose area for the ship's crew. The food under the deck grate suggested that it was often used as a mess hall, but the assorted lockers and loose pieces of half-assembled equipment along one wall implied that it was used for engineering and repair work, as well. Several floor grate panels had gaps for handholds, so that they could be lifted for access to the systems underneath. Prynn wasn't very familiar with the layout of Klingon starships, but several familiar-looking configurations made her fairly certain she was above the ship's main warp engine. *Where there are engineers, there are tools,* she thought.

Small motions and a painstaking attention to stealth made her inching crawl across the compartment excruciatingly slow. Once she reached the other side, she nudged open a toolbox with her chin and kept her bruised face firmly against the lid, to lower it slowly rather than let it fall hard against the deck. Her neck muscles ached with the effort. Finally, the box was open in front of her. In awkward, painful stages, she raised herself to her knees in front of the open box and took stock of its contents. None of the tools seemed suited to the task of cutting through the optronic cables. Some were too bulky, overly long, or just too heavy; others were unsafe to use so close to her body while working blindly behind her back.

Then she eyed the rough edges of the box itself.

Two minutes later she had sawed through the cables on her wrists with simple friction. Then she untied her legs.

Back on her feet, she assessed her situation. From somewhere forward—she guessed the bridge—she heard Taran'atar's voice. He sounded agitated, as if he were in a conversation with someone who was angering him, but Prynn could hear only his side of the discussion. Around her were various panels and narrow pipes, all marked in obscure Klingon alphanumeric symbols that she couldn't decipher. She tried to imagine the various systems and components around her as they would look on a schematic, then she tried to trace her way through the essential parts of a warp drive and a power distribution system. Seconds later, she was certain she had found a primary power tap that linked the core to the ship's internal systems. Then she paused, uncertain what to do with her discovery. *If Nog was here, he'd know what to do. He'd wire something to something else.* . . . She looked around for other connections to the power system.

An idea began to assert itself as she traced the various linkages through the access panels along the bulkhead. It was a crude plan, little more than a desperate gambit. There was, she figured, a fifty-fifty chance that she would fry herself into a cinder even attempting it. *For me, those are good odds.*

She began poking through the open toolbox for the needed items and some spare plasma tap coils. Holding a strange-looking tool in her hands, she mused, *I hope this is a dynoscanner.*

Working backward from target to source, she used an ion cutter to burn through the dark green-gray bulkhead next to the locked hatchway. She sloppily cut the first three sides of an irregular rectangle around where she believed the hatch's emergency forcefield circuit to be. Along the bottom of her incision, she worked with a lower setting, merely heating the metal of the bulkhead until it was soft enough for her to bend it by hand. Prying it forward with the claw-shaped end of the cutter, she bent it downward, out of her way.

Time to make an open circuit. Patching the positively charged spare tap coil into the power supply for the force-field generator was easy, as was cross-wiring its activator to the hatch's opening mechanism. She sabotaged the system to emit only the positively charged half of its repulsor field.

The negatively charged tap coil she connected to a floor grate in front of the hatch. With haste she lifted the grate and laid down a layer of insulating polymer beneath it, then lowered it closed. She packed its edges with more semi-liquid insulation.

Prynn stepped backward toward the main power tap from the warp core. The thick, rubbery black coils unspooled easily from her hands. Hooking the coils to the ship's primary power source would be a dangerous task even for someone who knew what they were doing. For Prynn, it was little better than a reasoned gamble. She'd had a fair amount of engineering training in Starfleet—almost all flight controllers benefited from having a better understanding of the systems that made their ships work—but this was alien technology, and she was trying to modify it with unfamiliar tools, in a hurry, to create a trap. *One of these blinking panels probably sets the circuits to safety mode for repairs,* she figured. *Knowing Klingons, the others are probably all self-destruct switches or something.*

Beyond the bulkhead, Taran'atar's voice grew louder.

Skipping the usual precautions, she searched with her eyes and fingertips for any multiplexed terminals into which she could connect the coils. To her irritation, all the nodes on the main power router were taken. *I could yank a couple noncritical systems,* she figured. Doing so suited the plan; it would sound alerts on the bridge and lure Taran'atar aft to investigate. The only major downside that Prynn could think of was that she wouldn't have any time to rig a capacitor to regulate the level of charge being delivered to the forcefield. It would hit at full force until its emitters shorted out. She knew that Jem'Hadar were extremely resilient and healed very quickly, but she had no idea how vulnerable they were to electrocution, or whether the trap she was laying might prove to be lethal.

I'm a hostage, she reminded herself. *He'll kill me when he's done with me. This is self-defense. I don't want to kill him if I don't have to, but if he dies . . . I can live with it.*

She disconnected the coils for two redundant backup systems from the router and hurriedly attached the spare coils that would deliver the charge to the door's forcefield emitter. There weren't many places to hide. She settled upon a mostly empty crewman's locker. It reeked of stale sweat and overripe boots. There she waited with bated breath and a fear-clenched jaw for Taran'atar to arrive.

His footfalls in the corridor outside were fast and heavy. Each step reverberated in the hollow spaces above and below the deck. A background hum that she had never even noticed suddenly went quiet as the magnetic locks on the hatch powered down. From her hiding place, she could see through a ventilation slat that the forcefield emitter charged instantly to full power.

The hatch opened. Taran'atar stepped inside. His foot touched the deck just inside the hatch. A flash-crack of white-hot energy pulsed around him for a fraction of a second, illuminating him in a fiery glow. Then the light and the blast of searing heat were gone.

Taran'atar fell forward with his eyes still open and landed facedown on the deck.

Acrid wisps of gray smoke twisted out of the cut in the bulkhead. The ends of the tap coils were little more than molten slag now, fused into the overloaded forcefield emitter and the charred, slightly warped floor grate. A sickly sweet scent of charred flesh filled the compartment.

Prynn burst forward from the locker and sprinted past

Taran'atar, who lay motionless on the deck. The sloped walls of the dim corridor blurred past her.

She ran through the open forward doorway onto the bridge. There were several stations on either side of her, but she had no idea how the Klingons organized their bridge operations, or if the various consoles could be reconfigured on the fly, the way that Starfleet companels could be. She scanned the layouts of the companels as she quickly passed by each one, trying to determine which would give her control over the internal security systems. The helm, located all the way forward, was easy to rule out. At the first station, an oscillograph closely resembled one of the gauges on a subspace radio console. *Communications.* The next was packed with screens, currently blank except for trefoil-shaped targeting crosshairs. *Tactical.* Then she reached a panel above which was a wide display showing a deck schematic of the ship. *Operations—jackpot.*

None of the controls on the main panel had any icon-style markings, only Klingon-language symbols. On a hunch, she tried tapping sections of the ship schematic overhead, starting near the aft compartment hatch. To her relief, the panel lit up, and several green points of light blinked rapidly near the aft hatch. *Guess I fried that pretty good.* Figuring she had little chance of locking Taran'atar in there—if he was even still alive—she instead pressed on the marking for the bridge hatch. As soon as it lit up, three colored dots appeared next to it. The first was red, the second green, the last white. One likely had been used to set the door to its currently open state; the other two, she presumed, closed the door and locked it, respectively. *There's only three; I think I can work this out by trial and error.* She pressed the red dot.

Nothing happened.

Right, she remembered. *Klingons* like *red. To us it's a warning color—to them it means security and comfort.* She pressed the white dot. Behind her the bridge hatch slid down from the ceiling to block the entryway. Halfway to the floor, a pair of scaly gray hands appeared beneath it and halted its descent.

Prynn searched the schematic above her for the cloaking device control but couldn't find it. She sprinted to the communications console and tried to figure out how to use its controls to send an SOS on a Starfleet frequency.

Centimeter by centimeter, Taran'atar forced the bridge hatch back upward. The grinding of metal and whining of servos was almost overpowered by his steady, escalating roar of fury.

In front of her, the Klingon control panel was just a jumble of shapes and colors, a puzzle with no answers. She berated herself for not thinking to steal Taran'atar's phaser while he was down.

The bridge hatch was more than three-quarters raised when its hydraulics gave out. Taran'atar slammed it fully open with a deafening, metallic clang.

He stepped onto the bridge. His skin was blotchy with burns. A feral snarl bared his teeth as he charged at Prynn.

She planted her feet and set up for a judo throw.

He slammed into her like a force of nature and hurled her backward, over the helm station, against the main viewer. Its screen fizzled momentarily with static as she struck it. She slid to the deck, stunned and unable to orient herself. His forearm locked around her throat and he pulled her off the bridge, back toward the aft compartment. She clutched at his arm, trying to loosen its hold so she could breathe. His muscles felt as unyielding as stone, and his skin was fever-hot, no doubt still suffering the galvanic effects of the jolt she'd given him. He dragged her through the open aft hatchway, then gripped her by the back of her neck and pinned her against the aft wall. She heard him fishing around through the tools and equipment on a shelf, looking for something. Then she felt the icy grip of Klingon-made magnetic manacles snapping into place around her left wrist. Pulling Prynn away from the wall, he carried her roughly to the middle of the compartment. He lifted one of her hands high over her head, next to a short curve of pipe drooping from the ceiling, stretching her upward until she stood on her toes. Then he lifted her other hand. The manacles, now extended through the closed semicircle of pipe, snapped shut around her right wrist. She dangled from the constraints, barely able to keep her weight on her toes rather than on her already badly chafed and torn wrists.

Taran'atar took a moment to remove from her reach anything that could be at all useful to her. Apparently satisfied that he had secured her properly this time, he stepped in front of her. "Don't do that again," he said, the gravity of his warning clear. "Next time, I will employ a more . . . *thorough* means of restraint." He let that warning sink in. "Is that clear?"

She didn't answer him. There was no point pretending that they had an understanding. Apparently thinking the same thing, he returned to the bridge without getting a response.

Alone again, Prynn realized she was out of options . . . and she began to accept the possibility that this filthy, cramped little ship was where she was going to die.

22

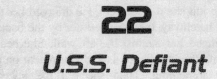

U.S.S. Defiant

VAUGHN STOOD ALONE AT THE AFT STATION ON THE BRIDGE. He had surrounded himself with star charts and recent intelligence reports on suspicious ship movements in the Almatha sector. It was a prodigious amount of raw information . . . and it was all just for show. Staring at it, he thought that it all seemed to blend together into a hazy mass. None of it really mattered to him.

A sip of tepid coffee left a bitter flavor in his mouth, but he didn't really care. His thoughts were haunted by Prynn. *Why did I always think there'd be more time? I spent years avoiding her; did I think she was going to come to me?* It had been months since he had made his first effort to bridge the cold gulf that had grown between them. She hadn't turned away his unannounced visit to her quarters, nor had she directly refused his invitation to meet again for dinner at a time and place of her choosing. To his dismay, that second reunion had never materialized. She had postponed it for her trip to Andor and had rescheduled it twice again since her return.

The lonely part of him had wanted to remind her about it, but Prynn had never liked being pushed. Rather than risk her canceling the dinner entirely, he'd convinced himself to give her space and time, to let her reciprocate his efforts at communication when she felt ready. *I should've tried harder,* he admonished himself. *Should've followed up, made sure she knew I really wanted to see her . . . hear her . . . know who she was. . . .*

Trying to clarify a mental picture of her, he was ashamed at how little he really knew of her private life. All he had ever really been certain of was that she had inherited Ruriko's countenance and poise, and that she had reflected his own dark, angry youth. Part of him wondered if the similarities in their natures, more than their differences, had been to blame for the length of their estrangement. *I waited so long to let go of my pride . . . and I think she was almost ready to meet me halfway. Or maybe she always was . . . if only I'd been willing to ask.*

He scrolled through a report about some smugglers working from an asteroid belt in the Ankaro system. It was sketchy at best, and he doubted that such small-time operators would be able to recruit someone like Taran'atar. He moved the file into the growing list of improbable targets.

Bowers's suggestion that Taran'atar would likely continue on his original heading, despite now being cloaked, seemed more plausible to Vaughn the longer he thought about it. Plotting the Jem'Hadar's original heading forward, he made note of which systems it intersected. With minor adjustments for local navigational hazards, there were easily a dozen possible destinations for the *noH'pach.*

Complicating the matter was the fact that Vaughn had no way of knowing how far Taran'atar intended to travel. None of the planets along the heading appeared to have any particular tactical value, but the longer the *noH'pach* remained in flight, the more star systems fell within its range. In the end, Vaughn stood by his decision to wait for better intelligence. If he risked flying blind at maximum warp and guessed wrong, he might actually put the *Defiant* farther away from Taran'atar, perhaps even so far that they would lose all chance of intercepting him. *Of course, if we wait here long enough,* Vaughn thought, *his lead will become insurmountable no matter what we do.*

On the large screen above his shoulder, he cross-referenced all the monitored smuggler activity in the sector with the *noH'pach*'s suspected course. There were some minor signs of correlation between the two sets of data, but nothing that he thought merited particular attention. This region of space was, essentially, an industrial zone of the old Cardassian Union. After the postwar collapse of the Cardassian government, an influx of smugglers and mercenaries had turned the sector into a sprawling haven for criminals of every conceivable stripe.

Fatigue pulled at Vaughn's eyes and left his mind dark and dulled with indecision. He resented the encroaching burdens of age, both physical and mental.

He imagined having to sort through Prynn's possessions when he returned to the station. Her casually messy quarters had amused him when he'd visited her; he could never live that way, wedded as he was to order and discipline, but it had gladdened him to know that she was free of an idiosyncrasy that he had long found to be as stifling as it was comforting.

One joy recollected led to another—the sound of Prynn laughing. He had overheard it once recently, in Quark's place, when she'd been talking with someone else. She hadn't known he'd been nearby, or maybe she had known but had gone on as if she hadn't. The moment had seemed too personal to interrupt, but Vaughn hadn't wanted to; he'd only wanted to sit and listen from a distance and hear her laugh again. Like a flame faltering and going out, the memory slipped away, pushed aside by the crushing knowledge that he would never revel in that bright voice again.

Grief closed its iron fist around his throat.

He bowed his head and refused to succumb to tears. *Not here—not in front of the crew.* He took a deep breath and tapped his reservoir of anger, which hardened his resolve and restored his mask of dark stoicism. His eyes opened, dry and blazing.

I wish I could talk with Benny—he corrected himself— *with Sisko. He would understand.* Vaughn had forged a special bond with Deep Space 9's former commanding officer during a profound Orb experience, one that had led Sisko to return to linear time and home to Bajor in time for the birth of his daughter. Since then Vaughn and Sisko had spoken on a few occasions; despite being much younger than Vaughn, Sisko possessed a quiet strength, a core of calm fortitude and insight that Vaughn desperately wished he could turn to now. The only person with whom Vaughn felt a stronger emotional connection was Captain Kira—and, for all he knew, she might soon exit from his life, as well.

Again sorrow assaulted his sense of control, kaleidoscoped his vision behind a sheet of tears, denied him air. He held his ground, cleared his vision, and slowly coaxed himself to draw one breath after another in a slow tide of gathering strength. Like a sun-scorched afterimage in his memory, he couldn't erase from his thoughts the memory of the blade in Kira's chest.

Vaughn knew that Starfleet would want to know whether Taran'atar had acted independently or on someone else's orders. Given his affiliation with the Dominion, the answer to that question might prove vitally important. As dangerous as it would be, Vaughn knew that he needed to capture Taran'atar alive so that he could learn, once and for all, what had sparked the Jem'Hadar's rampage.

Battling a Jem'Hadar was difficult enough; now Vaughn and the crew of the *Defiant* would likely have to accomplish that feat against one who had spent months studying them, individually and collectively.

Against the steady, low murmur of activity on the bridge, the double-tone that signaled an incoming transmission stood out. Vaughn turned and saw that Bowers was already reviewing the message over Forte's shoulder at the tactical station. The acting XO looked up and said to Vaughn, "Deep Space 9 is hailing us, sir."

Vaughn moved back to the center seat. "On screen."

The main viewer changed to show Dax, front and center, backed by several senior members of the ops crew, who were still at their posts hours after being summoned by the alert. All of them, Dax included, showed visible signs of fatigue. *"We've made some important discoveries, Commander,"* Dax said.

"Give me the high points, Lieutenant."

She nodded to someone off-screen, then stepped aside to let Major Cenn take her place on the viewscreen. Cenn nodded to Vaughn. *"Sir,"* he said with an acknowledging nod. *"The forensic investigation has confirmed that Taran'atar attacked Captain Kira and Lieutenant Ro. Mr. Nog analyzed and reconstructed several caches of data from the comm system in Taran'atar's quarters; they suggest that our Jem'Hadar may have been involved in the massacre of the Sidau village in Hedrikspool."*

Recalling the brutal mass murder of an entire village on

Bajor ten weeks ago made Vaughn wince. "Based on what, Major?"

"Among the data recovered from his system," Cenn said, *"were personal logs by Dr. Bashir and Chief O'Brien, in which they discussed their mission to the Sidau village. He also had some obscure academic research articles on the nature of the Sidau Orb fragment, written by Ke Hovath, the village's* sirah, *and numerous classified Starfleet records about the Orbs and the Celestial Temple. There were also several internal documents detailing Bajor's security protocols for foreign vessels visiting Bajoran space and facilities."*

Vaughn sensed that Cenn was holding something back. "What else?"

Taking a moment to compose himself, Cenn finally responded, *"Something I'd never heard of before—an alternate universe, one that was previously visited by station personnel."*

The alternate universe. Vaughn had read the reports of a closely parallel but drastically different quantum reality whose barriers with this universe were alarmingly permeable. Suddenly, he had a terrible sense of foreboding, and the destruction of the village and Taran'atar's assault on Kira and Ro began to seem more closely linked than he would have guessed. "Did anything in the recovered data suggest a motive for Taran'atar's involvement?"

"I'll let Dr. Bashir speak to that, sir."

Cenn moved aside, and Bashir took his place on the monitor. *"Lieutenant Nog identified a subliminal signal wave embedded in the communications Taran'atar received,"* he said. *"The waveform is an identical match for Taran'atar's brain-wave patterns during sleep. I think that whoever contacted him is using those pulses to control him. The attack on*

Kira, his flight from the station, even his current actions, might all be following a behavioral script that he can't resist."

"Are you saying someone bypassed his genetic conditioning?"

"I believe so, yes."

Concern deepened the creases in Vaughn's brow. This was the first real evidence that Taran'atar hadn't acted alone—and, in fact, might not have acted of his own accord at all. "Not many people could have done what you're describing, Doctor."

"Agreed," Bashir said. *"But Nog was able to recover a single-frame image of the person who sent these pulses."*

The image appeared on the main viewer as a small inset in the lower left corner. Though it was dark, soft-focused, and grainy, it was unmistakably Kira's face.

"The Intendant," Vaughn said.

"Unfortunately, yes," Bashir replied.

"We need to move quickly," Vaughn said. "Is there any way we can break the conditioning in the field?"

"We're already working on it," Bashir said. *"I'm developing a neuro-electric pulse to counter its effects, and Nog is designing a prototype emitter for it."*

"How long?"

"A few hours, at least. As soon as we have a working model, we'll send you the replicator specs."

"Very good," Vaughn said.

Bashir nodded in reply, then ceded his spot to Dax. *"We've just finished decrypting the origin point for the transmissions that Taran'atar received,"* she said. *"It's a Cardassian industrial planet called Harkoum, in the Geilod system."*

Tracing his finger along Taran'atar's suspected route,

Vaughn found the system squarely on the path. "Got it," he said.

"It's currently under Romulan oversight," Dax added.

Vaughn frowned, taking her meaning clearly. Despite the fact that Starfleet had an agreement with the Romulan Empire to limit the use of the *Defiant*'s cloaking device in the Alpha Quadrant—an agreement that had been honored more in the breach than in the observance—taking his ship cloaked into a system under their control would be certain to provoke them. Conversely, going in with the cloak down would alert Taran'atar that his destination had been uncovered. That, in turn, might lead to a confrontation that would draw in Romulan forces, who would be in a better position than the *Defiant* to capture the *noH'pach*—and its topsecret Klingon security codes. Vaughn simply nodded to Dax and said, "We'll keep that in mind. *Defiant* out." The screen switched back to stars. "Helm, set course for Harkoum, maximum warp."

Starlight was pulled in long smears across the main viewer as the deep, rapid throb of the ship's warp engines pulsed through the deck beneath Vaughn's boots. "Ensign Zucca," he said in a crisp tone of voice. "Assuming that Harkoum is Taran'atar's destination, and that the *noH'pach* is traveling at its maximum rated speed, what is our ETA to intercept?"

The brunette flight control officer checked her console. "The *noH'pach* will make orbit approximately eight minutes ahead of us, sir."

"Everybody listen up," Vaughn said. "I want a full sweep as soon as we reach Harkoum. If that ship's in orbit, find it. If it's in the atmosphere, I want its trail. Time is a factor on this one. Understood?" A chorus of "Aye, sir" worked its way quickly around the bridge. He nodded and snapped everyone into action with a single word: "Stations."

He felt that he now knew who had been pulling the renegade Jem'Hadar's strings; if he was right, it was imperative that the *noH'pach* be intercepted before it reached its final destination.

Few things frightened Vaughn, but an alliance between Intendant Kira and Taran'atar was undeniably one of them.

23

Kira

"ALL WE ARE ASKING FOR," GENERAL KIRA SAID, "IS TO BE permitted to help defend the fortress."

"The Eav'oq don't see it that way," Opaka said, her voice the very epitome of diplomacy. "This place has been in their charge since time immemorial."

"But it's been *our* fortress for generations," Kira argued.

"Are you so certain?" With a broad sweep of her arm across the wide arc of the battlements, Opaka said, "Do not be deceived by shells and façades."

"I know my keep," Kira said, her fury simmering.

"Of that I have no doubt," Opaka said. "I would think it likely that you know it better than the greater number of your kin and countrymen . . . possibly better even than some of its builders. But of *this* fortress you've seen naught but the outer walls. Until you've been inside, how can you be certain it is not merely a fortress much *like* yours, but different?"

"My generals and I would be grateful for a chance to enter and confirm our suspicions."

Opaka smiled. "And we return to the beginning, as always."

Kira shook her head, guided Jayol in a half turn, and pointed with her outstretched arm toward the far-off but ever-closer army to the south. "I know the Eav'oq have seen their enemy's approach," Kira said. "Why refuse our offer of aid?"

"Your aid is welcomed," Opaka said. "But the Eav'oq do not acknowledge your claim to their fortress."

"Yet they allow you to dwell with them, to speak for them."

"I did not arrive at their door demanding sovereignty over their shelter," Opaka said, her words gentle rather than scolding. "I came to them as a student and a teacher; they welcomed me as a guest."

The sun was high overhead now, and Kira's temper was as short as her shadow. "What if we negotiate a peace between the Eav'oq and their foes? Will we be granted shelter then?"

The older woman's countenance darkened. "I should think you would find that a futile effort."

Kira glanced at Jamin, whose face mirrored her own feelings of suspicion and concern. She looked back at Opaka. "Why?"

"The Ascendants will not negotiate," Opaka said. "For eons have they sought this fortress, which was hidden from them, mantled in mist. Now it has been revealed to them, and they are coming in force to claim it. In this, they will not be appeased, nor will they be dissuaded."

"Perhaps if they knew they would be facing two armies rather than just one—"

"It would make no difference," Opaka interrupted. "The Ascendants will destroy all who stand between them and the fortress. They will not be sued for peace. And they will not share dominion. Their only aim is to possess it . . . or be annihilated in the effort."

Kira considered all of Opaka's words with care. The army of the Ascendants grew wider across the horizon, like a spreading stain of shadow dividing land and sky.

She began, "If we can turn away the Ascendants—"

"You cannot," Opaka said, her tone ominous in its surety.

"But if we do—will the Eav'oq grant us haven?"

"Not until you arrive at the truth," Opaka said.

Kira was growing weary of riddles. "Which is . . . ?"

"You will know it when you walk its path," said Opaka.

"This is a dangerous choice," Jamin said.

"I know." It was obvious to Kira that he was upset with her; when he was angry, his voice became quiet, but only as a precursor to thunderous bellows of fury.

The two of them rode together. Side by side they inspected the preparations of the mounted soldiers who waited to form up into platoons and ride south to meet the Ascendants. Rank after rank of *zhoms* were saddled and bridled, brushed or bandaged, provisioned or watered. Soon it would be time to move out.

Jamin continued, "Meeting the enemy in the open is—"

"We don't know yet that they're the enemy," Kira said.

"Opaka certainly seems to think that they are."

Unable to hide a sly smirk, Kira said, "She also thinks that the Eav'oq own Parek Tonn. As with all things, I'd prefer to judge this for myself."

Jamin's *zhom* made a few snorting grunts, which were muffled by its bridle. He patted the creature's sinewy flank. "Easy, Denigarro," he murmured in the beast's large, tucked-flat ear. To Kira, he said, "He can tell we're riding into trouble." Looking sidelong at the legions of soldiers, he added, "They all can."

She decided not to indulge his fears and stuck to a review of the hard facts. "How many hours' ride to reach the Ascendants?"

"Moving hard, no infantry?" He looked up at the afternoon sky, then turned in a few different directions and sucked breath through his teeth, as if he was tasting the air. "The mounts are well rested. Maybe two hours. Before sundown certainly."

His estimate confirmed her own. "Which puts the Ascendants here at Parek Tonn a few hours after nightfall," she said.

"Assuming they don't halt their march at sundown."

Watching the army of the Ascendants start to take on recognizable shapes as its advance continued, Kira said simply, "I don't think they're going to halt their march for anything—not unless we give them a reason to."

"We should at least order the infantry to move on to Lonar, in case our parley fails," Jamin said.

"No," Kira said. "If we can't negotiate with the Ascendants, we'll be better able to defend ourselves behind the entrenchments at Parek Tonn than we will in the open."

"That would put us in a crossfire between the Ascendants and the Eav'oq," Jamin cautioned.

Kira looked back at the fortress, then out at the approaching army. She sighed. "We're already there, Jamin."

24

Harkoum

Putrefying flesh had filled the hold and cockpit of the *Otamawan* with a foul, choking odor. Grauq let go of the breath he had been holding; it billowed in front of him, a thick gray cloud of vapor in the frigid air of the small freighter. He had figured on having a few more hours before the stench of the ship's slain crew became unbearable, but even with the internal temperature gauges adjusted to freezing, the corpse of the Tiburonian man had decomposed more rapidly than the Chalnoth bounty hunter had expected. He made a note of this odd bit of biological trivia for future reference.

Several hundred kilometers away, the Romulan warbird began to break orbit. *About time,* Grauq fumed. Checking the sensors, he confirmed that his own ship, the *Githzarai,* remained in a steady, slow orbit a mere few dozen kilometers ahead of him.

Distortion rippled over the massive green hull of the warbird, which then vanished from Grauq's sight and the *Otamawan*'s sensors. Grauq waited a full ten seconds before engaging the *Otamawan*'s impulse drive and over-taking the *Githzarai*. He scanned it on his approach and noted that its shields were raised, just as he had expected. He powered up the *Otamawan*'s shields and reset their harmonics to enable them to pass without difficulty through those of the *Githzarai*. A few moments later, he maneuvered into close proximity over his stolen ship and penetrated its shields with the *Otamawan*'s. Then he released a surge of polarons into the shield emitters.

The *Githzarai* suddenly fell behind the *Otamawan*, its shields and main impulse drive both disrupted. An inability to balance polaron emissions was a weakness of his ship's primary power-distribution system, one that he had discovered the hard way when it had been exploited by a Breen privateer several months earlier. That mishap had cost Grauq a cache of weapons and a substantial amount of latinum. Now his ship's integral design flaw had just betrayed the Cardassian Woman, and he intended to make her suffer losses of a more intimate nature.

He circled back and snared the *Githzarai* in a tractor beam. Several hails to the small ship went unanswered. Suspicious, he swept the vessel with the *Otamawan*'s crude sensor apparatus. He was incensed to discover no life signs aboard the *Githzarai*. Pounding his fists on the console, he unleashed a string of vulgarities that lasted for half a minute.

A decoy. She lured me away with my own ship.

Grauq pushed up his loose sleeve to expose the armor-like band around his left forearm. The bracer was studded with computer interface controls that enabled him to guide his ship and activate its onboard systems from a remote position. Tapping in commands, he reinitialized the main power system, then activated the emergency transporter recall. The confinement beam gripped him snugly for a few seconds as the air shimmered white before his eyes.

When the glare died away, he was back in the hold on the *Githzarai*. He made a quick inventory and was not surprised to note that his hoverbike had been taken, along with his best pair of swords: a 23rd-century Terran *katana* and *wakizashi*, each with a monomolecular edge. He'd never had much use for firearms, but he kept his one sidearm as a hedge against emergent crises, such as the one he'd been forced to cope with today. Instead, he had amassed a sizable inventory of edged weapons; he gave the Cardassian Woman credit for at least being able to identify which two pieces from his collection—a matched set, no less—had represented the rarest and deadliest implements in his arsenal.

He didn't expect that she would be so careless as to forget to remove the homing device from the hoverbike. Regardless, there were not many paths she could follow back to the client, and it would be a simple matter to pilot the *Githzarai* back into the atmosphere and recover her trail en route. Barring any unusual complications, there was no reason he couldn't have her whimpering in the desert sands within the hour.

Lumbering forward toward the cockpit, he paused to retrieve a bottle of Aldebaran whiskey from his equipment locker, to cleanse the lingering reek of rotten flesh from his sinus. He wanted to appreciate the smell of the Cardassian Woman's sweat and savor the brine of her tears as he wrestled her into submission and broke her, bit by bit. He pulled the stopper from the bottle with his teeth, then let it fall and dangle by its delicate chain from the bottleneck. A hearty swig of the heady liquor numbed his gums and filled his throat with pleasant heat.

The cockpit hatch slid open with a dull scrape, and he stepped inside. He grabbed the well-worn, padded leather back of his seat and swiveled it toward himself.

Resting on the seat was one of his own high-explosive antipersonnel mines, the kind he used for securing base camps in hostile territory. The silent indicator on its proximity detonator stopped blinking as it registered his presence.

He had to concede a grim respect for the Cardassian Woman as the munition exploded in his face and scattered him and his ship in flaming streaks across the upper atmosphere of Harkoum.

25

Deep Space 9

ABOVE HIS HEAD, QUARK HEARD THE SOFT RUMBLE OF THE station's ventilation system. Its low hum ran beneath, between, and behind all the other tiny sounds in the intensive-care ward: gentle tones from a biofeedback monitor, Ro's shallow breathing, the quiet chirrups of the diagnostic computer in the next room . . .

. . . the gasp of the infirmary's outer door opening.

Quark sat up, lifting his head off the edge of Ro's bed. She was still unconscious, languishing in medicated slumber, but even had she been awake, her ears likely would not have heard all that his enormous lobes could. Slow, easy footfalls, just far enough apart to suggest someone with a long stride, drew closer. The rasp of rough natural fabric in motion grew clearer.

He tensed, though he couldn't think of a single reason why.

A tall figure, garbed in a dark hooded robe, emerged from behind the privacy barrier at the far end of the ward. The hood shadowed the visitor's face, making it impossible for Quark to tell who it was that stood there taking his measure in silence. Whatever the origin of those robes was, it wasn't Bajoran—at least, not one of the religious varieties. Quark had seen quite a few members of the Bajoran religious community in his years aboard the station, from monks and prylars to vedeks and kais. None of them had ever dressed like this.

The visitor took another step toward him, hesitated, then reached up and pulled back the hood.

It was Benjamin Sisko.

"Hello, Quark," he said in his rich but gentle baritone.

"Captain," Quark said, smiling almost reflexively as his shoulders released their tension. He couldn't describe exactly why, but seeing Sisko put him at ease. "Nice robe."

"I wanted to travel incognito," Sisko said with calmness and sincerity. Quark understood his reasoning; for months Sisko had dwelled physically in the presence of the wormhole entities, whom the Bajorans revered as deities known as Prophets. Ever since his return to "linear existence" on Bajor, more than a few Bajorans had become obsessive in their desire to inundate him with questions about everything from the true nature of the Prophets and the Celestial Temple to their fates and whether he had encountered the *pagh* of this or that beloved dead ancestor.

Sisko walked toward Kira's bed; the human stood over Kira, looking down at her with tender concern. He adjusted a chair that was next to her bed and sat down, paying no more heed to Quark or to Ro. All his attention rested on Kira; he reached out and gently laid his brown hand on her pale forehead. With his other hand he reached out and took hold of one of Kira's. She gave no sign of stirring, no hint of consciousness. He took his hand from her face and wrapped it around her hand, until it was enfolded fully in both of his.

Quark gently clutched Ro's hand in the same manner, then looked back across the ward at Sisko, who answered his gaze with a single, slow, respectful nod of empathy.

It was a small gesture, but it reassured Quark.

There really wasn't anything more to say, he knew. Neither he nor Sisko had come here in search of conversation or company. Carrying on a discussion above Ro and Kira, as if they weren't in the room, would have felt gauche, disrespectful. Until now, Quark had been alone in here, cut off from the rest of his life while he waited to see what would become of Ro's. Now at least there was someone else conscious in the room. Whatever other comfort that was worth, it was better than being alone.

The worried Ferengi returned Sisko's nod of acknowledgment, and they resumed their vigils for their wounded friends.

Nog hunched over a table in the middle of medical lab four and cobbled together a jumble of parts, culled from a phaser and several different medical devices, into something that could emit a neuro-electric pulse. He only half understood the principle behind the invention taking shape in his hands. Had his mission been to increase the phaser's accuracy, or its power, or its range, or its area of effect, he would have known precisely how to proceed. Instead, he was trying to rebuild its emitter crystal to release a type of energy completely unlike any ever previously used in a phaser, one that had to be strong enough to scramble the neurons of a Jem'Hadar but which would cause no physical trauma. It was a mental exercise that was giving him a terrible headache and a ravenous appetite.

Listening to Bashir mumble to himself on the other side of the lab for the first hour or so had been unnerving, mostly because of what the doctor's musings had suggested. Though the person who had designed the brainwashing pulse might have started with a broad-spectrum signal intended to overpower any Jem'Hadar's mental conditioning, the signals they were studying now had been customized specifically for Taran'atar himself. Bashir's current working theory was that Taran'atar had first been afflicted with a broad pulse and then was coerced into surrendering his personal biometric data, from which a more targeted control signal was created. Just imagining being turned into a spy against himself gave Nog a queasy shiver.

With each triggering of Nog's ion cutter, components fused together in a flash of emerald-hued light or were severed into their constituent pieces beneath a dense but slender twist of bone-white smoke. The sharp odor of overheated metal filled his nostrils as he worked. There were so many connections, so many false starts and dead ends; many of the items he was joining had never been intended to function in tandem. He had no idea how he and Dr. Bashir were going to test this device, either.

From behind him came the doctor's grim, heavy sigh. Bashir was seated in the dim green glow of the medical research lab's main computer terminal, directly behind Nog. He had been working for a few hours now, deconstructing Taran'atar's sleep-state brain-wave pattern to reverse-engineer a pulse that would free the Jem'Hadar from whoever had placed him under their control. But now the doctor was slumped in his seat, staring dejectedly at the oscillating patterns on the screen.

Nog watched him for a few seconds. "What's wrong?"

"I'm not sure I can continue."

"Why not?"

"Because this entire plan is unethical," Bashir said.

"Wait a minute," Nog said. "It was your idea!"

"And I'm beginning to think I was wrong for even suggesting it." Bashir got up and started pacing. "We have no idea what this pulse will do to Taran'atar," he said. "What if it causes brain damage? What if it erases his entire personality?"

"Call it an improvement," Nog muttered.

"That's not funny," Bashir said. "The first rule of medicine is 'do no harm,' but I'm supposed to create a device that will alter a sentient being's brain functions without his permission?" He leaned against the wall. "And what am I basing my work on? A pulse that looks like it was created by professional torturers. Using the fruits of this kind of research makes me all but an accomplice to the monsters who created it."

Putting down his ion cutter, Nog swiveled his chair to look at Bashir. "What a load of grub-*fudu*."

"Excuse me, *Lieutenant*?"

"You heard me, *sir*."

With derision heaped upon every word, Bashir said, "I had no idea you were an expert in medical ethics."

"It doesn't take a genius to know you're being a *reepok*." A confused expression on Bashir's face made it clear to Nog that the human needed a translation of the Ferengi vulgarity. "A person who doesn't know profit when he holds it in his hand. It's like you want to cut a collar off Taran'atar's neck, but you won't do it 'cause you're afraid he might get scratched."

A derisive smirk played across Bashir's face. "I'd hardly call wiping out his higher brain functions a *scratch*."

"If he had a brain tumor, you'd operate, right?"

"Only with his consent."

"So if you found him in the corridor, unconscious, with a brain tumor, you'd just let him die? Because he didn't give you consent?" Nog could see that he was chipping away at Bashir's reservations. "Or would you assume he wanted to live?"

"I see what you're driving at," Bashir said. "You want me to say that Taran'atar isn't rational enough to consent, that emancipating him would be like curing him." He shook his head, and he sounded exhausted. "It's not that simple, Nog."

"Why not?"

"To use your analogy, let's say he had a brain tumor and that it was causing him to behave irrationally. Does that mean I have the authority to force an experimental medical procedure on him? Am I empowered by his infirmity to erase his memory? Or risk leaving him in a permanent vegetative state? Or maybe even provoke a total synaptic failure and kill him?"

Nog had to admit that what Bashir said made a kind of sense, but it ran so completely counter to his every impulse that it made his lobes burn with anger to think about it. "But if he *is* being controlled," Nog said, "then isn't doing nothing the same as doing harm? Forget about harm to him. If we let someone else use him as a weapon, they can hurt other people—lots of them. And if he's been brainwashed with this pulse, then someone's using him as a slave, and that means they *are* hurting him. So if you don't break that control, you're hurting him and letting someone else use him to hurt others. What does your hiccup oath say about that?"

"*Hippocratic* oath," Bashir said, but his quiet tone took the sting out of his rebuke. He turned his head and stared at the waveform on the monitor where he'd been working. "If there was more time," he began, then he seemed to lose hold of his thought. "If only we could test it first . . ."

Nog wanted to ask, *On what?* It wasn't as if there were other Jem'Hadar on the station who were going to let themselves be brainwashed (even if it was possible to duplicate the effect that someone had achieved by exploiting Taran'atar's new need for sleep) just so Bashir could see whether or not he could reverse its effects without making grub stew of their brains.

Left in silence, the doctor seemed melancholy. Deep frowns born of conflicting emotions tightened Bashir's jaw. For a moment Nog felt distinctly ashamed that he had so callously argued for such a cavalier attitude toward another being's welfare . . . even if it was the cold-hearted *moogijokk* that had tried to kill his captain and his comrade.

"Perhaps you're right," Bashir said, to Nog's surprise. "If Taran'atar's mind has been forcibly altered . . . if he's acting without full free will . . . then he's very likely in a state of diminished capacity, unable to make a free or informed decision in his own best interest."

"Right," Nog said, nodding. *Is that what I said?*

"But using this data, even for a noble purpose . . ."

"Are you going to make a profit by using it?"

Bashir looked almost insulted. "Of course not."

"Is Starfleet? Or the Federation?"

"No."

"If you turn that pulse into a cure, who benefits?"

Slumping back into the chair at his workstation, Bashir sighed. "I just find that working with anything related to torture makes me sick to my stomach."

"I know what you mean," Nog said. "You don't want to see some of the Cardassian security devices I helped Chief

O'Brien remove from the—" Inspiration unfolded in his mind like a shimmering bloom of knowledge. "Cardassian devices! That's it!" He began calling up old schematics on a nearby computer screen, shuffling rapidly through them, narrowing down his selections until he found what he was looking for. He tapped his combadge. "Nog to Ensign Salmak."

"Salmak here," the Benzite woman responded over the comm.

"Salmak, go down to cargo bay three-eighteen and retrieve a box of disabled Cardassian small arms, and bring them to medical lab four right away. There should also be a few Cardassian medical kits. Bring those, too."

"On my way, sir." The channel clicked off.

Nog turned toward Bashir. "I think I've got it figured out," he said. "The reason I can't make the neuropulse work from a Starfleet phaser is 'cause it's Cardassian software. But I can make it work if I use Cardassian hardware." Scrutinizing Bashir for any signs of lingering doubt, he added, *"If* we're still doing this, I mean."

Drumming his fingers on the monitor in front of him, Bashir stared at the screen, regarding with a grimace his own moody reflection. He drew a sharp breath, then set his mind and his hands back to work. "I'll have the pulse finished in about an hour," he said. "Let me know when the emitter's ready."

Consciousness tugged at Ro Laren. It pulled her up toward the light, fighting against the inertia of her fatigue with the patience of a fisherman slowly reeling his spirited catch to the surface of a dark but warm ocean. Muddy hums of sound rose and fell on either side of her slow, deep breaths. Each exhalation droned inside her head, like a wind groaning softly in a deep cavern. She felt weightless yet anchored; she was at rest, on her back. The sounds of the computers and the faintly astringent odor of sanitizer made it clear to her, even with her eyes closed, that she was in the infirmary.

With difficulty, she willed her eyelids to open.

The lights in the room had been dimmed, but she still winced slightly as her irises adjusted. She was in the bed at the farthest end of the recovery ward. Her head lolled ever so slightly to the right, so the first thing she focused on was Kira, lying unconscious on a bed along the next wall. It took her a moment to recognize the man seated next to Kira, leaning close and seemingly whispering in the captain's ear. Then she realized it was Captain Sisko.

A hand closed softly on her left shoulder. She turned her head to see Quark standing beside her, looking down at her with equal measures of hope and fear. "Laren?"

Her voice was weak and thin. "You're here."

He shrugged. "What are friends for?" He smiled through a moment of silence that, to Ro's relief, felt not the least bit awkward. Then he said, "Are you okay?"

"You tell me," she said.

"I've heard them whispering a lot in the other room," he said. "Couldn't really help it. They've been trying to figure out how to give you the ol' 'good news, bad news' speech."

"What's the short version?"

He shrugged. "They think you'll be back on your feet in about a week. That's the good news."

"And the bad news?"

"That's when you start your physical therapy. Aylam and Tarses are debating whether it'll be four weeks or six before you can walk without cybernetic supports."

She sighed heavily. "My feet are getting cold."

He gestured at the blanket. "Should I . . . ?"

"No," Ro said. "It's all right." She permitted herself a small, cautious smile. "I'm just glad I can tell the difference." Looking around, she asked, "What time is it?"

Quark checked his chrono. "About a quarter till 0600."

Struggling to piece her memories back together, she recalled that the alert in Taran'atar's quarters had sounded shortly before 1830 hours the previous evening. It had been just over thirteen hours since she and the captain had been attacked.

Interrupting her ruminations, Quark asked, "Do you want me to get Bashir? Or one of the other doctors, maybe?"

"Not yet," Ro said. "I could use a few minutes of quiet."

He nodded, then remained silently beside her and held her hand. She steadied her thoughts and made the Herculean effort of wiggling her right big toe. Elated at her tiny success, she squeezed his hand in her feeble but warm grip.

"Quite a workout routine you've got there," he joked, obviously aware of how difficult that small achievement had just been for her. "You should eat to keep your strength up." He leaned close to her ear. "But between you and me, I hear the food in this place is terrible, and the service is worse. . . . Maybe I could bring you something from the bar?"

"I'd like that," she said.

His expression brightened. "I know just the thing." He started to step away, then hesitated. "I'll be right back. Don't go anywhere."

"Have I ever told you how funny you are?"

"No," he said, playing along.

She grinned. "Ask me why."

He returned her grin with his own toothy smile, nodded, and made a quick exit to fetch her something more edible than Starfleet's medical-recovery dietary supplement of the week.

The faint sensations in her leg and back became more prominent and grew into a dull ache. She had every reason to expect the pain would become much worse before it got better. That didn't worry her. Pain was better than numbness; pain meant sensation. Pain meant she was still alive and fighting.

She lay still and let the ambient sounds of the ward envelop her. Her hearing attuned itself to the sound of Sisko's voice, whispering half a room away. Turning her head, she watched him talking quietly to Kira. Before long, she found herself impressed by his low-key charisma and by the aura of strength that seemed to surround him.

His hands, she noticed, were clasped around Kira's right hand and had been since Ro had regained consciousness. His expression as he talked to Kira was relaxed, almost jovial, as though he were simply chatting with an old friend across a dining table. Ro strained to hear what he was saying to Kira, even though she knew it was impolite to eavesdrop so brazenly. Yet when he looked up moments later and met her stare, he smiled so graciously at her that she felt not a whit of shame.

"How are you feeling, Lieutenant?"

"I've been better, sir," she said.

"And you will be again, I'm certain of it."

Everything about him was so reassuring, but she couldn't say why. Despite her agnostic attitude toward spiritual matters, she couldn't help but wonder if Sisko's status as the Emissary of the Prophets was more than just an empty honorific. More than most people Ro had met, Sisko had . . . *presence.*

"If it's not too personal to ask, sir . . ."

He raised his brow inquisitively, then intuited her question. "You're wondering what I was saying to her."

"Yes, sir."

"I was telling her a story," he said. "An old Bajoran parable . . . about the three brothers from Jokala."

Ro still carried a dim memory, from her childhood, of the old homily about the value of family and the danger of greed.

"The one about the *kava* root?"

"Yes," Sisko said with a nod. "That's the one."

Although Ro didn't recall the story in any kind of detail, she knew the essential gist of it—and she failed to see what bearing it had on Captain Kira's current medical crisis. Not wanting to give offense, she gently began to ask, "Why . . . ?"

Sisko looked back down at Kira with a sad half smile and his eyes shining with tears. "Because she once did this for me."

26

The Alternate Universe— I.K.S. Negh'Var

INTENDANT KIRA RECLINED AGAINST A MOUND OF PILLOWS stacked on her bed, her arms outstretched, the curves of her body pushing rebelliously against the clinging fit of her bodysuit. On the other side of her spacious private chamber, a boyish-looking Bajoran research scientist named Ke Hovath was surrounded by snaking power cables and coils of data fiber, which all led to a freestanding control panel that faced a bare wall. His tools were scattered about his feet.

"I apologize for the delay, Intendant," Professor Ke said.

"No need." Kira took a piece of round, green fruit from a tray held by one of her Vulcan handmaidens. "As long as it's ready before we reach Harkoum."

He wiped a sheen of perspiration from his forehead. "It's almost done, Intendant." He set himself back to his task, changing the settings of countless tiny variables in the interface and recalibrating hundreds of elements inside the enormous piece of machinery it controlled.

She had expected him to protest her order that he complete this complex and delicate task alone, but he had so far refrained from complaint or any sign of self-pity. He didn't seem to notice as she slinked off the bed and sidled up to him, leaning over his shoulder. She let her breath tease the back of his neck as she spoke. "You're doing a wonderful job, Hovath."

The compliment made him pause. "Thank you, Intendant."

If only that fool Smiley could see what I've made of his little toy, she thought. *What a pity he won't live long enough to witness its true power.*

Moving away from him, she turned her eyes to the bulky assembly of coils and energizers that was suspended from her ceiling in front of the barren wall. To the untrained eye, these looked like ordinary components, unremarkable in any way. Imaging scanners, energizing coils, even the luminous shine of the phase transition coils failed to convey the true magnitude of the technological leap forward that she had commissioned from Professor Ke. She had long suspected that the young scientist was capable of greatness, ever since she had recruited him from the Sidau College of Physics to serve the Alliance's Research and Development Branch. But this . . . if it worked, then Professor Ke would exceed all her expectations.

"It's ready," he said. "All the modifications are made. We just need to activate its link to the power mains."

"Computer," she said. "Activate the new power circuit. Authorization Kira-one-eight-one-*shakom-doka.*"

The enormous assemblage of metallic parts thrummed to life.

She lifted her foot to step up onto the platform beneath the ceiling apparatus. "Stop," Ke said, and she did. "It's too dangerous. The area between the coils is highly unstable.

Let me lock it down first." He made a series of adjustments on the main console, and the coils' hum faded away. "The system wasn't made to harness these kinds of forces, you know."

Kira nodded. "Quite true," she said, curious whether Professor Ke had deduced the true purpose of the modifications she had asked him to make to this illegal piece of technology. "But this always was a dangerous invention."

"Yes, yes," Ke said. "But not like this. The original could be exploited easily enough, but its sole destination was so hostile that it wasn't worth the effort." He chuckled nervously. "This, on the other hand—it's absolutely . . ."

A sudden fear played across his features, a realization that perhaps he had just said too much.

"Go on, Hovath," Kira said warmly, with a broad smile. "I'm eager to hear your opinion as to what we've accomplished here. Or should I say . . . what *you've* accomplished here." With a wave of her hands she dismissed her Vulcan handmaidens, who slipped out a back entrance, as silent as a memory of ghosts.

She turned her attention back to Hovath. Playing to his ego had worked; his fearful frown became a prideful grin.

"If we can find a way to stabilize the system," he said, "we'd no longer be limited to the one other alternate universe. They'd all be open to us—an infinite number of universes." His excitement grew as he continued. "With infinite worlds and resources, we could transform the Alliance! And we could apply this kind of shifting to propulsion systems, slip in and out of other universes at will, launch surprise attacks anywhere. Whoever controls this would be all but unstoppable."

Kira smirked. "Well said." She crossed the room in elegant strides, brushing her hand across his back as she passed by him. "Have a drink with me, Hovath." He followed her to the other side of the room, where she opened a cabinet and removed two glasses, then a bottle of wine from the vineyards of the Tilar peninsula on Bajor. She set the glasses on top of the cabinet, then uncorked the bottle. A whiff of sweet cherry fragrance filled the air around her and Professor Ke. The deep-red wine fell like liquid silk into the two low, teardrop-shaped glasses. Kira lifted one and handed the other to Ke. "To your genius, Professor," she said. "And to the historic service you've performed for the Alliance."

"It's my honor to serve you, Intendant."

She savored the complexly sweet, aromatic beverage and swallowed it with a satisfied purr. Ke downed two large sips. Kira smiled and looked into his eyes. A few seconds later she saw it—the first glimmer of comprehension, followed immediately by the dark tide of panic. His breathing seized. She gently plucked the wineglass from his weak, trembling hand and set it with her own back on the cabinet. He fell to his knees and looked up at her in terror. *What a waste,* she lamented.

"I'd offer you some of the antidote," she said with mocking sweetness, "but I drank the last dose an hour ago."

27

U.S.S. Defiant

BOWERS JOINED THE OTHER SENIOR PERSONNEL OF THE *Defiant* at the bridge's aft consoles. He noted the harried, flustered demeanors of the officers who surrounded him and Commander Vaughn. There had been almost no time for them to prepare and even less time for them to check their data before starting the mission briefing.

Scanning the group's unsettled expressions, Vaughn said, "Who has the background on Harkoum?"

Science officer Rahim raised his hand slightly. When all eyes landed on him, he began. "For just over a hundred years, it was one of the Cardassian Union's biggest producers of raw minerals and refined alloys, including duranium." He tapped a key on his padd and transmitted his report file to all the other officers' padds. Bowers skimmed the text as Rahim continued. "Its lack of an indigenous sentient population made it ideal for large-scale industrial operations, which ranged from strip mines to ammunition plants. However, its resources were expended quickly, and by the end of the last century, most manufacturing and refining on the planet had ceased."

Sensing that this was a good point at which to jump in, Bowers said, "Once its industrial operations were scaled back, its distance from the Cardassians' core systems and its harsh climate and terrain made it ideal for another purpose: maximum-security detention facilities." He uploaded his own briefing document to the other officers' padds. "Prisoners sent to Harkoum routinely 'disappeared.' No official records were kept of anyone sent there, so it was a pretty convenient way for the old Cardassian elites to eliminate dissidents and dispose of foreign operatives."

Lieutenant Forte added, "According to Starfleet Intelligence, the prisoners who weren't executed en route or on arrival were used as slave labor."

"Only the lucky ones," said Nurse Richter, currently the senior medical authority on the ship. "Starfleet Medical has reports that Cardassian research scientists used several of the prisoners for experimentation—everything from testing the effects of biogenic weapons to trying out new surgical techniques or refining their torture methods."

Ensign Boehm nudged Bowers's arm and handed him a mug of fresh coffee. It was dark and sweet.

"What's the current status of Harkoum?" Vaughn asked.

"It was officially decommissioned after the Dominion War," Forte said, "but no prisoners were released or acknowledged even then." He noticed everyone looking at his padd, waiting for the update. "Sorry," he said. "I didn't have time to collate my files. As I was saying, sources inside the former Cardassian government reported hearing rumors of mass executions in some of the prisons on Harkoum. Others were allegedly abandoned by their staffs, and the prisoners were left in confinement to starve."

"Nothing like having an exit strategy," Vaughn muttered. "Rahim, how much company should we expect at Harkoum?"

"Limited commercial traffic," Rahim said. "There are still a few starports operating on the surface, near the last few working mines and refineries."

"Long-range sensors picked up a Romulan ship in orbit until roughly an hour ago," Zucca said. "Intel suggests it was the warbird *Verithrax*, deployed three weeks ago out of Panora. But even if they've left the Geilod system, they won't be far away by the time we get there."

"Then we'll have to make this a quick visit," Vaughn said. "Bowers, how many of Harkoum's detention facilities do we have coordinates for?"

"None of them, sir." Vaughn answered Bowers's statement with a skeptical glare. Bowers added, "Even after the Obsidian Order disbanded, its former agents and supervisors denied it ever operated any facilities, of any kind, on Harkoum. Even though we suspect there could be more than sixty of them still down there, almost all of them were built underground and concealed from visual and sensor scans."

Boehm handed a cup of coffee to Vaughn. He nodded his thanks to her, then continued the briefing. "Zucca, what's our ETA, relative to the *noH'pach?*"

"We're closing the gap, sir," she said. "We should make orbit about six minutes behind her."

"Bowers, Forte—where are we with seeing through her cloak?"

Vaughn looked at Bowers, who tried to deflect the question by looking at Forte, but the tactical officer wisely evaded eye contact with the acting XO. Taking it upon himself to deliver the bad news, Bowers said, "Not there yet, sir. We're still working on it."

Blinking away exhaustion and irritation, Vaughn said, "Best guess, Bowers: Will we have it before we reach Harkoum?"

"I don't think we will, sir."

"Then let it go," Vaughn said. "Focus on improving our sensor response time. As soon as we hit orbit, we need to pick up the *noH'pach*'s trail. If I'm right, it'll be heading into the atmosphere. No matter how good its cloak works in space, in an atmosphere it'll make a ruckus. Ionized particles, wakes of displaced air, superheated gas from its impulse engines, electromagnetic disturbances, the works. It might be invisible to the naked eye, but in the air it'll light up our sensors like a Christmas tree—and I want a lock on that ship, as quickly as possible, the moment we're out of warp. Understood?"

"Yes, sir. We're on it."

"Good." Vaughn sipped his coffee and nodded with satisfaction. "Look sharp, everyone. We're taking on a Jem'Hadar elder. There won't be any prize for second best."

28

Kira

ARMY ADVANCED UPON ARMY, TWO DARK WAVES OF METAL and men slowly lurching toward one another across the expanse of the barrens that lay to the south, between Parek Tonn and the sea.

Kira and Jamin rode at the head of the column of Bajoran cavalry. For the sake of speed, the infantry had been left at Parek Tonn, where they would fortify their position until her return—or until her outrider returned with orders for them to flee the Fields of Berzel and strike west to Lonar.

The thumping patter of *zhom* paws on the road and hard-packed earth infused the air with an expectant rumbling, a muted thunder that radiated from the long procession like power itself. Kira liked the higher vantage of the saddle, the sensation of height, of being able to see farther afield.

But what she saw now gave her pause.

Unlike the straight files of mounted warriors who followed her, the Ascendant army was moving in a wedge formation. Its mounted legions sat atop enormous reptiles with thick heads and wide-set legs. Each of the creatures was easily three times the size of a *zhom*, though not likely as swift by half. Several soldiers rode on the back of each lizard—one guiding the creature, the rest either spearmen to attack troops on the ground or archers to strike foes from a distance. The beasts in the rear echelons of the Ascendant formation towed massive siege engines: towers and ladders, pallets of artillery shot rolling on squeaky wheels, vats of smoldering pitch, mounds of sapping gear. Its supply lines, unlike those of Kira's long-exhausted battalions, were long and robust, trailing behind it, possibly reaching back even to the sea, more than two days' ride away.

"There must be at least twenty thousand troops," Kira said to Jamin, unable to hide her dismay.

Sounding as unfazed as ever, he said, "More than that, I think. Closer to thirty thousand . . . but that's not what concerns me." He pointed toward the rear ranks of the Ascendant wedge. "What do you think the range of those trebuchets might be?"

"It would depend on the counterweights," Ghavun said, revealing his eavesdropping presence behind them. "But it's likely they can best anything we have at Parek Tonn."

The two armies were less than four *kellipates* apart, and the western sky was a wash of bloodred patched with ragged, milky-pink clouds. Soon it would be dark. A course of action had to be decided upon. "We'll ride ahead and seek a parley," Kira said to Jamin, then she looked back at Ghavun, Nathech, and Renla, to make certain they knew that they were included.

She urged Jayol forward. Her *zhom* went from a trot to a gallop in a single stride. Jamin and the other generals flanked Kira as she proceeded directly toward the

Ascendants' point rider. The clank and thunder of the enormous army ahead roared like the ocean. In the long rays of the setting sun, the distant troops gleamed like tall, elegant jewels in the shapes of men.

At two hundred paces, the mass of the Ascendant army blotted out the southern horizon and loomed ahead of Kira, a dark wall on a relentless march. She reined Jayol to a halt. Flares of dying sunlight blinded her for a moment. She spread her arms apart, palms up and empty. "Hail," she called out. "I am General Kira Nerys of the Bajora! I come seeking a parley."

Lean and graceful, the Ascendant leader was slender, almost fragile-looking. He rode atop an enormous warlizard, flanked by a swordsman and a female archer, while a mahout controlled the animal. At first Kira admired the Ascendants' superbly crafted armor. It covered their entire bodies and shimmered in the sunset, like pools of mercury trapped in glass, or sheets of exquisitely carved and polished ivory. Looking closer, she shuddered when she realized that it wasn't armor at all but an organic exoskeleton, like that of the scavengers on the ocean floor.

Then she saw their eyes. Golden, without pupils, fluted at their outer edges, they reflected the fading crimson light and resembled pools of flame. And, like fire, they held no mercy.

The Ascendant army lumbered closer, its pace unchanged.

"Stand aside," the Ascendant Leader said, his voice as melodic as it was imperious. "We ride to the fortress."

Jamin's brow pressed down with grim concern. "Nerys," he said, "we should fall back."

Ignoring him, Kira kept her eyes on the Ascendant Leader. Even atop her mount, Kira felt the tremors caused by the advancing forces. Then one of the war-lizards roared; it was a shivering howl that rose and fell on a monstrous scale, a rolling cry that rent the air, both booming and shrieking at once. It was answered by thousands more like it, a cascading tide of deafening sound, pushing ahead of the Ascendants like terror incarnate.

Flickers of fire ignited throughout the angled ranks of marching giant reptiles, and Kira realized that flaming arrows were being nocked to thousands of bows.

"Fall back!" she ordered. She yanked on the reins and turned Jayol hard about, then gave his flank a kick with her heel to spur him to a run. His muscles coiled and he sprang away, with the rest of Kira's retinue following behind.

A deep moan, like a suffering ghost, pitched upward and grew louder. It was the sound of fear in flight—thousands of arrows, darkening the sky and falling like a hammer blow from above. Sick waves of anticipation roiled in her gut as she kicked again, spurred Jayol faster, harder, toward safety, toward the fortress. . . .

Impact. Silvery shafts of death fell from the sky. The burning triangular head of an arrow pierced her armor and plunged into the right side of her back. Several more arrows ricocheted off her armor, hitting with enough force to knock her forward and off her saddle. Dozens more drove into Jayol, into his back and flanks, into the back of his head, and the noble beast fell with a tragic whimper into the dry dust, his once-lustrous fur aflame beneath a plume of greasy smoke.

On either side of Kira, *zhoms* prickled with fire-arrows crashed snout-first to the ground, hurling their riders forward like rag dolls. The standard-bearer was dead, stuck with more arrows than Kira could count. Then another howl of beastly suffering, and Nathech and his mount collapsed behind Jayol's twitching body, mount and rider both clearly slain even before they fell, carried forward only by their momentum.

Renla and Jamin had both been hit, but they were still in control of their wounded *zhoms*. Only Ghavun remained unscathed. He circled back and interposed himself between Kira and the Ascendant horde. Jamin rode back and reached out to Kira.

Without a word, she took his blood-slicked hand and let him hoist her up into the saddle behind him. Her entire right side raged with pain from the arrow buried in her ribs.

The moment she was in the saddle, Jamin kicked his mount to a full run, back toward the already retreating ranks of Bajoran cavalry. Kira clung to Jamin's torso with her left arm, and she saw Renla and Ghavun racing only a few lengths behind them.

As the Ascendant Leader's war-lizard trampled the flag of the Bajora underfoot, another storm of fiery metal rain erupted forward, turned the sky to shadow, groaned as it split the air and converged into a cone of force. Thousands of arrows hit home in a narrow, concentrated kill zone, and Renla and Ghavun both vanished inside of it. The eerie cry of arrow flight was followed by the dull thuds of heavy bodies slamming into the road, engulfed in a cloud of dust and inky pitch-smoke from a thousand tar-coated arrowheads.

Kira and Jamin were out of range by the time the smoke cleared, and the corpses of Renla and Ghavun diminished until they were only dark dots left behind on the horizon.

Jamin's mount remained at a full run.

Wind whipped through Kira's hair, which flowed loose behind her, unraveled from its braid. Her head grew light, but she did not wonder why. The wound in her back bled copiously. Syrupy warmth coated the linen garment beneath her armor. Each pounding stride of Jamin's *zhom* spurred the bleeding and sped Kira toward the end of her days. Her sight faded with the last rays of sunset, and her world followed the hour into twilight.

29

I.K.S. noH'pach

PRYNN'S SHOULDERS ACHED UNDER HER HANGING WEIGHT. With even the slightest movement, the bones of her arms ground in their sockets like a mortar and pestle. She tried to remain still. The effort made her calves burn. Keeping her toes pointed and pressed against the deck twisted her feet with horrible cramps. Her mouth was parched from dehydration, but her uniform jacket was saturated with sweat. She felt beads of perspiration race down the gulley of her back.

In the sultry stink of the Klingon ship, each breath was a struggle. With her arms so fully extended, it was immensely difficult to expand her chest enough to inhale fully. Despite the agony the manacles inflicted on her wrists, Prynn was forced every few minutes to close her fists and pull herself toward the ceiling; holding her body several inches off the deck with her arms bent, she was able to gasp for air. The exertion forced her to hyperventilate slightly, which helped her increase the oxygen in her blood and delay her next pull-up.

Time had become indistinct. She was fairly certain she'd been in this compartment for more than an hour, maybe a few hours, but certainly less than a day. Beyond that she wasn't able to be any more specific. The incessant hum of the ship's engines, its never-changing crimson-twilight illumination, the monotony of loneliness in this barren space . . . together these things were like mental anesthetic.

Little games had not helped her maintain her focus. Counting to track the passage of time eventually detoured into daydreams of windsurfing on Pelagia Prime, or to thoughts of Shar's beautiful, wind-tossed, bone-white locks dancing like serpents in the gusts of an evening gale. Never in her life had she ached for someone the way she did now for Shar. Even as a child wishing for her father to come home, she hadn't yearned like this for someone else's presence. To hold Shar again . . . to see that quiet passion in his eyes, to hear him say her name . . .

What if I never see him again?

The question haunted her.

Her breaths grew short and weak. With burning biceps and gritted teeth, she pulled herself upward and huffed several fast lungfuls of air in and out, until the light-headed feeling passed. She relaxed her arms slowly and let her body extend, as if it were elastic, until her toes once more pressed against the metal grating below. *If Taran'atar abandons me here, I won't be able to do this forever. Sooner or later, I won't be able to pull myself up . . . and then I'll suffocate.*

She had tried scrunching her fingers together and slipping free of the manacles. They were fastened too tightly for that, and she had managed only to add to the already grievous cuts and abrasions that Taran'atar's twists of cable had left scoured around her wrists. During her first few pull-ups, she had searched in vain for any structural defects in the ceiling or the curve of pipe to which she was locked. When she had been at the Academy, she had remembered hearing tales of an Earth animal, a coyote, that was said to be so averse to ensnarement that it would chew off one of its own limbs or appendages in order to escape from a trap. Far from feeling that level of motivation, at the moment Prynn nonetheless understood it.

After another pull-up for breath, she tried inverting herself and looping one of her feet through the gap above the pipe, figuring that it would be no less uncomfortable to hang upside down for a short while, and maybe rest her wrists in the bargain. The space was too narrow. She unwound herself and stretched her tingling feet back toward the deck.

The hatch opened. Taran'atar barged in and moved at an angry quick-step, past Prynn, to the router she had sabotaged earlier. She twisted her neck to watch him over her shoulder. He pulled at the router. Pounded his fist against it. Low growls rumbled in his chest, deep and forceful enough for Prynn to feel them as much as hear them. She feigned disinterest as she observed his growing agitation. He started disassembling the router's connections. Small pieces of the assembly clanged onto the deck around his feet as stalks of stiff optronic cable sprung loose from the open panel in front of him. Even without knowing what it was he was trying to do, she was certain that he was making it worse rather than better.

In an openly mocking tone, she said, "Something wrong?"

He stopped working, and his posture stiffened. His back was to her, but she could feel the rage boiling inside him. "The damage you caused is interfering with the ship's internal circuitry. I cannot complete my pre-landing check."

"Perhaps I could help," she said.

In the span of half a breath, he turned and was centimeters from her face. His eyes were feral, his breath hot and ragged from his flared nostrils. "I like you where you are."

"Fine," she said scornfully, refusing to show any of the fear that had her heart racing. "Stop pulling all the cables. Even if you get the router fixed, you'll have a hard time putting them all back in the right places."

He stormed back to the open wall panel and resumed his work, albeit more calmly this time. "When I want your advice, I will ask for it." He shoved components roughly back together.

She was about to goad him again, but then he kept mumbling, either to her or to himself; she wasn't entirely certain.

"Obedience brings victory," he said, sounding to Prynn like someone talking in his sleep. "Victory is life. . . . But there is no life without the Founders, and the Founders have deserted us. . . . She said she was no god. . . . But if the gods are not gods, what am I? . . . A soldier? A fugitive?"

His hands had stopped working. Now he was leaning against the bulkhead, his head drooped forward, his vocalizations too low and mumbled for her to make sense of them.

Prynn had not seen many Jem'Hadar in her life, but she was familiar enough with their reputation as a species to know that no one in the Federation had ever seen one of them in a state anything like this. It resembled the worst stages of withdrawal from chemical dependency, but it was more psychological than physical. Taran'atar's body was quaking, as if he were teetering on the verge of collapse.

She heard his breathing: It was quick and shallow, the respiration of panic.

Softening her tone of voice to one that would be less likely to sound confrontational, she said, "Taran'atar . . . where are you taking me?"

"To the rendezvous," he said. "At Harkoum."

"The rendezvous . . . with whom?"

He struggled to steady himself. "I don't know." He shook his head. "No! I *do* know, but I am meant *not* to. I was told to *forget*. . . . To forget *her* . . . to forget *that* face. *Her* face."

"Whose face?"

"I . . . don't . . . *know*."

"Was that why you left Deep Space 9?"

With a fervent pride that she found alarming, he said, "No, I left the station because I attacked Captain Kira and Lieutenant Ro. It's very likely that I killed them."

Prynn felt her face blanch. "Are you going to kill me?"

Taran'atar didn't look at her. His eyes, wide-open and paranoid, darted from one place to another—along the floor, over the walls, at the ceiling—all the while evading Prynn herself. He looked like he was searching for an answer.

His hand fumbled inside the pocket of his coverall and took out a hysopray. It was loaded with his second ampoule of stimulant from the *Euphrates'* first-aid kit. Without hesitation, he pressed it to his jugular and injected the entire dose. He gasped and groaned, a sound of disorientation mixed with relief. His eyes rolled upward into his skull for a brief moment, and inchoate vocalizations rolled from his throat as the drug coursed through him. He slumped heavily against the bulkhead. Seconds later his breathing slowed and became regular, then he closed his eyes and inhaled slowly through his nose. Exhaling, he relaxed his body and straightened his posture.

When his eyes opened again, he was Taran'atar: calm, disciplined, focused, and lethal. He looked at Prynn.

"For now," he said, in a voice that sounded made for command, "you still have value as a hostage. If the *Defiant* overtakes us before we reach Harkoum, I will need to use you to limit your father's options. When you cease to be an asset, however . . . I will act as circumstances dictate."

Prynn didn't let her expression change; until now she hadn't known whether Deep Space 9 was even aware that she had been abducted. Taran'atar's capture of the *noH'pach* had only made her more concerned that, if and when her comrades went looking for the *Euphrates*, no one would be able to follow their trail. Now she knew they were looking and that Vaughn was in command.

If Taran'atar's worried about the Defiant, she reasoned, *they must be close.* This was no time for her to dwell on morbid possible outcomes; it was time to gather strength and plot her escape. Watching Taran'atar finish his repairs to the power router, she spied the control device for the magnetic manacles attached to a belt loop on the right hip of his coverall. It was exactly the kind of simple, no-frills device one would expect a Klingon engineer to make: it had only a single button, which alternately locked and unlocked the manacles.

And if I get free, she wondered, *what then? I'm still no match for him in a hand-to-hand fight. What's my goal?*

They were no longer on the runabout, which meant she no longer had to focus on preventing the ship's capture. And now that she knew he was headed for a rendezvous, identifying who he was in league with moved to the top of her priority list.

He closed the wall panel. On his way back to the hatch, he stopped and stood in front of her. "I have restored the internal security monitors," he said. "I will keep an image of you on the main screen at all times. If you escape those manacles, I will come back to this compartment and break your neck. Do you understand?" She stared back at him, mustering her fiercest glare of contempt. "I do not kill without reason, Ensign Tenmei," he added. "Please do not make me kill you."

Then he turned and left through the hatch, which shut behind him. Alone in the pungent, moist heat of the aft compartment, Prynn couldn't decide for herself just how precarious Taran'atar's state of mind really was. At moments he seemed perfectly in control, calm and lucid. Other times he resembled a wild tiger too long caged and now looking for something, *anything*, to sink its teeth into.

Feeling the manacles slicing once more into her raw, bloody wrists, she concluded that there was only one thing of which she was certain right now: He had been telling the truth when he'd promised to break her neck if she escaped.

Gathering her strength for the coming fight, she began another pull-up.

30

Deep Space 9

EZRI DAX STEPPED PAST THE PRIVACY BARRIER INTO THE recovery ward. The lighting remained on its standard night-shift setting, dim and diffuse. At the far end of the ward lay Lieutenant Ro, unconscious and, to Dax's eyes, peaceful. A tray of mostly empty dirty plates from Quark's bar rested on the deck at the foot of her bed. Quark sat next to Ro. He was asleep, his head resting on Ro's midriff.

On the left side of the ward, a few beds away, Captain Kira lay comatose. Benjamin Sisko sat beside her, clutching her right hand in his. Dax wondered if he was asleep, as well. She took a few soft, slow steps in his direction.

He turned his head slightly and noticed her out of the corner of his eye. Immediately, his expression brightened. "Good to see you, old man."

She stood behind him and placed her hands on his shoulders as a gesture of comfort. He felt warm. "I'm glad you could come, Benjamin. But I'm sorry it had to be for this."

"Me, too," he said. He nodded toward another chair on

the other side of Kira's bed. Dax moved to it and sat down.

"You look tired," Sisko said.

"I am tired," Dax said. "I've been up for about thirty hours now, and I've been on duty in ops for the past twenty-six. I haven't felt this dragged out since the war."

A slight and crooked half-smirk turned up the corners of Sisko's mouth. "Sounds like the job I remember."

"It's not what I expected when I applied for the command track," Dax said. "I figured on more action—"

"And less paperwork," Sisko cut in.

"Exactly," Dax said. "That's how it was at first, like the mission to Sindorin, or defusing the uprising on Trill. But lately, so much of the job is just . . . routine."

Sisko made a grunt of amusement and nodded. "Duty logs. Requisitions. Transfers. New protocols from Starfleet Command. Just one damned thing after another."

"Pretty much," Dax said. "Don't get me wrong, Benjamin. I don't regret switching to command. But running a space station isn't where I see myself five years down the road."

"The red tape is just as thick on a starship," he said.

"I know. But I want to be *out there*. Exploring the Gamma Quadrant. Making first contacts."

"The *Defiant*'s not anchored to the station, you know. From what I hear, you and Commander Vaughn made some remarkable discoveries on your last mission to the Gamma Quadrant."

"I'd call that the exception rather than the rule," Dax said. "Just three months in the past year. The *Defiant*'s a great ship, but you know better than anyone that she wasn't built for that kind of mission."

"Then what's the answer, Dax? Because it sounds to me like you're talking about a transfer."

Dax recoiled, surprised at his conclusion. "I didn't say that," she protested.

He smiled reassuringly. "Relax, old man. It's not treason to ask for a new billet. Sometimes it's the only way to move your career forward." After a short pause he added, "Where would you go, if you could choose?"

"A deep-space explorer," she said. "Maybe one of those new *Luna*-class starships I hear they're working on at Utopia Planitia."

"Those won't be in service for years, at best," he said.

She grinned. "I'm a Trill, Benjamin. I'm used to thinking long-term."

"There's nothing wrong with planning ahead," Sisko said, "as long as you don't lose focus on the here and now." He squeezed Kira's hand. "But I can guarantee she'd be sorry to see you go."

Dax's bright mood dimmed. "How is she?"

"Hard to tell," Sisko said. "Bashir tells me she's comatose. Her artificial heart is functioning, but beyond that he's not making any promises."

"Julian's always been one to hedge his bets," Dax said. Noting Sisko's intense, serious focus on Kira, the ex-counselor in her felt concerned. "How are *you?*"

"As well as can be expected," Sisko said.

"It's okay to admit you're worried about her, Ben. You don't have to play defense with me."

His aura of calm and confidence faltered; his countenance darkened. "I am worried," he said. "Mostly about Kira. But it's more than that."

"Has something happened?"

"Not to me," Sisko said. "Not yet, anyway. It's nothing I can point to and say, 'That—that's what's bothering me.' . . . It's more a feeling of something coming, something waiting to happen. Ever since the attack on the Sidau village, I've had moments, like Orb shadows, when I thought I could glimpse the future, but they always slip away. Over and over again."

Dax had rarely seen Sisko so unsettled. Ever since his return from his stay with the Prophets, he had seemed the very paragon of calm and centeredness. That newfound inner peace he'd exhibited made this kind of agitation all the more worrisome. "Do you think the attack on Kira had something to do with it?"

He shook his head. "I don't know. Maybe." After a heavy sigh, he continued, "I'm afraid it's just the beginning of something bigger . . . something worse."

"Ben, it's normal to harbor anxiety after something tragic happens to someone close to us. Especially after an event like this, it's natural to try to infer a rational cause for what was really just a senseless act of violence. . . . It helps us pretend the universe makes sense."

"Maybe you're right," Sisko said, shaking his head in a futile gesture of denial. "But lately I've been remembering something the Prophets said to me, during the Dominion War." Dax watched Sisko's eyes take on a faraway gaze as he reached into the deep shadows of memory. "They told me that I was 'of Bajor,' but that I would 'find no rest there.' After what happened in the fire caves with Dukat and Winn, I thought I'd finished with that. Now I'm starting to see it doesn't have an expiration date. These past few months with Kasidy and Rebecca . . . I've been living on borrowed time. Troubles are on the horizon, old man. I can feel it."

"Say you're right, Benjamin," Dax said. "What'll you do? Take your family off Bajor?"

"No," Sisko said. "The Prophets didn't say anything

about my family not finding rest on Bajor. Just me."

"You could always come back to Starfleet. Take that promotion they offered you."

That drew a derisive snort and a soft chuckle from him. "That's one direction I don't see my path leading. At least, not yet." A wan smile played across his face. "Besides, I kind of like wearing civvies all the time."

"So where do you think you might be headed?"

"I'm not sure." He looked down at Kira, staring at the blank tableau of her face, searching it for an answer. "But I get the feeling this is where I'm supposed to start."

31

U.S.S. Defiant

BOWERS HUNCHED FORWARD IN THE CENTER SEAT ON THE *Defiant*'s bridge. He had just finished his sixth cup of coffee in four hours. The caffeine was giving him a headache, and the dull throb of pain was fraying his nerves and undermining his normally cool demeanor. Around him, the other bridge officers worked quietly, only rarely interrupting his tactical planning for the coming engagement.

A soft double tone, from his left-side command interface, indicated an incoming transmission had been received. "Bridge to Vaughn," Bowers said, checking the message's origin.

"Go ahead," Vaughn answered.

"Priority signal from Deep Space 9, sir."

"On my way. Vaughn out."

Half a minute later, Vaughn quick-stepped back onto the bridge. Bowers relayed the subspace communiqué to the main screen, which snapped to an image of Bashir and Nog. As soon as Bowers stood up, Vaughn settled quickly into the center seat. "Talk to me, Doctor," he said.

"We've sent you replicator specs for a prototype," Bashir said, nodding to the ungainly device Nog was holding. *"It's fabricated from Cardassian parts, to make it compatible with—"*

"Skip the tech, please. Does it work?"

Bashir raised his eyebrows skeptically and looked at Nog. The young Ferengi took over the briefing. *"We don't know,"* he said. *"Probably."*

"Gentlemen," Vaughn said, "I don't doubt your skills, but if I'm going head-on with a Jem'Hadar, I want more to pin my hopes on than 'probably.'"

"I understand, sir," Bashir said. *"But we have no way of conducting a practical test."*

"But," Nog quickly interjected, *"both of our holosuite simulations worked perfectly."*

"Thank you, Lieutenant," Vaughn said dryly. "That's tremendously reassuring. Please tell me there isn't some complicated, ten-step process for using that thing, or some incredibly specific condition required for it to work."

"No, sir," Nog said. *"Line of sight. Pull the trigger."*

"How many shots will I get?"

"As many as you need," Nog said. *"It works off a regular Cardassian power cell, like a disruptor."*

Vaughn nodded. "And after I land the shot?"

"No way to tell," Bashir said. *"At that point, whatever conditioning he was subjected to should be broken, but depending upon his state of mind, he might do anything. For all we know, we might override all his Jem'Hadar conditioning."*

"He'd be cut loose from his obedience to the Founders?"

"It's possible," Bashir said. *"Whether he'd use that freedom to follow their orders willingly or to continue fighting, there's no way to predict."*

Bowers was quickly losing confidence in Vaughn's plan.

Vaughn continued, "Any other side effects I should know about?"

Bashir cast a glance in Nog's direction, then looked back at Vaughn. *"There's no way to be certain,"* Bashir said. *"But, in theory, there is a limited risk of brain damage, memory loss, or total synaptic failure resulting in death."*

"What about friendly fire?"

"The pulse is calibrated specifically for Taran'atar's brain waves," Bashir said. *"It shouldn't affect anyone else, except maybe another Jem'Hadar."*

"Good work, gentlemen," Vaughn said. Nog and Bashir nodded their acknowledgment. *"Defiant out."* The screen snapped back to the slow stretch of starlight over the ship's warp field. Vaughn turned his chair toward Bowers. "ETA to Harkoum?"

"Twenty-three minutes, sir."

Vaughn thumbed the intraship comm. "Bridge to engineering."

"Leishman here."

"We've just received the replicator specs for a new piece of equipment," Vaughn said. "I want one ready by the time we reach Harkoum. Understood?"

"Aye, sir. You'll have it."

"Bridge out." He swiveled his chair toward Bowers. "Is my strike team ready?"

"Aye, sir," Bowers said. "They're standing by."

"Good," Vaughn said. He turned away from Bowers and directed his attention to a weapons-drill report that Forte had just completed. Bowers moved unobtrusively to Vaughn's side, leaned over the commander's right-side companel, and spoke in a low voice. "Sir, I'd like to ask you—"

"No," Vaughn said without deigning to look up from the report on his console.

Bowers began, "It's highly irregular for—"

"I'm aware of that. The answer is still no."

Conflicting emotions rooted Bowers in place, staring at Vaughn's passionless profile. Over Bowers's objections, Vaughn had decided to lead the strike team on Harkoum himself. It only slightly worried Bowers that his CO was a centenarian and perhaps not ideally suited to the rigors of leading a ground-combat unit in a covert-ops assault to capture a Jem'Hadar elder. Of much greater concern to him was the possibility that his CO might be blaming that Jem'Hadar for the death of his daughter and that the stated objective of capturing Taran'atar might be merely a pretense that Vaughn was using in order to kill him.

Bowers had the utmost respect for and trust in, Commander Vaughn. But during his twenty-odd years in Starfleet, Bowers had seen other officers—just as noble, just as disciplined—succumb to lesser temptations or crack under less-oppressive conditions. Worse, Vaughn's own lapses during the incident in the Gamma Quadrant a few months ago only stoked Bowers's current concerns.

No doubt feeling the weight of Bowers's stare, Vaughn turned his head and finally looked right at him. "Something else, Mr. Bowers?"

He had to make a decision. Either accuse Vaughn of being emotionally unfit to remain in command and ask Nurse Richter to conduct a psychological exam as a precursor to removing him from the center seat . . . or trust that Vaughn was in control of his emotions and knew exactly what he was doing.

Vaughn was still looking at him. "Well?"

Bowers steeled himself, lowered his voice, and hoped he

wasn't making the worst mistake of his Starfleet career. "We need to speak, sir—in private."

Bowers followed Vaughn into the commander's ready room. Vaughn walked quickly, his annoyance with Bowers abundantly clear. As the door swished closed behind the acting XO, Vaughn turned to face Bowers and said gruffly, "Make this quick."

"Permission to speak freely?"

"Damn it, Sam, out with it."

Too frustrated to be diplomatic, Bowers blurted out, "Sir, what the hell are you doing?"

"I've *made my decision.*"

"What decision, exactly, have you made? To get yourself killed? Because if you've got a death wish, I'm scrubbing this op right now."

"The hell you are," Vaughn said, his tone low and dangerous. He moved for the door. "We don't have time for this."

Bowers blocked his path. "Make the time." Vaughn backed off half a step. Bowers continued, "Heins and Neeley are good field commanders. They can do this without you."

"Maybe," Vaughn said. "But they're not going to."

"With all respect, sir, that's not up to you. You command the ship, but the crew is *my* responsibility. Letting you lead the strike team is a bad call, and you know it."

"Why? Because I'm old? I'll slow them down? Or maybe you're afraid I'm in this for the wrong reasons."

"All of those had occurred to me," Bowers said.

Vaughn eased away from the dark edge of his anger. His eyes were bloodshot, and the circles under them had grown dark and deep. "Sam, I'm the only one on this ship who has any real history with Taran'atar. I helped him save the station from Kitana'klan. And since we got back from the Gamma Quadrant, I've had more face time with him than anyone else on DS9 except Kira and Ro—and they're in no shape to help us now. So, if Nog and Bashir's little gizmo works and snaps him out of whatever mind-control has him on the run, our best chance of bringing him in without a fight is to make sure he sees a familiar face . . . hears a voice he knows. And right here, right now, that best chance is me."

Heavy silence hung between the two men as Bowers considered Vaughn's argument. He admitted to himself that it had the ring of truth to it. Nodding slowly, he said, "Just tell me you'll let the team back you up all the way and not run off and try to face him down one on one."

"Sam, believe me—I really don't want to face off against a rogue Jem'Hadar," Vaughn said. "But this is the only way this'll work. . . . You'll just have to trust me when I tell you that I know what I'm doing."

32

Kira

PRISTINE WHITENESS, METATEMPORAL AND PURE, SUFFUSED Kira's consciousness. Luminous apparitions drifted on the edge of her vision. Reality was a blank template, a virgin parchment on which her heart's desires could be writ large.

Yet all she knew was sorrow.

Disembodied but aware, she was mind without form, thought without flesh, sentience outside of time and space. Images of Parek Tonn were vivid in her memory but also distant, as if from a dream. Opaka appeared beside her, and suddenly Kira was corporeal again, back in her uniform. She looked down at Opaka and knew that she was addressing a Prophet.

"A vision," Kira said. "You showed me Parek Tonn."

"The end of the journey," the Opaka Prophet said. "And the beginning." Wind blustered and dispersed the silvery veil of nothingness. Kira and the Opaka Prophet stood together on the blighted plains of Dahkur, beside the twisted hulk of a scorched tree whose silhouette was barely visible against the star-speckled sky. In the distance, the

Ascendant army moved toward them. To the north lay the fortress and the army of the Bajora.

"None of this is real," Kira said. "It's just an illusion. It never happened."

"Never," said the Prophet, now wearing the body of Odo.

"Yet," added another, guised as Shakaar.

A Prophet as Vaughn appeared beside her. "Always."

Another Prophet took shape on the other side of Kira. She turned and looked into the face of her late, beloved Bareil, who was dressed now in the vestments of a vedek. With a beatific half smile, he said to her, "Our hand must defend the fortress."

It was absurd. Waving her arm at it with dismissive bravado, she said, "But it isn't *real*."

Sisko's voice answered from behind her. "It's as real as anything you've ever known." She turned and was taken aback; Sisko was attired in unusual clothes of a style she had never seen before, and he wore a vision-correction device composed of two glass lenses in a frame that fit over his ears. "Look into your heart: The fortress *is* real—not just to you but to the Eav'oq and the Ascendants, as well."

Turning back toward Parek Tonn, she gasped to see it shining like a beacon in the darkness. Its light stretched in shafts toward the heavens, blades of fire dividing the night.

The sight of it swelled her heart with hope and awe.

And she understood.

"The fortress," she said. "It's faith."

"Yes," Sisko said. "And it's more than that."

"It's the Celestial Temple," Kira said.

"Yes," said Sisko, who sounded pleased by her new understanding.

Intuition flowed through Kira's being, truth and wisdom

together, power and light, the glory of the eternal and the bittersweet ephemeral beauty of the physical universe. It was the touch of the Prophets.

"The fortress in the vision," she heard herself say. "It isn't Parek Tonn. It only looks like it . . . because the faith of the Eav'oq and the faith of Bajor are built on the same foundation."

"Our hand is of Bajor," said the Prophet who wore the visage of Vaughn. "Our hand is of Idran."

His words led Kira to look down at the road under her feet, and to consider the point many *kellipates* distant where it met two more roads, at the Fields of Berzel.

"Three roads," she said. "Three peoples."

"Our hand rises where the roads meet," the Opaka Prophet said. "There is where our message guides our hand."

"I still don't follow. Do you mean you're *trying* to bring the Eav'oq and the Ascendants together? Even though the Ascendants might try to exterminate the Eav'oq?"

"All roads meet," said the Vaughn Prophet.

The Opaka Prophet continued, "Some cross."

"Some intersect," the Bareil Prophet said.

The Odo Prophet added gravely, "Some end."

The vision washed away, revealing the formless white tableau of eternity that was the Celestial Temple.

Kira was stunned that the Prophets were so blasé about the genocide of a race they had graced with their tutelage. She searched their faces for any hint of empathy or compassion. It dismayed her to find it absent, their stares blank, unfeeling. She pivoted, turning from one borrowed face to another as she harangued them all. "Is *this* what you want? Two species you've reached out to are on a path to war, and you're just going to let it happen? Is *that* your will?"

"Our hand must act of its own accord," said the Odo Prophet.

"In peace," the Shakaar Prophet added.

"And in war," said the Vaughn Prophet.

"In friendship," said the Opaka Prophet.

"And in enmity," said a Prophet masked as Gul Dukat. "Our hand must shape the future."

Crowds of silhouettes congealed in the blinding emptiness, pressing in on Kira and her audience of Prophets. As the shades drew closer, some resembled Eav'oq, with their multilimbed bodies and tubular trunks, gliding through the ivory void. Others, long and willowy, like stretched humanoids, revealed themselves to be Ascendants. And countless others were Bajorans, some known to her, some strangers. Her father and mother, people she'd fought beside in the resistance, persons living and dead. Their numbers defied counting; they stretched back into eternity, all three crowds, millions of faces.

The long, narrow eyes of the Eav'oq shone with an inner light, peaceful and revealing. The fluted, golden eyes of the Ascendants all raged with fire, licks of flame that could purify or annihilate. And in the eyes of every Bajoran, Kira saw tears—of sorrow, of joy, of pain, of relief.

"Not all the Prophets' children interpreted their message the same way," said Sisko, who stood beside her once more. "The Eav'oq used it as the foundation for a philosophy of peace and tolerance. Bajor developed a religion of empathy and reason . . ."

"And the Ascendants," Kira realized with a deep and heartfelt sadness, "made it into a crusade."

Gouts of fire erupted in a ring around Kira, Sisko, and the Prophets. It consumed the Eav'oq and Bajoran *boryhas* that had gathered around them. Screams of agony and horror unlike any Kira had ever heard drove her to her knees. She covered her ears, but the terrible cries of pain could not be shut out. Worse than the wails of the dying at Gallitep, worse than the tormented shouts of the wounded on the battlefield, this was the death knell of two peoples, two philosophies . . . two paths.

When the seemingly endless, racking howls of torment at last abated, all that was left in the eerie silence was Kira's own weeping, her bitter sobs of inconsolable grief.

"Our hand must not yield," the Opaka Prophet said to her. "The fortress must not fall."

Trembling now with the understanding of what was at stake, Kira lifted her head.

Parek Tonn emerged from the misty white void. Dark rocky ground revealed itself; the blank page of the Celestial Temple receded like a wave into the ocean. Kira stood above herself, beneath the towering majesty of the ancient fortress. Her ancient alter ego lay on the hard ground, attended by several retainers dressed in the raiment of the medical castes. Jamin, the spitting image of Sisko, hovered nearby, watching the ministrations of those who cared for his commander.

"Follow the path," the Opaka Prophet said. "When you know where it ends, you will know how to begin."

33

Harkoum

WINDBLOWN WAVES OF SAND SLID PAST ONE ANOTHER ON THE arid plain, a slow migration of soil from one hemisphere of Harkoum to another. Dawn slashed the bloody sky with shining streaks of ivory. Sawing melodies of insect-song faded with the passing of night. Soon, the heat of Harkoum's twin suns would break over the horizon and white out the details of the parched landscape, a vista of cracked earth and crooked gouges cut by rivers long since run dry.

Sheltered under a rocky overhang that would keep the sun off his back, Savonigar slipped on his polarized goggles to cut the glare. The tall, lean Nausicaan pulled back the tab on a field ration and picked at the container's contents. A dried, overly salted stick that might once have been meat. Some wedges of a yellow, sticky fiber that might once have been fruit or a Lissepian honeycomb. A goop of chemical preservatives with just enough legume paste in it to pass for an edible substance. Savonigar tossed the sticky hunk of fiber in his mouth. It was even chewier than he expected, but it was mildly sweet, with a hint of clover. *Definitely the honeycomb,* he concluded.

Savoring the rich flavors as he continued to move the chunk of honeycomb around in his mouth, he pocketed the salted meat stick and discarded the bean mush.

Unable to dislodge the last bit of honeycomb from his back teeth, he opened a canteen and drained the last of its water. He shook the final few drops into his throat, then sealed the empty canteen and put it back with his gear. He still had two full canteens remaining. Fortunately, he had planned on holding this position for quite some time.

Unlike his peers, who had scrambled to the farthest reaches of the planet in search of the Cardassian Woman, he had ignored the client's histrionic orders and made his base camp here, a few short kilometers from her primary base in the abandoned pit of Grennokar. The truth of the situation had been clear from the look in her eyes: The Cardassian Woman was a threat, one who meant to force a confrontation. Rather than waste time tracking an obviously dangerous foe over unfamiliar ground, the Nausicaan assassin had elected to let his prey come to him.

If the Cardassian Woman never made it this far, that was of no concern to Savonigar. He didn't need the money, so it didn't bother him if one of the others collected the generous bounty the client had offered. And unlike the boastful Klingon woman or that pitiably insecure Chalnoth, the Nausicaan had no desire for glory, no appetite for sadism. He was a professional.

At home on Nausicaa, he had been an anomaly. In a world populated with excitable, irritable thugs, Savonigar had stood out precisely because he'd been none of those things. Rarely had he raised his voice in anger. Insults that had provoked other young males to draw their blades had drawn only icy stares from him. But when his enemies had turned their backs . . . when they had retired to their beds . . . when they had let all thought of him pass from their minds . . . that was always when he had struck, in the dead of night, as calm as he'd been lethal. Passions ran deep among his people, but even as a youth his peers had called him *venolar*—"snowblood."

So, naturally, when he had attained the age of majority, the military had come calling. But not to make a soldier of him, as they had with his classmates. The powers that pulled the strings on Nausicaa had drawn darker designs for his future. He'd welcomed their sinister tuition, and he had learned those lessons well—well enough that when he'd decided to leave their service and go into business for himself, there had been no one who'd been able to do anything to stop him. And no one who had been able to find him again ever since.

There was a small kink in the camouflage netting that hid his position. He reached up and gently adjusted it to where it should be. The morning air grew hot. Blinding daylight crowned the peaks of distant mountaintops just above the horizon.

A wisp of dust kicked up out of the canyon in the distance.

Savonigar picked up his field glasses and focused them toward the faraway dust cloud. The image sharpened, and he saw another wisp, slightly closer than the last. It was coming from inside a narrow, twisting gulley below ground level.

There were many dozens of such fissures spiderwebbed across the lowlands of Harkoum, and he had expected that someone approaching Grennokar would use one of them for cover rather than speed across the vast range of open terrain. If there hadn't been so many paths, he would have mined the most advantageous approaches to Grennokar. As the intermittent spurts of dust revealed, however, whatever was causing them had eschewed all of the easiest passages in favor of a more difficult one.

He opened the case at his side and removed his pulse rifle. Its matte finish immediately adjusted its appearance to his surroundings, taking on the dusty, grayish-brown hues of the shale outcropping that hid him from sight. The weapon powered up silently. A dim reddish icon below its targeting scope indicated that it was fully charged. Taking his time, he stretched his body and lay down slowly, careful not to disturb the surrounding sand or rocks. Lying on his stomach, he leaned forward on his elbows and inched the barrel of the rifle through a narrow gap in the netting. He closed one eye and peered through the scope.

Blurred glimpses of a rider on a silvery personal vehicle. A *hoverbike,* Savonigar figured. *If I had to guess, I'd say it's the one Grauq was always polishing in his hold.* Billows of sandy dust and ripples of heat distortion made it all but impossible for him to get a clear look at the rider who was cloaked from head to toe in pale desert-survival garments. All the same, he knew who it was. It couldn't be anyone else.

The Cardassian Woman.

There were two forks ahead of her in the gulley, but both were too narrow for her to pilot through. She would have to continue straight on until much farther ahead. And long before she got to the next viable fork in the path, she would pass through a widened stretch of the miniature canyon, one that would force her to drive straight into his sights for at least ten seconds. *More than enough time,* he gloated. He shifted his crosshairs into the wide gulch and steadied his hands for the killing shot.

Overhead, a scavenger bird's hoarse screech cut the hush of morning like a sonic knife, then faded away, swallowed by the sky. Below, the plumes of dust sped closer more quickly than Savonigar expected. The Nausicaan was mildly impressed. *She must be quite a rider to go that fast in such tight quarters.*

A few more seconds. His finger hovered, loose and relaxed, in front of the trigger. The lightest touch would fire the shot. Gauging the distance, he estimated a quarter-second lead time.

She was still several seconds away from the wide gulch when a mechanical roar emerged from the incessant low moan of wind. His instincts urged him to look up, but his training kept his eye on the crosshairs. He had a bad feeling that he knew what was coming, but he hoped there was still a chance he could make the shot before everything went to hell.

There wasn't.

A sonic boom made a hammer of the thick morning air. One bellicose thunderclap shook the ground and churned up a mountain of sand that erupted toward the sky. It crashed down like a wave in his direction. A maelstrom of dust and small rocks, riding a blast of superheated air, tore away his camouflage netting and slammed him into the corner beneath the shale overhang. Savonigar covered his face with his forearms. Choking plumes of dirt pushed into his nose and mouth for several long seconds. Then the furious onslaught ended.

He shook himself briskly and clambered out from under the rock shelf. Looking back beyond it, he saw a tiny Klingon scout ship decloak. It hovered for a few seconds, then pivoted and glided toward a sheer face of rock—and vanished through it. *If the pilot knows about Grennokar's holographic cloak,* Savonigar reasoned, *then he must be an expected visitor.* Turning back toward the lowlands, he saw no sign of the Cardassian Woman—only an uninterrupted wall of dust wafting across the plains.

With that kind of cover, she'll reach the edge of the plain before I get another shot. He packed up his rifle and set out, likewise taking cover in the sandstorm that the arriving Klingon ship had whipped up. If he was quick and stealthy, he could intercept the Cardassian Woman before she climbed the short hill that led to the camouflaged entrance of Grennokar.

He hadn't planned to let the Cardassian Woman get this close to her target, but whether she perished a light-year away or a meter away from the client didn't matter to Savonigar.

As long as she died before reaching the client, he would be satisfied that his job was done.

"We're in orbit over Harkoum," Zucca said from the helm.

Vaughn turned his chair toward Forte. "Company?"

"A handful of freighters," the tactical officer said. "No sign of the *Verithrax.*"

"Starting sensor sweep," Bowers said from the opposite side of the *Defiant*'s bridge. Almost immediately, he added, "I've got a huge ion trail in the lower atmosphere."

"Confirmed," Rahim said from the science station. "We're also reading a lot of neutrinos and graviton spikes. Levels are consistent with a Klingon class-IV cloaking device."

Now on his feet, Vaughn said, "Do we have a lock on the *noH'pach?*"

"Negative," Bowers said. "We've got a clean read on its trail to the surface, but then it just stops."

"On screen," Vaughn said. "Show me where the trail ends."

The image on the main viewer changed to show the mostly featureless, brown surface of Harkoum. There was no evidence of a landing strip, starport, or other facility where the ship could have set down. Thinking out loud, Vaughn said, "Could she still be cloaked, on the surface?"

"No, sir," Rahim said. "We'd still be reading the neutrinos from her cloaking field."

Forte joined the speculation. "What if the *noH'pach* was using an interphasic cloaking device?"

"That's a Romulan technology," Rahim said. "And then we'd be reading a massive spike in chronitons."

"Forte, Rahim," Bowers said, snaring their attention. "Run a level-one tachyon scan on the coordinates at the end of the trail. Forte, look for an unusual lag in the return signal. Rahim, watch for signs of optical distortion on the surface."

Vaughn suppressed a wry grin. He had been moments away from giving the same order, and he was pleased that Bowers had done so without being prompted. The commander moved to observe over Forte's shoulder while the survey was carried out.

As the results appeared on Forte's monitor, he nodded. "You were right, sir. Signal lag, fourteen nanoseconds."

Rahim turned his chair toward the XO. "Affirmative on the distortions, sir. Minute fluctuations consistent with a disrupted holomatrix."

Bowers looked at Vaughn. "Sir, sensors indicate there's a sensor-shielded facility on the surface, concealed with a holographic blind and equipped with an active interference system that returns phony sensor readings. My current speculation is that the *noH'pach* is inside that facility."

"Good work, Sam," Vaughn said. "Can you cut through that sensor blind and get me a look inside?"

"We'll do our best, sir."

"As soon as you have a solution, upload it to the away team's tricorders." Vaughn moved toward the exit. "I'll be in transporter bay one. Bowers, you have the conn."

"Aye, sir."

Vaughn left through the aft starboard hatch and walked quickly back to the transporter bay. Chief Chao was at the control console. Three security officers, all lieutenants, were waiting for him in front of the transporter platform.

Lisa Neeley, a tall and athletic redhead, had the distinction of seniority, having served with Captain Sisko on the *Defiant* during the Dominion War. Calvin Moore, a dark-skinned human man, was slight of build but tough and wiry, and his eyes had the sharp gleam of a ground-combat veteran. The last of the three was Darrell Gervasi, a stocky man with a shaved head and biceps twice as large as Vaughn's calf muscles.

All three wore surface-operations blacks, solid-color uniforms designed for ground-combat troops. Vaughn hadn't worn SOBs, as the uniforms were commonly called, since the battle to liberate Betazed from the Dominion. He noted that the design was essentially the same: padded shoulders and knees and an ablative outer skin that dispersed directed-energy attacks. He was relieved to see that someone had wisely done away with the band of department-specific color that had previously crossed the uniform at mid-chest, wrapped over the shoulders, and stretched across the back; the dark-red stripes had simply made it easier for hostile forces to target a unit's command officers.

Utility belts on the strike team members' waists were loaded with backup power cells for their phasers, spare phaser sidearms, and tricorders. Gervasi also wore a narrow backpack, which Vaughn assumed contained a medkit and other staple survival gear. Dangling by an elastic band around each team member's neck was a pair of dark, matte-surfaced goggles.

"We've got your gear ready to roll, sir," Neeley said. She handed him his own set of SOBs. *A couple years ago, we'd all have beamed down in our regular duty uniforms,* Vaughn mused as he kicked off his boots. Without any self-consciousness, he stripped off his regular uniform coverall and shimmied into the battle gear. It felt heavier than he remembered, and he realized that it was because a layer of ultralight, armor-mesh fabric had been added as an inner lining, to protect personnel from projectiles and shrapnel. He transferred his combadge to the new fatigues, then pulled his boots back on.

Gervasi put a phaser rifle in Vaughn's hands.

"Ready to beam down, sir," Neeley said. "Heins, Minecci, Thron, and Stov are standing by in transporter bay two."

Vaughn nodded, then turned and thumbed a comm circuit on a wall companel. He knew it wasn't really necessary these days, but sometimes old habits came back to him. "Vaughn to bridge."

"Bridge here," Bowers responded.

"Where do we stand on that sensor screen?"

"We can bypass the scrambler," Bowers said. *"But there's kelbonite plating under the surface, and maybe something else under that. No way to beam through. Rahim recommends you beam down a couple klicks from the entrance."*

"And I thought all the fun had gone out of this job."

"Sorry, sir, best we can do. The new scanning protocols have been uploaded to your tricorders."

"Acknowledged. Vaughn out." He turned toward Chao. "Open a channel to transporter bay two." Glancing at Neeley, he asked sotto voce, "Who's senior down there?"

Neeley whispered back, "Heins."

"Channel's open, sir," Chao said.

"Heins, this is Vaughn. Is your team ready?"

"Aye, sir."

"All right, then. Everybody, listen up. I know you've all fought Jem'Hadar before. You've been on the ground, and you know how to handle yourselves. But this is something different.

"Taran'atar is a Jem'Hadar elder. He has skills far beyond those of most Jem'Hadar you may have faced in the Alpha Quadrant. And just to make our jobs interesting, we have to take him alive. I know you've heard by now what happened on Deep Space 9 to Captain Kira and Lieutenant Ro." As he continued, he felt inhumanly disconnected from himself, from the words that he was saying. "And you know that during this pursuit we've also lost Ensign Tenmei. But this is not about getting even or meting out justice. Our job is to capture him and return him to Deep Space 9. What happens after that is not our concern right now. Our only objective . . . our only priority . . . is to bring him in alive and not get ourselves killed doing it.

"Neeley, wrap up."

Neeley faced Gervasi and Moore, and she raised her voice to be heard clearly by the team at the other end of the comm. "Set all weapons for heavy stun. Activate IFF circuits." Vaughn adjusted his own weapon. It took him a moment to find the IFF—Identify Friend or Foe—circuit, which was located under a flip panel above the grip. It was a relatively simple invention but one that had saved count-less lives during the Dominion War: a sensor that temporar-ily locked down the firing mechanism whenever the target-ing sensor fell on a person whose combadge or other identification transponder was encoded with a recognized allied signal. It had reduced friendly fire incidents among Starfleet personnel by more than seventy-one percent as compared with their performance during the Cardassian conflicts less than two decades earlier.

Neeley finished her pre-mission checklist just as Ensign Leishman from engineering hurried in. She held a repli-cated copy of Bashir and Nog's neuro-pulse device, which looked like an overdesigned Cardassian tricorder. She handed it to Vaughn. "As requested," she said. The three security officers all regarded the device in Vaughn's hand with varying levels of distrust and disdain.

"That's the weirdest thing I've ever seen," Moore said.

With a derisive smirk, Gervasi said, "Does it come with a tripod?"

"Put a cork in it, both of you," Neeley said. Turning to Vaughn, she said more quietly. "It does seem a bit . . . unwieldy, sir."

Hefting the device in his hand, Vaughn nodded and looked at Leishman. "How hard will this be to use?"

"Just point it and press the power key," Leishman said. "It's not a combat weapon, but it'll get the job done."

"All right," Vaughn said, tucking the device securely on his belt. He stepped onto the transporter stage, and the security officers followed him. "Chao, scan the coordinates where the *noH'pach*'s ion trail ends. Assume that someone will be there, watching for company, and find us the closest possible concealed spot for beam-in."

"Aye, sir," Chao said, starting the search.

"Goggles down," Neeley said. Vaughn lowered his into place. They tinted the world in a surreal, amber hue. The color, he realized, of Jem'Hadar blood.

"Site locked in," Chao said. "Your cover's a bit low." She gestured with the flat of her palm for the team to crouch. The away team sank toward the floor.

Chao looked at Vaughn for the order.

"Energize," he said.

"We've made orbit over Harkoum, Intendant," said General Kurn, who had risen to greet Kira as soon as she stepped on to the bridge of the *Negh'Var*. The younger brother of Worf, the former Klingon regent, had been spared his sibling's disgrace through Kira's intervention. It was a favor he had yet to repay.

"Move us into geostationary orbit above the Grennokar Detention Center," she said. Kurn half-nodded at a subordinate, who rushed away to carry out the order.

The topmost latitudes of the burnt-orange planet curved across the lower third of the main viewscreen. Ashen masses of cloud obscured much of its surface. All around Intendant Kira, guttural Klingon voices barked orders in short, hard shouts. Slowly, the image of this neglected world seemed to rise, then it shifted until the shallow curve of its equatorial region dominated the right half of the screen.

An adjutant approached Kurn and spoke to him in a confidential hush. The general turned to Kira. "We'll reach position in four minutes, Intendant."

"Thank you, General."

Kurn pretended to watch the screen for a moment, but Kira could feel him mustering the will to speak. "My engineers want to know why your quarters require a direct link to the main reactor," he said. "As do I."

"An experiment," she said. "That's all you need to know."

"And is the regent aware of your 'experiment'?"

"No," she said. "And if you see to it that he remains ignorant of it"—she lowered her voice and leaned closer to him—". . . you may find yourself a step closer to taking his place, and restoring your family's honor."

For a very long moment, his expression remained guarded and inscrutable. She wondered if she had miscalculated: Did his loyalty to the Alliance trump the temptation of his ambitions?

Then he flashed his lascivious smirk at her. "I can keep a secret if you can."

Returning his salacious leer with one of her own, she said, "I need to return to my quarters now. Hold position over Grennokar until you hear from me. I'm not to be disturbed for any reason." She began to step away, then turned back, and, over her shoulder, beguiled him with her best come-hither glance. "When my work here is done, Kurn, I promise to show you my *deepest* gratitude . . . *personally.*"

Guiding the *noH'pach* forward with its navigational thrusters, Taran'atar felt perfectly calm as he piloted it toward a solid-rock cliff face. There was no hesitation in his mind or in his hands; his course could not have been more true had it been ordered by one of the Founders. He did not tense or brace himself against a moment of impact. A voice . . . *that* voice . . . *her* voice . . . was inside his mind, telling him to go forward without doubt or delay.

And so he did.

The sleek, narrow Klingon scout ship glided through the holographic illusion. On the other side it passed down a short, relatively low-ceilinged approach tunnel that led to a vast, circular space more than a kilometer across and marked by deep shadows, dark metal, and a uniquely Cardassian utilitarianism. A web of grate-floored catwalks radiated out from and provided the support for the broad, disk-shaped landing platform in the center of the facility's top level. Another catwalk encircled the topmost outer perimeter; a broad stairway led up from the perimeter catwalk to the concealed entrance tunnel, while other stairways throughout the space led to various sublevel platforms. Below that, Taran'atar saw only fleeting glimpses before the landing platform obscured the view.

He lowered the landing gear and set the ship down with the smooth, deceptively easy-looking grace of a veteran pilot. Only the slightest of tremors vibrated through the hull and deck as the vessel settled onto the platform with a final roar from the nav thrusters. The roar dwindled to a purr and then silence.

Standing up from the helm, Taran'atar considered whether he would be likely to need this ship again. Something told him that this would probably be the last he'd ever see of it. Unconcerned with its fate from this point forward, he chose to forgo the effort of locking out its controls. Stolen or destroyed, captured or recovered, he didn't care. He used the master operations console to unlock and lower the ship's port-side gangway. His Starfleet phaser and Klingon disruptor were tucked under opposite sides of his coverall belt, and the *d'k tahg* was secured under his belt at the small of his back. The control for the magnetic manacles was in his pocket.

At the exit ramp, he paused. To his left was the hatch to

the aft compartment. He thought it highly unlikely that Ensign Tenmei could have freed herself of the manacles in the scant few moments since he had ceased observing her on one of the bridge's secondary monitors.

Prudence compelled him not to take her continued captivity for granted. He drew the disruptor, cleared his mind of expectations, and opened the hatch. On the other side, still firmly secured to the ceiling pipe, was Tenmei. She noted the disruptor in his hand. "Made up your mind, then?"

Remembering the trap she'd laid for him many hours earlier, he reached slowly forward and tested the hatchway with caution. "Yes," he said. "I will remand you to whatever authority is in charge here."

"Great." She rolled her eyes. "You're a real prince."

"Good-bye, Ensign Tenmei." He turned and left. The aft hatch closed behind him. Moments later, he was striding down the exit ramp to the landing platform. The cavernous echoes amplified every sound in the facility, which was alive with the pounding pulse of air-circulators and the mechanical whine of hydraulic-powered elevators. A gust of air swept over him. It was dry, hot, and untainted with odor. Unlike Klingons, the Jem'Hadar valued cleanliness and order on their ships. The rich stench of the *noH'pach* had grated on his nerves, even after he'd thought his senses had become acclimated to it enough to block it out. Away from it now, he felt a tide of relief.

He turned his attention to the six armed irregular mercenary personnel who had, in the past several seconds, expertly and almost silently surrounded him on the platform. *Skilled,* he noted. *But poor unit cohesion. They've set themselves up for a crossfire. No doubt a lack of leadership.*

One of them—a jet-skinned male with a dark-magenta

twist of chin hair and ritualistic facial scars—stepped forward. His sidearm was holstered, and his rifle was slung behind him. He moved with authority and balance. "You must be Taran'atar," he said. "I'm Jaid. You're late. The client's waiting for you."

"I know," Taran'atar said. He fished the manacle controller from his pocket and handed it to Jaid. "There is a prisoner on my vessel. Do with her and the ship as you see fit. I'm done with them." Jaid seemed about to respond, but Taran'atar shoved past him with ease and moved directly toward a staircase that led to one of the lower sublevels and several elevator platforms. Descending the staircase, he saw the lines of a circular abyss converge beneath him at a point far below, lurking under a blanket of steam glowing with dim crimson light.

He crossed a long catwalk to the outer perimeter walkway and began circling around toward the closest elevator.

It is time to meet my new god.

A hint of reflected light on the sand was the only warning.

Savonigar dropped his rifle and drew his blades, turned and crouched, and lifted his two swords in a defensive cross, all in one flash-fast maneuver.

He parried the Cardassian Woman's lunging attack. Metal edges rang and gleamed. He recognized the weapons in her hands: Grauq's Terran swords. Clearly, she had an eye for quality.

They circled one another in slow steps, unblinking as they took each other's measure. He saw his advantages immediately. Strength. Length of reach. Weight.

Hers were just as easy to deduce. Speed. Narrower target. Lower center of gravity.

He feinted with his long blade. Lunged with his short sword. She deflected his thrust and spun inside his defensive perimeter. Her shorter blade—the *wakizashi*—slashed through his body armor with ease, lacerating his abdomen.

She tried to duck-and-turn clear. His right knee shot up and caught her in her ribs. Several of them snapped and buckled inward, fragile targets.

Parrying his quick slashes and cuts, she stumbled backward.

She circled him again, her breath heavy and ragged. Reading her body language, he knew how desperately she wanted to clutch at her side, protect her wounded flank. That was the obvious place to press his attack. *She'll know that.*

The rasping croak of a nearby lizard was sharp and loud in the mortal silence. The combatants' footfalls were light, phantomlike on the shifting earth and sun-baked stone.

She shifted her grip on the *wakizashi,* held it in a classic knife-fighting position, the flat back of the blade against her forearm. The *katana* she still held proudly in front of her—part challenge, part deterrent.

Savonigar pondered the threat of those two blades. Both, like his own, had monomolecular edges. One lucky slash or thrust could negate all his advantages. With swords, speed was often the most critical factor.

For all his skill, in this fight she held the advantage.

She lunged in, drew his defense with her *katana.* Pinned it with her *wakizashi* and her momentum. She made a desperate attempt to cut his legs out from under him. He blocked it, pushed back. *Time to change the terms.*

He forced her off-balance, put his strength to use. Twisted her wrist and spun the *katana* loose. It arced from her hand, over a mound of rock and out of sight.

Her left hand sliced upward. Then his own longsword was airborne along with half his right hand, in a delicate mist of his dark orange blood.

Before the pain took hold, he wrapped his bloodied right arm around her left, slipping it between her arm and the *wakizashi,* preventing another blow from that atomically subtle edge. With his left hand he thrust his short blade forward.

She turned in his grasp, and he missed her. His blade sank up to its crossguard in a slab of rock.

Struggling, they fell sideways. The blade snapped off, leaving him with an empty handle. He cast it aside and punched at her face. She lifted her arm, blocked it. Her knee slammed into his groin, but he was armored and padded. It was a dull hit.

His right knee shot up to crush her ribs. She twisted like an eel and dodged the blow. He slammed his left elbow on the raised bone and cartilage between her neck and shoulder. It shattered like crystal.

He flexed his right arm and broke the bones in her left arm. She gave up a throaty growl of rage. Spinning for momentum, the burly Nausicaan flung her across the narrow dirt path.

She struck the boulder on the other side, slammed face-first against it. The *wakizashi* flew from her fingers and vanished into the crags of the surrounding rocks. She clung to the boulder for a second, then pushed away, staggering backward.

Her right eye socket was mashed and swollen. Blood ran freely from her nose and pooled over her lips. She spat it out and stumbled slightly to her right. The viscous sputum turned into a dusty glob of mud on the trail behind her.

She showed Savonigar the bloodied grin of a predator.

Their blades gone, they stalked each other once more, in ever tightening circles. He tore a strip from his sleeve and wrapped it, tourniquet-tight, around the wrist below his bleeding right hand.

But he kept his attention on the Cardassian Woman.

Damage to her right eye would dull her peripheral vision. Broken ribs would impair mobility on her left side. Her useless left arm would make that side even more vulnerable.

He sprung forward. As he expected, she dodged to his right.

His elbow struck her midstride, smashed in her nose. She spun with the impact, absorbing the blow.

He realized too late she was inside his circle of defense.

Her foot slammed into the side of his right knee.

It snapped and buckled beneath him. A torrent of agonizing pain. He crumpled toward the dusty ground.

She tried to move behind him. He pulled a knife from his right boot and thrust it upward. Caught her square in the gut.

He drove the blade up and in, tearing her intestines but, he could tell, missing her heart.

He yanked his blade free.

She slumped behind him. Her knees hit the ground.

He coiled for another strike. Felt the cold bite of metal in his upper back. Then, from his shoulders down, he felt nothing at all. He vaguely sensed the resistance of his flesh as the woman pulled her knife free of his spine.

Savonigar pitched backward and lay on the trail, staring up at the pale blue morning sky; it blanched in the glare of twin suns beginning their long climb toward the midheaven. He lolled his head to the right and saw that his tourniquet had come loose. His hand was bleeding again, surrounding him with a spreading stain of vermillion lifeblood. It made the sand granules glisten darkly in the daylight. His eyes drifted from the tableau of his own expiration to see a small lizard perched on a rock, staring at him—one wild thing beholding another—while resting its leathery chin on a fist-sized stone.

He heard the sandy scrape of the woman pulling herself across the ground. It took him several seconds to turn his head; he felt ethereal, detached from the grim truths of the moment.

She rooted through his pack, a few meters away. The woman had dropped her *d'k tahg*—Jonu's *d'k tahg*, Savonigar realized as he saw the black-winged emblem on its pommel—on the trail behind her. Her drag-tracks were speckled liberally with her own blood, which coursed in regular beats through her fingers clenched futilely over her abdominal wound.

It wasn't hard for him to intuit what she sought. "The surgical pack," he rasped, "is under the bottom flap."

Suspicion colored her glare, but she checked where he said and found the field surgery kit. She sat back against the rock wall opposite him and, working with one hand, flipped it open beside her. Its assorted implements shone with antiseptic brightness, all of them neatly arranged and secured with small elastic loops. He wondered how much she knew about its use.

Her blood-slicked fingers didn't fumble or hover. She plucked the small medical scanner from the large top pocket, activated it, and propped it on a rock on the other side of her. It gave off a soft, high-pitched hum as it scanned her and catalogued her multiple wounds. She found the osteofuser first and powered it up. Then she closed her eyes . . . took a few deep breaths . . . and with three fast, wrenching movements set her own broken radius, ulna, and tibia.

And she didn't scream. Tears rolled from her eyes; a groan that verged on a shriek struggled but failed to get past her gritted teeth; her eyes went from squeezed shut to wide with horror and pain. Then she settled, her hyperventilation slowing to something less frantic.

She picked up the osteofuser and patiently mended her arm, paying no heed to the darkening pool of blood gathering in her lap. Then, with both her arms functional again, she reached up and gripped the two cleaved portions of her neck bone.

With a grotesque crunch she forced them back in line, then fused them whole.

Next she selected a microcauterizer. Threading it gingerly into her abdominal cavity through the jagged, bleeding gash Savonigar's knife had torn, she watched the medical scanner rather than her hands. Savonigar remembered the only time he had ever used the microcauterizer; he'd nearly cooked all the muscle in his leg in his haste to repair his femoral artery before he bled to death. Unlike some of the fancy Starfleet devices he'd heard about, this one wasn't automatic or self-guiding. It could rejoin severed tissue and knit it back together with tiny cauterizing "welds," but if one didn't know how to use it, it could easily do more harm than good. He also remembered that it had been excruciatingly painful.

The Cardassian Woman, despite massive blood loss and what had to be phenomenal suffering, seemed calm as she guided the device and repaired her savaged intestines.

He tried to speak, but his mouth was sticky with thirst

and dust. Swallowing hard, he managed to say, "Where did you . . . learn to do that?"

Without taking her eyes off the medical scanner's display, she said, "Cardassia."

Minutes passed while she worked.

"In a perfect world, I'd rest after this," she said, at a point after Savonigar had lost track of the difference between minutes, hours, and a lifetime. "But if it was Taran'atar on that Klingon ship, I'm out of time." She used a hypospray to suction away the excess blood. "If he's in the pit already, it might be too late." She sealed her gut wound with a dermal regenerator, then stood up. Walking on shaky legs, she returned to Savonigar's side and retrieved a field scope from his belt. She propped herself against a low boulder and peered through the device, toward the top of the narrow trail.

"Company," she said. "Humans, most of them. A Vulcan and an Andorian. Two squads, alternating cover as they advance. Standard attack formation." She seemed to ponder that for a second, then nodded. "Starfleet," she muttered as she put away the field scope in her pants pocket. Moving slowly, limping and unsteady, she retrieved her *d'k tahg* and tucked it under her belt. She looked at Savonigar as she picked up the rifle he'd dropped when she'd first attacked. "I'm taking this," she said.

He bared his fangs—as close as Nausicaans came to grinning. "You fought well."

Her mien was inscrutable. "As did you." She turned to head up the trail toward the client's redoubt.

"Good hunting," Savonigar said in a moment of unbridled professional admiration.

The Cardassian Woman paused. She looked back at him with an expression of respect, then set down the rifle and hobbled to the medkit. With shaking hands she loaded the hypospray with a massive dose of pale-gold medicine and injected herself with only a tiny fraction of it.

Then she reset the hypospray, carried it to Savonigar, and kneeled beside him. "Do you believe in gods?"

"I believe in the Four Winds."

"If you want, I'll release you to them."

He gave a small nod. "You are a noble adversary."

She pressed the hypospray to his neck. Its soothing coolness infused his body and mind with a whisper-hiss of dark relief. "Go to them," she said.

And his *tegol*, freed at last from the prison of his flesh, soared with the wind, to the Heart of the Sky, where his ancestors awaited his coming.

Gritty and pitted and cracked, the intimidating wall of sheer rock stood like a tower before Vaughn and the strike team. Though it was illusory, it might as well have been completely real, thanks to the interactive forcefield with which it had been reinforced. Like many modern holograms, it was effectively indistinguishable from the real thing. It even reacted to light and shadow, completely in harmony with its environment. And it was enormous, tall and wide enough that when its forcefield had been lowered, the Klingon scout ship had no doubt passed through it with room to spare.

Hunkered down in the shelter of some tall rocks several meters away from the wall, the strike team waited patiently while its tech specialist, Thron, studied the hologram with his silent tricorder.

They had been stalled for nearly three minutes out here in the open, and it had felt to Vaughn like an eternity. An eerie wail of wind snaked between the rock clusters, pushing flurries of sand that, to Vaughn's eye, skittered over the boulders like an army of lice on the move. Dry heat, odor-less and unforgiving, leached the moisture from his nose and mouth.

Neeley moved in a low crouch to join Thron. "How much longer?"

The Andorian lieutenant didn't look up as he answered. "Too soon to say. Penetrating the forcefield without draw-ing attention to ourselves might not be possible."

Vaughn crabwalked over to Neeley and Thron, sup-pressing the grimace of pain caused by the grinding scrape under his aged kneecaps. "Forget subtle," he said, keeping his voice down. "Just get us in there."

Thron nodded to acknowledge the order, then he waved over Gervasi. As the brawny man approached, Neeley ges-tured to Vaughn that they should move clear and avoid bunching up. He followed the long-legged redhead back to another outcropping of cover.

Gervasi kneeled with his back to Thron, who opened flaps on Gervasi's pack and removed a trio of small objects. With a slap on the backpack, he signaled Gervasi to move back to other cover. The Andorian's hands worked quickly, programming the devices and extending their tripodlike feet. One by one he checked them with his tricorder.

Next he waved over Stov and Minecci. The Vulcan and his human partner were at Thron's side in seconds. He handed each of them one of the devices he'd prepped, and he picked up the last one himself. Pointing at the holo-graphic barrier, he whispered some instructions to the two men and made some simple hand gestures that Vaughn understood as instructions on how to secure the devices in place.

Thron looked at Neeley and gave her a thumbs-up sign.

Neeley glanced at Vaughn. He gave a curt nod.

She returned the thumbs-up sign to Thron. Moore set up his rifle in a defensive position as Thron, Stov, and Minecci broke cover and scrambled over open ground toward the barrier, separating as they went. Stov split away to the right and Minecci to the left, while Thron charged headlong toward the center of the barrier. The Andorian was the first one in position, and he planted his device flush against the illusory stone. Moments later, Stov and Minecci did the same, at either end of the hologram. Thron held up his fingers and counted down from three while Minecci and Stov watched. When Thron's fist closed, all three of them activated their devices.

The hologram flickered for only a fraction of a second. The forward trio flattened themselves on the ground and reached for their rifles. Vaughn saw Neeley tense beside him, her finger lingering over the trigger of her rifle, which was pointed at the wall in case something terrible should emerge.

Nothing came.

Up at the barrier, Thron slowly pushed his hand forward until it disappeared inside the hologram. He pulled back his hand and activated his tricorder. Looking back down the gradual slope at Neeley, his hands conveyed his findings in quick signs and motions.

"Tunnel on the other side," Neeley whispered, relaying the report to Vaughn. He was able to understand Thron's field signals just fine—perhaps better than Neeley did—but he saw no gain in undermining her confidence or authority in the field. She continued, "Large space beyond. Multiple life signs there. And a lock on the *noH'pach*."

"Have him fall back," Vaughn whispered back. "Let Heins take point, then Stov and Minecci. We'll follow them in."

Neeley mimed the orders quickly to the rest of the team. Vaughn concentrated on taking deep breaths. Once the action started, there'd be no time to stop and collect himself.

Lieutenant Heins advanced up the slope as Thron retreated. Regrouped with Minecci and Stov, Heins leveled his rifle and stepped through the holographic wall. Stov and Minecci followed him through a few seconds later.

A few meters ahead, Vaughn saw Thron monitoring the forward trio's progress with his tricorder. Vaughn stole one last deep breath, then lifted his rifle to a ready position. "Move up."

He followed Neeley out from their concealment. They converged with Gervasi and Moore on Thron's position, then the five officers advanced together in a loose formation toward the holographic barrier. The suns were at the team's backs and still low on the horizon, stretching their shadows ahead of them.

Vaughn and Neeley stepped through the disrupted illusion of stone and emerged together on the other side in a vast, high-roofed tunnel of rough-hewn rock.

Heins, Stov, and Minecci were several meters ahead, all of them staying close to the wall on the right.

As opposed to the powerful sunlight that had warmed Vaughn's back a moment ago, the tunnel was steeped in shadow. He glanced back as Gervasi, Thron, and Moore entered. The landscape behind them had been reduced to dim outlines and a blank gray dome of sky. One of the functions of the holographic barrier, Vaughn realized, was to block out excess light and heat.

Perpetual night, he thought as he followed the team's example and lifted his goggles back on top of his head. *Exactly what you'd expect to find in a Cardassian prison.*

Ahead of him, muffled but unmistakable, was the clank

and throb of an industrial facility. Abyssal echoes and
reverberated, droning hums swallowed any smaller sounds.
He suspected that even the sharpest scream would be lost in
that heavy din.

He and Neeley moved up behind Heins's team on the
right. The others followed them. When everyone was in
position, Neeley signaled Heins to press on. The tall, fair-
haired officer nodded, then stalked forward, his body
ducked low and his rifle level and steady in his hands. The
ground inside the tunnel was surprisingly clean, which
helped them step softly as they advanced toward the far end
of the long passageway.

When he was still several meters shy of the end, Heins
held up a closed fist and halted the team. He waved the flat
of his palm slowly down at the ground, and the team
behind him all dropped to one knee. After checking his tricorder for several seconds, he motioned to Neeley and
Vaughn to move up and join him. As they reached his side,
Vaughn's eyes were able to pierce the veils of steam that
wafted upward in the yawning area beyond the tunnel. The
facility was round and roughly a kilometer wide, and
empty space dropped away below a network of catwalks
and platforms that radiated from a central landing pad, on
which sat the *noH'pach*. Its starboard side faced them, and
it was surrounded by a handful of armed, nonuniformed
personnel whom Vaughn took to be mercenaries.

Short, simple hand gestures passed rapidly between
Vaughn, Heins, and Neeley.

Vaughn asked, *Where's Taran'atar?*

Below us, Heins indicated. *Descending.*

Neeley pointed at the mercenaries. *How many?*

Ten, Heins signed. *Four there. Six on the perimeter.*

Nodding at Heins's tricorder, Vaughn extended his hand.

He checked its readings and noted the deployment of the ten mercenaries. He tried to lock in Taran'atar's bio-signature, but the signal was quickly becoming weak and distorted.

There was no more time for hand signals. Neeley and Heins leaned in close as Vaughn gestured for them to listen. "I'm going after Taran'atar," he said, "and you're going to cover me. Don't go any deeper into the facility than you have to, and hold your fire until fired upon. Heins, take your men and pin down the mercs on the right flank. Neeley, hit the ones on the platform. When I'm ready to be extracted, I'll let you know."

Heins jabbed a thumb toward the *noH'pach*. "We could capture the ship and beam him out."

"Negative," Vaughn said. "I can't get a clear read, even inside two klicks. There must be a scrambling field in here to prevent that sort of thing. When we bring him out, it'll be the old-fashioned way: over our shoulders." He tucked the tricorder in the left breast pocket of his uniform. "Questions?" Both officers shook their heads. "Positions. Hold for my order."

Vaughn moved to the point position on the right. Heins redeployed the team in a skirmish line along the edge of the tunnel. Neeley led Gervasi and Moore to the middle of the passage. Gervasi shed his pack, then the three of them dropped supine and began inching forward on their stomachs, propelling themselves with knees and elbows, rifles held level above the ground as they crept toward the edge.

Heins led Thron, Minecci, and Stov in front of Vaughn. The Andorian and the Vulcan both crawled into sniper positions, while Minecci and Heins set themselves up at the corner. Minecci crouched low; Heins stood to fire over Minecci's head.

Neeley and Heins signaled ready. Vaughn filled his chest with one last, deep breath and steeled himself for a risky dash through a mad crossfire. Moving as stealthily as he was able, he left the safety of cover and descended a narrow metal ramp to the catwalk that ran the facility's perimeter.

He was most of the way to the catwalk before he heard the mercenaries' first shouted alarm. Then the screech of disruptors filled the air above him, and it was answered by the angry hiss of phaser fire.

Vaughn sprinted, eager to reach a nearby stairway that led down to the next level, which he hoped would give him some cover from the enemy personnel above. Then all he'd have to worry about was whoever was waiting for him down below, in the pit.

Flashes of light spat up fountains of sparks in the darkness around Vaughn. He dodged a near-miss disruptor shot and resisted the urge to fire back; it would only pinpoint his position and make him an easier target. Ducking his head, he barreled forward at a full run. The stairway was only a few long strides away.

A bright blue blast of energy burned into a thin metal support beam directly behind where his head had just been.

Gritting his teeth, he let his rifle swing on its strap behind him. He grabbed the stair railing; his momentum whipped him around the tight turn into a steep drop. He planted his other hand on the opposite railing and slid down on his palms. His boots hit the deck grate with a solid clank.

For the moment, he was out of the line of fire. He checked his tricorder. Taran'atar was still descending slowly, probably in an elevator. Vaughn detected no other personnel on this level, and he located another lift-type apparatus, a few dozen meters away, through the maze of catwalks and half light.

Roving searchlight beams, broken up by the overlapping grids of metal beneath him, reached upward like probing fingers of brightness. Above him, the fury of battle raged on.

He put away the tricorder, lifted his rifle, and continued forward toward the nearest elevator.

There hadn't been much point in trying to stop Taran'atar from storming off. Jaid hadn't been in the mood to have his neck snapped by an edgy Jem'Hadar, and, in any event, the client had made it clear that she wanted Taran'atar's arrival expedited.

That left the matter of the Jem'Hadar's ship, though. Not to mention the prisoner he had said was still aboard.

Manacle controller in hand, Jaid climbed the port-side gangplank not knowing what to expect. Naturally, he was ready for the stench. He'd visited Klingon worlds before and had even signed on a few years back for a brief stint with some Klingon mercs who had acquired an antiquated bird-of-prey. Blood, garbage, uneaten food . . . there was no end to the variety of festering things one could find in the dark crevices under a Klingon ship's deck.

Still, disgusting was one thing. Deadly was another.

In the interest of caution, he stopped at the top of the ramp and scanned the ship for traps. Satisfied that it hadn't been rigged to snare or slay the unwary, he continued inside.

It smelled exactly as he'd expected. In its favor, though, the air on board was noticeably cooler than that outside.

The bridge, which was more of an oversized cockpit, checked out. All the drive systems were powered down, as were the majority of the internal systems except for life-support. The modern equipment in this compartment confirmed the newness of the vessel. It would fetch a good price on the black market—assuming, of course, that the client chose to part with it. A ship with a cloaking device— even a vessel this small—was a prize not to be discarded lightly. He had every reason to expect that she would want it looked after with care.

Jaid turned the manacle controller end over end in his hand. He looked through the open hatchway. The aft hatch was shut. Nightmare visions paraded through his imagination as he tried to guess what the Jem'Hadar might have confined in there.

Checking his scanner again, he noted that the life-form on the other side of the hatch was human. And female.

Intrigued, he walked down the corridor to investigate.

The hatch wasn't locked. He opened it.

The human woman dangled by her wrists; her toes barely scraped the deck. Her hair was unruly and black, her body lean and supple. A bluish-purple bruise marred one side of her lovely, golden-brown face. Over her shoulder, she regarded him with a hard and unforgiving stare. She had a nature of fire.

The Nalori mercenary grinned. *My lucky day.* "Hello," he said, swaggering forward to claim his prize. "I'm Jaid."

Prynn watched the Nalori man drift closer to her. His depraved intent was apparent. So was the manacle controller in his hand. As he drew nearer, he tucked it under his belt. She noted its location even as she maintained eye contact with him.

He circled her as he ogled her body. "I'll say this for the Jem'Hadar . . . he certainly knows how to bring a lovely gift for his hosts." She conserved her energy, remaining still, keeping her eyes forward, tracking his movement by listening to his footsteps. "I think I'm going to enjoy you a great deal," he said, his sick glee infecting his words with a sound like a suppressed laugh. "If you please me, you can look forward to weeks of my personal attention. Displease me . . . and you'll get to know my entire crew. Maybe a few at a time. Maybe all at once."

"I don't know what you deserve more," she said as he stepped back into her sight. "My disgust or my pity."

"You're hardly in a position to be doling out pity," Jaid said, unable to keep that perverted smirk off his face. He took a step closer to her. "But I'll be teaching you a few new positions soon enough."

She spat in his face.

He recoiled, wiped away her saliva with his left hand, then slapped her hard across the face with his right.

Feeling her bruised cheek glow red and hot, she lowered her head as if to hide her eyes. As she suspected, the Nalori wanted to savor the moment by looking for fear or shame in her gaze. He stepped right in front of her and cupped her chin in his palm. Lifting her head to make her look at him, he said, "That was foolish of you, darling."

From outside the ship, faint and echoing off the bulkheads, came the unmistakable sound of a disruptor shot.

Jaid's head snapped around as he realized what it was.

Prynn's knee kicked up and forward, crushing his groin.

He doubled over. She pulled herself higher. Slammed her other knee into his jaw, snapped his head backward. Finishing her pull-up, she wrapped her shins around his throat, locked her ankles together, and crushed with all the strength her anger would give her.

His hands flailed at her as his flat-black eyes started to turn midnight blue. Not finding any advantage, he reached down and fumbled desperately to draw his sidearm.

Prynn pulled herself higher, fighting against his

writhing weight, and got just enough extra height to kink her right knee sharply forward.

Jaid's weapon had just cleared its holster when his neck snapped. He went limp. The pulse pistol fell from his hands and clattered on the deck.

Slowly, Prynn straightened her arms and lowered the dead Nalori to the floor. Undulating from her torso, she built enough momentum to drag him directly beneath her. Then she let him go and stood comfortably on his chest. Stretching one foot downward, she lined up her toe along the bottom edge of Jaid's belt and tapped the only button on the manacle controller.

The restraints snapped open, and her arms fell free. She rolled away from Jaid's body as she collapsed to the deck. Her first minute of freedom was spent slowly and painfully forcing her hyperextended arms back to her sides.

Outside, the sound of phasers and disruptors grew more intense. She grabbed Jaid's pulse pistol, then plucked his scanner from his belt. With the weapon in one hand and the scanner in the other, she moved in fast strides to the portside exit hatch. She scanned quickly for Taran'atar's biosignature. It was faint, garbled, and moving away—down, deep below her current position.

She considered closing the hatch, powering up the ship, and making her retreat. But the weapons fire outside . . . she *knew* that sound: Those were Starfleet phasers. *If Starfleet's here, it's got to be to stop Taran'atar,* she reasoned. *But if they're pinned down, he might be escaping.*

Still, the cockpit called to her. Flying she understood. She was a pilot, not a soldier. And the aching bruise on the side of her face reminded her that Taran'atar had slapped her unconscious with hardly any effort at all.

She checked the power cell on the plasma pistol. It was

fully charged. *I didn't come this far to run away,* she decided.

Brandishing the pistol, she descended the ramp quickly, before she could change her mind. She sprinted away from the *noH'pach,* toward a narrow stair to a catwalk that led out toward the perimeter. Far in the distance was a bank of freight lifts.

Dashing across the catwalk, she stopped. And looked down.

A nightmarish circular abyss dropped away beneath her. Countless levels of prison cells and industrial machinery were stacked in rings along its perimeter, most of them dark and deserted, a few glowing with pale chemical lighting. Based on the height of the closest levels, she quickly estimated that this pit was nearly ten kilometers deep, a yawning maw of despair whose distant bottom level glowed like an ember beneath blankets of fire-hued smoke and steam.

Above and behind her, the firefight raged. Blinks of crimson crisscrossed lances of orange phaser energy. Shouts and cries of pain drowned in the cavernous echoes of the domelike ceiling, which was itself festooned with more catwalks and rigging, and from which occasional blasts of blue plasma fire rained down on the Starfleet personnel below. Her position was exposed; there was nothing she could do from here to help her Starfleet comrades. Turning away, she continued her mad dash across the narrow catwalk to the elevators, determined to track Taran'atar to the darkest circle of this Stygian pit. As for what she would do then . . . she resolved to figure that out when the time came.

34

Kira

THE GENERAL AWOKE FROM HER DREAM. ITS FACES AND voices, though foreign to her, had gifted her with understanding. Fluttering open her eyes, she beheld in the ruddy glow of torchlight the attentive stare of Shirab, the apothecary, who loomed over her like a scavenger bird above carrion. She tried to sit up, but at once her head spun, faint and dizzy.

"Easy, General," said Shirab. "You've bled a great deal. The nightmint I gave you will help restore your strength, but you must let the wound heal."

"Always overcautious, Shirab." Kira reached out her hand to Jamin. "Help me up." Jamin hesitated as Shirab cast a glare in his direction, but then the tall general shouldered past the brewer of elixirs and took Kira's hand. With help from the healer, Jamin raised her to her feet. Taking stock of the situation, she realized that most of her forces had advanced to the very edge of the entrenchments, perhaps wary of approaching closer to the gate for fear of provoking a barrage by the Eav'oq.

The stars above told her it was just after midnight.

Jamin spoke softly, his concern tempered by discretion. "Are you all right?"

"I'm but hurt," she said. "Get me a mount. We ride for the gate." Sensing his confusion and reluctance, she added, "Now."

Gritty sensations tickled her skin while she waited for Jamin to procure her a *zhom*. Recalling her collision with the ground after Jayol had been so callously slain beneath her, she realized that her armor and robes had likely become logged with grit and dust. Her armor's breastpiece and backpiece had been removed, probably by Shirab while he had tended to her wound. The two pieces lay on a blanket next to where she herself had been set down. Spying her squire, Zeir, passing nearby, she called out to her and bid her to help fix her armor.

The squire was securing the last of the straps that held the two pieces in place when Jamin returned with a fresh *zhom*.

Their ride to the gate was slow. Each gentle, padding step of her reddish-brown steed provoked flares of pain in her wound.

When they at last arrived at the gate, Kira said to Jamin, "Help me down." He dismounted, moved to her side, and took her hand as she eased herself off the saddle to the ground.

She let go of his hand, took a few steps forward, and kneeled beneath the gatehouse. "Gatekeeper," she cried. "Opaka!"

Without delay, Opaka Sulan and the gatekeeper appeared high above, peering down from the high rampart.

Kira shouted up to them, "I was mistaken." Her voice was dry and hoarse. "This is not our fortress," she said.

"We built upon the same bedrock, the Bajora and the Eav'oq, and the great towers we've made look much alike at first glance. We both share this natural foundation . . . but this place is yours."

Opaka replied, "What is your wish, then? To withdraw? To return to your own fortress and leave the Eav'oq to defend theirs?"

"No," Kira said. "My army will make its stand here, against the Ascendants."

"We have not asked this of you," the Gatekeeper said.

"Regardless," Kira said, "it will be done. To defend your foundation is to defend our own." She stopped. Her mouth was dry; blood loss had left her parched. She swallowed hard and continued, "Let us stand with you. Seeing your keep might help us better know our own, and our passion to defend it might show you how precious it truly is."

Kira extended her hand to Jamin, who helped her back to her feet. Calling up to Opaka and the gatekeeper, she added, "A hand can wield a weapon of war, and it can be extended in friendship. I come to you with my hands open, on behalf of all my people. But even if you will not take our hand, we will still make our stand here—in the open, without defenses—when the Ascendants come. I pledge to defend you with Bajoran faith and blood. And all I ask in return . . . is that you take my hand in friendship."

Opaka and the gatekeeper returned in silence to the gatehouse. Kira wondered whether they had listened to her at all. Then, from behind the gates, came the deep clang and clack of massive mechanical levers and gears moving, unlocking, retracting. Grinding shrieks of metal, scraping groans of wood and stone . . . and with a screech of iron against bedrock, a sliver of firelight appeared in a gap between the towering gates as they swung outward, opening toward Kira and Jamin.

As the gate doors parted and spread wide, the short but radiant form of Opaka appeared in the warm glow of light flooding out from inside the fortress. She walked out and approached Kira. The older woman was unarmed, and there was no hint of challenge in her manner. Arriving in front of Kira, she extended her own hand. Kira grasped it.

"Stand with us," Opaka said. "Bring your people into the fortress of Idran."

Kira nodded to Jamin, who turned and waved back across the trenches to the rest of the army, signaling them to come forward into the keep. As he gathered up the reins for his and Kira's mounts, Kira let Opaka lead her through the gates, into the bustling clamor of Idran.

Its towers and blockhouses were alive with wordless song, an unnerving siren-call of rising and falling scales and musical circumlocutions. The crash of water, the sound of complex machinery, the clatter of wheels rolling over flagstone, all of it was overlaid by the unearthly voices and their seemingly atonal melodies. Thousands of Eav'oq moved about inside the keep, some walking the roads in peculiar bobbing gaits, propelled along by several of their ribbonlike appendages. Others climbed between levels, using their limbs like prehensile coils, their bodies surprisingly agile and limber.

The lines of the structures inside the walls were unlike anything Kira had seen inside Parek Tonn: Whatever doubts might have lurked in the back of her mind about the Eav'oq's claims vanished as she beheld this alien architecture. Water-powered platforms for lifting supplies, water-driven clocks, ornate bridgework spanning several sectors of the interior . . . it was a marvel of engineering, a masterwork in stone, wood, and iron.

Opaka led Kira up a tall and curving staircase to one of the lower battlements, which looked out on one side toward the Fields of Berzel, and on the other down into the city behind the gates. As Kira's eyes scanned the courtyard of Idran and then its battlements and towers, it was what she didn't see anywhere that most caught her attention—and fueled her alarm.

She turned to Opaka. "Where are the armaments?"

"What armaments?" Opaka asked, her tone sincere.

"The trebuchet, the ballista, the archers, the pikemen— how do the Eav'oq plan to repel the Ascendant siege?"

"They don't," Opaka said. "The Eav'oq are pacifists. They will not end sentient life, for any reason."

"They said they'd defended this place against the Ascendants before!"

"And they had," Opaka said. "By concealing it . . . by hiding the road that led here. But now that road is exposed, and the Eav'oq cannot hide the fortress any longer."

As the Bajoran troops marched swiftly in a narrow column toward the gates of Idran, panic swelled in Kira's heart. *Arrows against siege engines? What kind of strategy is that?* She and Jamin would have less than two hours to plan a defense before the Ascendants arrived. It would not be enough.

The Ascendants would have every advantage—superior numbers, better weapons, and the ability to strike unanswered from a distance. Kira tried to tally the advantages of her position and concluded that there were none.

In the darkest hour of night, the battle would be engaged.

Watching the Ascendant army lurch closer with each passing minute, Kira tightened her grip on her sword and let go of any hope that she would live to see the dawn.

35

Harkoum—Grennokar

DESCENDING INTO THE DARKNESS, TARAN'ATAR LOOKED UP.

He was being pursued.

On one side of the massive circular complex, opposite his position, a freight platform had begun its slow crawl downward. Directly above him, along a track parallel to the one that his own lift platform was following, a second elevator cab trailed his. Beyond the lattice of metalwork at the top of the line, a firefight's telltale flashes came and went like fireworks.

Rushing gusts of air and the low mechanical grind of the elevator were all he could hear, but *that* voice—*her* voice—taunted him in his memories. The stimulants he'd injected on the ship were already proving unequal to the fatigue in his limbs and the confusion in his mind. He wanted to shroud, fade away, disappear into the smoke and shadows until he reached his destination . . . but he couldn't focus enough to shroud. The great talent bestowed on his kind by the Founders remained out of his reach. Without invisibility, he would have to rely on stealth and speed to evade his pursuers.

I still do not know where I am going . . . or why.

More troubling to him than the fatigue, or the loss of focus, or even the shattering of his faith in the Founders themselves was the utter uncertainty of his objective. All his life he had lived under a code of order and discipline. Guided by the chain of command, never in his life had he ever labored without knowing *why.*

The reason had been simple: A Founder wished it. The Vorta commanded it. His First gave him an order. Nothing more had ever been necessary for Taran'atar. In his opinion, complex justifications and nuanced rationales had been for those afraid to act. Appeals to free will had been a sop for those who'd lacked the discipline to obey orders.

Then his shoulder had snapped Ro's back. His knife had leaped from his hand and pierced Captain Kira's heart. Awash in her own blood, she had looked up at him with dying eyes, and his lifetime of oaths and loyalty had been forfeit.

There was no guilt in him as he thought, *I betrayed Odo.*

Part of him wondered whether Odo might not have intended this all along. *He wanted me to observe and comprehend these people and their cultures. They prize free will; they act irrationally and defy authority. Is this what he wanted me to learn?* The paradox of his rationalization struck him. *Have I done Odo's will by defying it?*

The more he pondered it, the less implausible it seemed.

Perhaps the Founders guided me to this outcome, he told himself. *Odo sent me into exile to test my will. The imprisoned Founder denied her divinity to test my faith.* He looked down at his hands and thought of all they had wrought in the past day. *Maybe they have always meant for me to be free. A test. To see if I remain loyal when I have the freedom to betray them.*

If his suspicions were true, then he felt cruelly manipulated—enough to justify willfully abandoning his life of service for the unfettered existence of a renegade.

However, if his theory was no more than a pathetic excuse, then he had tricked himself and deserved to languish for the rest of his days as a pariah.

Lingering knots of heavy vapor swallowed his lift platform as it neared the bottom of the pit. The vast space that loomed larger above Taran'atar with each passing second was obscured from his view by the reddish haze, and the hoarse turning of the lift gears was lost in a thumping din of arcane machines that rose up around him.

As the brakes began to engage, he told himself the truth.

I am not here for Odo. And I am not here because I wish to be. I am here because she commanded me to come . . . and because I cannot refuse. He pictured her face. His fists and jaw clenched.

I have come because I am a slave.

Every second of the ride down, Vaughn's knees shook a little bit more. Thanks to whatever scrambling field was at work in the lower levels of this place, his tricorder was useless for scanning. He tucked it away.

His eyes had adjusted slightly to the dimness of the lower levels of the pit. He saw another elevator descending a kilometer or two below him. Moments later, he caught sight of second lowering platform directly above it, at a slightly higher level than his own. He took the field scope from his chest pocket and peered at the lower elevator. Riding on it was a burly humanoid figure. He couldn't make out any more detail than that, but he was certain that it was Taran'atar. Shifting his gaze upward, he couldn't discern anything except the bottom of the trailing platform. If there was someone on it, he couldn't see any sign of them.

If somebody's up there, they're not shooting at me, so no point in drawing their attention, he decided.

Soon he would reach the bottom of this hellhole. Each level he passed was a labyrinth of identical-looking corridors and dark, decrepit cells. Knowing the Cardassians' pre-Dominion War reputation for Kafkaesque jurisprudence in general, and the Obsidian Order's predilections in particular, Vaughn shuddered to imagine what kinds of physical and psychological horrors had been conceived in this benighted abscess of the universe. How many lives had vanished into this place? How many people had drawn their last breaths here while dreaming of homes under distant stars? For his entire career in Starfleet, Vaughn had lived with the risk that a mission gone wrong could land him in a place of horrors such as this; as he fell farther from daylight with each passing moment, he realized, with morbid irony, that in fact it just had.

The neuro-pulse mechanism was still tucked on his belt. He lifted the flattened-hourglass-shaped device and accustomed his hand to its weight. It lacked the clean balance of a phaser. *I hope this thing works.* He didn't even want to imagine what would be a worst-case scenario for a brain-altering device's effects on an already unhinged Jem'Hadar.

Even if it works, he wondered, *what do I do then? What do I say to keep him from killing me?* He didn't want to lie to Taran'atar. It would insult his intelligence to pretend there wouldn't be consequences for what he did to Kira and Ro; the mitigating factor of external mind-control would be unable to reforge the broken bonds of trust between Taran'atar and the rest of the crew on Deep Space 9. *I'm no exception,* Vaughn confessed to himself. *So what if he was being controlled? He was lucid enough to choose his tactics. Calm enough to kidnap Prynn. Focused enough to trick me into killing her. Am I supposed to forgive all his sins just because he serves a new devil?*

Vaughn focused on bringing in Taran'atar alive, and exposing Intendant Kira for her role in the attack on Captain Kira and Lieutenant Ro and the massacre of the Sidau Village on Bajor. More than a century of living had taught Vaughn not to hang on to anger; it was poison for the soul. But the part of him that was still raging and mired in anguish, the grieving father in him, wasn't listening to reason. All he could do was hope that, when he caught up to Taran'atar, he would have the strength to keep his fury in check and the courage to reach for the neuro-pulse device and not his phaser.

More than a minute after the lower platform vanished into the thick haze in the bottom of the pit, Vaughn's lift was swiftly enshrouded in the obscuring lake of roiling gases. His best guess was that he would have at least four minutes' head start on whoever was on the lift above his.

He secured the neuro-pulse device on his belt and lifted his phaser rifle. He would have to track Taran'atar into this labyrinth the old-fashioned way.

The lift thudded and bounced to a halt. Its sliding, wire-mesh safety-cage gate clattered open.

It was roughly one-point-seven kilometers to the other lifts' arrival points. There was no way to tell which way Taran'atar had gone after touching down. And for all Vaughn knew, he was walking into a trap—there could be dozens of hostiles waiting to intercept him.

Keeping his eyes in motion on his surroundings, he crouched as low as was comfortable and moved out, rifle at the ready.

****

Lieutenant Quin Heins had never been one to cling to a bad idea when a better one was available. So, when the strike team started taking fire from above, he gave the order to break for cover, sparse as it was, farther inside the facility.

Shots raced every which way as the strike team charged in.

Heins tried to be at least slightly cautious, but Moore charged headlong, snapping off shots with his sidearm in every direction and relying on the weapon's IFF circuit to prevent him from accidentally stunning one of his own comrades. The scattering field inside the facility prevented their weapons' targeting sensors from locking on to targets, but Moore was more than capable of lining up his shots the old-fashioned way—with a sharp eye and plenty of patience.

Winded from the zigzagging sprint, Heins ducked behind a metal barrier next to Minecci and Stov. The Vulcan was stoically tending a disruptor wound to his foot that he had suffered on the charge forward. Minecci peeked up over the edge of the barrier and snapped off another shot at whoever was lighting up their position with plasma-blast ricochets.

Heins fired off his own volley, then said, "You guys okay?"

Minecci nodded. "Solid."

"My wound is superficial," Stov said. "I can continue."

"All right, you'll cover us," Heins said. "Minecci, we'll flank right to that empty guard post. Take point on my go."

"Aye, sir."

Several meters away, tucked between two towering stacks of empty metallic shipping containers, Neeley, Gervasi, and

Thron fended off their own barrage of disruptor fire from several locations. With a quick wave, Heins got Neeley's attention; he telegraphed his intentions with a few simple gestures. She gave him a thumbs-up and indicated her group would lay down suppressing fire for his run. He nodded.

Turning to Minecci and Stov, he held up three fingers, then folded them down: Three . . . two . . . one. "Go!"

Phaser noise rang like a clarion as Stov and the others opened fire, blanketing enemy positions with short blasts intended to keep their foes' heads down while kicking up sparks, smoke, and dust. Heins and Minecci sprinted toward the guard post.

A blast of enemy fire came from an unexpected position. The first shot clipped Minecci's knee. The second slammed into Heins's shoulder like a hammer made of fire and spun him half-around. Both men stumbled and landed hard on the narrow catwalk, sitting ducks for whoever had just sniped them.

Another pulse-weapon shot came from the opposite direction and passed over their heads. By its angle, Heins knew it hadn't been aimed at them. Whoever had fired it wasn't part of the Starfleet strike team but had just eliminated an enemy sniper from a range of more than a kilometer.

There was no time to look around and search the shadows. Heins grabbed Minecci's arm and pulled him to cover near the guard station. Only when they were shielded did Heins spare a moment to peer through his own targeting sight in search of whoever had just saved his and Minecci's lives.

A dim shape, vaguely feminine in profile, slipped out of sight in a location where there was no stairway. Whoever she was, she was agile enough to risk climbing through the open metal framework between the top deck and the next sublevel.

Have to remember to thank her, he thought. Another volley of hostile fire tore across the far side of the guard post. *If I get out of here alive, that is.*

Vaughn moved through the corridors of Grennokar's bottommost level, senses sharp, his rifle drifting back and forth in a slow arc ahead of him. His knees hurt. His back was stiff, and he had forgotten how heavy a phaser rifle could start to seem when one had been holding it for too long. Featureless walls stretched between unoccupied rooms and identical intersections. Wind moaned through the concourses, disturbing the hanging emergency lights. Empty stretches of gray floor receded and curved away into the distance at every turn.

Hands taut on his weapon, Vaughn listened to every random sound in the open rooms around him. Drips of water from broken pipes. The snap of sparks from a damaged computer panel. Papers fluttering in wayward breezes. The skitters and shrieks of voles scrambling over a pile of broken, sodden furniture. An open door on a cabinet creaked slowly back and forth, buffeted by the airflow from a ventilation duct.

No other footsteps except his own, lightly splashing in the puddles that dotted the passageway.

Another set of rooms opened up on his left. They were burned shells, filled with the charcoal-hued remains of what Vaughn guessed might have been a research lab. He remembered what Rahim had said about the Cardassians using their prisoners for experimentation; Ruriko herself had filed reports describing such things during her undercover work in Cardassian space.

Motion on his right. He turned and aimed.

A junction relay dangled from the ceiling, suspended at the end of a tangle of optronic cable. More detritus scattered across flooded floors, more fire-gutted walls and overturned remnants of what resembled an office.

Reaching the next intersection, Vaughn prepared to continue forward toward the far side of the facility when a dim blue glow on his right captured his attention. His eyes struggled to pick details from the cobalt twilight. All he could glean was the impression of a larger, more open space, one that perhaps had been spared the ravages he had so far seen on this level.

Starfleet protocol recommended that he continue forward, then track Taran'atar from his last known position.

Instinct made him turn right.

He was hyperaware of the sound of his own breathing. *Remember your training.* He forced himself to relax and not hold his breath. As he got closer to the dark-blue warren of spaces ahead of him, he began to see patterns and shapes emerge. In the middle of the sprawling lab were rows of tall, cylindrical containers, all of them linked by thick bundles of cables, tubing, and pipes to a vast network of machinery that dominated the elevated ceiling. High banks of computer consoles blocked his view of the cylinders, which he quickly realized were the source of the intense blue-violet illumination that bathed the room in sapphire hues.

Vaughn halted. The space was too open for his comfort.

He took a knee and tried using his tricorder. Flurries of garbled data hashed across its display. He turned it off and tucked it away. Pressing the stock of his rifle against his shoulder, he peered through its holographic targeting scope. Its crosshairs panned slowly across the periphery of the room. No movement. No telltale shadows. He kept his rifle in ready position as he stole forward, into the main part of the lab.

The cylinders rose up in front of him as he cleared the corner of the computer bank. Stenciled on their sides in Cardassian characters was the name of this facility: Grennokar. As the transparent fronts of the cylinders came into view, he gazed into their cerulean radiance and stopped walking.

Inside the cylinders, floating in thick fluids percolating with slow-rising bubbles and shining under the intense blue glare of stasis field emitters, were dozens of Jem'Hadar.

There were adults and adolescents. A few had open wounds where their ketracel-white shunts had been located. Some bore injuries that looked combat-related. Others were marred by the gruesome scars of autopsy. All of them drifted in the eerie blue energy fields, unmoving, eyes open but unseeing.

All dead, he realized. *Test subjects.* Revulsion knitted Vaughn's brow with anger.

He passed by the first row of ten cylinders. The second row was flush against it. Past that was an open space, in the center of which stood a metallic, bed-sized, blood-crusted platform surrounded by trays and rolling drawers filled with surgical instruments. Above it was a bank of several independently focusable light fixtures. The air here was cold and had the bite of sterilizing antiseptic. Everything except the platform shone like it had never been used, but Vaughn knew otherwise.

On the other side of the surgical platform was another pair of back-to-back cylinder rows. From where Vaughn was standing, all of them appeared full, just like the ones behind him.

In front of each cylinder was a small interface panel. He moved to the nearest one and checked to see if it had power. It sprang to life at his touch and presented a dense block of information—in Bajoran. Vaughn had seen enough of the language in the past year to recognize it when he saw it, but not enough to read it without a translation aid. Searching the rest of the interface, he noticed an icon indicating that the page had been translated from a Cardassian document.

He reverted to the Cardassian version. He wasn't exactly fluent in that language, but he'd picked up enough of it during the eighteen years of the Betreka Nebula fiasco to be able to glean the important details from most documents.

The display in front of the cylinder was packed with technical information about the subject, such as his Jem'Hadar name and rank, morbidly clinical vivisection findings, the details of where and when the subject had been hatched, and where he had been captured.

The abundance of data did not surprise Vaughn; Cardassians were notorious for their attention to detail. What surprised him was the fact that it had been translated into Bajoran . . . then he remembered Cenn's revelation that Taran'atar had transmitted data about the alternate universe.

The Intendant knew enough about Jem'Hadar brainwave patterns to control Taran'atar, he thought. *Looks like this is where she did her homework.*

Time was short; intercepting Taran'atar was a priority. But Vaughn knew that it was equally vital to preserve what he'd just found. He fished the tricorder from his pockets and tapped with mounting impatience on the Cardassian display interface, trying to make the two devices talk to one another. Fortunately, the strides that the Deep Space 9 team had made over the past eight years in reconciling Starfleet and Cardassian software made the task much easier than it might have been before they had assumed control of the abandoned Cardassian space station.

The download progressed quickly. Vaughn was relieved that whatever was preventing him from using the active scanners of the device didn't interfere with data-transfer operations. *With all these computers down here, I guess that wasn't an option.*

Whoever had most recently been working in this lab had disabled all the mainframes' encryptions and lockouts—another piece of evidence that suggested an interloper even as it speeded the download. His tricorder display flashed an "operation complete" symbol on its display, which then went dark again, back into stealth mode. He put it back in his pocket.

Time to get moving, Vaughn told himself.

He continued toward the other side of the lab. At the far exit, he paused. He leaned sideways and peeked down the dark corridor. In the steam-occluded gray distance was a steel-frame staircase—and a fleeting glimpse of a Jem'Hadar moving swiftly past it, alone and armed with a handheld weapon.

Vaughn checked his rifle's setting. Heavy stun. He moved out into the long, straight stretch of metal walls and decks, his every step echoing his presence.

Overhead lights stuttered on and off. The drone and thump of air-circulators grew more oppressive as he neared the corner. Before peeking out to scout Taran'atar's position, he crouched low, then leaned out, his head at around knee-level.

A phaser shot hit the corner centimeters above his head. He recoiled as sparks, dust, and smoke erupted in front of him.

Dammit, he fumed. *Didn't even see where it came from.*

He backed up a few steps. Got a running start. Rolled across the passage, to the shadows under the staircase.

On one aching knee, he aimed his weapon between two steps. He surveyed a multilevel labyrinth of crisscrossed metal stairways, ladders, catwalks, and corridors. Resetting the holographic sight to infrared, he swept the industrial vista again, but it all glowed with ambient heat, more than warm enough to mask the glow of most humanoids. Viewed in nightvision, the somber crimson glow turned pale blue-gray but was brightened by only a small degree. The entire facility flickered with spectral light.

Still there was no sign of Taran'atar. *Maybe he's shrouded,* Vaughn realized. *If he's invisible . . . he could be anywhere. Right next to me.* He shook off those paranoid suspicions. *Can't think like that, it just leads to paralysis. Have to keep moving.*

Leaving cover seemed foolhardy. Knowing that Taran'atar could be anywhere in this infernal complex—perhaps invisible—brought home to Vaughn just how vulnerable he was, alone down here, without backup or an exit plan other than a miraculous victory in close quarters against a Jem'Hadar elder.

Well, if I have to do this blind . . . so will he.

Vaughn swiftly sniped the light fixtures in the immediate area. Darkness fell, oppressive and gravelike. To the best of Vaughn's knowledge, Jem'Hadar could not see in total darkness any better than most other species. And he had not seen any weapons larger than handheld devices when Taran'atar had passed the stairway, so it was unlikely that he had one with a targeting scope. It was a thin advantage, but it was all that Vaughn had. With a dark road cleared to the next major point of cover, he set the targeting sight for a dim display, so as not to give away his own position, then he peered through it with one unblinking eye as he advanced.

Thirty seconds later he was back under cover. He scanned the two possible directions that Taran'atar could have followed from this intersection. One led back toward the upper levels. Vaughn ruled that out. *Why go to the bottom level only to climb back up on foot?* The other direction sloped downward, into the engineering sublevel beneath the center of the complex. The very nadir of the pit.

He lifted his rifle and scouted the path. Pitch dark. Barren, no cover until emerging at the far end, and no telling what would be available there.

It was the perfect place to walk into an ambush.

Nothing for it, he told himself. *That's the mission.*

He followed his rifle into the stifling gloom.

Every step made his heart pound more ferociously. His pulse was hard and painful in his temples. He felt his breath catch in his chest. It was like a bad dream, plodding anxiously down a corridor that seems to grow longer and whose end retreats from you, no matter how hard you run.

Then he stood at the end, at the corner, his back to the wall, his rifle clutched tight, the emitter crystal down. Here the passage opened into a depthless maze of pressure vessels and snaking conduits, all of it deeply alive with the thrum of machine systems and the hiss of rushing gases and fluids. Broken light filtered down from above, through multiple layers of steel mesh and overlapping arrays of pipework and structural supports. The floor was ankle deep with filthy, chemical-slicked water.

Ripples in the water were already dissipating. Vaughn studied them through the rifle scope, watching how they overlapped, noting where they were long or short, observing their intervals. His best guess was that Taran'atar had gone left, but the signs were unclear. Steeling himself, he waded cautiously into the final sublevel, moving slowly to avoid kicking up any splashes that would reveal his position.

He ducked through a gap between two enormous storage tanks. A disruptor shot ricocheted off the pipes near his head, and he hit the deck. More shots lanced out of the darkness.

Crawling on hands and knees in the ammonia-laced water, he took refuge under one of the storage tanks. Another short barrage showered his location in ephemeral orange sparks.

He tried to determine where Taran'atar was firing from. A few seconds later, he found it—a raised platform in the middle of the sublevel, with solid barricades around it. An extremely defensible position.

Some fortuitously placed auxiliary tanks shielded Vaughn for the moment, but as soon as Taran'atar realized that Vaughn was unable to retaliate from here, he would no doubt shift to a better vantage point. Vaughn knew that he had to take the high ground before that happened.

He craned his neck and looked up. Narrow ladders scaled the curving exteriors of all the largest storage tanks, leading to catwalks that ringed them near their upper quarter, roughly twelve meters above ground. *If I can reach one of those,* Vaughn realized, *I can get into firing position without breaking cover.*

Scaling the ladder, however, posed another problem. He had no way to get to it without exposing himself to an easy shot—not unless he could keep Taran'atar busy while he made the climb.

He took the tricorder from his belt and worked quickly. Within moments, he turned it into a remote-control for his phaser rifle. Perching the slaved weapon securely across two parallel pipes, he test-fired it with the tricorder control. It snapped off a quick series of shots that scoured Taran'atar's redoubt on the platform. Vaughn selected a minute-long, randomized firing sequence, then moved into position for his jump to the ladder.

He waited for a few return volleys of fire from Taran'atar, then he triggered the sequence. The rifle screeched as it unleashed a staccato barrage on the center platform.

Vaughn clambered out from under the storage tank, grasped the rungs of the ladder on its side, and started climbing. He was exhausted already, his shoulders and thighs raging with the burn of lactic acid buildup in the muscles.

Below him, the rifle's onslaught continued. In the back of his mind, he counted off the seconds and urged himself upward.

As he pulled himself onto the level catwalk near the top of the storage tank, the phaser rifle's firing sequence ended. He crouched low and waited until he heard a few return shots from Taran'atar's weapon. Then he used his tricorder to select a new firing pattern, triggered it, and lurked forward.

He held the tricorder in his left hand and lifted the neuro-pulse device from his belt with his right. Leishman had advised him that its effective range was roughly five meters; Vaughn figured that when he reached the end of the storage tank, he'd be just barely in range. He promised himself he wouldn't hesitate when he got there; he would aim and take the shot.

The front curve of the storage tank was directly ahead of him. If he stood up, he would still be almost entirely behind cover, but he should have a clear shot at Taran'atar.

A few seconds later, his rifle's second firing sequence ended. He waited for Taran'atar to stand or lean out from cover to return fire. There was no sound from below, however.

Sick with dread, Vaughn put away his tricorder and slowly straightened, steadying the neuro-pulse emitter with both hands. He cleared the curve of the tank and aimed downward to take the shot. His view of the center platform was all but omniscient.

Taran'atar wasn't there.

Vaughn sensed disaster coming, like a wave at night, dark and inevitable. Survival instinct compelled him to pivot about-face, the device at eye level.

Silently and faster than Vaughn could fire, Taran'atar deflected the neuro-pulse device down and aside, against the storage tank. The impact shattered the bones in Vaughn's right forearm. He cried out in agony as the device tumbled away. It smashed on the flooded concrete floor below.

Taran'atar backhanded Vaughn, knocking the old man to the edge of the catwalk. Vaughn's footing slipped, and he slid beneath the railing. Flailing about with his left hand, Vaughn grasped a vertical beam. He dangled off the edge as Taran'atar moved forward, drawing a phaser from his belt.

The auxiliary tank that had shielded Vaughn minutes earlier was directly below him. He let go of the railing. His ankle twisted slightly as he struck the curved top of the smaller tank. He landed with excruciating force on his broken arm, slid down the side, and splashed onto the hard, puddled floor. He hobbled back toward his rifle.

Like a meteor crashing into the sea, Taran'atar dropped in a crouch to the ground directly ahead of Vaughn. The impact of his landing launched a crown of water. He straightened, eyes gleaming with violence, standing between Vaughn and escape. A fleeting shaft of light glinted off the phaser in his hand.

Backpedaling, Vaughn knew that he was only delaying the inevitable. Behind him was a dead end of overlapping pipes and valves, a wall of machinery. He stepped on something oily under the surface; his balance faltered. He fell backward and landed hard. Pain shot through his hips and back as he crabbed in reverse across the floor, pushing himself with his feet and one good hand, through the gray-brown water, away from the advancing Jem'Hadar.

Vaughn's back struck something hard. He had nowhere left to run.

Taran'atar quickened his pace and aimed the phaser at Vaughn. Then a flash of energized plasma sizzled past Taran'atar's shoulder and caromed off the pipes above Vaughn's head. The Jem'Hadar spun to face his new foe.

Vaughn didn't dare believe what he saw.

Standing ten meters away, Prynn held her pulse pistol aimed squarely at Taran'atar. "Drop your weapons," she commanded in a deadly tone. "And get away from my father."

36

Kira

SURVEYING THE BATTLEFIELD FROM THE WALLS OF IDRAN, General Kira Nerys looked out upon thousands of pinpoints of flame gathered in the darkness like a sinister vigil.

Even before the fires had been lit, the coming of the Ascendants had been announced by the steady beat of war drums, deep and powerful, like the pounding of a frightened heart shaking the foundation of the world. Cries of trumpets and other terrifying, otherworldly noises rose from the shimmering ranks of the approaching army. Roars from their giant lizards split the night and provoked panicked howls from the legion of *zhoms* huddled with their riders behind the fortress's gate.

At Kira's request, the Eav'oq had withdrawn from the battlements and sought refuge in the blockhouses and towers behind the walls, leaving the ramparts clear for her archers to deploy. On either side of her, the wooden creaks of bows being strung was met by the squeaks of pulleys, as the fletchers hoisted buckets of battle-arrows up to the archers, who set them in long rows between the crenellations. Whetstones rasped against the bright edges of blades being sharpened for combat.

Bitter smoke, invisible against the curtain of night, wafted up from the Ascendant army, which stomped to a halt. The war drums fell silent. A lone rider, traveling under the white banner of parley, weaved through the narrow paths that crossed the deep entrenchments. As she drew within fifty *pates* of the gate, Kira called down to her, "That's far enough. Speak."

The rider reined in her reptilian mount, which was smaller than those that carried soldiers. It was longer and leaner and clearly capable of carrying only one person. The creature made a rasping growl-snort as it halted. Its rider, an Ascendant herald, shouted back up to Kira, "Abandon this fortress now, and your deaths will be merciful."

"We will not surrender," Kira said.

"Your presence here is a heresy," the herald said, her scorn evident. "Those who dare the fortress must die and burn."

"I would offer you the same counsel," Kira said.

"Renounce your heresy," the herald said. "Open the gate."

"Never."

At that the herald guided her slender lizard to turn about, and she wound her way back through the paths to rejoin the rest of the Ascendant army in the dim firelight beyond the trenches.

Kira nodded to Jamin, who stood several dozen paces away on the same lower rampart. In his booming baritone, he called out for all to hear, "Archers! Stand ready!"

Four thousand arrows were nocked against creaking sinews.

Jamin bellowed down into the courtyard, "Brace the gate!"

Every squire and noncombatant member of her army surged forward to set angled supports against the mighty, iron-banded gates. The ends of the braces were sunk an arm's length into the ground, and dozens of men added their weight to each one, while dozens more in a tight line pressed their shoulders against the gates themselves.

In the enemy ranks, the blazes of fire grew larger and brighter. Clarion calls resounded. War drums resumed their unflagging thunder of death on the march. A single voice, amplified by means of a hollowed-out tusk from a giant tundra *kulloth,* called out a terse battle cry: "Die and burn!"

And the Ascendants began their assault. They raced forward, their infantry leading the charge, winding through the few paths between the trenches. To the Bajoran archers, Jamin called out, "Hold!" Until the Ascendants reached the last stretch of the path—the one and only that led out of the trench paths to the gates—they would be out of range. But as they emerged onto the open slope beneath the battlements, they would converge in a bottleneck, just at the edge of the longbows' reach.

It was a strategy that had served Parek Tonn well, and it promised to prove equally fortuitous for Idran.

Then several dozen eyes of fire blinked open in the sky. Blazing missiles, hurled aloft by the Ascendants' trebuchets. Just as Ghavun had warned, these massive siege batteries were more powerful than any the Bajora had ever known.

In all the battles Kira had seen—and there had been many—never had she witnessed a catapult that could strike a target from much more than a third of a *kellipate.* But the Ascendants had just fired a massive salvo from nearly two-thirds of a *kellipate*—and judging by its azimuth and trajectory, it was on-target for the walls and heart of Idran.

She could order her men to take cover, but then the infantry below would advance up the slope unchallenged.

Fearful faces, anxious glances, all turned in her direction. She drew her sword and pointed at the charging infantry below, even as a storm of fire fell from above. "Aim!"

The infantry rounded the final turns toward the bottleneck—and halted. They were going to wait for the hammer to fall before finishing their charge.

"Cover!" Kira shouted, and she pressed herself against the battlement wall as the first salvo struck home.

Large sections of the lower battlement erupted in fire and were blown to pieces. Rock fragments whizzed past in every direction. Metal spheres, studded with spikes and sheathed in flames, slammed into the curved towers, shattered the spans of delicate bridges, broke apart on impact, and unleashed sprays of caustic acid and sulfuric brimstone. Fractures spiderwebbed through the outer walls from parapet to foundation. Bodies fell in wide arcs, hurled into the air, broken and burned, some dead already, others crying out in terror as they plummeted to the ground far below. Thunderous crashes exploded one after another. Sparks and cinders fell like fiery rain.

Then the barrage from afar paused for a breath, and the shuddering booms of rams striking the gate began.

"Archers!" Jamin shouted above the pandemonium. "Fire!"

Even in all the flames and carnage, thousands of longbowmen rose from the ashes, drew back their arms, and unleashed a dark storm on the enemy troops below. That horrible *whoosh,* the banshee groan of an arrowflight that descended and tore gaping holes in the front ranks of the Ascendant charge . . . but another wave of bodies filled the empty spaces, like mercury flowing into a void.

The battering rams swung forward again. Each ram's head burned brightly. Every impact smeared the gate with another streak of flaming pitch. Already the iron bands of the gate glowed red with transmitted heat.

"Take out the rams," Kira ordered. Then another barrage of fireballs was hurled into the air by those distant engines of destruction. "Volley and cover!" she cried out above the din.

Another moaning fall of arrows interrupted the rams for a moment. Then the archers ducked to cover, and the onslaught against the gate resumed as another wave of fire and stone beat down on Idran from above.

Like the hammer of a dark god against its anvil, enormous rough-hewn boulders and polished spheres of studded iron fell on Idran with devastating power.

Upper wedges of the outer battlement were torn away. They rained down in man-sized bricks of broken rock on people and animals in the courtyard.

A crushing blow disintegrated the base of a tower in the heart of the fortress; it turned to a cloud of sand as it collapsed and crushed a half dozen more buildings. The roar of its falling swallowed the screams of the dying.

Sheets of burning oil turned the inner thoroughfares of Idran into pits of fire. Impenetrable black smoke vomited up into the night, turning all to flame and shadow.

The ramparts trembled under Kira's feet. At any moment, the entire upper third of the outer walls would fail. "Fall back!" She pointed to the upper battlements. "Go for high ground!" Catching Jamin's eye, she pointed with her blade toward the courtyard, where their *zhoms* awaited them.

Kira and Jamin scrambled down the curving staircase to the courtyard while their archers withdrew to the highest battlements of Idran. A few paused to fire a few more shafts at the enemy personnel battering the gate; then a new barrage of catapult shots hammered the lower battlements, whose ramparts crumbled and became a cascade of broken stone and dust.

Crossing the courtyard, Kira stumbled. Jamin reached out and steadied her. She nodded her thanks, and he let go of her. They neared their mounts. "We have to stop those trebuchets," she said.

"They're too far out of range," Jamin replied. "The archers can't hit them."

At the main gates, flames licked between the timbers, smoke poured from knots in the wood, and the iron bands and hinges glowed like the heart of a smith's furnace.

From the upper battlements, another cloud of arrows screamed down and disappeared beyond the broken outer walls, into the enemy ranks outside.

"In a few moments, those gates will fall," Kira said. "When they do, we charge."

Jamin was taken aback. "Through the trench paths?"

"It's the only way, Jamin," she said. "We have to destroy those siege engines. Without them, the Ascendants can't take the inner battlements. The archers can hold them here."

"It's a suicide charge," Jamin said as they reached her mount. He helped her into her saddle as he added, "They've held their archers and cavalry in reserve. When we try to cross the pathways to the Fields of Berzel—"

"You know of another way, Jamin?"

Another trebuchet assault pounded into the city.

The outer walls began to collapse.

Buildings within the walls imploded, belching up flames. Swirls of fire and acid rained down, searing man and beast.

The main gates splintered beneath another hit from the battering rams and buckled inward. Roaring geysers of flame climbed the gap between them as the crossbar bent and the angled supports snapped like twigs. The last few hardy souls who had been holding the line fled, shedding garments now set aflame.

"If we're going out the gate, we'll need momentum," Jamin said. He summoned two scuffed and singed foot soldiers.

"Round up a platoon," he told them. "Go over there and get behind that undetonated sphere. Roll it over here, in front of me. Go!" The men scrambled away, recruiting others as they ran toward the sphere. Within seconds, they had a team of ten strong backs pushing the sphere with them, rolling it in a mostly straight path, making slight detours around chunks of broken granite, until they wrestled it to a stop where Jamin had said.

They looked up to him for further instruction. He pointed at the gate. "Send out a squad to clear the path from here to the gate. When I give the order, roll the sphere toward the gate, as fast as you can, and let it go. Then get clear, because we'll all be right behind you."

It happened quickly, mostly because the men were thankful for anything to focus on other than the steady beat of rams against the crumbling gates, the distant pounding of war drums, the low rush of arrows cutting the air, the rhythmic death chants of the Ascendants poised to break through the gates and enter the fortress of Idran.

Another barrage stormed over the walls, and several shots landed in the midst of the cavalry formation. *Zhoms* howled with agony and rage, drowning out the pitiful cries of the dying men and women who had been struck down with them.

The last of the angled braces splintered and fell away. The crossbeam broke in twain. The iron bands came unbound, and all that clutched the timbers of the gates together was smoke and memory. Jamin dropped his arm and cried, "Forward!"

Infantrymen charged, pushing the sphere ahead of them, rolling it until it picked up speed on the slight downward grade to the gate and accelerated away from them. They dodged wide, sprinted clear. Kira raised her sword. "Cavalry . . . charge!"

She kicked her *zhom* and urged him forward into a full run. At her side, less than half a pace behind, Jamin raced with her into battle, his own sword extended behind him, tensed to strike and parry as the moment demanded. War whoops of men and the primal yowls of *zhoms* fused into a cacophony of rage.

The gates heaved inward, against the natural direction of the hinges, and parted almost wide enough for a man to pass through. Sword tips and spearheads lunged through, stabbing at nothing.

Then the massive steel sphere crashed into the gates, reduced them to smoky kindling and twisted metal, and rolled roughshod over the mass of troops gathered beyond. Its path swerved wildly as each new life it ground into the dust set it in a new direction. Fanatical as the Ascendants were, they had enough sense to dodge clear of the gargantuan, ersatz boulder, which rolled away to one side.

Kira urged her *zhom* toward the line of densely packed bodies blocking the gate. With a small tug on the reins, the animal leaped, cleared the shattered and burning debris on the ground, and plowed violently through the enemy's front rank. Kira swung her sword in a wide arc. It cut through a foe's exoskeleton and flesh with little resistance. She figureeighted her swing to sever the arm of another foe on her left. Her blade blurred through the dancing orange firelight.

Jamin's sword swung through the same narrow gap between their mounts, and more Ascendants fell.

But they were everywhere, on every side, rank upon rank, a vast throng, all regrouping swiftly and charging forward, pressing in on the racing cavalry. Bodies were trampled under heavy *zhom* feet, gored by the running strokes of daggerlike claws. Waves of tumbling bodies rippled away from the impact of the charge. Dozens of Ascendants were slammed aside into the trenches.

Hacking blows from Kira's sword felled bodies with every swing, but there was no time to parry counterattacks. Jabbing spears lunged at her; glancing strokes of swords slashed across her thighs. Speed and momentum were her only defenses.

Jamin guarded her left. His *zhom* and hers ran so close together that they could barely navigate the narrow passes through the trenches, but no enemies could come between them.

Side by side, they led the assault, pushing forward, battering a path through the hapless infantry who stood between them and the Fields of Berzel.

Huge ballista—missiles like oversized arrows—ripped through the air, striking with enough force to send *zhoms* and riders hurtling off the path and into the mass graves of the trenches.

A thrown spear arced out of the night. Kira twisted to her left and tried to bat it away with her sword. The wound in her back burned and bled, and she barely deflected a killing blow. The head of the spear gouged across the back of her neck. Hot, stinging pain turned to an excruciating burning as she pressed on.

Dull thuds shook her *zhom* as more Ascendant troops were knocked aside, into the depths, underfoot. Metal rang against metal, and wet sounds of carnage filled the night.

Then a droning roar rose ahead of them.

Low, like the cold breath of a mountain.

Deep as summer thunder rolling over the sea.

Arrowfall. The largest that Kira had ever heard.

And its pitch was rising.

The Ascendants had unleashed an arrow storm into their own infantry, apparently considering them expendable— acceptable losses in order to halt her cavalry charge.

There was no place to hide, no chance of turning back.

Kira drove on, sword flashing in the predawn starlight, committed to stay the course, to follow the path to its end.

A lucky thrust from the enemy jabbed a short blade up and under the breast piece of her armor. She felt its bite in her chest—

Death fell with a breathy hush.

Thousands of bodies, friend and foe alike, were pummeled to the ground by the arrow storm.

Silvery shafts impaled Kira's thighs, tore into her arms, sank deep into her torso. Her *zhom* was skewered from head to tail. The impact of arrows driving into his head all but nailed him to the ground, bringing him from a full run to a complete stop. Kira was thrown forward. Racked with pain, she lay in the blood-soaked dust and felt like she was drowning, trying to breathe underwater. Salty froth pooled in her throat.

Lifeblood ran from her. Unable to hold her hand closed, she let go of her sword. It tumbled over the edge of a trench and vanished into the shadowy abyss.

A wooden groan signaled another trebuchet volley. Dozens of burning orbs made their silent passage of the starscape and floated down toward Idran. Kira watched, her eyes too dry to shed tears, as the outer walls collapsed, the towers inside fell, and the final row of battlements began to succumb. Defeat was only a matter of time now. The Bajora had been eradicated, the Eav'oq exterminated, the fortress taken.

She turned her head. Jamin lay dying beside her. His legs were pinned beneath the quivering body of his *zhom,* Denigarro. As the sharp cadence of marching feet drew near, he opened his mouth and let the pooled blood drain. Barely able to form words, he rasped to Kira, "Not . . . enough. Should have had . . . allies."

Kira knew he was right. Defending the fortress had been a doomed proposition from the beginning. The only way to break the siege would have been to keep another force waiting in reserve, to strike the Ascendants from the rear after they had committed themselves. *Too late now,* Kira knew. *No second chances.*

Wedged under the breast piece of her armor was the grip of a dagger, of a kind she had never seen, sunk into her chest up to its crossguard. She had expected the arrows, but the blade in her chest had been a surprise; she had never seen it coming.

Vision and strength failed her. The fight was over.

Ascendant soldiers gathered above her, their alien faces and eyes of golden fire showing her neither pity nor respect.

She let go of breath and of life and allowed her *pagh* to be borne away on wings of darkness, back whence she came, into the uncreated womb of night.

Illumination was everywhere; light was everything and everyone. There were no more dark places, no shadows, no shades of gray, no taint of the ambiguous. Luminous truth was in every thought. The hand of the Prophets grasped the future and was one with its terrible beauties.

For a moment, the Prophets eschewed their masks. No speaking in tongues, no adopted faces. Kira's vision resolved itself in her mind, and she saw in it the shape of things that never were, and of things that might yet come to pass. The future was malleable, fluid in its designs, its potential like ink on a quill, waiting for a hand to guide it to paper and set its form.

Waiting for the hand of the Prophets.

She did not need to ask if They could hear her. They were with her, and she could sense Them within her and without. All was seen and heard, and Their will was manifest in her *pagh*.

From the white void a small form grew larger and resolved itself into the image of Opaka. "Our hand is in motion."

"I understand," Kira said. "I'm ready."

Then, like a fond memory brought to mind, Sisko was beside her. His hand on her shoulder was warm and comforting, but his voice resonated with a grim warning. "No, you're not," he said. "No one is *ever* ready."

37

Harkoum—Grennokar

THE PULSE PISTOL SHOOK IN PRYNN'S HAND. SHE HAD expected to find someone from Starfleet here fighting Taran'atar, but seeing her father had pummeled her with an unexpected mix of emotions: surprise at the seeming co-incidence of it; sudden terror that he was in harm's way; and, most shocking to her, an almost childlike elation that her father had charged into the darkness to protect her from monsters both real and imagined. The irony that she had become his rescuer did not dilute her pride in him.

Taran'atar's amber gaze was locked on her, cold and unflinching. "Drop your weapons," she repeated, the confidence in her voice starting to waver. "Toss them away—carefully."

With an attitude that bordered on the cavalier, the hulking Jem'Hadar discarded his phaser with a flick of his wrist. The weapon vanished into the grayish muck beneath a storage tank. He reached for the Klingon disruptor tucked in his belt.

"Thumb and one finger only," Prynn said.

Never taking his eyes off her, Taran'atar did as she said. He flung the pistol-type weapon away. It clattered to rest in the distant shadows.

Prynn took a few slow steps forward. "Now the *d'k tahg.*"

His fingertips closed around its pommel. Delicately, he pulled it free and let it dangle loosely in his minimal grasp. Extending his arm to his side, he let the dagger fall. It splashed into the water on his right.

Then he slowly folded his hands behind his head and began to crouch forward, his posture one of classic surrender. She wished she had thought to bring the manacles from the *noH'pach.*

From behind Taran'atar, she heard her father's voice croak out in desperation, "Shoot him, Prynn! Shoot! That's an order!"

"He's unarmed," Prynn said. Taran'atar closed his eyes and submissively bowed his head.

"Damn it, Prynn, shoot—"

An upward blur of motion faded into empty darkness, and he was gone. A fraction of a second later her brain caught up to the situation and realized that Taran'atar had just shrouded and sprung upward from his crouch. He was airborne and about to strike, unseen until the moment of impact.

She fired wildly, left and right, up and down in shallow arcs, pivoting ferret-quick, trying to fill the empty air ahead of her with charged plasma. Bolt after crimson bolt seared the darkness with strobe-bright intensity.

A splash of water right in front of her. One last shot.

Taran'atar reappeared, tucked in a deep crouch landing. His huge, gray left hand swatted her pistol from her grasp and into the air with comical ease. His right palm slammed into her solar plexus and winded her as it launched her backward. She landed on her back, half-submerged, gasping for air like a beached grouper, unable to fill her lungs.

Taran'atar stood between her and Vaughn and looked calmly back and forth between them. His expression was masklike, lethal in its disdain. At the terminus of the dead end, Vaughn lay shivering in the water, half in shock, cradling his twisted right forearm. Prynn could only guess what she looked like, her face bloodied and bruised, her uniform soaked with filth, her wrists torn up from her captivity.

A voice both feminine and condescending, and eerily like Captain Kira's, echoed from a PA system that Prynn couldn't see. *"Did you find the hypospray that I left for you?"*

Taran'atar nodded. "I did," he replied, gazing upward toward the disembodied voice as if he'd been speaking to God.

"And the beacon?"

He reached into his pocket and pulled out a palm-sized device, the details of whose interface Prynn couldn't discern. "I have it," Taran'atar declared.

"Then it's time."

"Obedience brings victory," he said. "And victory is life."

As Taran'atar began to enter commands into the device, Vaughn rasped out, "The captain's not dead."

Taran'atar paused briefly and looked away from the device in his hand. Lost in thought for a moment, he regained his focus and continued entering commands.

"You've had Prynn with you all this time . . . haven't you?"

The Jem'Hadar looked askance at Vaughn. "Yes."

More tapping on the device. Prynn was still trying to figure out what her father was doing. For her own part, she finally succeeded in pulling in a feeble half breath, staving off her swelling panic for a few more moments.

More confidently now, Vaughn said, "And you hesitated up on the catwalk. You waited for me to turn around." Taran'atar's frantic tapping of the device interface slowed, then stopped. He looked up at Vaughn, who added, "Prynn and I are both unarmed. We're incapacitated. . . . You could kill us both right now."

Those hard amber eyes shifted from Vaughn to Prynn and back. Taran'atar made one last tap on the device.

"You are not my enemy," he said.

Then a nimbus of twisting folds of space-time enveloped him, spun his image into a radiant, golden reverse silhouette, and vanished into itself, taking him with it. The light blinked out of existence, leaving behind only empty darkness and delicate ripples where the water under Taran'atar's feet rushed back in to fill its own vacancy.

Still fighting for breath, Prynn was too dizzy to stand. She half-crawled, half-limped through the shallow, tepid water, ignoring the scrape of the concrete against her knees, pushing herself onward to her father's side.

"Dad . . ." It was all she could say before she choked down another mouthful of air. There were tears in his eyes as he reached up with his left hand and gently stroked the side of her wet, dirty face. In a way that she would have thought impossible only a day before, the small gesture of parental comfort touched her deeply. Her own hand reached up and clasped his. She exhaled slowly and eased air back into her lungs.

"We have to get out of here," Vaughn said. "Help me up." She draped his good arm over her shoulders and lifted from her knees. He pushed with his legs. A few awkward seconds later, they were both standing. Once she was certain he was steady, she guided him forward, out of the dead end.

That voice—Kira's but not Kira's; snide, haughty, and cruel—echoed over the PA system again. *"What a heartwarming reunion,"* she said. The venom behind her words encircled Vaughn and Prynn with malice. *"I'm sure the two of you could go on and on. Unfortunately, my use for this base is about to come to an end—and so are you."*

Strobe lights, mounted on the walls at regular intervals, flickered and pulsed as a deep male voice began repeating slight variations of a monotone, prerecorded announcement. Prynn didn't speak Cardassian, but the ominous cadence of a self-destruct countdown sounded markedly similar in most humanoid languages. All around her and Vaughn, the sound of power generators grew louder and higher pitched.

"Who the hell puts a self-destruct in a prison?" she said.

"The Obsidian Order," Vaughn said. "Run!"

Most days Vaughn wouldn't have been able to keep pace with his daughter, but he followed her, fueled by adrenaline, up the sloped corridor, back past the staircase, away from the lab, and around the curve toward the same set of lifts that she and Taran'atar had used. The drone of the countdown, the blaring squawk of klaxons—all of it overpowered Vaughn's senses. Their mad dash to the lift had the surreal quality of a nightmare; the throbbing pain that swelled up his right arm almost to the shoulder was the only thing keeping him rooted in the stark reality of the moment.

The safety cage of the lift shrieked and scraped mightily in its tracks as Prynn pulled it open. She ushered Vaughn inside, then followed him in and closed the gate behind herself. With his left hand he punched the button for the top level. The lift lurched upward, shaking as if it suffered from a palsy. Tendrils of foul-smelling gray mist clung futilely to the open mesh of the passenger car as it ascended; they released their hold as it rose out of the bowels of Grennokar and climbed anemically back toward the exit, ten kilometers above.

The panorama of the silo-shaped facility was humbling in its dark and sinister majesty. Endless rings of pain and suffering, all identical and reeking of futility, stretching down, one below another, into the bedrock . . . it was the epitome of Cardassian penal architecture.

And it was starting to implode.

White-orange blossoms of flame bloomed in the misty gray nadir of the pit. Vaughn watched geysers of black smoke jet upward and mushroom beneath the lift car as it continued to climb. The meters seemed to drag past. Prynn huddled next to him as his eyes gazed imploringly upward. He hugged her close to him as a thunderous explosion shook the facility. Loose bits of debris tumbled downward, like iron rain from the network of scaffolding and catwalks far above.

She looked at him and asked a question in a way that sounded as if she already knew the answer. "Why did you ask if he'd had me with him?"

He looked at his daughter with a sad, trembling smile. "He set a trap for us. . . . I thought he used you as bait . . . thought he'd killed you." After a moment, he laid bare his pain and told the truth. "I thought I . . . thought *I'd* killed you."

"At Nahanas," she said.

"Yes."

Chunks of something dense and metallic struck the top of the lift and rang it like a church bell. Prynn flinched and nestled closer under the shelter of his arm. Distant explosions rumbled far below, booming like thunder under water.

She wrapped her arms around his waist and didn't ask him any more questions. The lift continued its slow climb. About halfway up, he retrieved the tricorder from his pocket and scanned to see if the distortion had receded enough to get a signal through. He was able to lock in the combadge signals of his strike team up above, but he couldn't get a response from the *Defiant*.

No way to burst-upload the data from the lab, he mused darkly as he put away the tricorder. He tapped his combadge. "Vaughn to Neeley."

The delay in her reply was brief. *"Neeley here."* He heard the sounds of weapons fire behind her voice.

"Neeley, the base's self-destruct is armed—"

"We know, sir, we're waiting for you."

"Don't wait. I want you and Heins to take the team and fall back, get outside to safe ground. That's an order."

"What about Taran'atar?"

"He got away," Vaughn said. He didn't intend to add any details, then he realized he didn't really have any. "Fall back now. Vaughn out." He winced as incandescent forks of jade-colored electricity arced across the chasm of the silo. Then a regular cadence of detonations roared beneath them, punctuating the staccato cacophony of machine thunder buffeting the lift.

Fire rushed through the corridors of each level, a serpent of flames consuming all in its path, growing and ascending, its forked tongue lashing out into the middle of the emptiness at the heart of this metal abyss. Conduits reaching up far past them glowed cherry-red with heat.

Closer now, the radial sprawl of the top level spread out above them, its dark assembly of metal illuminated from within by patches of ruddy glow. Couplings groaned and shrieked asunder. More debris pattered and clanged heavily off the roof of the lift car, which grumbled upward, its gears working in a steady thumping cadence.

Hot gusts billowed through the open mesh. Vaughn blinked the tears from his eyes as Prynn prodded him back to his feet. A blast of steam erupted sideways from a ruptured conduit, blinding him as it momentarily scoured the passing lift.

"Almost there," she said. Then a jaw-rattling detonation tore something loose from the landing platform structure above them. A length of heavy piping and a section of catwalk swung loose, buckling at the end that met the silo wall, falling away from the center and toward the outer wall—right at them.

Prynn pulled Vaughn to the floor, and they huddled together. The falling wreckage bashed in the outer face of the lift car and hurled Prynn and Vaughn against the other side. The dented metal box ground to a whining halt.

Fear pushed Vaughn back to his feet. He strained to focus his vision through the thick mesh of the safety cage and the torrents of steam and smoke and vapor gushing from every opening on every level of the complex. He saw the next interlocking gate for the safety cage; they were stopped half a meter shy of the next level. He turned to Prynn. "Help me force the doors."

Working together, they pried aside the gate of the safety cage to reveal the lower half of the interlocking gate on the next level. "I can reach the release," Prynn said. "Can you boost me with one arm?"

He bent at the knees, wrapped his arm around her waist,

and lifted her up. She reached into the narrow gap between the lift car and the outer wall, grasped the emergency release lever, and opened the door. Already up, she planted her palms on the ledge and vaulted herself clear of the lift, onto the deck above.

Then the lift's gears made a horrible metallic yelp as it lurched down a few centimeters with a jarring bump that knocked Vaughn off-balance.

Prynn reached her hand through the gap toward him.

"Dad, c'mon!"

Visions of the lift dropping and severing her arm paralyzed him. Another hideous creak swelled in the lift's gears.

She yelled with the bravado of a commander. "Now!"

He jumped up and grabbed her arm. Her strength surprised him—she yanked him up and pulled him clear of the gap in a single dexterous motion. They collapsed onto the deck, but she was quickly up again and kneeling solicitously beside him.

"Are you all right?"

"Yes," he lied. "Let's go." She helped him to his feet. Then, with a deafening cry of distressed metal, the lift car broke loose of its tracks and plummeted like a stone into the swelling sea of fire and shadow below.

Vaughn let her pull him into motion, and he sprint-stumbled in front of her, scrambling up a quaking staircase. He was afraid to look back, like Orpheus leading Eurydice out of the underworld. In every direction fires danced and advanced and smoke belched from disintegrating floors and ceilings. Grennokar was immolating itself from the bottom up.

They reached the top of the staircase and turned toward the catwalks that stretched out toward the center platform, where the *noH'pach* stood waiting. "The ship," Vaughn shouted, pointing ahead of him at the Klingon scout vessel. Prynn nodded as she ran half a step behind him, out from under the stony ceiling into the open pandemonium that raged like a storm from Hell.

They charged across the half-kilometer-long bridge, all other concerns left behind. Tiny bits of shrapnel from exploding machinery high overhead pattered down, leaving smoky twists in their wakes. Smoke erupted up from under their feet; steam hissed and made white ghost-walls that obscured their view of the treacherously swaying path ahead. Sirens howled while the same voice droned through its countdown in Cardassian. Alert lights flashed and strobed, explosions rocked the facility, heavy slabs of rock fell from the domelike roof. Vaughn gasped with panicked intensity as he ran, his entire reality reduced to a concussive chaos of jolts and relentless forward motion through a blistering gale.

A dozen incendiary detonations erupted in rapid sequence around the perimeter of the landing platform. Metal warped and folded over on itself with a heart-wrenching groan, a deep and ominous sound, like the death knell of an undersea leviathan.

The myriad catwalks and bridges folded downward, answering the Dantean summons of the lake of fire below. The *noH'pach* and the broken disk of the landing platform vanished into the rising flames, which roiled upward out of the greasy black smoke and revealed themselves like the petals of an obscene flower.

Without a word, Vaughn and Prynn turned back and sprinted up the drooping walkway, toward the pit's perimeter, to the encircling catwalk that was now their only hope of escape. He looked back. Sections of the catwalk splintered off and broke away under the stress of their own weight. And the end of the walkway was quickly catching up to him.

Prynn was a few meters ahead of him when the catwalk fractured behind her feet, between them. The gradual incline he had been climbing steepened. He tripped and fell on his belly.

Vaughn felt gravity's inexorable pull. He slipped backward. His hand flailed for purchase, sought out the railing of the doomed catwalk segment. He missed the first one.

The lower half of his body slid over the edge toward the abyss. He grabbed the last, bent rung.

Above him, Prynn had turned back and was at the edge of the last reliable section of the bridge. "Dad! C'mon!"

Wind-whipped streamers of smoke swirled around him. The inferno licked at his heels.

Prynn reached out, her hand more than a meter shy of his. "Dad! Climb!"

"I've only got *one arm*, Prynn! I *can't* climb!"

She stretched herself farther over the edge, almost daring gravity to cast its spell on her. "You can reach me!"

"Dammit, I can't!" he protested. "Get out! Run!"

"No," she shouted, growing more hysterical by the second. "Take my hand, please. . . ."

He could see it in her eyes. She wouldn't leave him here.

Even if it meant tumbling into the flames, she wouldn't give up, not as long as there was even the slimmest possibility that she might pluck him from the edge of destruction.

The fracture at the end of the broken segment of catwalk groaned mournfully. Prynn remained stretched across it, her hand reaching futilely downward.

Below him, the flames burned like damnation.

He thought of all the times he had failed Prynn, all the

moments when he'd answered the call of duty and neglected his sacred charge as a father.

He remembered Ruriko.

I deserve to die like this, Vaughn thought. He looked up through misting eyes at his daughter. *But she doesn't.*

"Run, baby," he said, with all the tenderness in his heart. And he let himself fall.

She was reaching as far as her arm would extend, but it wasn't far enough. *Just a little farther,* she thought, shaking, straining, willing her body to stretch, but her father was nearly a meter beyond her fingertips. "You can reach me!"

"Dammit, I can't!" he shouted back. "Get out! Run!"

"No!" she yelled over the roar of explosions, battling back against the fear, the powerlessness, the hopelessness of watching her father hanging by his fingertips over the fire. She could see that he was broken, beaten . . . *old.* He didn't have the strength or the leverage to climb with only one arm. She knew it, but she couldn't give up, couldn't turn her back on him. She'd done that for years, had thought it was so easy, and now it was suddenly impossible. Her open palm stretched into the unbridgeable empty space between them. It was all a blur beyond her watery curtain of tears. "Take my hand, please. . . ."

Her father looked down, mesmerized, into the flames. Then he looked back up at her, his eyes full of sorrow, darker, and deeper, and more nakedly honest than she'd ever seen.

His tearful gaze burned with the paternal love she had longed for as a child and had thought she could live without as a woman. For the first time in her life, she saw herself in her father's face. And she knew instantly what he meant to do.

"Run, baby," he said.

She lunged forward as he let go of the railing.

He was plummeting, succumbing to simple physics, and she was diving after him, one hand outstretched, one trailing behind her. Her fingertips brushed his sleeve cuff. The wet fabric slipped in her grasp as her other hand swung out to arrest their fall, to cheat the reaper and the law of gravity all at once.

Her free hand slapped the railing but missed.

She clawed at the open spaces in the catwalk grating.

Their momentum was too great. She couldn't take hold.

They were in free fall. The catwalk receded above them.

His cuff twisted free of her fingers. He grabbed hers.

Flames rose to meet them, father and daughter, as they clutched one another and plunged together into perdition.

Then the burning sea parted beneath them to reveal a massive darkness, its fiery silhouette winged and insectile.

Prynn met it feet-first. The impact was blunt and brutal. Even as she rolled through the fall, her ankles splintered, and her knees buckled as the ligaments tore apart. Her arms could have helped break her fall if not for the fact that she was holding on to her father and doing all she could to shield him from the trauma of this not-so-soft landing.

They were rising, ascending out of the hellish vortex of impregnable darkness and searing light, borne aloft on the back of the *noH'pach*. Through the soot and the grime she briefly glimpsed the Imperial Klingon trefoil emblazoned on the wing. *Thank God the away teams never follow orders.*

Flashes of explosion shredded the roof at the top of the silo. Wedges of rock and chunks of metal smashed down on the *noH'pach*. Prynn and Vaughn huddled together, with him clutching her, and her hanging on to a narrow gap between two hull plates. The ship climbed through the firestorm, pivoted toward the tunnel, and accelerated forward.

Behind them, the silo's roof collapsed into the flames.

The tunnel blurred past. Wind ripped over them, blasted at them, forced their faces against the intensely warm hull.

A final, cataclysmic boom, and the pit vomited up a plume of white-hot fire that chased them into the tunnel.

The *noH'pach* broke free into daylight and veered clear to port.

Blazes of fire jetted out behind the ship and dissipated into the desert morning. The butte above the silo sank into itself, and the well of horrors once known as Grennokar collapsed into a pool of slag deep beneath the surface.

Unbearably bright, the light of Harkoum's twin suns beat down on the tiny, scorched Klingon ship. The *noH'pach* made a wide, slow turn into the desert, in search of a place to land. Riding on top of the ship, her body trembling from adrenaline overload and too numb with shock to feel relieved at having been narrowly delivered from destruction, Prynn Tenmei embraced her father.

38

The Alternate Universe—
I.K.S. Negh'Var

INTENDANT KIRA SMILED AS THE CONTROL SYSTEM confirmed the cross-dimensional transporter lock. The homing beacon in the other universe had been activated and was working exactly as planned. As she stepped forward, palms pressed together in front of her chin, the machine powered up and automatically initiated its transport sequence. An electric tingle coursed through her. Whether it was an effect of the transporter or the result of her own fervent anticipation, she was uncertain.

With a resonant drone that evoked the music of the spheres, space-time unfolded and revealed new facets of itself. A cylinder of shimmering golden light swirled into being and became blinding. The Intendant averted her eyes as it flared with the momentary breaching of the universal barrier. When at last she looked back, the familiar violet-blue whirlpool of charged atoms reassembled into a humanoid form.

Large and imposing, the creature that took shape before her carried himself like a soldier. Proud of bearing, with pale eyes peering through the fading halo of the transporter beam. His skin was gray and tough-looking, and his face had the spiny armored quality of a deep-sea creature or a reptilian predator. Clearly, he was of a species meant to be strong, to make war, to conquer. The sort of ally she had long dreamed of.

He stepped off the platform and stood an arm's length in front of her. She regarded him with awe and reverent respect, but most of all with elation. Her smile was reflexive and wide.

"Taran'atar," she said, "in the flesh." He nodded slightly. She continued, "Welcome to my universe. You've already been a better ally than I could have dared hope for. To finally stand here with you is an honor, and a pleasure long overdue."

"Thank you," he said. With a wan smirk and a tilt of his head, he added, "I, too, have looked forward to this meeting."

His hand was around her throat, so quickly that she had been lifted several centimeters off the ground by the time she realized she'd been assaulted. Her hands reached reflexively to loosen his grip on her windpipe, but struggling against a being this powerful was futile. Belatedly she reached for the alert signal on her belt. His other hand tore it off and cast it away.

Asphyxiated, panicking, she became hyperaware of the smallest details around her. The faint lingering perfume of her bath a few hours ago. An almost too-clean scent of the air on the ship. Her quick but weakening pulse. The dry friction of his leathery fingertips on her neck.

His eyes were cold and remorseless.

The machine powered up behind him, activated once again by a remote beacon from the other universe. A roar like the ocean surged in her ears, and she realized it was the rushing of her blood. Gasping raggedly for air, she became aware that he was holding her tightly enough to weaken her but not enough to kill her. At least, not yet.

Again reality turned itself inside-out under the energizer coils of the cross-dimensional transporter. Another humanoid form began to emerge from the glowing nimbus, this one smaller than Taran'atar, less bulky. Once more, Intendant Kira shut her eyes to the harsh flash of light and waited for it to diminish before she opened them to see who had just crossed over.

Moving with feral grace, Kira Nerys stepped off the platform. She was garbed in civilian clothes, and her hair was styled differently than the Intendant recalled from their last meeting; it was a now a perfect match for her own. She had a dagger in her hand.

Kira regarded the Intendant smugly and said to Taran'atar, "Put her down." The Jem'Hadar set the Intendant back on her feet. Kira pointed at the deck. "Kneel," she commanded.

The Intendant hesitated. Taran'atar pressed on her shoulders and forced her to kneel before Kira.

"My, my," the Intendant said. "Haven't you gotten fierce since last we met?" She looked up over her shoulder at Taran'atar, then back at Kira. "And more cunning, too. I certainly won't underestimate his loyalty next time. I hate to admit it, but you played this well, Nerys. Bravo."

Kira listened, her expression intense and malevolent. Then a glint of cruel amusement lit up her face with sinister glee. "You have *no idea* who you're dealing with," she said.

And in a silvery flash, she cut the Intendant's throat.

Shocked and sinking into herself, the Intendant swayed on her knees. The room spun out of control.

Blood, warm and wet, sheeted down the front of her bodysuit, puddled between her knees.

Silent screams fluttered inside her, trapped in her breast, robbed of her voice.

She pitched backward.

Collapsed to the deck.

Stared at the ceiling as the room faded out from the edges, the final darkness pressing in on her, erasing her from the world, erasing the world from her, devouring all that she was and had ever known, swallowing her *pagh* and condemning her to walk the bitter last path of all flesh.

As the light went out of the Intendant's world, she heard Kira's icy instruction to Taran'atar: "Get rid of the body."

39

Kira

COLD AND BLUE-GRAY, FILLED WITH THE SOFT HUM OF LIFE-support systems, softly lit and deeply shadowed . . . Kira recognized Deep Space 9's infirmary as it revealed itself to her by degrees. One breath followed another, slow and deep, and she gradually became aware that it was her own breathing, that she was back in the temple of her own body . . . she was alive.

Her left hand was cold and lay at her side. Her right hand was upright and warm. She turned her head. Benjamin Sisko was at her side, holding her hand. His reticent half smile and bloodshot eyes projected brotherly love and concern and filled her with a sense of peace, security, and comfort. He was with her, and there was nothing to fear. Everything would be all right now.

"Ben," she said, her voice weak, a mere whisper.

His voice was deep, quiet, and soothing. "I'm here, Nerys."

Tears welled in her eyes. "Am . . . am I . . . ?"

"You're all right," he said. "You made it through surgery, and you're going to be fine."

Memories of the attack in the corridor felt far away, hazy behind the obscuring clamor of events that had swallowed her up, dreamlike, during her vision of the Celestial Temple. "A knife," she said. "In my chest . . ." She recalled its impact and winced.

"I know," he said. "Taran'atar attacked you and Ro."

Powerful emotions coursed inside her. Cold terror twisted beside fiery rage; Taran'atar's betrayal both saddened and infuriated her; her heart filled with bitter disappointment that he had violated Odo's trust and hers. "Why? Why did he do it?"

"Julian thinks someone was controlling him," Sisko said. "Beyond that, nothing's really certain."

Sudden and profound guilt took hold of her, and she felt ashamed for thinking only of her own fate. "Ro?"

"She's all right, Nerys," he said, nodding toward Kira's left, where Ro lay sleeping. "It'll be a few weeks before she can walk again, but she will. Bashir promised."

She nodded, and the flurry of panicked musings in her mind began to settle. Clarity returned with effort, and she began to feel more conscious. "Where's Taran'atar now?"

"He fled the station," Sisko said. "Vaughn went after him in the *Defiant*. We're still waiting on an update."

"We need to get a message to Odo," she said and tried to sit up. The horrible pain in her chest knocked her back flat on the bed. She gasped for breath.

"Easy, Nerys. Dax already has a hail out to Odo. As soon as he replies, we'll let you know."

Kira gingerly massaged the aching flesh over her sternum. There was no trace of a scar, not that she had expected there to be. Starfleet's dermal regenerators were among the best she'd ever seen. "Feels like Julian had a hell of time putting my heart back together," she said with a rueful grin.

"Actually," Sisko said, "he didn't."

"What do you mean?"

"He wasn't able to fix your heart, so he gave you an artificial one."

An irrational charge of fright tingled Kira's skin with cold, prickly goosebumps. Hearing that her heart had been removed and replaced with a biosynthetic organ, she half-expected it to immediately seize and plunge her back into the arms of the Prophets. Reaching reflexively for her chest, she pressed her palm down and waited to feel a heartbeat. And there it was—smooth, regular, natural . . . and completely familiar. "Feels just like it always has," she said, sounding mildly shocked.

"What'd you expect?" He grinned at her. "A drum solo?"

She chuckled and smiled back at him. "Well, sure, why not?"

"I'll ask Bashir," Sisko said. "Maybe he can add one."

"Please, don't give him any ideas," Kira said. "The last time *he* had an idea, *I* had the O'Briens' baby."

Sisko's laugh was deep and rich, and if it had a color, Kira was certain it would be golden. More than anything else—the cool clean air, the crispness of the sheet covering her legs, or the gentle beating of her new heart—his laughter told her that she was still alive, delivered from the edge of eternal shadow for a few more precious bits of time in the world of the living.

She reached out and took his hand. "I'm glad you're here, Ben. It means a lot to me, to know that . . . well, that you . . ." Brushing a lonesome tear from her cheek, she continued, "That you would take time away from Kasidy and Rebecca to be with me, it's just . . ." She smiled sadly. "Thank you."

"When we heard the news from Dax, Kasidy *told* me to go to you. She said you needed me more than they did." He gently tightened his grip around hers. "But the truth is, I probably need you more than you need me."

Noting Kira's look of gentle surprise, he added with a teary smile, "After all—what good would I be without my right hand?"

40

Harkoum

TO VAUGHN'S RELIEF, THE *NOH'PACH'S* LANDING WAS SOFT. IT touched down on the desert sands, a few kilometers from the smoking ruins of Grennokar. Flittering packs of small creatures skittered away to the shadows under distant patches of vegetation as the landing gear made contact. Sunlight beat down with awesome force, pressing in on the gray back of the ship, which seemed almost to strain under the burden of it.

He and Prynn were tucked between two protruding masses on the ship's hull. Her arms were locked around his torso in a fiercely protective embrace. She pressed her head against his chest, her ear directly over his still-racing heart.

The thunder-rush of the impulse engines ceased and was replaced by the mournful cry of the wind.

His right arm lay in his lap, twisted and broken, throbbing with deep and terrible pain. He lifted his left hand and gently stroked a sweat-dampened twist of dirty hair from Prynn's forehead. She lifted her head and looked up at him, all traces of malice or bitterness erased from her expression. Tears rolled from her eyes, washing paths of clean flesh down her grime-darkened cheeks. Bruised and blackened, eyes red with tears, to Vaughn she looked angelic, the most perfect vision of grace and beauty he'd ever witnessed in all his decades traveling between the stars. Tears overflowed his own eyes. *My daughter.*

Part of him still reeled in disbelief at the fact that she was alive. His guilt and his sorrow were still too raw to be easily cast aside, even as joy swelled in his soul.

Her tears turned bitter, and her hands closed, white-knuckle tight, on his damp and filthy black fatigues. Anger and fear shone through her grief. "Why did you let go?"

"I had to," he said, flashing back to that awful moment above the fire. His throat tightened and went dry, as if to stop him from saying anything more, but he pressed on. "I had to make you . . ." He remembered the sensation of falling. His voice broke. "Make you leave me and save yourself."

She wrapped her arms affectionately around his neck and kissed the top of his head. A sob heaved in her chest as she said, "I wouldn't leave you, Dad . . . I'd *never* leave you."

"I know, baby . . . I know." He abandoned his ancient yoke of stoicism and let his tears fall. It was time at last to weep—for himself, for Ruriko, for the years he could have had with Prynn but had squandered—and he was not ashamed. He clutched his only child and cried with her, and he was in all ways grateful.

The past would always be with them; he knew that. Nothing had been undone, no wrongs had been expunged. Neither of them had said *I'm sorry* because neither had had to. Forgiveness was too explicit a boon to grant, too dear an act of grace to hope or ask for. This was something rarer and far more fragile and a hundred times more precious: a new beginning.

From a few meters ahead of them came the metallic echoes of magnetic locks being released from an exterior hull hatchway. Prynn wiped the tears from Vaughn's face and turned with him to watch as the hatch dislodged with a pneumatic gasp and swung upward, blocking their view of the person who had opened it. They listened to footsteps on metal rungs and the dry scrape of someone clambering out onto the sun-baked, debris-littered outer hull.

Out of the corner of his eye, Vaughn saw tiny figures double-timing across the dunes a few hundred meters away. He counted quickly and realized that all seven other members of his strike team were accounted for on the ground.

Then a slender Cardassian woman of average height cleared the hatchway and stood in front of them. Her dark hair was filthy and tousled; her face had been beaten; her drab and desert-friendly garments were torn and shredded and bloodstained. She moved awkwardly, as if nursing a deep injury.

Vaughn knew at once that he'd never met her before, but she looked discomfitingly familiar.

"You're alive," she said. "Good. I waited as long as I could for you—almost too long, as it turns out."

"Then I guess we owe you some thanks," Vaughn said, not bothering to hide his suspicion. "Care to tell us who you are?"

"Listen to me," the Cardassian woman said. "I failed my mission, and that means we're out of time. We have to warn Captain Kira Nerys that she's in mortal danger."

"You're a bit late for that," Prynn said darkly.

Vaughn added, "Taran'atar already made an attempt on

the captain's life, and we know he's working with Intendant Kira from the parallel universe."

The Cardassian woman boiled over with fury and frustration. "You have *no idea* who you're dealing with."

Sensing that his day was about to once more take a turn for the worse, Vaughn felt his mood darken. "Why don't you enlighten us."

"She's a renegade from the Obsidian Order." She hunched suddenly, in agony, winced, and clutched at her gut. Fighting her way upright, she continued, "She's a deep-cover agent—an infiltrator, an assassin who knows thousands of ways to kill, and torture, and seduce, and distract, and confuse you. Her handlers altered her surgically to look like Kira Nerys, but before the switch was made something went wrong. The op fell apart, betrayed from within. Kira escaped, and her look-alike vanished. No one knew if she'd been killed, or went mad, or was captured . . . no one except the bastard who betrayed her. *His* name was Gul Skrain Dukat. . . . *Her* name is Iliana Ghemor."

Vaughn grew even more suspicious. "And you know all this . . . how?"

"Because," she said, *"my* name is *also* Iliana Ghemor."

As the dimensional transporter powered down, Taran'atar checked its readout and confirmed that every last trace of the body had been dispersed into the ether between realities, atomized and scattered beyond any hope of reclamation. There was still the enormous slick of dark blood on the deck to contend with, but his new god had not instructed him to do anything about that . . . at least, not yet. She had instructed him to dispose of the body, and that he had done without delay.

He turned to see her at the far end of the rather lavish residential compartment, being attended by a lone Vulcan servant. The slender, dark-haired woman helped Captain Kira's doppelgänger into a tight-fitting, textured black garment. The Vulcan woman's fingers were agile and swift as she finished by placing the Intendant's metallic headpiece upon her mistress's brow.

Eyes afire with excitement, the red-haired woman listened attentively while the Vulcan whispered in her ear. She answered in the same hushed tones, and the handmaiden nodded a polite confirmation. The Bajoran grinned. "Thank you, L'Haan," she said. "Your rewards will be many and extravagant." The handmaiden bowed, then backed away to a respectful distance.

Taran'atar's new god descended the tiered levels of her quarters. She halted on the tier above him and looked him in the eye. "Your service has also been most impeccable," she said, with a haughty grandeur that reminded him of the tone so often employed by the Founders.

He said nothing. In his imagination, his hands choked her, broke her, twisted her until her bones cracked and her muscles tore apart. But his hands could not obey his desires. Rooted in place, rendered mute, he was in thrall to this woman he hated, and he didn't know how to set himself free.

She turned away from Taran'atar and raised her voice.

"Kira to bridge."

"Kurn here, Intendant."

"Set course for Regulon, maximum warp. It's time to rejoin the fleet . . . and time for you to replace that worm Macet as its commander."

"As you wish, Intendant," Kurn said. *"We depart at once."*

"Excellent. Kira out."

She stood for a long moment with her back to Taran'atar and L'Haan. Her attention was fixed on the palm of her right hand, where she wore a golden bracelet bejeweled with a single luminescent green stone. Then, with a flourish, she spun on her heel to face them and spread wide her arms. "We stand on the edge." she said, almost giddy. "We have the key to reality itself, and all we have to do is reach the door." Prowling forward, she moved with the economy and grace not of a warrior, but of a seasoned assassin. Then she halted, and a haunted expression took over her face and put a fearful light in her eyes. "All those years in exile . . . all those years in the dark . . ." Just as quickly as it had come, the moment of melancholy vanished, and a manic gleam lit her mien once more. "And now we have a battle fleet, an army at our command, the multiverse at our fingertips."

Outside the sweeping, panoramic windows that wrapped around her quarters, the stars were pulled taut, stretched long across the black canvas of eternity as the *Negh'Var* jumped to warp speed. She turned to face the view, as if beholding the shape of her future in its surreal, drifting distortions of starlight.

She spoke in the dreamy monotone of a sleep-talker. "We have far to go and much to do. Reality is infinite . . ." Hatred infused her voice as she added, "But it only has room for *one* Kira Nerys."

THE SAGA OF
STAR TREK: DEEP SPACE NINE
WILL CONTINUE IN

FEARFUL SYMMETRY

ACKNOWLEDGMENTS

Always first in my heart and first in my acknowledgments is my beloved wife, Kara. Her love and support make bearable the solitary nocturnal labor of writing a book for months on end—not least because she frequently reminds me to take a night off now and then, so that our friends can remember what I look like.

Of course, I wouldn't have been able to write *Warpath* or anything like it if not for the efforts of a great number of incredibly talented people. Leading the pack, of course, is editor Marco Palmieri, who is rightly regarded as the visionary behind the post-finale Deep Space Nine novels. Looming large, as well, is fellow author David R. George III, whose riveting Worlds of Deep Space Nine book about the Dominion, *Olympus Descending,* brought to critical mass a whole new set of story arcs for the post-finale Deep Space Nine saga.

Who else? Some know him as "Worf Boy." Several remote tribes of the Amazon Basin speak of him in hushed myths as the "Shaggy Coffee God Who Types Like the Wind." I speak, of course, of my good friend

Acknowledgments

Keith R. A. DeCandido (aka KRAD the Tireless), who added a few more of my markers to his Karmic account for his advice on the peculiarities of small Klingon scout ships and for e-mailing me a copy of his original manuscript, "Horn and Ivory," as a touchstone for the Kira story line in this book.

Another person who came through for me via the Internet was Alex Rosenzweig, who generously answered my late-night SOS for vital information that was in a book I had misplaced.

My gratitude also to Dayton Ward, who shared his martial expertise to help me hone the edge of several hand-to-hand combat sequences in this book. Anything lame that slipped through in those scenes is entirely my fault.

Thanks, of course, are also due to Paula Block and John Van Citters of Paramount Licensing, for their ever-astute input. Paula also deserves kudos, along with Terry Erdmann, for the *Star Trek: Deep Space Nine Companion*, which was invaluable to me while working on this book. Other references that I could not have done without are *Star Charts* by Geoffrey Mandel; the *Star Trek Encyclopedia* by Michael Okuda and Denise Okuda; and the *Star Trek: Deep Space Nine Technical Manual* by Herman Zimmerman, Rick Sternbach, and Doug Drexler. The condensed time line in the front of S. D. Perry's novel *Unity* helped, too.

All of this, of course, was set in motion by the remarkable people who created, wrote, produced, designed, and starred in the television series *Star Trek: Deep Space Nine*, for which I had the amazing good fortune to collaborate in the writing of two episodes, "Starship Down" (which I cowrote with John J. Ordover) and "It's Only a

Paper Moon" (for which John and I wrote the story, and Ronald D. Moore wrote the teleplay).

And though I have thanked my parents before, I can never truly thank them enough. When, as a child, I told them that I wanted to be a writer, they prepared me for the hard work that lay ahead but also encouraged me to follow my dream. I'm still pursuing it all these decades later, but only because Mom and Dad showed me the way.

ABOUT THE AUTHOR

David Mack is a writer whose work spans multiple media. With John J. Ordover, he cowrote the *Star Trek: Deep Space Nine* episode "Starship Down" and the story treatment for the *Star Trek: Deep Space Nine* episode "It's Only a Paper Moon." Mack and Ordover also penned the four-issue *Star Trek: Deep Space Nine/Star Trek: The Next Generation* crossover comic-book miniseries "Divided We Fall" for WildStorm Comics. With Keith R. A. DeCandido, Mack cowrote the *Star Trek: S.C.E.* eBook novella *Invincible,* currently available in paperback as part of the omnibus *Star Trek: S.C.E. Book Two—Miracle Workers.*

Mack's solo writing for *Star Trek* includes the best-selling, two-part eBook novel *Star Trek: S.C.E.—Wildfire* (republished in the paperback omnibus *Star Trek: S.C.E. Book Six—Wildfire*); "Waiting for G'doh, or, How I Learned to Stop Moving and Hate People," a short story for the *Star Trek: New Frontier* anthology *No Limits;* a pair of *Star Trek: The Next Generation* novels, *A Time to Kill* and the *USA Today* bestseller *A Time to Heal;* and *Harbinger,* the debut volume of a new *Star Trek* book series, *Star Trek Vanguard.*

About the Author

His upcoming titles include the Wolverine novel *Road of Bones* and a number of *Star Trek* projects.

An avid fan of the Canadian rock trio Rush, Mack has been to all their concert tours since 1982. He currently resides in New York City with his wife, Kara.

Learn more about David Mack and his work on his official website: www.infinitydog.com

Return to the 23rd century.

SUMMON THE THUNDER

by Dayton Ward and Kevin Dilmore

Coming in July, 2006
From Pocket Books
Available wherever books are sold

Also available as an eBook

www.startrekbooks.com

Turn the page for a preview. . . .

"EVER SEE ANYTHING QUITE LIKE THIS?" DR. FISHER ASKED.

"Well," said Dr. Jabilo M'Benga as he stepped closer to the body of the nude Denobulan male lying atop the examination table, "I've seen stabbings, puncture wounds, and impalements, but nothing on this scale." At the center of the Denobulan's chest where his thoracic cavity and its associated organs were once harbored, only a gaping, circular hole remained. The polished steel of the table was clearly visible on the other side of the ghastly wound.

"Me neither," Fisher replied, reaching to the shelf set against the bulkhead above the examination table to retrieve a fresh pair of sterile surgical gloves. Working his right hand into the first of the gloves, he added, "And after fifty years out here, that's saying something."

The two doctors currently were the only living occupants in Starbase 47's morgue, itself an unassuming area of the station's four-level medical complex. Housed within the hospital's lowest deck and situated near Vanguard's core, well away from more active sections of the station, Fisher knew that the physical placement of the morgue owed much more to the glacial pace of change regarding the traditions of medicine than it did to the facility's function. While 23rd century post-mortem medical practices had advanced far beyond the need for such archaic conventions as refrigeration and chemical preservatives, thanks to the development of stasis fields and other such useful technology, what still remained were the superstitions and general discomfort of the living that seemed to accompany the physical presence of the dead.

Keep the morgue in the basement, Fisher mused. *Can't be giving anyone the creeps now, can we?* As if to hammer home the point, the temperature in this room even seemed to be several degrees cooler than the rest of the hospital.

As he returned to the subject of his study, however, even Fisher had to agree that the sight of this ill-fated being might be enough to give anyone pause. The Denobulan, stripped of all garments that might have indicated his rank or station in life, lay before them blank-faced and motionless on the examination table extending from one of a bank of stasis units along the rear wall of the morgue.

"I thought you might want to be in on this one, Jabilo," Fisher said, "given that a physician attached to starship duty might run across this sort of thing more often than those of us bound to a mere starbase."

Fisher could not resist the sly remark, which he tempered with inflections of good-natured sarcasm in the hope of couching somewhat the underlying edge of bitterness behind it. He had devoted a good deal of his time these past months preparing M'Benga to assume the role of chief medical officer for Starbase 47, a task Fisher attended with the true desire of ensuring the station—and his dear friend

Diego Reyes—was left with a capable physician and surgeon upon his impending retirement.

That desire was dashed, however, when the younger doctor filed a request with Starfleet Medical to transfer to the next available physician's posting on a starship. Fisher had swallowed his disappointment long enough to sign off on M'Benga's request—but had since put little effort into restraining his words on those occasions when his displeasure at the idea made itself known.

If M'Benga was fazed at all by the jab, he did not show it. *Guess his tour of duty in a Vulcan medical ward lends him the occasional stoicism,* Fisher thought, *or the simple indifference to my situation, at least.*

"According to his file," M'Benga said, already down to business, "Mr. Bohanon here was part of the research team on Erilon. Was he involved in an accident?"

Fisher shook his head. "He was attacked. At least, that's what I was told. By what, I don't know." Once more he directed his attention to the massive hole in the Denobulan's chest, which had remedied the victim of his lungs, heart and a significant portion of his spine.

Reaching out to trace the outline of the wound with a gloved finger, M'Benga said, "It looks almost surgical in its precision. Whatever did this, it struck him with tremendous force."

"If not for the strength of his rib cage," Fisher replied, "whatever hit him likely would have just torn him in two." Tapping a control set into the wall next to the table, he activated a spotlight which he then directed to better illuminate the cavity. "See how it tapers inward from front to back? He was stabbed—skewered, really—by something that got wider as it went deeper." Dipping his own gloved hand inside the wound, he gently probed its edges with his fingers. "Its sides are uniform and smooth, but it doesn't seem to be from some sort of heat cauterization."

"What else might cause that?" M'Benga asked.

Shrugging, Fisher replied, "Acid. An alien enzyme, maybe. It could simply be a function of his being transported almost exactly at the time of his injury, and the transporter buffer just . . . tidied things up."

"You're suggesting he was literally beamed right off the object that killed him?" M'Benga frowned at that suggestion. "If that was the case, then why wasn't that object, or even a piece of it, brought up with him?"

Fisher nodded in approval at the observation. "Good question, but you're assuming the deadly force here was inflicted by a physical object. If he was hit—for example— by a shaped antiproton beam, that might explain a few things."

"But wouldn't such an attack leave some residual energy that might be detected at the wound site?" M'Benga asked.

"Not if the stasis field that Mr. Bohanon entered on the *Endeavour* shortly after his death nullified any energy traces we might hope to find." Fisher smiled, noting the younger physician's knit brow as he considered that possibility. "It's a tangled web we attempt to unweave in an autopsy, Dr. M'Benga, but we have one thing going for us."

"And that is?"

"It's pretty obvious how this poor fellow died, which means we get to spend more time trying to discover what was used to kill him."

He reached for a laser scalpel set atop a tray positioned next to the stasis bed and by applying a deft touch with the device, Fisher carved away a sliver of muscle tissue from the surface area of the cavity and placed it in a waiting specimen dish. Handing the sample to M'Benga, he said, "Let's see what a molecular scan can tell us."

The younger doctor led the way across the room to a nearby workstation which offered an array of scanning equipment as well as a standard computer interface terminal. Fisher watched as M'Benga placed the tray under the sensor array and keyed a series of instructions to the small keypad set into the worktable. The sample dish was bathed in a soft blue light, the forensic scanner sending its findings to the computer for further processing and analysis. Within seconds, data began to coalesce on the workstation's display monitor.

And Fisher's eyebrows rose.

"What the hell is that?" he asked as he studied the information being put out by the computer. "Anabolic activity? These cells are *alive*?" He leaned closer to better scrutinize the computer monitor, but the data displayed upon it did not change.

"That's impossible," M'Benga said. "Something must have contaminated the site."

"They look like new metabolic pathways," Fisher said. Watching the computer-enhanced image of the cell sample, the doctor could plainly see that some as yet-unidentified substance had come into contact with the exposed areas of the open wound, and even now was slowly but surely working to break down the Denobulan's cells, only to rearrange them into something resembling a crystalline structure. "It's an enzyme, and it's mineralizing the muscle cells somehow."

But what the hell for?

Beside him, M'Benga asked, "Could it be a form of viral infection native to Erilon that was arrested when the body was placed into stasis, and only became active once it was exposed to an atmosphere?"

"The *Endeavour*'s CMO scanned the body for infection, but found nothing," Fisher replied.

M'Benga nodded toward the screen. "Shouldn't he have found this?"

"He wasn't allowed to autopsy the body," Fisher said. Frowning as he said that, he nevertheless kept his thoughts on that decision, as well as who had made it and issued the appropriate orders, to himself. "Besides, if there was any kind of contamination, our auto-containment procedures would already have kicked in and sealed this place off. We're not looking at any kind of contagion." Turning away from the workstation and moving back to where Bohanon's body still lay, he called over shoulder, "Get a portable scanner."

It took only a moment to survey the rest of the ghastly wound in the Denobulan's chest and confirm Fisher's suspicions. Holding the scanner up so that he could see its collected data, M'Benga said, "The same readings. Every exposed area of internal tissue is in the process of gradually being altered at the cellular level."

"Putting him in stasis halted the process," Fisher said. He indicated the control panel on M'Benga's side of the table. "Jabilo, put him back in. I want to study this, and we need to preserve what we've got as long as we can."

"Yes, Doctor," M'Benga replied, pressing the control that retracted the examination table and its current occupant back into its storage drawer. The door hissed shut and a gentle hum exuded from the bulkhead as the small chamber's stasis field activated.

"Have you detected a rate of progress?" he asked as he rejoined Fisher at the computer workstation.

Pointing to the monitor, Fisher replied, "Already plotting one out." The screen displayed a small graph inset atop the main image of the ongoing cellular metamorphosis. "Not that it's going to help us much. The process is tapering off. At this rate, it'll neutralize completely before it extends more than a millimeter or two into the surrounding tissue."

"The process might need more of its catalyst in order to continue," M'Benga said. "Maybe something native to the planet?"

Fisher offered a small grunt of affirmation. "Could be, but maybe all it needs is more living tissue." Turning back to the workstation, he began to key in a series of instructions. "We've got everything we need to try a computer model. Let's see what kind of luck we have with that."

In response to his requests, the computer screen generated a new graph. Fisher watched as the function graph did not slope toward the zero baseline but instead spiked quickly.

M'Benga, who was watching the computer's progress along with him, drew in a loud breath. "If he'd been alive, he'd have been fully compromised by the process."

"In a matter of minutes," Fisher clarified, "and depending on the size or location of the wound, I'm guessing it wouldn't have been a pleasant experience."

The sound of a pneumatic hiss behind them caused both men's heads to snap toward the morgue's doorway as Rana Desai entered the room.

"Did I scare you gentlemen?" she asked, her tone suggesting that she hoped she had.

"You didn't, no," Fisher said, looking at M'Benga, "but we've got a case of the willies all the same. How can we help you, Captain?"

"Well, I'm not looking to interrupt," Desai said, glancing at M'Benga a moment before returning her gaze to Fisher.

After a moment in silence, the younger physician nodded. "I ought to excuse myself, anyway," he said. Looking to Fisher, he added, "I'd be very interested in hearing about any . . . developments, Doctor."

"I'll keep you posted," Fisher replied, waiting until his colleague had left the morgue before turning to Desai and offering a sly smile. "I'm beginning to think you like hanging out in the basement."

Desai shrugged in mock defensiveness. "Okay, so the occasional investigation happens to bring me down here once in awhile, but maybe it's not the morgue that I like so much as your charming company."

"Ah-hah," Fisher said, feeling more than a little unconvinced. "Well, if you're down here, I'm guessing the *Endeavour* incident's still on the fast track."

"In a fashion, yes," the captain said, pulling a chair closer to Fisher's workstation and settling herself into it. "We've gotten some preliminary reports from those who survived the attack. Everyone's accounts line up. The whole thing amounts to an expedition and a landing party that ran into something unanticipated and overwhelming. Based on their interviews, there's just nothing that anyone could have done differently. This all seems . . . well, routine, for lack of a better word." She released a tired sigh before adding, "Damn, I know that makes me sound cold, but how else do I say it?"

"How about, 'Accidental in the line of duty?'" Fisher offered. "You're saying no one's to blame."

"Not every investigation in our office is launched with the hope of being able to turn up a mistake or a scapegoat," Desai said, her defensiveness this time sounding genuine.

"You don't need to tell me that, Rana," Fisher said.

"Well, I have to tell Diego," she shot back. "Every time."

A tone from the computer terminal echoed in the morgue, and the doctor smiled. "Well, I guess you'll have some good news for the commodore today." Indicating for Desai to join him, he turned the monitor so that she could see the information displayed upon it.

"What are we looking at?" Desai asked.

Fisher did not reply at first, his attention instead riveted on the results generated by his computer model. "Oh, my," he finally said, trying to absorb as much of the detailed report as he could at once.

"Oh, my what?" Desai said, reminding him that he had an audience.

"I don't rightly know," he answered, ignoring the twinge of excitement he felt in his gut and the sensation of feeling his pulse increase. He even felt goose bumps rising along his arms. "I've never seen anything like this."

He stared at the whirling virtual representation of the enzyme's DNA strand—realizing as he did so that "strand" seemed a wholly insufficient term to describe what he was seeing. It was a genome, yes, but wondrously complex, encoded with far more raw biochemical data than he ever had seen in one place . . . more than he even imagined might be possible.

"Fish, talk to me."

The physician let Desai's plea hang unanswered, so intent was he on what he was seeing. The genetic structure dwarfed the human DNA strand and—according to the computer's own messages, at least—appeared to baffle even the vast storehouse of knowledge available to him via Starfleet Medical. He entered a rapid-fire string of search requests, each one coming back unanswered or not understood by computer or the massive database with which it was communicating.

This is incredible.

Somewhere in the middle of that convoluted web of genetic code, Fisher imagined he saw the keys to uncounted medical and scientific advances, be they cures for disease, repairs to genetic defects, even enhancements to the human genome itself. There was no end to the speculation of what this might signify for the future of all known races in the universe.

Assuming somebody can figure the damn thing out.

"Doctor," Desai said, more forcefully this time, "does this have anything to do with what happened on Erilon?"

Without looking up from his viewer, Fisher said, "I wish I could tell you."

That the alien enzyme scraped from the Denobulan corpse seemed to have the power to turn tissue into a crystalline substance was one thing, but to detect a genomic structure within that enzyme—a DNA molecule the scope of which had never been uncovered by Federation science to date-Fisher knew the implications were staggering.

And to think I could have retired before seeing something like this.

"Fish," Desai said, her expression now one of concern, "what the hell is this about?"

Stroking his silvered goatee, the doctor replied, "Well, it looks like we'll both have something to share with our friend the commodore."

"Well, then, my timing is perfect."

Reyes's voice rang through the morgue, loudly enough that it startled Fisher and visibly shook Desai. The doctor looked up to see the station's commander striding their way. "But here I am without an invitation to the party—again."

Fisher crossed his arms, smiled wryly at Reyes. "And as usual, you don't have a problem assuming that it wasn't intentional."

Desai quickly chimed in. "It's not as much fun down here as you might think."

"It never is," said Reyes, letting the words hang in the air for several seconds before turning to Fisher. "Zeke, we need to talk."

"Yes, we do," the doctor replied, instinct telling him that the commodore's timely arrival was more than simple coincidence.

"Is this about the Erilon incident?" Desai asked. "If so, then my team's finished their preliminary report, and . . . ."

"I'm sorry, Captain," Reyes said, cutting her off. Fisher noted the almost apologetic look in his friend's eyes as he regarded Desai, "but I'm afraid this is a security matter. Stop by my office in an hour, and I'll take your report then. That'll be all for now."

Desai's eyes went wide, and the doctor noted the tightening of her jaw, but she only nodded in response to the sudden turn of the situation. "Aye, sir," she said, glancing toward Fisher before turning and making her way out of the morgue, leaving a grim-faced and even-tired looking Reyes standing before him.

"Something tells me this is going to be pretty interesting," Fisher said.